Game Of Twins

By
Tom Ranseen

Table of Contents

Prologue

October 30, 1663

Hartford, Connecticut

Gasps filled the silence when Judge Thelonious Neville gaveled and announced that the defendant, Abigail, was innocent of the charge of witchery. Abigail smiled, reveling in her triumph over the judge, whom she often discretely "entertained." The pair had thus perpetrated a travesty upon Hartford justice.

Taking Reverend Hiram Johnson's lead, onlookers protested throughout the small courtroom. "She's a witch! She's evil! She must be hanged! Hang her today!" Judge Neville slammed his gavel with such force that the head broke off. He stood, all six-foot-four of him, and glared down at his court. The bystanders filed out with their heads down. Only Reverend Johnson remained, shaking his finger at the judge. Then he, too, left.

When the courtroom was empty, Abigail, considered the most beautiful woman in Hartford, walked up to the bench, kissed the judge, and winked. As she turned to leave, he playfully patted her backside and watched her long, auburn tresses bounce on her shoulders. Outside in the brilliant sunshine, she hugged her twin daughters, Pamela and Molly. They headed home to enjoy a fine midday meal of venison with currant sauce, sweet potatoes, and apple pie for dessert. Sitting at the dinner table, Abigail smiled at her daughters. She'd been so fortunate to have two identical twins who had her long, flowing auburn hair, unusual dark eyes, and faces that Athena would be jealous of; she was sure both would become more powerful witches than her.

The thirteen-year-old twins spent the rest of that glorious fall day exploring another half mile west of the big tree into an area that villagers considered dangerous – with Mohegans still hunting from time to time. Once last summer, Pamela thought she'd seen an Indian dashing through the forest as swiftly as a deer but wasn't sure if it was her imagination. One day, she hoped to meet an Indian face-to-face.

As the sun waned and the night air chilled, the girls decided to forego their favorite game: sitting quietly in the naturally carved-out section of the enormous oak tree, about twenty feet up, each trying to speak the other's thoughts word-for-word – a game and a discipline their mother encouraged. The girls began to realize that with enough concentration and with reasonable proximity, they could "hear" a neighbor's or stranger's thoughts as well – thoughts they often found disconcerting. The twins invented their own game: one would vocalize a recent silent conversation she'd overheard in the village, and the other would try to guess whose thoughts those were.

After a bite of leftovers from lunch that included a generous piece of apple pie and a cup of tea, the twins joined their mother in the main room in front of the large fireplace. Abigail sat in her favorite chair with a candelabra lighting an ancient book. The twins sat on the floor; before them, there was a set of ivory pieces and mahogany board brought from England by their grandmother. While their mother read, they played their favorite indoor game, chess; with a unique rule: they could not read one another's thoughts while playing.

Shattering their calm evening, one flaming torch, then another, crashed through the front window, setting the drapes on fire. The flames quickly spread, snaking along the floor, and within seconds, the tablecloth was ablaze.

Abigail stood and told her twins, "Cover the fire with blankets and throw on as much water as you can. If I don't come back in, go down through the pantry and run. Run far away and fast. You know where the coins are. I love you both."

With a last glance at her daughters, she grabbed a shawl and opened her front door, only to find two dozen Hartford citizens staring her down. Their spokesperson was Reverend Hiram Johnson. The stick-like, craggy-faced, white-haired man bellowed at her, "Justice was not done today, witch. We're here to make sure it is."

Defiantly, she waved her hand from one edge of the crowd to the other and extinguished all torches. She yelled to the darkened mob, "You will leave my house and never return to harm me or mine. Disobey at your peril." Many of the men howled and shrieked in terror. But then, in the darkness lit by a full moon and her own burning home, the old man walked toward her and said, "Witch, hanging is too good for you. We will do unto you what was done unto our Christ — and worse."

A shot rang out, and Abigail fell on her front walkway. The reverend yelled, "Stop! She must suffer more."

Robert Freeman, the blacksmith, yelled out, "Get her twins! They're witches, too!"

The musket blast was unmistakable. Pamela told her twin, "Go down now." Molly saw no fear, only calm, on her sister's face and scrambled into the dirt cellar, which had an exit twenty feet behind the house. They'd extinguished part of the fire, but the smoke was now choking. After she found the book, Pamela grabbed her mother's reading candelabra and set the other window drapes on fire. Through the smokiness, she ran to the cellar door, pulled it shut, and climbed down.

The crowd stood and watched, their cheers deafening, as the whole structure went ablaze. Freeman exclaimed, "It's God's will — burning her witch daughters, too."

The mob dragged Abigail by her bootheels to a field on the outskirts of Hartford where fellow citizens had erected a crucifix, a stack of tinder and logs at its base. Her powers were nil in her current state as she bled from the bullet wound on her shoulder, but she wasn't too weak to understand what was happening. She could only hope her twins had followed her directions before the house burned down.

Johnson ordered, "Tear off her dress so we can see her teats. There must be a Devil's mark." It took two of them to do as he ordered. Indeed, Abigail had several dark birthmarks on her chest and her back.

"You see? Do you see where the Devil has burned his signs into her? Hanging is too good for her!"

The crowd chanted back in approval as they hoisted her up onto the wooden cross.

"Burn her!"

The gunsmith, Jacob Myers, climbed up a short ladder on one side, and Freeman ascended the other. She screamed as they both drove large nails through her palms into the wood – which kept her upright while two others nailed her feet to the base. The witch crucifix before him, Johnson shoved a black wooden cross into her cunt before he lit a fire at her feet. Abigail's eyes blazed as she said her last words: *"He will have his revenge on all of you."* Hartford villagers watched with satisfaction – knowing another witch had been eliminated from their Puritan town. The only Hartford witch ever burned instead of hanged.

The twins watched from the edge of a large tree nearly one hundred yards away. Molly started to scream, but Pamela clamped a hand to her sister's mouth and told her, "No, she's gone." Molly turned her head and sat on the ground, silently sobbing. Holding her mother's book, she stood and watched the murderers bask in the glow of her mother, who'd been tortured, crucified, and burned to death. She turned to her sister and said, "Take the creek path to where we play our games. Go now – I will be along shortly."

"No, I want to stay with you," her sister begged while grabbing her arm.

"There's something I must do. Go! If anything happens, Judge Neville will help you."

Molly got up and ran while Pamela waited for several more minutes. Then she walked toward her mother's smoldering carcass on the cross; the smell was dreadful and got worse as she approached. Pamela announced in her loudest voice, "Her twins have come out of the fire. You will burn in eternal hellfire! Every one of you! I have made it so."

Those still drinking in front of the atrocity turned in surprise. They'd all assumed the twins had burned in the house, and most stood dumbfounded. The blacksmith, Freeman, yelled, "We're going after them. Samuel and Mark, fetch your dogs. They can't get far."

Pamela ran off through the meadow as fast as she could, then into the forest to rendezvous with her sister. She got to the oak and climbed the limbs to their secret place in the hollow of the back of the tree. But where was Molly?

In her fright and haste, Molly took the wrong fork of the path. She backtracked and tore off her petticoat to run faster, but the sounds of canines told her villagers were catching up. Panting from exhaustion, she kept running until she finally saw the tree in the moonlight.

Pamela also heard the dogs and started to climb back down until she heard men's voices and saw flickering torches sprinkled about the forest. She ducked back into their hiding place and peeked around the edge of the tree.

Molly shrieked as two dogs caught up to her and attacked. Hugging the tree, Pamela could see the men about forty paces away. One of the curs had her sister by the neck, the other by her leg.

Molly screamed louder, "Help, please help me! Please!"

One man yelled, "Kill!" On command, the bulldogs began ripping off pieces of her sister's flesh.

The reverend shouted, "We know you're here, witch. Your sister is dead or will be soon. Come out and you'll get a fair trial."

Pamela knew it was a lie but couldn't help but let out a bloodcurdling "Molly!"

Reverend Johnson and the others followed the voice up the giant oak tree.

Then, an arrow pierced the moonlight and punctured the sternum of the gunsmith, the only man carrying a musket. A second arrow hit the dog whose fangs were around Molly's neck. The next struck another man in the head, and he dropped his torch. The other men froze in fright. Foolishly, Johnson stood up and walked toward the tree as the next arrow sliced into his gut.

"Indians!" the men yelled and ran helter-skelter back toward Hartford with the remaining dog – leaving their fallen townspeople behind and never looking back.

A single Mohegan brave walked out from the blackness.

He was not frightening. He was majestic. His head was shaved bald on both sides, and a thick tuft of black hair ran down the middle with three long feathers attached. A necklace of huge white bear claws hung around his neck. The Indian was dressed in long, dark leather pants tied in the back and a vest of black fur. On his feet were leather shoes without heels. He was maybe twenty or so, but Pamela had no idea. His bronzed, sharp-edged face, perhaps the one she'd glimpsed once before?

She was stunned but scrambled down to tend to her sister. Molly lay in the dirt before the big tree, her jugular sliced, and her body covered in blood. She was dead. Pamela looked into the eyes of the Mohegan brave. With tears flooding her eyes, she said, "Thank you."

The Indian brave nodded as if he understood and strolled toward the reverend, who lay on the ground gurgling blood, trying to speak. The Indian knelt before him and – in the blink of an eye – sliced off the top part of his white scalp with his tomahawk. He got up and handed the piece of bloody flesh and tangled white hair to Pamela. She reached out her hand, took it, and nodded. Then he handed her his weapon.

It had a smooth wooden handle and a razor-sharp, glistening edge; it was heavier than she'd thought it would be. She dropped the scalp in the dirt and gripped the handle with two hands. She stood over Johnson. "This is for my sister and mother. I will see you in Hell, reverend!"

As he tried to speak, she buried the tomahawk into his chest, cracking his sternum and puncturing his heart. Blood sprayed her dress.

The Mohegan carefully removed the arrows and tomahawk from the dead men and wiped them off before putting the arrows back in his quiver and sticking the tomahawk in his thin belt. Pamela bent down and kissed her sister for the last time. She picked up her mother's book and smeared the inside cover with a bit of Molly's blood. The back inside cover she smeared with blood from the Reverend's scalp. The Indian took off his fur vest and handed it to her. She put it on and followed him west, deeper into the woods than she'd ever been before.

And that was the beginning of Pamela's first revenge for the gruesome deaths of her mother and twin sister.

As generations after would realize.

Part I - The Tigress

Chapter 1 – The Mayhem in Cascade

Easter 2015

Atlanta

The gray Acura with dark-tinted windows slowed as it passed the well-kept bungalow. Blood red and starburst yellow tulips lined the long sidewalk from the street to the front door. That Holy Saturday, the historic Atlanta neighborhood of Cascade Heights came alive with verdant greens and vibrant colors exploding from every orifice. Mother Nature dared anything to stand in her glorious way.

As the Acura resumed average speed, the passenger remarked, "It really is a lovely, peaceful place."

About an hour away, on the other side of bustling metro Atlanta, Donnie and Jeb Dixon had been drinking Budweiser and smoking weed since noon in their ramshackle little wood-framed house on the fringe of Covington, Georgia; their normal behavior on Saturdays unless they decided to respond to an emergency plumbing call. Which they rarely did on weekends and wouldn't do today. Donnie was rail-thin, six feet, and wore a scraggly red beard. Jeb was 300 pounds if he was a pound. His skull was bald, with stubble covering his face. He was three inches shorter than his brother. No one ever guessed they could be brothers.

Donnie and Jeb were watching an early-season Braves game. The clean-up hitter struck out with men on second and third. Jeb jumped up and bellowed, "Goddammit, why can't these assholes hit the goddamn ball! We got too many niggers and spics who make a zillion bucks and ain't worth a damn." Donnie ignored his big brother and went out to the fridge to get another beer.

There was a bang on the door. "Don't worry about getting up off your sorry fat ass," Donnie spit at his brother. "I'll get it."

Donnie stumbled to the front door, opened it, and thought he saw heaven. A woman wearing a Pizza Hut cap, a woman unlike any he'd ever seen in his life; long blonde hair; a sleeveless midriff top with no bra and eye-popping cleavage; jean booty shorts and heels. She carried three large pizzas tucked into her bare tummy under her boobs. His lips could utter not a word.

"You boys hungry?"

After staring for more than an appropriate time, he said, "Ma'am, I could eat a horse, but I don't think we ordered any pizza. Maybe you got the wrong place?" He turned and hollered, "Jeb, you ordered pizza?"

His brother yelled back, "No, dumbass!"

The super-hot pizza babe looked Donnie dead in the eyes. "A plumbing client of yours who wants to remain anonymous told me to deliver these to you boys. You want 'em or not?"

Donnie couldn't find his tongue again. The babe started to turn to leave.

"Wait! Wait! We want the pizzas."

"You're Donnie?" she asked.

He stammered, "Yes, ma'am, I am."

"With his mouth open in shock more than anything, he took them as she beamed, "Need to grab more surprises from my car."

"Donnie, who the fuck is at the door!" his brother bellowed.

Jeb Dixon finally got up off his fat ass and walked to the door as the looker pranced up with two bottles of Jack Daniel's Black.

Scanning the beautiful blonde from head to toe, he, too, was left speechless.

"You must be Jeb. Here's the rest of your gift." She handed him the bottles and said, "Sure hope you boys enjoy."

Donnie begged, "Hey, baby, can't you stay and party?"

"Sorry, boys, I'm sure yawl would be fun, but I gotta get back deliverin' pizzas."

As she blew them a kiss, the two brothers watched her swish her world-class ass down their weather-beaten sidewalk.

The Dixon boys looked at one another. "Get a couple glasses, Jeb. Nutt'n better than pizza and whiskey."

Jeb nodded. "Pussy woulda been nice too. That was one fine bitch!"

Jeb and Donnie Dixon might have stayed home all evening watching the flat-screen and eating pizza without her visit, but a couple of drinks of the roofie-infused whiskey would ensure that both were out for the night. It was her job to extinguish the possibility of any alibi they might have while she was on the other side of Atlanta later that night.

Easter Sunday, April 5

Atlanta

Since she'd been a child, Suzanne Delacroix loved attending Atlanta's historic Ebenezer Baptist Church with her parents. Easter had always been her favorite holiday. Her policeman father, Hollis, usually wore his seersucker blue pinstripe suit, and she remembered how he'd turn women's heads. But her mother, Mei, was another story. Mei rarely dolled up, but on Easter, she would wear a bright, slinky dress and matching hat. All of Suzanne's friends said her mom looked like a movie star, and she did.

She smiled at the photo of her parents on her dresser. They'd given her more love than any child could ever hope for. Plus, they'd left her a wealthy woman – from the life insurance policies and money inherited from her mother's share of her family's Chinese grocery stores. But she'd give it all up to see them one more time.

Suzanne slid into a brand-new, yellow silk dress with a matching hat and heels she'd bought earlier that week. Bedecked like a long, spring daffodil, she was thrilled about Easter Sunday. She was going to the 10:30 a.m. service – but would need to leave early to get a pew where she could see the preacher.

Standing in her Easter outfit in front of the full-length mirror, she heard her all-too-familiar, truncated Clint Eastwood ringtone for police calls: "You've got to ask yourself a question: 'Do I feel lucky? Well, do ya, punk?'" It was a code 48, but at least not in the Atlanta projects. Within thirty seconds, her longtime partner, Dusty, called and said he'd pick her up.

Already, she didn't feel lucky that gorgeous Easter morning. Stepping out of her virgin Easter duds, she groaned out loud, "Fuck me." Though she'd sworn off cussing many times, that righteous resolution never stuck. A woman of strong Christian faith could usually filter out expletives who took the Lord's name in vain. But not others. Her tirade of expletives continued. Her Aussie, Zeke, hated her swearing and high-tailed it into the laundry room to hide. She pulled on tight jeans, a sleeveless top, a light leather jacket, and boots, then grabbed her shield and shoulder holster with Glock and headed out the door.

Over the years, Suzanne and her partner, Dusty Rayfield (aka "Deadeye"), got dealt more than their fair share of ungodly calls as Atlanta PD's top Homicide detectives. That morning was no exception. Dusty, a fireplug of a guy, cueball bald and a half-foot shorter, was waiting in front of her condo near Piedmont Park when she walked out. Now in a horrible mood, jealous of the Easter churchgoers she saw on the sidewalk, she climbed into his car. He handed his partner her signature Starbucks: chai tea, no water. She grabbed it and chided, "Nice way to spend the Easter holiday with my freak'n partner."

She slurped her tea and pouted for a couple of minutes. Dusty knew better than to interrupt her silence. Finally, after several hits of the caffeine dessert, she managed, "Sorry, Deadeye. Thanks for the Starbucks. I just wanted a quiet, relaxing holiday."

"Yeah, right, in your next lifetime," he grinned. The blue lights went live as they headed toward Cascade Heights, which was only about fifteen minutes away, depending on traffic.

She'd been in the area several times, but in her seventeen years as a cop, she'd never had a case in "Cascade," as the inhabitants called it. A southwest Atlanta neighborhood with historical importance; a gem bordered by the 285 Beltline to the west and I-20 to the north; filled with parks, recreation, and large wooded lots; and the lowest crime rate in the city.

In 1962, Cascade was at the bleeding edge of the civil rights movement when a young surgeon, Dr. Clinton Warner, a WWII vet and a founder of the Morehouse School of Medicine, purchased a house and twenty-one acres of wooded land in the area. In retaliation, Atlanta Mayor Ivan Allen erected a cement barricade at the corners of Peyton and Harlan Roads with the intention of keeping blacks out of the white Peyton Forest neighborhood. It quickly became known as the "Peyton Wall" or "Atlanta's Berlin Wall." Still, it stood for only seventy-two days and was a watershed for the downfall of racially inspired planning and zoning restrictions nationally. Cascade Heights became the poster child for white flight out of major cities – but evolved into a prominent, predominantly black suburb that had been home to baseball great Hank Aaron, Ambassador to the United Nations Andrew Young, former mayor Shirley Franklin, and many other black luminaries.

Cascade was even more beautiful and charming than Suzanne remembered. An oasis of calm on the edge of Atlanta's unremitting urban sprawl. But that Easter morning, the neighborhood was out of kilter. A gaggle of police vehicles lined both sides of the street. The police cruisers' lights strobed purple against the enormous maples and flowering white dogwoods, magnolias, birches, and firs. The old neighborhood was dead quiet, save the birds chirping, seemingly without care. The house was an older but well-kept, two-story beige and white trimmed bungalow tucked into a pretty piece of wooded property near the dead end of the short street—a mile or so from where the infamous Peyton Wall once stood.

Dusty parked his black Mustang behind a police SUV, and the Mutt and Jeff cops emerged. When Suzanne wore heels, she was more than a head taller than her partner, but it never bothered him. Dusty followed her up the sidewalk, which was lined with dozens of red and yellow tulips. The tulips, she noticed, were the exact hue as the crime scene warning tape that cut across the walk and extended to both sides of the house. Several neighbors dressed in their Easter finest were gathered outside the tape, waiting anxiously to hear any news. An impeccably dressed older black man in a white suit, white shirt, powder blue bow tie, and white straw hat – no doubt on his way to church – took a step forward and asked her, "Ma'am, do you know what's going on here at the Monroes'?"

She stopped for a few seconds but deflected. "Sorry, sir, I don't, but I'm about to find out."

No need to flash their APD detective shields to the uniforms inside. There wasn't an Atlanta cop who didn't know and respect them.

As they walked through the front door, it was eerily quiet. Too quiet. Then they stopped dead in their tracks at the entrance to the dining room off the main hallway.

In her seventeen years as a policewoman, Suzanne had seen a few hundred crime scenes. But nothing like the one before her. Not even in the ballpark. The cops who preceded them could barely glance at the carnage on the huge mahogany table. They'd positioned themselves outside the dining room in the two doorways from the kitchen and hallway to give space to the two detectives. The police officers had been well-trained not to contaminate a crime scene by tromping in masse across the floor. By rote, she and Dusty pulled on their gloves and shoe covers.

The hardwood floor was laden with dark, semi-coagulated human blood and lots of blurred footprints. Shortly after she and Dusty arrived, Suzanne heard the CSI team enter, and she knew the Fulton County ME wasn't far behind. This was a biggie.

Two girls' bodies lay parallel, an arm's length apart, on the large rectangular dining table. Their calves – and feet with ankles tied – hanging off the edge in early-onset rigor mortis, mouths taped, and their arms laid out perpendicular to their bodies; a hand of each folded against the side of the other, palms facing up. The mother sat slumped over on a dining room chair in the corner, completely clothed, bound, and gagged with her throat slashed from ear to ear. Her head slumped – it looked like her eyelids were taped open, presumably forced to watch her daughters' ordeal before she was murdered. Collateral damage, Suzanne surmised, after an initial scan of the grisly scene.

Maybe the girls were twins? It was hard to tell. Both were nude, and there were no clothes of any type on or near the table. They were girls of color but now a chalky light brown. Most of their blood stuck like gobs of uneven, dark acrylic paint to the table and floor.

Innocence annihilated forever.

The dead teenagers lay on their backs on the slab of mahogany in a place Suzanne knew they'd all prayed and eaten many meals together. Like their mother, throats were slashed from ear to ear, but they were also cut identically from throat to pelvis in two straight lines and then again horizontally, directly beneath their small breasts, with two separate slashes. Not eviscerated, but sliced in a precise pattern, in perpendicular directions. Two sacrilegious human crucifixes were also branded with crosses.

Both butchered, no doubt, with the unusual hunting knives that were firmly embedded like gruesome exclamation points in the hardwood floor between the girls' dangling legs. The knives had been thrown with serious force to stick straight up like that. Whoever did this knew his way around cutlery. But what type of murderer or murderers would leave weapons, especially as unique as these?

On each side of the dead girls were bloody, yellow Confederate battle flags with red swastikas embroidered into the top portion. Curious, but it was impossible not to focus on the worst: a black-lacquered wooden cross impaled into each girl between their legs. Their bodies were laid out as crosses; crosses carved into their skin; and black crosses stuck perversely inside each of them.

She stood motionless – trying to process the mayhem while smelling the all-too-familiar pungent aroma of blood and dead human flesh. A sinister, rancid odor of evil also permeated the dining room. Two murdered children and mom on the holiest of Christian holidays. Then it struck her. The girls looked familiar, but she wasn't sure why.

Still, absolute silence. Everyone seemed to be in a catatonic state. She bent down as close as she could and crouched to look more closely at the two huge knives stuck in the floor. Smooth white handles with a natural stone pattern and inlaid with a curious symbol – like a weird-shaped "H" with the middle bar pointing out, or no, maybe like two black crosses jammed together.

By then, in any typical Homicide case, Detective Delacroix would have already asked, "Okay, what do we know?" She would have begun to dissect and organize the facts of the case and bark a series of orders. Then immerse herself in the scene. This time was different. Her eyes were glued to the horrific knives. Where had she seen that design before?

It wasn't the blood and gore or even the horror of two dead kids and their mom. While she stared at the knives, something snapped at her core. She felt woozy as she got to her feet. She turned her head quickly enough so as not to contaminate the gruesome crime scene before her. Then the unflappable detective projectile vomited – hurling her cheese omelet, toast, and chai tea into an empty corner of the dining room.

After throwing up her breakfast, she walked around the blood splatter into the adjoining kitchen, leaving six uniformed officers, the CSIs, and her partner dumbfounded. Dusty saw his longtime friend and partner shaking and, in a daze, which he'd never seen. He grabbed her by the arm gently yet with purpose.

"Let's go, Suzy, you've got the flu or a stomach bug. I'm phoning in another team," which he did while holding her elbow. "CSI and the ME have plenty of work on this one for now." He handed her a few sections of paper towel from the kitchen to wipe off her face and clothes and told the uniforms to button the place up and say nothing to anyone, especially the press.

So stunned by her visceral reaction to the horror in the quaint dining room, zombielike, she took Dusty's hand, and they walked back down the front steps and sidewalk as the onlookers stared and her colleagues watched in disbelief. The distinguished black gentleman in his Easter finest was still there. "Ma'am, what happened in there? Please tell us."

Dusty told him. "Sir, I apologize, but we can't comment now. The police inside are handling it. There will be news soon."

Thankfully, the TV vultures hadn't swooped in yet. With her head bowed, the only thing Suzanne saw walking back up the sidewalk was the crimson tulips, and she felt an urge to puke again. At his car, Dusty helped her in like he might do with an elderly person. He told her, "Suzy, it's okay. I'm going to take you home."

As he turned off the Monroes' street, CNN and Channel 2 vans barreled around the corner toward the desecrations.

He had no clue what to say. She was in a strange state, but he didn't think it was a shock. After five minutes of silence, he asked, "So what the hell happened in there?"

Looking straight ahead, she replied, "It's not the flu or food poisoning – and I'm not knocked up."

He tried to give her encouragement. "Suzy, you'll be okay. You're the Tigress."

"The Tigress," she mumbled. "Yeah, right."

As he drove up Peyton Road to I-20, her mind drifted back to when she'd gotten that nickname.

It happened one Saturday afternoon years ago when she and three good ole boy colleagues were hanging out in the grungy little third-floor lounge at Atlanta PD headquarters. They were all bored and drinking stale, lukewarm coffee, waiting to hear if the perp was going to lawyer up after popping two conventioneers in a drug deal gone bad outside the Omni. Either way, she was going to have more work to do unless Narcotics took over. Not likely, that spectacular summer day.

The ceiling fan recirculated male cop BO – enhancing her

claustrophobia. She was about to escape for fresh air but realized nobody was paying attention to the ancient Sony perched on a file cabinet in the corner of the little room. The Braves were getting powdered by the Reds, 9-2. The remote had been missing for as long as she could remember, so she got up and switched it manually to the TPC at Sawgrass. Standing, she watched as Tiger Woods, only a shot off the lead, hit a towering 9-iron dead at the pin tucked far right on the infamous, treacherous island green. He put it eight feet away; the crowd went crazy. She stood riveted as Tiger stalked the line from every angle. After she sat back down, Mack Hines, the most Neanderthal of the three, got off his fat ass, walked over, and turned the channel back to the ballgame that he hadn't been watching. She asked him to please turn it back. He retorted, "Fuck you, Delacroix. Golf is a fucking pussy game." Then he doubled down, adding, "Tiger fucking Woods is a fucking chink, nigger pussy." She got up and turned the channel back to golf.

The whole room went silent except for Johnny Miller, babbling about Tiger's left-to-right breaking putt.

The woman of similar lineage to Tiger's told him. "Hines, you wanna take that back?" The paunchy alpha cop in a pitted-out short-sleeve shirt, stretched by his gut, sneered and said nothing. Without another word, she stepped a foot in front of his red-glazed, pumpkin face. Eyeball to eyeball, in less than a blink, her right knee hit him with a crunching thud, compressing his balls to the thickness of silver dollar pancakes and sending him directly to the scuffed linoleum.

She towered over the obese detective, looking ten feet tall with the edge of her boot heel poised for another shot – daring him to make the next move or say anything else that stupid.

He managed to cough out, "Okay, jeez! I take it back. Jeez, Delacroix. Are you fuck'n nuts?"

She switched the channel back in time to see the replay of Tiger sinking his lightning-fast birdie putt. As Hines lay on the floor, groaning and cuddling his crotch, his compadres lifted not one finger. Instead, they laughed hysterically. Then it blurted out of Jake's mouth, "Wow, don't want to ever fuck with the Tigress." After that episode, the nickname stuck. And no one at APD – male or female; black, white, or brown; big or small; rich or poor; religious or atheist – ever fucked with her again.

That was also about the same time her legend took off like a brilliant shooting star, one no longer tethered to her father's. Hollis Delacroix, the revered Deputy Chief of Criminal Investigations, had never given his daughter a free pass. And he couldn't have been prouder of her.

But that Easter, walking from the Monroe's, she was thinking that if her dad were still around, he wouldn't be too proud. Who would be? *Tigress,* she thought, what a fucking joke. And no one even knew about the debilitating nightmares she'd suffered for two decades.

Suzanne finally spoke as they got to Midtown. She asked Dusty to take her to the Homicide Unit of the Atlanta Major Crimes Division on Ponce De Leon.

"Seriously, you wanna do that?" Dusty appealed.

"Do it," Suzanne replied in a tone with which he was not familiar.

He parked the Mustang in the underground lot, and they took the elevator up to Homicide. Her mind wandered again. It hadn't been a banner last two years. Her Delta pilot husband of thirteen months left her for a younger model, a twenty-three-year-old South African blonde-bombshell stewardess. Then her beloved captain, Isaac Gates, retired and was replaced by the less-than-mediocre Joe Tucker, whom she trusted not one iota. But worst of all, her dear mother, Mei, passed away suddenly from pancreatic cancer last May. Atlanta homicide cases kept piling up like the putrid garbage on Carter Street. Today, the depravity of the horrific triple murder put an exclamation point on all of it.

And the nightmares – she knew would keep coming.

Homicide was quiet that Easter morning. She walked to her spartan metal desk adorned only with her PC, a stack of files, a lamp, and a few family photos. She had a ton of vacation days and knew that she could take time off and chill out. Stoically, she sat down at her desk, took a few deep breaths, and wrote a short note. She sealed it in an envelope and addressed it to Captain Tucker, known mainly for his attempts to screw any good-looking, young female employee at APD. Thankfully, Tucker was not in his office, so she left the envelope, her detective's shield, and her Glock 22 on his desk.

Before leaving, she walked up to the few colleagues who were there, shook their hands, gave them big hugs, and offered kind words. She picked up her limited stuff and asked Dusty if he could give her a lift to her place in Midtown.

He could barely stammer a few words while driving up Peachtree. "I can't believe you're doing this, Suzy. You can't do this!"

"Sorry, partner. Been a long time coming. Today's the day. You're the best partner any cop could ever have. I'm going to get out of town for a while." They both got out of the car, and she leaned down and kissed him on the top of his shiny head, which she'd never done in the decade of knowing him. "You gotta promise me one thing, though, Deadeye. You will get the fucks who committed these murders."

"I'll do my best, but I'm going to miss you a lot," Dusty told her with tears rolling down his cheeks.

"Me too, but I'll be around," she told him, her tears streaming as well. He watched her enter her building and drove off, hoping it was a bad dream but knowing it was the worst Easter ever.

Where should she escape to? Money was no object. She loved the West – Montana and anywhere around Yellowstone, Santa Fe, Sun Valley, Santa Barbara, or Napa; or maybe she'd hop on a plane to St. Barth's or another Caribbean island she'd never been to or go to Hawaii; or even visit Hong Kong, where she and her mother always said they'd visit but never got around to doing. A bucket list item never to be crossed off, one that always made her sad. Another dozen possibilities popped into her brain as she toweled off from her shower.

After flopping down on her big bed, Zeke, her Aussie Red, put his head on her shoulder, licked her face, and looked at her, his irresistible, lively, begging eyes saying, "You can go wherever you want, but I'm coming with. So cut the bullshit – you know where we're going."

She packed in twenty minutes. Looking over her bedroom to check if she'd forgotten anything, she grabbed her mom's antique cross necklace, platinum studded with generous diamonds, an expensive gift from her father on their twentieth anniversary. She'd never hung it around her neck until then. Looking at herself in the mirror, she decided it would be a fixture. Indeed, it was more beautiful and permanent than a silly wedding ring.

Maybe they could make it by seven o'clock if the traffic wasn't too horrible driving south through Alabama with the likely other hordes of spring break vacationers.

Driving through Alabama, she couldn't get it out of her mind. The only other time in her whole life she'd vomited was nearly two decades ago. Back then, she wasn't sick or pregnant either. It happened only a few miles from where she now lived in Atlanta.

Chapter 2 – The Frat Party

Twenty-one Years Ago – March 29, 1994

Georgia Tech University – Atlanta

Suzanne wasn't a big party girl at Spelman College and not the Greek type. She wasn't keen on going to the fraternity party at Georgia Tech, but her friend Kim Thomen talked her into it.

"I'll probably be the token non-white, non-sorority girl at the party."

"Way worse than that," her friend kidded. "Safe bet you'll be the *only* Afro-Chinese chick there who stands six feet tall. It'll be a blast. You need to get a life and get out of the library and off the golf course for a change."

She gave in. "Okay, I'll go, but we're not staying out all night."

"I'll make sure we're back by daybreak," quipped her terminally spunky friend.

As the day of the party approached, Suzanne found herself anticipating it more and more. She'd already called Kim a half dozen times to consult about the dress code. "Let's go for it," Kim told her. After much consternation and a shopping spree to Lenox, Suzanne finally chose a short chiffon, black dress: strapless and low cut. Plus, new black heels lifted her a few inches over six feet.

Because they'd no doubt have a few cocktails, they decided to splurge and share the short cab ride up to Tech and then back and crash at Suzanne's place after the party.

"Girl, you look amazing!"

"Thanks. You look great yourself." Her friend was a foot shorter but had that perfect body that big athletes lusted for: cute, petite, blonde, and curvy. Suzanne had always wondered why the little girls liked the big guys and vice versa. She liked guys who were in good shape, intelligent, and funny; within reason, she didn't care so much about their height or ethnicity.

On that comfortably warm, early spring evening, they arrived at the Antebellum-styled, sprawling, three-story, on-the-Georgia Historic Register building a block off fraternity row near the Tech campus. Suzanne realized she'd walked by it many times on the way to watch Tech football games with her dad, but she'd never set foot inside a Georgia Tech fraternity house in her nineteen years.

On the grand veranda of Delta Sigma Zeta stood an endless assortment of handsome white boys and more knockout white girls than Suzanne had ever seen accumulated in one place – and she hadn't made it inside yet. At a quick glance, she didn't see even one other woman of color but wasn't too surprised.

Bubbly Brenda Daniels, who'd gotten them an invitation, greeted them with hugs. "Thank yawl for come'n. Lemme show you off to a couple of the brothers and give you a quick tour of the place. But othawise, you all make yaselves at home," the Zeta little sister told them in perfect, syrupy southern Atlantese. Brenda could have been Kim's sister. She was a curvy, little, blonde-haired cutie.

The stately frat house, built after Sherman burned down the city in 1864, was a huge stone building with four mammoth, white, three-story pillars in front and an interior lined with rich dark walnut throughout. Tonight, it had turned into an enormous nightclub with countless college partiers gabbing and chowing down on fancy hors d'oeuvres while pouring down alcohol.

Brenda introduced Suzanne and Kim to a couple of guys, one a dark-haired hunk, and one of only a few boys whom Suzanne had spied so far tall enough to look her straight in the eye. "Suzanne, I'd like you to meet Thad Sutterland." As if a knight from long ago, he bowed and kissed each girl on the hand, then pecked Brenda lightly on the cheek and tugged her around her waist.

"Thad's one of the top lacrosse players at Tech. But watch out. He's quite the ladies' man," Brenda warned them with a pixyish smile.

"Thank you so much for coming to our little party. I'm the designated photographer for this evening. Do you mind?" Thad held a thin Captiva Polaroid camera and snapped a few photos of Suzanne, flanked by the two petite blondes. He excused himself and winked. "No doubt I'll be seeing more of you this evening, Miss Delacroix." With all the other distractions, the other two girls weren't paying that much attention, but Suzanne felt Thad's eyes devouring her.

Usually, Thad was partial to tiny spinners like Brenda or Kim Thomen. Still, he was stunned by the beauty of the statuesque girl with Asian features and a glossy, light mocha complexion. He'd never seen such a stunning creature in his twenty-one years.

Brenda introduced Kim and Suzanne to more partiers, then disappeared into the throngs. Suzanne met a half dozen boys who were on the Georgia Tech lacrosse team and discovered Delta Sigma was *the* big lacrosse fraternity while also including many jocks who played other sports as well. In the early '90s, lacrosse was hardly a major sport on the level of football or basketball, or even golf or tennis. In 1994, it wasn't even a scholarship sport; but despite being only a club sport, lacrosse had garnered its own signature aura. A rough and tough game for entitled males. It was a cool, elite sport played by bad boys with an edge – who thought football was beneath them. Lacrosse boys rated above other college athletes where it counted most: the opinion of Southern belles.

Suzanne had seen a few high school lacrosse games and thought that it was an entertaining sport: fast-paced, high-scoring, hard-hitting, and obviously requiring a lot of skill. Even though most of the lacrosse boys were shorter than her, she hadn't met one yet who wasn't good-looking. A few of them even danced with a bit of rhythm. Standing six-foot-three in her heels, the multiracial girl with the magnificent body and beautiful face got nonstop attention and more pick-up lines than she'd heard in her whole life. After a couple of drinks, she found herself flirting more than she could remember.

Suzanne sipped the free-flowing, violet-colored party punch from her crystal goblet that always seemed to be magically full. Each time she turned around, even when she escaped out front for a little fresh air, Thad seemed to be there clicking off another Polaroid. His lacrosse friend Andrew topped off her goblet while Marty dropped in a lime—more than once.

After yet another candid photo-op, Thad asked, "So, are you having a good time, Miss Delacroix?"

She told him, "Absolutely. Yawl throw a great party."

Thad leaned into her breasts and whispered, "You are the sexiest girl here by a light-year. See you later, beautiful."

She meandered through the mob of Tech's beautiful college crowd. The impeccably dressed Georgia Tech students became perspiring dance fiends as the DJ played Janet Jackson, Warren G, Nate Dogg, Prince, Reel to Real, and even Marvin Gaye oldies, which she loved. A lot of the cuties had kicked off their heels, and dudes had ditched their coats and ties and unbuttoned most of their shirt buttons. The strobes lit up the smoky haze that engulfed the frat house; the party spilled from the main lobby, living room, and library into the cafeteria and out onto the cooler veranda.

Back inside, with the funky DJ's music blasting away, she danced and mingled and drank – and tried to remember "sip, don't gulp; sip, don't gulp" the tasty purple potion with floating limes in her bottomless goblet. But she'd lost count.

More than a few times, the preppy boys accidentally, on purpose, brushed or grabbed her ass. She shrugged it off as harmless touching – part of the price of admission – but realized this was a party that could get out of control. Thad continued popping up with his lacrosse lap dogs – clicking her picture and refilling her glass.

She had no idea of the time but wanted to leave. Even with her unique vantage point, though, she couldn't spot her running buddy. Searching for Kim and stuck in the middle of the party masses, Suzanne suddenly felt woozy and more than a little drunk. The walls of the considerable library were both spinning and closing in on her. She needed to escape the din of smoke from cigars, cigarettes, and joints; and the smells of sweat mingled with perfume.

It was like the haze had sucked the oxygen from the room. She wove her way through the main mob scene – her head now banging like a bass drum. She desperately needed to lie down for a few minutes. She found a deserted side hallway, not included on her earlier tour. At the end of it was a short flight of stairs. Even hanging onto the banister, she could barely step down. In front of her was an unoccupied half-screened porch at the far back of the rambling frat house. Finally, fresh air. She plopped down on the couch and passed out in the darkness.

Groggily, she opened her eyes and realized the top of her dress was pulled down to her waist. She heard a click and then more clicks, coupled with bright flashes. Semi-blinded by the staccato bursts, she tried to sit up but failed and slumped back down.

"Suzanne, I'm so glad I finally found you in this madhouse. I thought that my room upstairs would be more comfortable for us, but this will work fine after we get a bit more privacy." Thad pulled down the wicker blinds and locked the glass door.

Lying on the couch, she heard a different kind of click and saw the glint of a thin, shiny triangular blade. Thad smiled down at his prey, leaned over, lifted the middle of her strapless half-bra, and sliced it between the cups with the razor-sharp stiletto – exposing her substantial breasts. There were more bursts of blinding light, but she could only see globes of brazen brightness.

Thad eased her over to give him room to sit on the edge of the sofa. Grinning ear-to-ear with malevolent glee, he pulled up Suzanne's dress, then sliced off the skimpy thong at her hip. The wisp of black lingerie fell to the porch floor. More flashes of light. His hands greedily groped her from top to bottom. She tried feebly to stop him but couldn't.

"Here, let's sit you up." He was strong enough to grab her shoulders and pull her to a sitting position. The smile he'd given her on the veranda hours earlier had transmuted from welcoming and friendly to ominous and evil. Switchblade in one hand, with the other, he unzipped his khakis and freed his stiff manhood. Suzanne was too incapacitated to put up any resistance. She could only mumble, "Please, please don't hurt me. Please."

Thad couldn't remember being this excited since he'd raped twenty-one-year-old Mindy Fuller in her Virginia Highlands apartment five years earlier. He'd thought it was hilarious that his lawyer, Laura Cantrell, threatened to have Mindy charged for sexual assault of a minor. He guessed Mindy got paid a bunch of money. Whatever. Laura and his dad made it all disappear – no charges, no record, no nothing – like all the others. Life was good as a Sutterland in Atlanta.

"Can't believe I've never done a black bitch or an oriental chick either," he said, holding his dick in his hand and his knife in the other. "I guess I'm getting this as a twofer," Thad laughed. "My old man told me there ain't nothing better than wild black cunt. Not sure he's ever had oriental-nigger pussy like you, though. He'll be jealous as hell."

It was like she was watching herself in a movie – but unable to change the scene. She thought, "This can't be happening to me." Time crawled, second by second.

"Please don't. Please," she begged in a near whisper.

"Please? You do want it, don't you, Suzanne? I knew it."

Thad stood, his legs straddling hers, and bent down—his erection inches from Suzanne's face. "I want you to lick it and suck it first. They all love it. Then I promise I'll fuck you like you've never been fucked," he told her, still brandishing his frightening switchblade, the tip of his cock now kissing her raspberry lipstick.

His parents were filthy rich. Thad had cars, boats, Jet Skis, 24/7 access to their two private jets, multiple homes on three continents, and anything else money could buy. Strangely, though, the knife, a slim custom-made stiletto, was his most prized possession. By age fourteen, he'd discovered that it could be effective with the ladies. It was a fun conversation piece that he'd learned to throw with uncanny accuracy – and could hit the bull's-eye of a dartboard from fifteen paces. Or better, he used it as a sexy turn-on when removing their clothing – as well as an implied threat – before getting his way with them. Plus, it was a good weapon and constant companion, especially with so many nigger lowlifes rummaging around the streets of downtown Atlanta.

"Please, no," Suzanne again murmured, still unable to get her bearings or put up any fight as he pressed his erection into her lips – his engorged penis intent on entering her mouth. She pursed her lips and kept her teeth closed, but it seemed futile.

"Open wide, Suzanne, like it's a big, tasty ice cream cone," he told her.

Suzanne was drunk and drugged but not unconscious, which she thought might have been better. She wanted to pray. Which is what her mom had taught her to do, especially in times of trouble. But before she could: a God-thing.

As Thad's tip slid between her lips and sought her tongue, Suzanne vomited involuntarily and explosively – shooting an *Exorcist*-like deluge of purplish, smelly goop all over the stud's hard dick, crisply pleated tan khakis, and white bucks. Regan, the Exorcist girl, would've been proud.

Enraged, Thad stood over her – gobs of putrid, purple puke dripping off his rapidly deflating erection, staining his slacks and favorite shoes. The lacrosse jock could only spit out, "Gross me out, you fucking worthless, nigger bitch, chink cunt! Jesus fucking Christ! Gross me fucking out!"

He backhanded her across the face, and she collapsed on the couch; the blow hurt, but she heard his long switchblade snap back into its handle. He unlocked the porch door and disappeared. If there was one thing Thad hated, it was a mess, especially himself as a mess. He had to get cleaned up, then deal with her.

At least she was alone and alive. "Thank you, Lord Jesus," she prayed.

Still confused in a dense, dark, and unfamiliar alcohol- and drug-induced fog, Suzanne was a smelly disaster. Her little black dress was around her waist, her breasts and crotch were bared, and she'd thrown up all over herself as well as Thad. But through her haze, she realized that he could be back any minute. Maybe with reinforcements. Throwing up and her extreme panic seemed to sober her a bit. She felt horizontally glued to the couch but willed her body to start working muscle by muscle. She had to get moving and get out of the frat house.

Unstable and uncoordinated beyond anything she'd ever experienced, her brains scrambled, and her skull felt like it was in a winepress; Suzanne managed to pull herself to a sitting position. The slightest movement sent shockwaves of pain through her head, but the pain seemed to wake her up more. Her bra and panties were hopelessly damaged; she left them in the muck and pulled up the top of her tiny dress. That would have to do for now. She wiped off bits of vomit from her gown – and then her face with a pillow. The taste in her mouth was wretched, hellish. Sitting, she fumbled to find her purse and heels on the purple-stained wood floor. After trying to scrunch her feet into her heels, she decided it was a bridge too far to walk in her heels; they were problematic even on a good day. She braced herself on the end of the couch and willed herself to get vertical. It took a few unsuccessful tries, but she stood and wobbled to the porch door like a rum-drunk sailor.

Gingerly, she climbed a level of stairs and traversed the dimly lit hallway barefoot; she only slipped once but didn't fall flat on her face. She braced herself on the hallway walls like a few of her fellow inebriated partiers were doing and ducked into a little bathroom. She locked herself inside and did a double take in the mirror. Like she'd walked out of *Night of the Living Dead*.

The vanity was gross from overuse that evening – including a slimy, spent condom in the sink. Her lipstick was smeared from Thad's attempted forced entry. Her long, jet-black hair, which she'd carefully curled earlier that evening, was messy and ratty. Her light brown skin wasn't dark enough to hide the bruise that was popping up on her cheek. Pieces of purple spotted her black dress and bare skin.

Using wet toilet paper, she wiped remnants of her own vomit from her dress, neck, arms, and legs. She quickly applied new lipstick and a dab of makeup to cover up the bruise, then brushed her long hair. Parched like she'd been stranded in the Mojave, she leaned down and sucked in as much water from the faucet as possible. When she opened the door, the music was blaring even louder than earlier.

Relying on pieces of furniture and a few obliging arms, she teetered through the vast crowd. Fireworks of agony pounded her head, not from Thad's blow but from whatever had been in those drinks. She thought she saw Andrew, one of Thad's boys, on the far side of the main dance area. Her panic returned as she wove her way through the masses. Without heels, she was a little shorter, a little less conspicuous – but not that much.

She had to find Kim.

After a couple of minutes of wading through the crowd, she spied her friend talking to a good-looking, muscular black athlete. She sat on his lap in the corner of the frat library with the guy's hands on the tops of her bare thighs. Suzanne was as direct as possible: "Kim, we gotta go."

"Suzy, the night's young. I'm having so much fun!" her friend slurred.

"Now!" She didn't mean to be rude, but there was no time to lose.

Kim took notice of the volume and tone of her friend's voice. "Are you okay?"

"No, I feel terrible, and *we* have to leave *now*."

Her ripped black friend, wearing his cut-off gold and black Georgia Tech football number fifty-two jersey and a big gold chain, chimed in, "Easy, girl. She ain't going nowhere. This sweet thang, she be with me."

Barely functioning but vertical, Suzanne was out of patience and time. She bent down and got in his face. "Listen, asshole, my father is an Atlanta police chief. If you even stand up again before we leave, he will know. And I promise he'll let your coach know you've been keeping a young lady, a white young lady, against her will. You want that, number fifty-two?"

Suzanne had never, ever played that kind of racial braggadocio card, but it wasn't a typical night. Kim pried herself off the big guy's lap and handed him back his massive paws. He sat incredulous as the two girls hightailed it out of Delta Sigma Zeta.

With petite Kim holding her statuesque friend around the waist, they hustled as best they could down the front steps and headed for Fourth Street. A couple of blocks from the frat house, Suzanne started to get her sea legs back in the night air. As the two girls walked as rapidly as they could down the street, Thad – after a shower and sporting fresh clothes – stood atop the Delta Zeta veranda. The party was a long way from ending. No doubt she was *the* primo piece of ass he'd ever laid eyes upon in his life. Oh, how he wished he'd had a chance to do much more with her. But he was no longer angry. It didn't work out tonight—a challenge for another night.

The two young women walked as quickly as possible down the dark street, both in their bare feet, holding their heels and purses. Kim asked, "What the hell's going on?"

Suzanne replied, "For starters, I was drugged. I used to have a bra and panties, but he cut both off with a knife. He fondled me and threatened me with the knife. He slapped me and tried to stick his dick in my mouth."

Kim was genuinely stunned. "Suzanne, we've gotta call your dad."

"That's exactly what we're going to do when we get to a phone."

"Who did it?"

"Thad."

"Thad, the lacrosse player? I can't believe it. He seemed like such a nice guy."

"Trust me, he's not. He's a monster. I passed out on a back porch, and that's where he assaulted me."

They finally reached Techwood, which had only periodic traffic but at least a couple of streetlights. Kim pointed to the first convenience mart and gas station that, thank goodness, was a twenty-four-hour operation. Suzanne wasn't sure if they looked more like typical drunk college girls or hookers at 1:45 a.m. on the streets of Atlanta. She didn't care. The clerk in the convenience mart gave them a strange stare but let Suzanne use the phone.

Her mother, Mei, was out of town at a conference in New York. She woke her father up. "Daddy, I need your help. I was at a Georgia Tech fraternity party. I got assaulted, almost raped. But I'm okay. I'm with Kim. We're at a convenience store on Techwood, off campus."

Hollis Delacroix, deputy police chief of the Criminal Investigations Division, tried to remain calm, but the anger was already mushrooming. He figured it would be fastest to have her driven up to Buckhead by one of his officers. "Okay, baby, stay right there. I'll have you picked up in a few minutes. Stay put."

Within three minutes of hanging up, two black and whites with blue lights blazing appeared in front of the store, and four uniformed policemen piled out.

Chapter 3 – The System

Saturday, March 30, 1994

Atlanta

The APD cruiser drove Suzanne to Buckhead, where her parents lived in a comfortable one-story brick home on Delmont Drive, a block off Peachtree in the heart of Buckhead. Dressed in his pajamas and slippers, six-foot-four, 240-pound Hollis met his only child on the front stoop of the house where she'd grown up. He hugged her and asked, "You okay, baby?"

She assured him that she was, but she wasn't. Hollis saw the bruise on one cheek. "He hit you?"

"He slapped me pretty good."

With his giant arm around his pride and joy, Hollis walked her inside and fetched a blanket and ice for her face, along with a Polaroid camera. "Suzy, I'm going to take a couple of pictures of your face before we ice it—in case we might need them."

"Okay, I guess," she told him. She flinched as he snapped the photos, the flashes of light bringing back the terror.

"Daddy, I wanna take a shower."

Hollis told his daughter gently, "In a few minutes. We need to talk first." He handed her a glass of water and a couple Advils. First, the killer question. If Hollis didn't hear the right answer, they would be driving ASAP to Piedmont Hospital. Then he would call in his cavalry to pick up the boy at his frat house or wherever he was and throw his ass in jail with the latest collection of lowlifes. "Suzanne, you're telling me this guy didn't rape you. He didn't have vaginal intercourse with you?"

"No. Daddy, he fondled me all over. He was trying to force his way into my mouth, but he didn't have intercourse with me. He threatened me, cut off my underwear, pressed the knife against my crotch, and hit me before he left. If I hadn't barfed on him, I'm a hundred percent sure he would have raped me."

"Suzy, I know that this wasn't consensual, but did you talk to him, and did others see or hear you with him?"

"After we got introduced by Kim's friend Brenda, he talked to me off and on and kept telling me I was the hottest girl there and that he'd see me later. He got creepier as the night went on. He took Polaroids of lots of girls at the party and definitely a bunch of me, sort of like he was stalking me." She couldn't bring herself to mention the porno photos that she was now sure Thad took of her on the porch.

Hollis wished he'd been surprised by the events that his daughter relayed, but unfortunately, he wasn't. What Suzanne described was yet another in the increasing number of attempted or consummated rapes that he'd heard about on Tech's fraternity row and near other Atlanta colleges and universities. He knew a small number were ever reported; a small percentage of those were ever prosecuted; and a minute number of rapes ever became convictions. The system continued to be an abysmal failure when it came to sexual crimes. He was a top cop but knew there was no way he could run the Special Victims Unit.

After patiently listening to the rest of his daughter's story about her harrowing evening at the Delta Sigma Zeta house and jotting down notes, Hollis asked a few more questions but knew his daughter needed to rest. The last one:

"Do you remember his full name, the boy who assaulted you?"

"Thad Sutterman, Sutterberg. No, it was Sutterland. Thad Sutterland."

"What exactly does this Thad look like?"

"Good-looking white guy, brown hair, muscular build, not your height, but over six feet. Apparently, the Georgia Tech lacrosse team stud."

He had more questions, but it was 2:30 a.m. "We'll talk more about this in the morning. Mom will be back tomorrow afternoon. It'll be okay, I promise." He hugged her again and gave her a new ice pack. "I'm so sorry, Suzy. We'll figure out how to get this guy. I love you, Suzanne."

"Love you too, Daddy." In bed, it came to him. The Sutterland name. He wondered if Thad was related to Franklin Sutterland, the commercial real estate and business magnate. He wouldn't be surprised. He needed a little shuteye and would find out tomorrow.

In an old set of PJs and her familiar cozy, lavender bedroom that she'd known for seventeen years before moving to her apartment near the Spelman campus two years ago, she knew she'd be safe tonight. Her head was starting to calm down. She lay down between the crisp sheets, with an ice pack on her cheek, and fell asleep.

Hearing the shrieks, it took him only a few seconds to grab his .357 Magnum and race to her bedroom. His daughter was tossing and turning like she was having a seizure. Gently, he woke her up. "It's okay, baby, you had a bad dream."

"Daddy, it was horrible. He was coming at me with a knife again. It seemed so real. Can I sleep in your room tonight? Please?"

As he'd done when she was a child and had a nightmare, Hollis took his daughter's hand and led her to her parents' bedroom. She said a short prayer and was immediately out.

Soon after, Hollis got out of bed and made a pot of coffee. He watched the sunrise through his kitchen window – thankful for another day but anxious about the morning.

By six o'clock, Hollis had guzzled three cups, showered, and shaved – his sharp mind whirring and itching to take off. He waited until the respectable time of 6:30 a.m. to phone two colleagues. He asked each of them if they could meet him downtown at headquarters at 8:30 a.m. His daughter had been assaulted last night at a Georgia Tech fraternity party, and he needed their off-the-record advice on how to proceed. Neither complained about coming in.

Next, he called his wife at her hotel in New York. The call woke her up. Hollis started with, "Mei, how's New York?"

She knew him too well. "What's wrong, Hollis?"

"Suzanne was assaulted last night; she wasn't raped. But she's okay."

"What, Hollis?" she said, her voice trembling.

Hollis gave her the short version and said that he was on his way to get advice downtown before any next step. He told her that Suzanne was still asleep, and he had a cop car parked on their street.

"I'll see if I can catch an earlier flight. Tell Suzanne I love her."

Hollis left a note for his daughter: "Suzanne, the doors are locked. There is a police car parked up the street until I get back, probably late morning. Call my direct line at the station anytime if you want. I talked to Mom, and she'll get on a flight as soon as she can. Love, Dad."

Fifteen-year veteran Assistant District Attorney Jodi Stillwater and Detective Marsha Myerson from the Special Victims Unit, two of the best at their jobs he'd ever known, arrived at his office at the Criminal Investigations Division building on Peachtree at 8:30 a.m. sharp. He hoped the Dunkin' Donuts and coffee would mitigate a tad of the inconvenience.

"I want your take on the options. No bullshit. All off-the-record before any steps are taken. If there's a case, then there's a case. But otherwise, I don't want to put Suzanne into the system." A possibility that was already making him uneasy.

The three talked for two hours, and the news he got wasn't good. Or maybe it was. He wasn't that surprised. After they left, Hollis threw out his coffee and poured himself a half cup of Black Jack as he pondered what he'd try to sell to his daughter and wife.

He learned that her attacker was indeed a scion of the billionaire Sutterland family. Thad was well known to Marsha and Jodi. He'd been accused of two rapes in the past year, five in the past five years – and got off scot-free. They were sure there'd been others. Franklin was the mayor's biggest contributor. They played poker twice a month. Hollis' two colleagues told him that his being deputy chief could even make it worse for him and Suzanne. They admitted it sucked but deemed it a rigged deck. Marsha told him, "Hollis, you're not going to want to hear this, but Thad is off limits. Well, maybe an exception being if a dozen people saw him do a rape or murder and were willing to testify."

Hollis stroked his mustache while he mulled it over. Unfortunately, he knew they were right. Even as one of the top-ranking cops in Atlanta, he couldn't get any justice for his daughter. Not even from the system he was sworn to enforce and protect. The system sucked.

When Suzanne finally entered the kitchen at one o'clock Saturday afternoon, he was bracing himself for the inevitable blowback. "Mom called, and we talked for about an hour. She couldn't get on an earlier flight and then hers got delayed, but she should get home by five. So, how'd it go downtown?"

He procrastinated. "I'm famished." He got a couple of plates, grabbed chips and ginger ales, and put the Goldbergs pastrami sandwiches on the kitchen table. While sitting at the kitchen table with her eating lunch, he gathered his thoughts. "Suzanne, you remember what the knife looked like?"

She frowned. "Didn't you already ask me that last night? I don't know. It was dark on the porch. It was long and shiny. I heard a click, so maybe a switchblade. Is that so important?"

"Suzanne, in and of itself, it's not, but it's an easy question you'd get asked before a defense attorney would start shredding you. What were you wearing? How many drinks did you have? Do you even know what happened? Why did you seem to be so friendly with Thad at the party? To name a few."

He closed his eyes for a few seconds as he swallowed a bit of his sandwich but then tried to stick to the script that Jodi and Marsha advised earlier. Leaving out the repugnant Atlanta politics, he ended with: "Baby, I'm sorry, but going ahead with any charges is a bad idea. It isn't going to get you any justice."

Her amber eyes bore into his. Her lips parted in disbelief. He saw the anger etched in her beautiful face. She interrogated him. "You mean this punk is going to walk, and there's nothing I can do? Nothing you can do? You're a deputy chief, for goodness sake."

As anticipated, this got off to a rocky start, but he continued. "We *can* press charges, but they'll never hit court. I know you were assaulted, and so do Jodi and Marsha. They know that this all stinks, but they recommended letting it go."

"Let it go?" she asked incredulously, her eyes riveted on his.

For the next hour, Hollis used all the persuasion and patience he'd learned over his years as a father and a cop to try and convince his headstrong daughter that pursuing charges against Sutterland wouldn't be worth the effort and pain.

She was shocked that she was being encouraged to be silent, which was foreign to her upbringing. "Daddy," she pleaded. "Why not toss him in jail and throw away the key?" Her eyes were on fire; she was as pissed as he'd seen her since age three.

"Suzy, you're a legal adult. If you want to press charges, I'll drive you downtown now. I will. But I'm asking you to trust me on this one. Please. I agree Sutterland deserves punishment, and you are not the first woman he's assaulted. I'm going to handle this my way, and I promise as long as I live, you'll never have to worry about him again."

"Daddy, what are you going to do?" she asked him, seriously.

"I need you to trust me that I'll handle it."

Mei got home late that afternoon and spent an hour behind closed doors with her daughter—after agreeing to talk about anything other than what happened last night. Later, the three went out to eat at Bones, one of their favorite Buckhead spots. For two hours, the three enjoyed themselves, eating steak, salad, rolls, and a heavenly chocolate cake while hearing about Mei's trip, telling stories, and laughing—like last night had never happened.

Hollis had always been awestruck by his wife's beauty: perfect porcelain skin, long coal-black hair, tall with a superb figure, and the features of a Chinese empress. In bed that night, as he held her in his arms, she told him, "You know what I think about an eye-for-an-eye and that Jesus tells us to love our enemies. But Hollis, what happened to our precious daughter was wrong and deserves justice. I am sorry to say that, but it does."

"We'll trust God. He'll handle this like He always does."

"Okay, my love. We'll see what He does."

Suzanne stayed in her own bedroom in their home on Delmont, where she'd grown up, surrounded by her golf and basketball trophies, paraphernalia, and Marilyn Monroe prints. She had a hard time falling asleep, anxious about last night's dream and wondering what her father had up his sleeve for Thad.

The next thing she knew, it was morning. No bad dreams and lots of bright sunshine streaming through her window. Suzanne told herself, "It will be fine today." What had happened to her hadn't been a dream, but it was now in the past.

Chapter 4 – The Blues Brothers

Five Days After the Frat Party – April 4, 1994

Atlanta

Thad had underestimated the two old farts – whoever they were – and vowed he'd never let anybody assault him like that again. A block from his Tech parking garage, two old fogies in dark suits and old-fashioned hats – looking like they'd walked out of *The Blues Brothers* – beat the shit out of him. They took his clothes, but not his money or other personal effects. They did take his favorite knife, a custom stiletto that his father had given him for his thirteenth birthday – with the warning never to lose it.

Thad put the pedal to the metal and launched out of the Tech satellite and up Northside Drive to West Paces and the mammoth white brick mansion where he'd grown up and still lived when he wasn't in school, his haven for this evening.

Once again, he'd have to promise to be more careful with girls. A promise he'd not kept – even remotely – in the past. His fun with Miss Delacroix had been five days ago, and he hadn't told either of his parents yet. A mistake. He'd have to fess up about his fun with Suzanne Delacroix Friday night and being mugged earlier.

Driving up Northside Drive in his Bimmer, a beach towel draped around him, the car heat blasting, and his body throbbing with pain, Thad re-jiggered his stories of the party and beating. From his mother Maddie, he could hide nothing – but she'd give him a break. He longed for her soothing touch. She'd know exactly what he needed this evening.

Three years ago, he'd been surprised when his brother Jeremy opted to leave town and play lacrosse at Syracuse. On the field, the twins – knowing precisely what each other was thinking – were a formidable duo in high school lacrosse; Georgia high school state champs three years running. Jeremy, though, wanted to go away to school. Thad could have gone to Syracuse, too, but he'd miss his mother too much. Despite Jeremy being more like her, Thad knew he'd always be her favorite.

He punched in the gate code to his parent's estate and used his key to open the ten-foot oak front door. "Anybody home?" He yelled louder, "I need help!"

Maddie was in the living room downstairs and rushed to the marble foyer. Aghast at the sight of her bedraggled son with only a towel around him, she asked, "Thad, baby, what in the world happened to you?" He told her he'd gotten mugged down by campus. She took his hand and sat him on the couch.

"Franklin, come here *now*!" She told her son, "I'll be back in a minute, baby."

As her salt-and-pepper-haired, Richard Gere good-looking husband strolled down the spiral staircase from his upstairs study, she rushed by with a thick terry cloth robe, washcloths, and ice packs. She ripped off the beach towel and held the black robe as he fit his arms into the sleeves.

"What's all the ruckus?" his father calmly asked but was ignored. Sitting next to her son on the leather sofa, she dabbed his face with a warm cloth to remove the blood and pressed a big cold pack to his battered face. Then she opened the bottom of his robe and applied another pack to his testicles, his abdomen tightening with the frigid shock shooting through his groin, settling, though, as her fingers moved underneath his robe and touched his flesh, lingering lightly. Her touch felt better than a hundred ice packs or even a few lines of cocaine.

"Thad, you don't look so good, son," Franklin said. "Lemme get you a drink."

Maddie gently alternated the cold pack to each side of his bruised face while she eased a hand under his robe, making sure the ice pack was well positioned on his swollen balls.

Franklin doled out the drinks and sat in his favorite chair. "So, what the hell happened?" he asked while his son gulped the cold vodka. Not mentioning the lost knife and photographs, Thad told his parents part of the scoop about the fraternity party five nights earlier. He was fooling around with a beautiful oriental-black girl on the back porch after she'd had some drinks. He touched her but didn't rape her. She threw up, then she left the party. That was it. Tonight, two strange old guys in suits jumped him; they were sending a message to stay away from the girl.

Franklin chuckled. "Thad, maybe that'll teach you a lesson, son. But hell, you know when these girl things happen, I've got to know right away so Laura can take care of it." He smiled at his son. "Sounds like you almost reeled in quite a beauty." Thad gushed about her, and his father smiled. Maddie told them, "I'll be upstairs. Keep those packs on, Thad baby," she reminded him.

"Yes, Mother."

Stepping up the staircase to her boudoir, Maddie thought if only he'd been given more powers, more incidents like these might have been avoided, but Jeremy had received the lion's share, and he was the disciplined one. Although they were identical twins, she'd always been most fond of the second boy who'd emerged from her. Thad's dark brown eyes had always made her melt. She was so glad he was nearby at Tech.

Downstairs, Thad apologized profusely. "Sorry, Father, I screwed up." Franklin dismissed the apology with a flick of his hand. "Tell me more about the guys who hurt you." Thad described his beating at the hands of two strangers, adding, "They said they didn't care who the fuck my daddy was." Franklin was tired of cleaning up his son's messes but seethed at the assailants' comment.

The Chairman and CEO of Hawthorne Holdings, the multinational juggernaut based in Atlanta, told his strapping boy, "Thad, tomorrow morning you'll skip classes and go tell Laura exactly what happened. She'll be the best judge of what to do and get anything handled as necessary; she'll also check out this girl and her family. Here's your punishment: Other than talking with Laura, you'll do nothing else with the girl. Leave her be. There's one thing you will do. Get back to training and earn your black belt. I'll give you until the end of the year. Discipline and patience, son."

Thad was crushed that his father forbade him from pursuing Suzanne Delacroix, but he got it. "Yes, sir."

Though aggravated with his son, Franklin sympathized, and his anger smoldered. There would be the right time and place to settle the score.

Upstairs, Thad took off his robe and started the shower. In the mirror of his master bath suite, he perused the purplish contusions on his cheeks and chest, his big, fat, cut lip, and his swollen testicles. Leaning against the shower wall, he let the warm water rain down on his aching body. He replayed the episode with the fantastic Asian-black girl and got immediately hard, even with his aching balls, wanting her more than anything he'd wanted in his whole life.

As he toweled off, his mother appeared in a diaphanous black gown. Lovingly, she smiled at her bruised and battered son. "My sweet boy, I will make you feel better." She lifted her gown over her head and let it drop to the hardwood floor. She took him by the hand to his bed and pulled back the covers. As her son lay on his back, she carefully rubbed into his injuries an aromatic yellow salve from an old family recipe. Thad gazed at his lovely forty-three-year-old mother kneeling on the bed. A willowy brunette with a lissome body, striking oval face, and emerald eyes, she was lightly tanned except for her voluptuous, enhanced breasts and pale triangle of skin framing her dark brown, perfectly trimmed pubic hair.

Seeing her and feeling her touch made Thad forget all the pain. He'd never been able to resist his mother and never wanted to. He was aware her powers made him putty in her hands. No girls he'd ever been with did anything close to what his mother could do to his body. Maybe the tall, exotic girl from the party? He vowed one day he would find out.

Mei was asleep at the Delacroix home, only a few miles away, in Buckhead. Suzanne was back at her apartment. "The Blues Brothers," Sammy Baker and Floyd Gerrard, showed up at Hollis' – not wearing hats or sunglasses. He poured them all healthy pops of Tennessee whiskey. With the door shut in his small study, he listened to their firsthand report of how they'd "educated" Thad Sutterland. Afterward, Hollis opened his desk drawer and pulled out his hidden stash of bills to pay his old cop buddies for their services. But they wouldn't take a dime. They said they owed him way too much from the past. He told them, though, that they would be paid for their intermittent but ongoing surveillance of Thad. Both ex-APD detectives nodded as Hollis pressed a grand retainer into each of their palms.

They were men of few words, but Floyd told his old friend, "Hollis, that is one arrogant prick. I can tell he's a sicko who preys on girls and will never stop. He may play lacrosse, but he's no tough guy. He is a bad seed – there's something off about him."

Sammy added, "We humiliated and beat the shit out of him without doing permanent damage. Yeah, he struck me as creepy." He took a microcassette tape out of his coat and gave it to Hollis. "In case you want to hear it yourself."

Hollis hoped that his vigilante decision to handle Thad outside the system would not put his daughter in more danger – that this night would even the score and close the chapter.

Regardless, with Thad and his family in town, he knew there was always a chance she could remain in harm's way. Sammy and Floyd would keep an eye on Thad from time to time but couldn't tail him 24/7. He'd taught Suzanne how to shoot a handgun, and she had a Beretta in her apartment. Plus, she'd taken hundreds of self-defense courses during her teen years and had been tutored by a friend who taught her Krav Maga, which she loved. He outweighed her by ninety pounds, but she could take him to the mat without difficulty. His daughter could take care of herself a whole lot better than any female or male her age. Past that, all he could do was pray to God each day for her protection.

Sammy handed him Thad's exquisitely crafted stiletto. "That's quite a knife," said Hollis. He hit the release and snapped out the blade. No doubt the same one Sutterland had used on his daughter.

He thanked his old friends and sat back down in his favorite chair with another drink. He wished he'd been there to cut Thad's nuts off with his switchblade. The payback he'd never tell his daughter about would never be enough.

He walked his old friends out to their car, then unlocked his separate garage, where he did woodworking and rock polishing. He couldn't resist playing the tape. A little muffled but understandable. His blood boiled as he listened to the boy of privilege, the big man on campus, the star lacrosse player, the piece of shit who had assaulted his beautiful daughter. He returned to his office with the knife and tape and perused his collection of wooden boxes, many handcrafted by enslaved Americans. Although the maleficent weapon that had imperiled his daughter had no place in his house, he decided to keep it. From the top shelf, he pulled one of his favorites, a slender ebony humidor. He put the knife and tape inside the false bottom and put the box back on the shelf.

Chapter 5 – The Seashore

Easter Sunday, April 5, 2015

Seaside, Florida

There were lots of fancier beaches in the U.S. and around the globe, but Seaside, Florida, had always been her little slice of paradise. She loved it and couldn't wait to get back. Or maybe it was simply the intense need to flee. Surprisingly, it was smooth sailing through Alabama and even past Montgomery, where the interstate ended – with no major road construction or traffic glitches.

The sun was sliding from view as they arrived in Seaside. Suzanne was famished and knew Zeke was, too. But like a child, she was compelled to feel the wet sand between her toes and hear the crashing waves. She parked and, without unpacking, told her pet, "Come on, Zekey, let's hustle."

God painted the sunset skies with generous swathes of orangey pinks and burnt yellows framed by dusty blues – majesty tough to see through the big buildings of downtown Atlanta. But even more magnificent was the endless Gulf and the pure white beach. As the sun dove toward the dark water, Suzanne tossed off her sandals and waded knee-deep into the fizz of the surf; Zeke followed and was drenched within seconds. She stood in the cool saltwater and watched until the Gulf swallowed the entire golden ball.

Standing in the surf, her toes sinking in the sand, she smiled. Growing up, even though her dad had been a cop and her mom a housewife and volunteer, Suzanne had always known that her family had no financial troubles. She'd never lacked anything her parents thought was important for her, whether it be golf lessons or clubs, nice clothes, or her Spelman college education. They paid all expenses without ever using a credit card. But until her mom had moved on to heaven last year, she had no idea how much she would inherit. She was stunned. She was also glad that her short-term ex-husband had wanted a prenup – presumably to keep *her* out of *his* money. He had no rights to hers. She wasn't Oprah, but she'd never have to work a day in her life again if she didn't want to. And better than that, she could give a lot of away to worthy causes.

Her mom loved Seaside as much as she did, and when she died, Suzanne decided to take the plunge. She'd admired the cute aquamarine two-story Victorian on West Ruskin many times over the years. But then, about ten months ago, it had a tasteful "For Sale" sign in front. She bought it without negotiating. It was never going to be a rental but rather her home away from home, exclusively for her own use. So far, she'd not invited a man into her Seaside domain. There was no one to invite. Maybe one day.

The forecast was for tons of sunshine, except for the always possible short afternoon thundershowers. Perfect beach weather. On the second day at Seaside, Suzanne felt one hundred percent refreshed. She and Zeke fell into a relaxing routine. Before the serious sun worshippers arrived with their towels, umbrellas, folding chairs, coolers, and paperbacks, she'd already run a couple of miles on the beach. Zeke fetched his tennis ball in the Gulf and left grudgingly. They went for coffee and a bite to eat outdoors. Zeke got his breakfast – preferring an egg, bacon, and cheese biscuit above all else. Why not? Hell, they were on vacation. Maybe permanently. She went back to the beach for a few hours to swim and read while she let Zeke snooze in the house.

With her iPhone turned off all but ten minutes a day, she only returned a handful of texts, no calls or emails. She texted a few friends and colleagues, whose numbers popped up; to assure them she hadn't jumped off the deep end. The most she told anyone was that she was taking a break and having a terrific time at the beach, and she'd let them know when she'd be back.

On Friday of that glorious, sun-drenched, relaxing week at Seaside, Suzanne got a text from her old friend and golfing buddy, Kip Davies. Kipling Horatio Davies was a senior partner at Stuyvesant, Knight, Fitzpatrick & Burns, *the* top-shelf multi-practice law firm in Atlanta. He was considered by many to be the top criminal attorney in the city. Suzanne often kidded him that he was her buddy from the dark side – defending dirtbag criminals of all flavors and often getting them off so that they could wreak more havoc. He kidded her back and said that he kept her in business. Outside of her APD colleagues, he was the only guy who, at times, called her Tigress; it wasn't because of her golf game. Instead, he told her once that tigers were the most gorgeous, the most exotic, and the most dangerous of all creatures. He texted: "Heard thru the grapevine u left the force. Let's catch up when u can. K."

They first met in Fulton County District Court several years before on the opposite sides of a big drug-related murder case. Suzanne was immediately impressed – even while being interrogated on the witness stand. Kip was strikingly attractive in a Robert Redford, chiseled way with sunbaked wrinkles etched around his eyes and forehead, deep blue eyes, medium height with a slim build, and sandy hair. He didn't seem like the typical sleazy criminal defense attorney she'd so often encountered. He was as smart as a whip but also seemed genuinely human, self-deprecating, and charming – with his own special sauce of Southern charm. But she saw he could go for the jugular whenever needed. She was there in court when, on cross-examination, he'd sliced, diced, and laid to waste the prosecution's forensics expert witness.

From Seaside, Suzanne texted her friend back: "Thanks - at Seaside. Awesome here. Let u know when I'm back, S." The other folks she'd texted were a few close friends, including Dusty. One call she didn't acknowledge was Bobby Price, the investigative reporter for the *Atlanta Journal-Constitution*, who was considered by many to be the southern version of Woodward and Bernstein rolled into one. She had no desire to talk with Mr. Price on vacation, or preferably ever.

On Sunday morning, Suzanne woke after a dreamless night to booms of thunder and flashes of lightning, illuminating her bedroom through the thin window shades. She loved the pitter-patter of rain on the tin roof and always found morning storms peaceful and comforting. As he did at home, though, Zeke jumped into the bathtub, where he felt safe from the wrath of Mother Nature. As the storm continued, she snuggled under the covers and gave thanks for the week at the seashore. She clicked the TV remote. The weather, which had been so fine the whole week, had turned ugly. Nearly a one hundred percent chance of rain most of that day and the next. It was time to leave her little paradise on the Gulf. Time to get back home and start figuring out what she would do with the rest of her life.

While she drove up the two-lane highways through Alabama in the rain, Suzanne's thoughts kept drifting back to her parents. How could they both be gone before either reached age sixty-five? She knew exactly where they were and that they were together again. Still, she missed them terribly.

Her mother Mei's family, had immigrated to the U.S. in the early 1950s. After graduating with honors from Georgia Tech with degrees in both mathematics and physics, the beautiful Chinese woman went on a blind date with a handsome black policeman. Despite her family's initial lack of enthusiasm for their daughter betrothed to a black man, they were married four months later. Then, a year later, they had their only child, Suzanne Zhang Li Delacroix. At that point, her father was welcomed with open arms into Mei's family. Mei always wanted to be a teacher and was offered an assistant professorship by two deans. Still, she chose to walk away from academia. Through the Ebenezer Baptist Church, which Hollis had attended, she got deeply involved in a host of causes to help the downtrodden of Atlanta. Both her husband and her daughter thought that she was as close to a saint as any human they could possibly imagine.

As her husband's star rose in the Atlanta PD, Mei went to the big dinners and high society functions that were required – but confided to her daughter that she was uncomfortable at those functions. She felt much more at home with the less fortunate of her city than the wealthy and powerful. But Suzanne remembered how her dad beamed, showing off his beautiful, intelligent wife occasionally. After what had happened to her in college, Suzanne felt compelled to follow in her father's footsteps, which her father never encouraged but understood. From time to time, though, she was sorry she'd not taken her mother's road, one also riddled with human struggles but without the daily violence and mayhem.

Kiddingly, her dad would call his wife "Mother Mei," a wry take-off on Mother Teresa, but her mom had a sly sense of humor. She kidded back that she had married him mainly for his Christian last name, Delacroix, meaning "of the cross," and because he liked traditional Chinese food. On her deathbed a few months earlier her mom told her, "I couldn't have had a better daughter. I am so proud of you and your accomplishments in sports and school and then in becoming a policewoman and detective like your father was. You are going to be the first female, and the first female of color, to lead the Atlanta Police Department. You've grown into such a beautiful woman on the outside, but more importantly on the inside, and I am most proud that you have a strong faith and know Christ. Do not despair. One day, you'll find a good man worthy of you."

After her mother died, Suzanne didn't give up on God but wondered, "Where the fuck are *You*?" She continued to attend church, but her faith was wobbly at best. Why did God take both these two loving, good people instead of the trash she arrested and put behind bars – or many of her colleagues whom she knew broke a lot of rules and never got caught? But then she realized that both her parents had many more years on this Earth than the Monroe girls were given.

With Zeke in the passenger seat, his long fur plastered to his pointed head stuck out the window after the rain had stopped, Suzanne drove down the busy two-lane roads – mostly travelers returning with kids from the beach after spring break. Brighter old memories came alive. Her mom had loved to get away from the big city and took Suzanne to Seaside or Jacksonville – and even once, Captiva. Suzanne loved the fresh air and sand and water and swimming in the Gulf.

During the times her dad went with them, he usually played golf while she and her mom stayed near the water. Her dad was never a beach guy. He got bored quickly – but was also embarrassed that he'd never learned to swim. He'd wade out a bit into the ocean surf and get his toes wet. He always looked funny; a huge black guy with an oversized blue life vest like a mammoth black and blue Michelin man. But when he was wearing his life preserver on a fishing boat, he was perfectly content. He got lots of grief from his Atlanta fishermen buddies for wearing one but didn't care. He loved being *on* a boat wearing his adult floaty, but not *in* any water.

That made his death seven years ago even more bizarre.

Chapter 6 – The Lake

Seven Years Ago – November 2008

Lake Sidney Lanier, Georgia

Hollis Delacroix's Blackberry buzzed. "They bitin' yet?" his cop buddy, John Carleton (also a deputy chief at APD), asked.

"Getting my gear together, then I'll be on the water. Weather's not great but not horrible. When you come'n up?"

"Taking a quick break. I'll try to get there by late morning. Leave me a few stripers."

While Carleton's cabin was rustic and a half-century old, the small fishing boat that he owned was state-of-the-art: small, lightweight, and electric, stable even with two big guys standing in it fishing. Even Hollis, the aquaphobe, felt comfortable on the small boat in the water with his blue Overton life vest. Carleton kept the boat chain-locked and covered on a small boat trailer next to the cabin, along with an extra outboard engine and a much larger, older Gosling that they used when more guys were fishing.

Hollis could easily handle the small Twin Troller electric boat by himself. After checking the charge and snapping into his blue vest, he pulled it down to the small landing area, dragged it off the little trailer, and tied it to the dock. After getting his rod and gear and bait on the boat, he pushed off and headed out into the still, inky water of Lake Sidney Lanier, created more than a half-century before by the Army Corps of Engineers, which built the Buford Dam and named the resulting lake after the famous Georgia poet, writer, and musician. Doubtless, there were other fishermen on the vast manmade lake, with its hundreds of finger inlets, but he saw no others as he launched from Carleton's dock.

Hollis was a creature of habit. He always headed to his good luck spot first, which was only about a third of a mile out near the head of a wild cove on the other side of the lake – where he'd caught his biggest stripers over the years during the cooler weather. Anticipation pulsed through his veins as he readied his hook with the herring bait. Firmly yet lovingly, he held his Abu Garcia rod with Shimano reel, and despite the freshening of the cold breeze, he smiled broadly as he looked out over this lonely portion of Lanier. He sat on the back seat and cast his line out into the dark water – deep, but nothing close to the two-hundred-foot depths near the reservoir.

Within twenty minutes, Hollis got a serious bite and had a feisty fish on the line. It felt like a bass, a big one, running full tilt. *"Game on,"* he said with glee – and stood between the two seats to get more leverage. Entranced for the next ten minutes, while he tried to reel in the fish – his rod flexing periodically as the fish ran – Hollis realized that his small boat was rocking…but not from shifting his weight. It wasn't that windy. What the fuck?

Two hands were on the edge of the little boat, rocking it. A dark, masked head rose from the opaque water. The big cop had his .357, but it was in the waterproof bag under the back seat with his other belongings. He dropped his rod, which disappeared into the water and lunged for the bag. But a man in a mask and miniature Draeger rebreather grabbed his leg and pushed him sideways. Hollis lost his balance and fell into the cold, dark water of Lake Lanier.

At least he had his vest on and his head above the surface. But suddenly, the man grabbed his leg and pulled him under. By instinct, he kicked and struggled free, bobbing back up to the surface and gasping for a breath of air. Hollis knew he had to make it to the nearest shoreline, but it seemed miles away. With his vest on, he tried to doggy paddle but only made it a few body lengths until his assailant again pulled him under the surface.

Fear of the wet abyss paralyzed his brain. He panicked and swallowed a big mouthful of water. Gagging, his head broke the surface for a whiff of air, but the man was strong and relentless. Hollis went under again. Flailing, he instinctively tried to grab him, but no luck. Terrified, he gulped down more water. Again, he managed to find the surface, but the masked man pulled him down under again and again.

"Not this way, Lord," he thought, his fear mushrooming. *Please, not like this.* His final thought was of his girls, Mei and Suzanne. *"I love you both."* The man let him rise to the surface again and saw no movement. Again, he grabbed him by the boot and swam hard, pulling him down one more time for good measure. Hollis Delacroix had taken his last breath.

The killer worked fast. He unclipped the four snaps of the life vest. It floated on the surface; Delacroix began floating downward in slow motion. The man flipped on his headlamp and noticed that he'd lost a boot in the struggle. No way he was going to find it, but no matter. Delacroix drifted lifelessly past him, his eyes still open with a strange, knowing smile, staring dead at his killer.

It was pouring rain now, the cold wind whipping the pines and naked trees on the shoreline. The killer grabbed the floating vest and dropped it back on the deck of the small boat – leaving it where it would be more believable than Delacroix simply falling overboard with it on.

He swam underwater to the far shore. Before emerging, he used his miniature periscope to scan the lake. Only one boat that he could barely see at least a half mile away. He pulled off his fins, climbed out, retrieved his backpack hidden under a pile of brush, and made a cell phone call. "The accident happened." He hadn't had to use the backup syringe laced with aconite.

The recipient grinned and said, "Excellent." And hung up.

He took off his wetsuit, but as he unhooked his belt, he muttered, "Fuck!" When he'd rearranged the usual implements on his dive belt to make room for the syringe tube, he must not have fastened the sheath for his longtime, favorite knife.

The murderer walked through the woods until he reached the white van with "Sam's Window Repair" emblazoned in blue on the sides. The van bumped down the deserted gravel road. Mission accomplished. Two birds with one stone.

For Suzanne, it often seemed like yesterday. That blustery, hellish day the weekend before Thanksgiving in 2008 when her father drowned in Lake Lanier. Despite his fear of water, he loved to fish. He enjoyed it like he did golf, for both competition and camaraderie – and a way to escape the cop rat race. She'd imagined him and Carleton and other guys kicking back, drinking bourbon, playing cards, watching ballgames, and telling colorful tales. It was a guy's place that she'd heard much about – but had never seen until that awful November day.

This is what got pieced together:

After talking to John Carleton on his cell, Hollis went out on the water by himself. No one exactly knew what happened next. The weather was not great – off-and-on, rainy, and cold – so the lake had a fraction of its usual weekend inhabitants and visitors. By the time Carleton got there, seeing the smaller electric boat adrift a few hundred yards from the dock, he called 911 and then the main emergency number downtown. He untethered his other boat, launched it, and roared out to the electric fishing boat; then Carleton told his office to locate Suzanne ASAP.

Suzanne and Dusty had been working on a shooting in a familiar spot in South Atlanta. Dusty blue-lighted it the whole way up to Lake Lanier, doing one hundred miles per hour on the interstate. They made it in only forty minutes while Suzanne continually checked in on the radio. The rain lashed down, and the wind picked up. They located the little lake house, which was surrounded by several police and rescue vehicles.

Her dad, whom she believed always wore a life vest if he was going to get near a dock or any water – much less in a boat – was found drowned a half hour after she and Dusty arrived. She could barely see the boats on the lake but heard them radio in: "We found him." A diver had found Hollis' body nearly straight down from the pilot-less electric boat.

Suzanne couldn't believe or accept that her dad was dead. She watched as the rescue boats made their way back. Several men carefully lifted Hollis' body and laid him on the rickety wooden dock. Standing in the frigid, pouring rain, drenched to the bone, Suzanne was numb. Her father lay peacefully like he was sleeping. She started shaking her head, "No, Daddy. No, you can't leave me. You can't leave us. No." She stood alone with him on the dock for ten minutes while the others backed off. She knelt and kissed his forehead – her tears mingling with the cold rain.

Carleton tried to console her. "If I'd been here with him, this would've never happened. I'm so sorry, Suzanne, and for Mei too. He was a great man. I'll miss him."

Suzanne regained her composure and insisted that she tell her mother in person. Dusty drove her back to Buckhead in silence. Mei was inconsolable that evening, and Suzanne took the week off and stayed with her night and day, the two crying, consoling, and grieving together. Dozens of friends brought huge amounts of food, most of which Mei asked to be driven to food pantries sponsored by the church. Mother and daughter left home only for the visitation three nights later and then the funeral.

An "accidental drowning," Fulton County's Chief Medical Examiner concluded without fanfare after the autopsy. No big surprise. No heart attack or other medical condition factored in. No evidence of foul play. Hollis'.357 had been on the boat in a waterproof bag with his shield and cuffs, items that were never far from his person – as well as his wallet and car keys. His oversized blue life vest lay unsnapped on the deck after being retrieved near his boat on Lanier . It was surmised that Hollis had either not put it on at all or had taken it off. John Carleton confirmed that in recent years, while fishing with him on Lake Lanier, Hollis would, from time to time, unsnap his confining vest and even take it off for short periods, especially when the water was calm. Still, he'd never seen him in or near the lake without his blue life vest nearby. As a non-swimmer, it was further presumed that Hollis had been fighting a fish and had lost his balance. His rod and reel were gone. After going overboard, he panicked, was unable to reach the boat, and drowned.

In the aftermath of her father's death, Suzanne didn't know why, but her gut told her that her dad's drowning was no accident. All of them, even Deadeye, wrote it off as a sad mishap, mainly because of her father's inability to swim. For months, she spent much of her spare time trying to figure out how the drowning could have been a murder. But she came up with nothing.

Seven years later, she believed there was a cold case to be solved. But it was colder than the depths of Lake Lanier.

Chapter 7 – The Board Room

April 12, 2015

From Seaside to Atlanta

Suzanne owned two places with no mortgages, had a boatload of money and investments, had her Aussie, Zeke, a few friends, and belonged to arguably the best golf club in Atlanta. She was divorced with no man in her life, had no job, and had lost her mom and dad. She had the absolute freedom to choose any new direction. She had no clue.

Had she been too headstrong and screwed up, resigning from APD so hastily? Tucker had even left a scathing phone message: If she was done with her little unpaid, unapproved vacation and her moping, he'd be willing to give her a second chance – and not write her up. Fuck you, Tucker, she thought.

It was the only thing she'd known for seventeen years. Despite her dad's initial admonitions, right out of college, Suzanne applied to become a policewoman and started as an Atlanta beat cop. She rocketed up the ranks, working in Narcotics and then Homicide. She made detective at age twenty-seven and inspector first grade by twenty-nine, and she knew that made her father proud. For the past seven years she and Dusty Rayfield had led Atlanta PD in closed homicide cases. The Tigress was a superstar. Until she quit last Sunday.

Now, what the hell would she do?

She and Zeke arrived back from Seaside late Sunday afternoon. Hotlanta had heated up, now in the mid-eighties, and it was three weeks until May. It was good to be back, but as she used her security card to enter her condo, the peace of her vacation had vanished like a puff of smoke in the breeze. After a short walk with Zeke in Piedmont Park, she grabbed her mail and then took a long, hot shower – trying to relax but dreading the mountain of calls and emails to wade through. After pulling on a T-shirt and gym shorts, Suzanne poured herself a glass of cold Conundrum and gazed out her fourth-floor window onto the Piedmont traffic below. She'd get to her emails and calls tomorrow.

She was okay with her sudden departure from APD, but she was not OK with not solving the Monroe murders. Maybe not being on the force would give her more freedom to think and work outside the box.

The big guest room/office in her spacious condo had a mega closet with high ceilings like the rest of the room. That's where she stored her four-by-six-foot, rolling bulletin boards. She called it her "Board Room."

Although she'd heard that many police departments in big cities had gone NCIS or Homeland digital with giant, interactive – and even three-dimensional – digital screens, Atlanta was not one of those. Suzanne liked being able to see the nitty-gritty pieces of evidence right in front of her on the big, old-fashioned, erasable bulletin boards. Few cops even used them, but she liked hers at home. Sure, the give-and-take at the station could be productive, but she did her best thinking alone. For years – on significant or particularly confounding cases – she'd copy or "borrow" critical information and set up her boards, then share what she came up with. iPhone photos made that remarkably easy. Often in chaos, her Board Room was now empty.

She had four enormous, double-sided, rolling crime – aka evidence – boards. Right now, three were completely blank. The fourth in the far back she hadn't touched in seven years. It had "Hollis Delacroix" in black marker at the top. A few photos of her father in fishing gear when he was alive and a handful of questions in faded red. The blank space on the board was disappointing. Pitiful, she thought. She touched his friendly face in one of the photos and said, "I'm going to focus on these murders now. One day, I will find out what really happened to you."

She rolled out a blank board and wrote MONROES at the top, but she was too tired to continue. With Zeke at the foot of her bed, Suzanne had another dreamless, peaceful night's sleep. Maybe her short vacation to Seaside and her resignation from the Atlanta PD had been genuinely therapeutic.

Monday, April 13

Midtown, Atlanta

On Monday, Suzanne made her first cell phone call in a week to her ex-partner, Dusty Rayfield. She told him flat out, "Deadeye, I'm not coming back, but I'm gonna help you catch the dirtballs who committed the Monroe murders. How 'bout you drop by later for an early dinner? Oh, and sneak out any good files."

She could almost see him smile over the phone. He told her, "Will do, Suzy. We don't got jack shit on this yet. Been a circus, especially with Tucker in the middle of it."

Suzanne missed her longtime partner Dusty Rayfield, a tough, smart, honest-to-a-fault guy from Macon, Georgia. He loved being a cop and, for the past seven years, had been Suzanne's partner extraordinaire. His incredible skill was his accuracy with a handgun, which he attributed to his granddaddy, who taught him to shoot at targets and critters with an old Colt .45 at age seven. Deadeye was uncanny with his own Colt 1911s, but also any other handgun. At twenty-five paces, he could wear out a bull's-eye. Even more fun, though, he could hit a quarter thrown into the air from the same distance. And he could shoot two simultaneously, with a Colt in each hand. He was the only cop on the Atlanta PD she knew who always carried two guns of that size. He was the best shot she'd ever seen. Better, he was the best person she knew.

She always felt secure with Dusty as her backup. His pockmarked face was ravaged by teenage acne; he'd never married, though she knew he wanted to. She saw him as a beautiful gem on the dirty battlefield between good guys and bad guys.

She needed to get up to speed on the Monroe murders, especially after ignoring newspapers and TV news for a week. She went online to the *Atlanta Journal-Constitution* first and then to dozens of other news sites. Other than reports indicating that the three women were brutally murdered with a knife or other sharp instrument and that Confederate flags were found, there were no other specifics about the crime scene she'd visited a week earlier. Many in the media were postulating the murders were racially motivated – and predicting what the fallout could be in Atlanta and elsewhere. Even though they didn't come right out and publicly say it, it was obvious there'd been no progress the past week.

She spent the afternoon collecting preliminary info for the new board. When he arrived promptly at five o'clock that evening with four thick files under his arm, Suzanne met him at the door and handed him a Dos Equis. "Time to get to work, Deadeye."

"Nice to see you too, Suzy," he grinned.

In his jeans, T-shirt, and basketball shoes, he sucked on the longneck and followed her back to her Board Room, where he'd been only a couple of times. A large pepperoni and sausage pizza sat on the big desk along with dozens of Post-its, notepads, markers, pens, pencils, Scotch tape, and balls of string in a rainbow of colors. The window shades were open, but the bumper-to-bumper Midtown traffic was made virtually inaudible by her soundproofed windows. She liked the noises of the city but also the option for peace and quiet.

"Sit," she directed. "Let's eat first. And it is great to see you."

After devouring her first piece, she asked, "So, who'd they stick you with?"

"Fran Schultz – can you believe it?"

"Ooh, that's bad. Sorry, buddy. Hopefully, you'll be able to stay out of Grady's psych ward. Tucker is screwing with you. You know he wasn't crazy about me. Now you're going to get the fallout, I'm afraid."

"Fuck Tucker," he said and guzzled the remainder of his first beer." The good news is I'm on the Cascade Murders Task Force; Mia Gonzales is heading it up. I won't have to deal with my new partner too much for now. The Bureau got called in to check out the white supremacy angle and do the heavy-duty evidence testing. Mia wanted me to ask if you'd be a civilian expert on the Task Force?"

Coyly, she told him, "I'll think about it."

Under MONROES were the names and cut-out photos of the murdered women: Lisa, Leslie, and Linda Monroe. After wolfing down her second slice of pizza, she flipped through his police files and photocopied key photos and tidbits of information. A whirling dervish, she moved with purpose back and forth, writing, photocopying, cutting, taping, erasing, rearranging, and tossing – several colored markers stuck in the top elastic of her booty shorts. Neither worried about the legality of duplicating confidential police files. Tucker would have his badge, but Dusty could give a rat's ass. Still, the files needed to be returned that evening. The floor of the Board Room now looked like a class of second graders had been given free rein with unlimited art supplies for the day.

"So where are we on this?" The question she never got around to asking last Sunday morning at the murder scene.

He filled her in on info she couldn't possibly know yet.

"Who found them?" asked Suzanne.

"Anonymous call from a burner phone that morning: 'Here's where you'll find three dead niggers. The country is for whites only.' Then gave the Monroes' address and hung up. A cop in the area got there first, before any civilians. Thank goodness."

"Anyone see anything?"

"An elderly lady, Flora Nethers, lives alone in a house on the other side of the street. She couldn't sleep that night and went out to sit on her front porch. She couldn't remember what time, but thought it was around midnight. Saw the lights on across the street at the Monroes', which she said was unusual at that time of night. Said there was a truck at the dead end of the street near the Monroes' house on her side. Wasn't there in the morning when she got up. The detective said she was ninety and didn't seem to have her show together; she was probably blind as a bat. But her timeframe checked out with the approximate time of the Monroe deaths between midnight to 1:00 a.m."

Maybe she saw more than people think? She made a mental note.

"They were raped?"

"A lot of internal damage from the wooden crosses, so the ME said it's impossible to tell. But yeah, probably raped, then tortured, then killed. Big surprise, no DNA."

"Drugged?"

"ME said a weak morphine and pentobarbital injection. Probably, so they could be controlled better," he said.

"Multiple killers?"

"Probably two, maybe another one. They did a pretty good job of smearing their bloody footprints – and likely wore shoe covers. Tons of fingerprints around the house keeping the FBI busy."

"And you know, none will pan out."

"Yep," he agreed. "Probably wore medical or thin plastic gloves as well."

"What else about the Monroe girls, other than what I've already read about?"

"Fourteen-year-old fraternal twins looked almost identical but weren't. Lisa was about an inch taller than Leslie, but they both had similar slim body builds. Leslie's eyes were a lighter shade of brown, more amber, like yours. But they had similar facial features. Both looked like their mother, Linda, but weren't spitting images. Both were straight-A students, didn't date, and both had budding singing careers, having won an amateur duo competition held at Chastain Park as a local warm-up for Mary J. Blige. Also, both were in their church choir and active in church youth activities. They were supposed to sing at your church on Easter morning."

"At Ebenezer?" She stopped in her tracks. "That's where I've seen them! They sang in the teen choir. The world is too horribly small."

"Why, Lord, why these beautiful girls?" She knew God didn't owe her any explanation, but she was going to respectfully ask *Him* when her day came, *"Why were those beautiful young girls murdered on Easter?"* She felt guilty for missing their funerals on Thursday.

"What about the knives?"

"A pair of identical custom hunting knives, varying only with the imperfections in the onyx handles. We've already tracked them to the knife maker, a guy named Jeremiah Robert Hall, outside Santa Fe, New Mexico. Helped that he etched his initials, JRH, at the bottom of his blades. That's the good news. The bad news: Jeremiah, a lifelong four-pack-a-day guy, died ten years ago of lung cancer. For forty years, he had a shop on the outskirts of town and ran a cash-and-carry business. No plastic. No checks. Apparently, not much accounting either. Doesn't look like he ever paid Uncle Sam a dime.

"In his heyday, Hall was one of the go-to guys out West if you wanted a custom, decorative knives with handles made of stone or bone, and price wasn't relevant. Individually, they sold for hundreds of dollars, even back then. They're all collectors' items now, and most go for four figures and up. Always happens when an artist is in the ground. There's more in the file about the knives, but no known records of who bought them. Not even any photos of his creations. His son Rory, who still lives in Santa Fe, remembers at least twenty-five years ago, when he was a kid, that his dad made a few dozen white onyx-handled knives with the unusual black design inlaid on each side of the handles. He also vaguely recalled his dad telling him that the guy who commissioned them walked in, examined them, and paid him double what he asked in cash. On one condition: he never uses the same design again. They shook on it, and his pop said it was his biggest sale ever – by many thousand dollars. A few of his custom knives are on sale on eBay—but not like the hunting murder weapons. The Bureau's tracking down any known owners of Hall's knives to see if there might be any in our area."

Suzanne perused the eight-by-ten color photos of the enormous knives alongside a yardstick. Each measuring eleven inches of steel with five-inch handles made of tapered white, gray-streaked onyx with the unusual, inlaid black double-cross symbols on each side; razor-sharp, with serrated tips, high-quality stainless-steel blades. Suzanne couldn't take her eyes off the photographs of the knives that had been used to butcher the Monroes. Appalling yet magnificent weapons. She taped the photos to the top side of the board and wondered if she'd ever seen that design before.

"How'd the press get the Confederate flag information?"

"Don't know. This thing was supposed to be buttoned up tight. Had to be an insider. Hines suggested maybe you did it. Not even Tucker went for that. So, who knows? The *Constitution* got it first, and then others piled on. Erin Burnett was positively jizzy; I think because this happened so close to CNN's intergalactic headquarters. It's been her lead every night for a week. Like anticipating a race war worth many juicy news cycles. Last night, she started one of her famous countdowns: 'It's now been seven days since three black women were murdered in the peaceful, historic Cascade Heights neighborhood in Atlanta…'"

He hesitated and then said, "Hell, I guess the Indians could get real restless unless the mayor can show progress. A Confederate statue over in Decatur got trashed this morning. You probably saw that the governor weighed in—weeny-talk as usual.

"With three murdered black women and the Confederate-Nazi flags on the table, there's a full-court press to go after every pathetic white boy within a couple hundred miles who is wearing Jeff Davis's flag or has it emblazoned on his Ram pickup, has a gun rack, or chews Skoal. The problem is, as you can imagine, that's a big number. The mayor and the chief gave the mandate to go after white supremacists, apparently meaning the Aryan Brotherhood, the Klan, and other gumball groups high on the Southern Poverty Law Center's radar. Maybe a new flavor of ultra-radical white supremacy hate thing only the Feds knew about? Mia's coordinating the Feds, and Tucker is coordinating locally and with law enforcement across Georgia."

He stopped and said, "I don't know, Suzy."

"Don't know what?" she asked, bemused at the thought that a slew of rednecks were getting dragged through a serious wringer for a change.

"Doesn't have the feel of a stupid white supremacy hate thing. Hell, there was maybe twenty grand of jewelry sitting on the mom's bedroom dresser. Nobody that dumb wouldn't have lifted it – unless money wasn't important."

She smiled, even more sure who the murderers were not.

"How about the crosses?"

"Not much to tell, at least yet. Two black wooden crosses with four pointed ends: about a foot long and five inches across. Hand-carved ebony by a pro, but no initials. But here's what's interesting. They're notched, so when slotted together, they form the unusual double cross – like what's on the knives – and the shape in which the twins' bodies were positioned. So far, I don't think anybody's found anything, online or in the databases, like these crosses – or the way they were used."

Suzanne taped copies of the cross photos next to the knives. Crucifixes, without a Jesus image. Unspeakable instruments of sexual assault, torture, and death. For comfort, she touched the cross around her neck. She knew what it meant. The cross has been a Christian symbol since the time of Constantine, but there have been countless versions with many meanings over thousands of years. Christianity had no monopoly on the symbol. There must be a dark story behind the two crosses used to desecrate two precious girls. She believed in her God of Light one hundred percent, and so she must believe in the supernatural. Otherwise, nothing made sense. She'd dealt with unspeakable evil for years. Was it such a giant leap to think a supernatural Evil was battling back every chance it could?

"What else?"

"The usual rule-outs. It's not a family thing. No brothers. Mr. Monroe died years ago. Uncle in Baton Rouge is in a wheelchair. Mom, who was a middle school teacher, was well-liked. No family enemies that we've heard about. Oh, almost forgot, the alarm was on."

She remembered seeing the rectangular alarm sign stuck in the ground at the edge of the driveway near the house. "Whaddya mean it was on?"

"When the first cops got there and knocked on the door and didn't get an answer, they picked the lock, and the alarm went off; so I guess it was set. Not sure what the alarm company system was able to tell us if anything, but I'll find out."

"So, they knew how to turn it off and on. "Interesting and another reason not to go down the white supremacy path. Any other similar MO in Atlanta or anywhere?"

"Not sure what the FBI is checking out. If not done by a white extremist group, that would only leave a whole lot of psychos, sociopaths, wackos, devil worshippers, or other assholes even more fucked up. Sure looks like a ritualistic sex thing to me."

She nodded in agreement.

He asked, "Why leave the knives at the murder scene?"

"To make a point. Sorry, that's a horrible joke, but I think it's true. The murderers were showing off – using one-of-a-kind weapons to underline their murders. Mocking us. Daring us to join a sick game. Dusty, I don't know, but I think they've done this kind of thing before."

"Yeah, maybe the Bureau is considering a serial killer – or killers – possibility…. Hey, there wouldn't be any street cameras nearby, would there?"

"Not at the end of the street. I know the city has installed hundreds more in the last few years. I heard there are more cameras in Atlanta per person than in any other place except Beijing and London. I'll check where the closest ones are. Not sure what CCTV video would show unless we've got a clue what to look for."

Dusty put his empty longneck down and asked, "Okay, Suzy, tell me what *you* think is going on."

She wasn't a Quantico-trained profiler, but Dusty trusted her smarts and intuition a lot more than anyone he knew in any law enforcement agency he'd ever worked with.

Suzanne took a deep breath. "No question, they wanted the two girls. Mom was a sidebar. Multiple people planned and did the murders. I agree with you. No way it was the Aryan Brothers, the Klan, or a known white hate group thing, but it could be a new group or cult with a related, bizarre occult twist. These killers are sophisticated. Ritualistic murders are not inconsistent with the randomness of serial types – if, indeed, there have been others like this. The Monroes were chosen. Why, I'm not sure. Could be their number just came up."

Peak traffic over, she hit a button near the light switch and opened the bank of Board Room windows vertically halfway, allowing in fresh air filled with less strident sounds of the city. She paused and looked down on Piedmont and the tops of vehicles buzzing by in both directions. The thicker city air wasn't Seaside's, but comfortably familiar. She snapped out of it and peppered Dusty with more follow-up questions. At ten, she suggested they call it an evening.

On the way out, Dusty again asked her about the Task Force. Mia Gonzales had clawed her way up the testosterone-dominated FBI ladder to become second in charge of the Atlanta Field Office. It was no mean trick for a woman who was a second-generation Mexican American. She'd always liked Mia but hadn't seen her for months – since she ascended to the fifth floor of the Bureau's palace on Buford Highway.

"Lemme think about it, Dusty." But she'd already made up her mind.

Dusty Rayfield smiled as he climbed into his car. *"A woman scared of no person, place, or thing,"* Dusty thought as he left. *"She is amazing."*

But he had no idea of his former partner's private terror – which she'd never shared with a soul.

Chapter 8 – The Reporter

Tuesday, April 14

Cascade Heights – Atlanta

Suzanne was thrilled when her iPhone alarm went off at 5:45 a.m. because she'd slept the whole night without a bad dream. She popped out of bed and took a three-mile run around Piedmont Park with Zeke. It was already warming up, the city air thickening like it always did. Probably one of those short Atlanta springs that would morph quickly into an Amazonian summer.

After breakfast, she started slogging through her messages and emails from the past week. Kip Davies texted that he'd love to take her to lunch at the Capital City Club downtown tomorrow at 1:00 p.m. He was sorry that they couldn't also play golf, but they'd golf next time. There was no one else she'd like to eat lunch with more but texted back, "Thanks, see u there!"

Her cell rang. She figured he'd call again sooner rather than later.

"Suzanne Delacroix. You do have a phone. I was wondering."

"Bobby Price. What can I do for you?"

Over the years she and her father had encountered the *Constitution*'s top investigative reporter more than a couple of times. Now in his mid-sixties, he was still good at his job but could be a royal pain in the ass.

"If I didn't know better, Suzanne, I'd say you've been ignoring me."

"Been on vacation, Bobby. Catching up."

"So, I heard you resigned from the APD. That true?"

"Yep, I'm gone."

"Too bad. A scandalous reason, or you just got tired of shooting black guys? Oops, I meant bad guys," he mocked.

"Fuck you, Bobby, and you can quote me."

She heard him chuckle. "Amazing coincidence that you quit right after the nastiest, most high-profile multiple homicides in Atlanta since Wayne Williams' killing spree. I heard you were at the crime scene. Figured you'd be running it."

"Decided it was time to move on."

"Right," he replied with more than a hint of sarcasm.

She couldn't resist: "Hey, Bobby, it sounds like the press thinks the Aryan Brotherhood killed the Monroe twins and their mom."

"That's horseshit, and you know it. Filler copy for now – though the cops and stupid media hacks are loving it. It wasn't the AB or the Klan, was it, Suzanne?"

"No clue, but I'm sure you'll figure it out."

"You wouldn't still be working the case, would you?"

"Like I told you, Bobby, I left the force."

"Not what I asked."

He paused. "Oh, by the way, I don't think this was the first time these guys murdered twin girls. In case you're interested, check out the Blount twins' kidnappings in Anniston, Alabama, in 1973 and the Brevard twins' murders in our backyard in Woodstock in 1974. Not to mention the Oosterhuis twins' kidnappings in Birmingham in 2002. Three sets of female teenage twins were kidnapped or murdered. I believe all the girls ended up dead, and the crimes are related even though they are spread over a lot of years. The kidnappings are still cold cases. The Brevard murders were officially solved when the black suspect was himself murdered in jail. Pretty convenient, huh?"

She didn't respond, so he continued. "I remember when your father was a young Homicide detective. Worked on the case of an Atlanta drug dealer found dead in Anniston. It was the same time as when the Blount twins disappeared. He never found the murderer.

"Go figure that," she replied, but Bobby's comments were intriguing. When she'd been a struggling, green homicide detective, she remembered her dad telling her about his first big murder case. He'd thought it was intertwined with a double kidnapping, but he never solved the case. She knew it always bothered him.

"Suzanne, can you at least tell me how the Monroes were murdered? Anything unusual? Off the record? All I heard was that there were Confederate banners and lots of blood, probably from a knife."

She ignored the question. "Gotta fly, Bobby. Talk to you another time," she told him and hung up. She knew full well that Bobby Price wasn't going to disappear forever, but she needed to digest what he'd told her before she traded any information.

Bobby Price knew her well enough that he was ninety-five percent sure that Suzanne was still on the case, even if she'd quit APD. Or if she hadn't been on the case, she was now. He'd bet good money she was going to help get him a great story. For now, he had no problem letting her do the heavy lifting. He would be back in touch.

Her Board Room was a disaster, so she spent a half hour cleaning up the clutter. Dusty called and asked if she could be ready by 10:30 a.m. "We got an appointment to see Flora Nethers at her home in Cascade Heights."

Dusty parked in front of Mrs. Nethers' small single-story brick house. Almost involuntarily, both walked over to the Monroes' and stood silently at the end of the sidewalk. The beautiful old home was now devoid of activity, but at least it was no longer defiled by yellow crime scene tape.

Transfixed on the Monroes' house, Suzanne said something he'd never heard her say. "When I find 'em, Deadeye, they're not going to prison."

He nodded his head in solemn agreement, and they walked back across the street.

Suzanne rang the doorbell and waited patiently until Flora Nethers made her way to the door. She introduced APD Detective Dusty Rayfield and herself as a police consultant. "Can we sit out here on your front porch, Mrs. Nethers?"

"Lordy, it's a fine spring morning. Let's do that. My, you're a pretty girl," the old woman said. Suzanne blushed.

Flora used her walker to nimbly avoid the cracks in her tidy but deteriorating cement front porch. Gentlemanly, Dusty tried to help her get seated on what was obviously her favorite perch, but she'd have none of it. Suzanne made small talk with her for about fifteen minutes while Dusty listened impatiently.

She was an itty-bitty raisin of a black woman – frail-looking but not your typical one-foot-in-the-grave, depressed oldster. She wore a pair of old-fashioned, flared-edged brown glasses that looked like they were from the Truman era. Her baggy, faded, floral dress looked even older than her glasses.

"Mrs. Nethers, we're sorry for the inconvenience, but can you please tell us again what you saw that night?" Suzanne asked.

"Call me Flora. Couldn't sleep a damn. A might chilly, but I needed air. Put my shawl on and sat right where I am now. Maybe a quarter after midnight. Full moon. A truck or I'd guess you'd call it a van, was parked a little way down the street, not quite at the dead end. My side of the street. Never seen it before."

"Could you describe it?" Dusty asked.

Flora Nethers turned her head and focused on the spot where the van had been parked. After a minute, Suzanne could tell Dusty was antsy for an answer. She gave him a barely visible shake of the head to let her talk.

Then she spoke emphatically: "Well, the way it was parked, I only saw the back. It was a light color. It had writing on it and a big faucet."

"Like a plumber?" Dusty asked.

She straightened up a bit and stared directly into his eyes. "Yes, sir. Could be." As if a lightbulb went off, she continued. "Yep, probably was a plumber. White with a big blue faucet and wrench. Hard to tell with the one streetlamp."

He asked, "Anything else about the van?"

"Letters and numbers, but I don't remember what they were. Hope you catch them bastards. Fine folks, the Monroes."

Suzanne got an idea and asked, "Flora, how many people did you see that night?"

"After I went back in and shut the door, I looked through my front window. Saw three of them walking down the Monroes' sidewalk to the van."

She and Dusty were shocked. "Three? You're sure?"

"Sure as I am there are three cardinals sitting in the dogwood tree in their yard right now. There were three white folks, two tall and one shorter, dark hair; dark clothes; wearing caps like the Braves. I love baseball. They were all carrying bags."

Suzanne had to strain to barely see a couple of the birds and wasn't sure what kind they were. With his twenty/fifteen eyesight, Dusty could see them but had a hard time believing bespectacled Flora Nethers could at that distance.

She and Dusty both thought the same thing: Holy shit. As close to a quality eyewitness as they'd ever want.

"Flora, did you tell the other policeman that you saw three people?" Suzanne inquired politely.

"I see pretty damn good. Don't remember recent stuff that good all the time, though. Then, I do. The other PO-lice banged on my door the next morning before I got going good. I didn't like him much. No manners. I was gonna tell him about the people, but before I could, he just left without even saying thank you. I like you two. Was hoping somebody nice would ask me."

Suzanne asked, " Flora, did you get a good look at their faces?"

"No, they had their heads ducked. Saw a little of their faces; their hands were white. I think the shorter one was maybe a woman."

"Why do you say that?"

"Don't know. Maybe she just walked more like a female."

Instead of interrogating Flora more, Suzanne thanked her again and said they might need to come back and talk. In the meantime, if she remembered anything else, Dusty handed her his card. "Please call me anytime, Flora."

"I'd like that. For you all to come back."

Suzanne thought, cool lady; hope I can have my shit together half as much as she does at age ninety. Her brain tripped into overdrive. No doubt the murderers used the plumbing van that Mrs. Nethers saw. Believable that the Monroes had a bad toilet leak, even on Easter Eve. But they weren't called. They came as strangers without invitation. They'd done their homework and knew exactly what they would do. Three white people, one maybe a woman, came to kill. They came and left in a plumber's van.

They learned a lot from ninety-year-old Flora Nethers. Dusty knew it was coming. She told him, "That was seriously shitty detective work, making assumptions about an elderly lady who's sharper than most of our colleagues – I mean *your* colleagues."

"You got that right," he replied, shaking his head. "Our bad."

"You all need to check out the video feeds for all cameras ringing the area a mile or so out. I can only imagine how many hundred hours that will take. No doubt Tucker won't be thrilled at the tons of overtime – but if your folks can see a similar van, and maybe get a plate, we might find the killers."

Dusty said he'd run with the van lead from Mrs. Nethers but added, "Suzy, the higher-ups are already in love with the white supremacy thing. Fry a couple crackers for the deaths of three black women. That will get the mayor another four years, for sure. Maybe a congressional seat."

"Yeah, well, let Tucker and the other dickheads think that. You and I both know it didn't go down that way. And the plumbers brought along a woman? No fucking way."

After getting back, she headed to East Lake to get outdoors and play a quick round of golf. Hitting the little white ball on the spongy, perfectly manicured Zoysia grass always freed her mind. By herself, with no other groups in the way, she zoomed around the front nine in a little more than an hour. On the tenth tee, though, she couldn't get Bobby Price's theory out of her mind. She put her driver back in her bag and decided to check out that possibility.

Suzanne called Dusty on the way home and confirmed dinner at 6:30 p.m. – and told him to bring Chinese, use his card, and let himself in. He was one of two people who had both the code into her building (without needing to be buzzed up) and keycard into her condo. The other was her friend, Katie Leopold, Zeke's pet sitter and dog walker. Living on the edge of Midtown, Suzanne had always been comfortable that her building was secure, even without a guard stationed on the first floor. The condo association contracted with a top-notch 24/7 security service and had surveillance at all entrances, elevators, and hallways. Besides, she had Zeke – and in her condo and car, she had enough firepower to stop a small army.

Zeke greeted Dusty at the door and licked his hand. Suzanne was in the kitchen when he came in. Before attacking the Board Room, they sat down and gabbed while scarfing down wonton soup with crispy noodles, egg rolls, and ginger beef on brown rice while sipping a peppery Zin.

Dusty said, "That's a gorgeous necklace you're wearing. Don't think I've seen it before."

"Dad gave it to Mom on their twentieth anniversary. Needs polishing, and I need to make sure all the stones are secure. Since leaving the force, I've decided to wear it all the time – to remember them both."

As Dusty finished off his Chinese food and wine, he got an idea. "Hey, I've got a friend whose store is right next to an old jeweler up in Sandy Springs. Says the guy is awesome. How about I get it polished and checked out for you? Sorta like an APD going-away present."

"I don't know, Deadeye."

Dusty Rayfield had no clue whether he could pull off what he had in mind – in addition to the cleaning and maintenance of her necklace – but he'd check it out tomorrow. It was worth a shot.

She pasted the Monroes' photocopied pictures on a new board,

TWINS MURDERS, with four columns: Monroes, Blounts, Brevards, and Oosterhuises. Dusty asked, "So where are we going with this?"

"You remember the Oosterhuis twins?" she asked him.

"Yeah. Birmingham, several years back. Kidnapped, never found."

"Correct. In 2002, Kelley and Karley Oosterhuis were fifteen-year-old high school sophomores. Identical, willowy blondes. Top students, star volleyball players, models under contract with AM&T, one of Atlanta's top agencies, and active volunteers at their Methodist church in Birmingham. One evening they walked home together after a volleyball match at Mountain Brook High School, about a mile away from their home in the ritzy Birmingham suburb. The twins disappeared without a trace. For the first couple days, it was hoped a ransom demand would come. It never did."

"On one obscure crime blog, though, I found a small lead. On two different occasions, a cyclist whose daily route took him through the Mountain Brook area noticed two different commercial vehicles parked at the elementary school near the Oosterhuis home. Different vans in the same spot about the same time of day, one a week before the twins disappeared and another the day they went missing."

Dusty interjected, "So, we've got the murders of teenage twins and the disappearances of another set of twins eleven years ago, and an unknown van or vans?"

"There's more. Mathilde and Mareissa Brevard, two teen twins, were brutally murdered in Woodstock in 1974. I haven't located much information about their murders yet. An issue with those: a black farmer, Orville Johnston, was charged with the murders but was killed in jail a few days after he was arrested. Doubtful the murders were ever thoroughly investigated. No details that I could find in the press. The year before, in 1973, Cherry and Merry Blount, teenage twins, were abducted after a football game in Anniston, Alabama. Still a cold case. I think they might all be related."

"Sounds like a stretch, Suzy – over what, four decades? Where'd this come from?"

"Bobby Price."

"No shit?"

"No shit."

She spent the next half hour filling in the columns with what she knew now. A few commonalities of the victims: twins (but not all identical), ages thirteen to fifteen, beautiful, murdered or abducted (and likely murdered), and the van used (at least in two). Multiple perps per case.

Suzanne asked, "Think you could get Sheila to run down any old files on the Brevard murders up in Woodstock? I'll owe her."

"Will do. Hey, I need to get back to the hacienda." She took off her necklace and walked back to her bedroom and put it in a small, square jewelry box.

At the door, she handed him the box. "Remember, Deadeye, it's your ass if anything happens to this."

"You're on to me," he laughed. "I'll be in Rio or another ritzy place with a hot chick on each arm after I fence it." But he was hoping she wouldn't kill him for what he was going to get done to her necklace.

Suzanne looked at the new board and knew she was barely scratching the surface. She needed to find out a lot more, but she needed sleep.

That night, Suzanne's dream came back with a vengeance. It always did. It was never the same but often included Thad or a mysterious dark-haired guy and a shiny blade or blades:

She walks up the sidewalk naked, people lining both sides. She doesn't want to go in but does. The door opens, and she sees two black girls sitting at the dining room table eating dinner, covered in blood. A man sharpens one knife blade against another. She hears, "Your turn, beautiful." She lays back on the dining room table as he carves a large cross on her body. No pain at all. "See, that wasn't so bad, was it? But you may not want to watch this." Another man holds her down as he aims the sharp point of a black cross between her legs.

She awoke shaking in a cold sweat and walked out to the sofa while clutching her pillow. Thank God she had Zeke to keep her company the rest of the night. Nights like this she thought she'd go insane. It was the cross she'd borne for two decades, but she continued to pray to be freed of its torment. She'd promise to catch the bad guys who murdered the Monroes – if these dreams could finally end. But did that now include the other girls, too? Maybe, if she could make such a bargain. A bargain with whom? God? She knew He didn't make bargains.

Suzanne had run from her job as the top APD Homicide cop, but she could only run so far. Each night when her head hit the pillow, it was like playing Russian Roulette. The Tigress had never been able to outrun her own fears.

Chapter 9 – The Sheriff

Noon, the Next Day – Wednesday, April 15

The Capital City Club – Atlanta

Suzanne was familiar with each of three of the Capital City Club's super-exclusive venues. East Lake, where she belonged, wasn't chopped liver but wasn't like the old-money splendor of the Capital City Club. As soon as she walked in, she felt the stares – at an Afro-Chinese woman invading their privileged club that remained ninety-eight percent white, except for the help. Kip Davies, she knew, didn't give a rip and reveled in having her as his anomalous guest. He was sitting at his reserved window table in the classically formal, white-table-clothed Peachtree Room at the Capital City Club on Peachtree Street, its original in-town location. He jumped up from his seat and gave her a kiss on the cheek and a hug – a little but not too chesty.

"Suzanne, it's so good to see you again. You look fabulous as usual, my dear." She'd done serious primping to get ready for lunch at the hoity-toity club and was wearing a new outfit: a tight, short – but not too short – turquoise skirt, peach blouse, turquoise jacket, and turquoise heels.

She smiled broadly. "Hi, Kip, great to see you too."

"How's civilian life? You going to kick back and play a bunch of golf at East Lake? If your handicap drops, don't whine about getting fewer shots from me."

She laughed. "Had a nice vacation in Seaside with Zeke. No golf last week, but I did play Tuesday. Rusty short game. So, what are the folks around town saying about the Monroe murders?"

"Ah, what they are calling the 'Cascade Murders'? The folks I talk to are still shocked. Major rumblings in the black community that these murders were racially motivated. The mayor, of course, is promising no stone left unturned until the killer or killers are brought to justice – and is doing whatever he can to calm the racial rhetoric without pissing off his political base. Got a mess on his hands right now, no doubt."

He asked her what she knew off the record, and she tossed out a few preliminary thoughts. He was intrigued. "Interesting. Honestly, I hope they are found and fried."

"I want to get them myself," said Suzanne.

"Ex-cop. Now Atlanta vigilante?" he chided.

She didn't reply. After a pause in their conversation, Kip asked, "Why'd you quit?"

She couldn't avoid his beautiful blue eyes. "Kip, it's complicated. When I was at the murder scene...," she said, her voice trailing off. She wished she could be more upfront with her longtime friend.

Usually not at a loss for words, Kip leaned over and touched her hand tenderly and did not press for more.

Over lemon sorbets, Kip looked into her huge amber eyes and popped the question: "How about coming to work for me? I mean, with me. We need a lead investigator. I fired ours a couple of months ago, and we haven't replaced him yet. You'd report only to me; you decide what cases you want to accept or not; you can farm out the others; you know the system; you've got great contacts; you're smart and ask the tough questions; you know where to look; and you get results. And you can tell me when I'm full of shit. And yes, we can still be friends."

She smiled. "Okay, you can keep going. I need to hear more great stuff about me. You're serious about me switching over to the dark side?"

"Deadly." He laughed loudly enough to attract the attention of nearby tables. "Hey, a lot of our clients aren't the Devil incarnate. We do all sorts of cases: corporate, criminal, civil, tax. We need our own investigations of the facts: surveillance, interviews and depositions, locating witnesses, research, strategic advising on cases, and the like. You'd be perfect. Look, it's up to you, but sooner than later you need to jump back on the horse, Suzanne. Maybe a different horse would be good for you. Think about it and give me a call. No rush."

On the way out, he kissed her on the cheek again. It was a lunch she didn't see coming, but she emerged from the distinguished club into the Atlanta sunshine with a big, hopeful smile on her face.

No street cop, but arguably Atlanta PD's best data analyst, Officer Sheila Cummings could ferret out whatever there was on any topic anywhere on the planet. They'd worked together a lot over the years and even had drinks periodically. The spectacle-wearing, petite blonde had come on to Suzanne once early in her career. After they straightened out who was interested in what gender, they became fast friends.

Sheila showed up at her condo at four o'clock in the afternoon. Her embrace was a healthy breast hug and a teasing but firm ass grab. "I miss you so much. Can't believe you're gone."

"Great to see you, Sheila."

"You're gone but not gone? Hey, I gotta fly to a thing, but here's what I found so far, and we can talk tomorrow. Sorry, not much from the Woodstock PD or Cherokee County PD. Not sure when they got their first computers. After looking a bit at how they keep records, it's a wonder they can find anything other than the last couple of years — much less decades ago. The important stuff on the Brevard twins' murders, I haven't the foggiest. Could be lost."

Sheila handed her the two thin, worn files and was off as Suzanne never got a word in edgewise, not atypical for Sheila with an iPhone glued to her ear.

Suzanne poured herself a half glass of wine and read the rudimentary files at her dining room table. Basic info on the 1974 Brevard murders in Woodstock: arrest report and cursory notes but no crime scene photos; in fact, no photos at all. No autopsy reports; no physical evidence. Nothing terribly illuminating. There were two policemen who'd signed off on the old documents. Sheriff Johnny Sumner and Deputy Sheriff Louis Giles. While Sumner was probably dead and buried, the Sheriff of the City of Woodstock, Georgia, as displayed on its website, was none other than Louis R. Giles, who had to be in his sixties or older. Maybe Giles could provide insight and know what happened to the murder files. She took Zeke for a walk to jog her brain for inspiration.

It was a long shot, but she called and briefly introduced herself. The woman who answered said politely, "Lemme see if the Sheriff's available, ma'am."

In less than thirty seconds she heard, "Sheriff Louis Giles at your service," in his backcountry, lazy southern drawl. Giles, which he pronounced with two and a half syllables, and Louis, with a "Lou" and a long "e."

Before she could get started, he said, "Ma'am, I never met you or your mother, but I saw pictures of you both. I went fish'n with your daddy many a time up at Lanier." He chuckled. "He always wore that big blue vest – anywhere on or around the lake – and looked funny as hell."

She gasped. "My father, Hollis Delacroix?"

"Yes, ma'am. One of the finest men I ever knew, besides being a kick-ass Atlanta cop. He often talked about you and how proud he was that you became a Detective."

In her wildest dreams, this wasn't what she'd expected. Holding her iPhone with both hands, tears streamed down her face while she tried to regain her composure.

"Miss Delacroix, you still there?"

"Sorry, Sheriff. Still have a hard time thinking about him at times."

"I understand."

She regained her composure. "Sheriff, yes, I was a cop and an APD Detective for seventeen years. Until I quit a couple of weeks ago."

He waited to see what she was going to say next.

Sitting with his boots up on his big glass-top desk on the second floor of the modern Woodstock Police headquarters, the past rushed back fast and furiously at Louis Giles as sat in his corner office. He took a deep breath and broke the silence. "Your daddy helped me out on a murder case about twenty years ago. We got the guy, and it turned out it was one of the Gwinnett cops who lived in the city. I heard Hollis drowned in Lanier a few years back. I went to the funeral but didn't stay to meet folks. Can't tell you how sorry I was. What about your mom?"

Suzanne told him she'd passed away in the last year, then said, "Sheriff, this may sound crazy, but I think the murders that happened in Cascade Heights two weeks ago may be linked to the murders of the Brevard twins in 1974 in Woodstock. Back when you were a deputy."

"Miss Delacroix, I'm thinking you're dead on."

She almost dropped her iPhone.

Giles knew it could all come home to roost one day. He was shimmying out on a long, flimsy limb with Hollis's daughter. But he owed her dad, and even more, he owed the victims to set the record straight. Now it was his turn to face the music and deal with the consequences. It could be dangerous for him and Suzanne, but it sounded like she could take care of herself. Maybe at age sixty-five, he'd have a shot at traveling up instead of down when his time came.

This time, she broke the silence. "Lemme ask you, Sheriff. I was at the Monroe crime scene in Cascade Heights. The worst thing I've seen in my life."

She hesitated. "Were there two black crosses…?"

"I was at the Brevard crime scene, Miss Delacroix. Yep, two black crosses. Wish I'd never seen that."

Chills shot down Suzanne's spine.

Many times since 1974, Giles had tried to sort it all out but never could. Thankfully, it hadn't crossed his mind much lately until two weeks ago when he saw the TV news and read stories in the newspaper. Twin black girls and their mother murdered in a nice area of Atlanta. Apparently, victims of stabbings – with Confederate flags at the scene – but not a lot more detail. Two days later, he received a package. This time, double the cash he'd gotten in the mail nearly four decades ago. The message was clear: stay away from the murders, past and present.

He began, "Suzanne, this is between you and me – at least for now. And I'm telling you, I ain't proud of it. I ain't proud of any of it. Lotta holes in this, but here's part of the story:

"FBI Special Agent Derbert Hinke started hunting the murderers of teenage twins Natalie and Nellie Haverford in New Canaan,

Connecticut, in 1950. Assigned by Hoover himself. Hoover thought the commies did the murders since there were communist banners at the scene. A cold case until Hinke found out that twin girls, Merry and Cherry Blount, were kidnapped in Anniston, Alabama, in 1973. His first break in over two decades. Said he found other clues that linked the Blount kidnappings to the Haverford murders in 1950. Hinke heard about the murders of Mareissa and Matilde Brevard murders the next year in Woodstock and got his ass down to Atlanta. I was deputy sheriff back then. I showed him the crime scene and the farm where they got killed. Beautiful daughters of one of the heaviest hitter bankers in Atlanta, Barron Brevard, who had a big ranch in Woodstock. Slam dunk case when a black farmer, Orville Johnston, who owned the farm, was found inebriated at the crime scene on his own land. But Barron knew Johnston and knew his daughters hung out on Johnston's farm from time to time. He didn't believe he killed the girls."

He paused.

"Until Hinke and I made sure he did believe."

"Pardon?"

"Hinke and I went into Johnston's house the day after the murders. Hinke found a few Polaroid photos of the Brevard girls before and after they got murdered. Plus, several of the Blount girls were killed in almost the same way, but indoors. Yes, with black crosses. Hinke then had three very similar murders of twins; black crosses, he told me, with the Haverfords as well."

"Where did he find the photos?"

"Hinke knew exactly where to look -- inside a cutout Bible in Johnston's nightstand. He knew he was hunting multiple murderers. He knew there was no way Johnston could have done any of the murders."

"Hinke knew Johnston got set up – and so did you, right, Sheriff?

"Yes, ma'am."

"What happened next?"

"Hinke proposed a deal: He got all the Polaroids except two of the Brevard girls, which I kept and then turned over to my boss, who showed them to Barron Brevard. Barron changed his mind about Johnston and arranged to have him killed in the Canton jail – to avoid all the trial hassle. Hinke gave me money and an expensive ring. After Johnston got murdered in jail, no one cared anymore, and a couple weeks later I got him the case files."

"But it didn't end there, did it?"

"No. A week later, Barron Brevard committed suicide, which didn't surprise many folks after losing his daughters. But his grief, I don't think, was the only reason."

"And that was?"

"Guilt."

"That he had Johnston killed?"

"Yes and no."

"A few days after Barron Brevard died, I got a package in the mail. Ten thousand dollars cash and two Polaroids."

"Of?"

"When the girls disappeared that Easter afternoon, people wondered what happened to their black lab that went with them everywhere. In fact, Barron put up a $20K reward for his return. One photo was of the entrance gate to the Brevard ranch; the other was of the dog. His head had been positioned like the horse's head in *The Godfather* in Barron's bed."

"Oh my God. So Brevard saw the head and knew Orville Johnston was innocent."

"That would be my best guess. He got rid of the dog head before he blew his head off with a shotgun in front of a huge mirror in the hallway of his ranch."

"Holy shit. These fuckers murdered the twins, set up Orville Johnston, and pushed Brevard to suicide?"

"Yes, and I was part of all of it."

"What happened with Hinke?"

"We talked a couple of times, but he didn't tell me a lot more. I heard he died of a heart attack or something else in D.C."

Giles paused. "But a few years later, I learned more."

"Which was?"

I mentioned that your dad and I fished a bunch up at Lanier. I bought a decent cabin; we had fun and didn't talk a lot of business. Except for drinking one night, he was talking about his first murder case that he never solved. An Atlanta drug dealer was found in the trunk of his car in a creek outside Anniston, Alabama. He told me he met an FBI agent who was investigating kidnappings of twin girls."

"The Blount twins."

"Yes. Hinke and your dad kept in touch a bit. It was in 1975: Your dad told me that Hinke wanted to meet him in Atlanta for dinner and that he had a good idea who'd killed the multiple sets of twins – and knew who killed the guy in Anniston. But that was it. Hinke never showed up for dinner and was found dead in his D.C. apartment the next morning. Hollis went to his funeral. All those cases died."

"Until now. They got Hinke killed, too, didn't they?"

"That would be my guess. At that point, they didn't know what I knew or didn't know. I was tempted to tell Hollis what I knew about Hinke and the details of the other murders – but decided it would be dangerous to him…and his family."

She took a deep breath and tried to digest it. She wouldn't condone a lot of stuff that Giles had done, but she also realized that he was probably right. At least back then – by not telling her headstrong father more about Hinke – indeed, he may have saved his dad's life, her mom's life, and hers.

She told him, "Other than me and you, there is one other person who thinks the murders and kidnappings since 1973 are all related."

"That would be…?"

"Bobby Price of the *Constitution*, but I don't think he has squat. It's more of a hunch, and I've dodged him so far."

Sheriff Giles had her head spinning, and she needed to digest his revelations. She suggested, "Sheriff, why don't you and I have dinner tomorrow night on me?"

"Sounds good, and I'll show you the ring that Agent Hinke gave me as part of my deal. Once owned by Hoover himself. It'll pay a few of my nursing home bills down the road if I need it," he chuckled.

Louis Giles remembered the photograph of Suzanne's mother and could tell by her voice that she was a looker. Super-smart, to boot. Probably a lot like her dad. He already felt better and desperately wanted to tell her the rest of his story tomorrow night. He'd kept his deep, dark secrets for too many years. He was well respected in Woodstock and had plenty of money, but he'd never felt good about any of it.

Before hanging up, she said, "Sheriff, I'm working on another crime that happened up in your neck of the woods. I may need help with it."

He waited.

"Sheriff, my father didn't drown by himself in Lanier. I think he was murdered."

Sheriff Louis Giles' eyes popped wide open. "Be glad to help if I can."

After talking to Suzanne, Giles drove the thirty-five minutes to his lake home on the north side of Lanier. It wasn't a palace, but he'd been told its price had tripled since he'd bought it in the late '70s with some of his blood money. He pondered Suzanne's belief that her dad was murdered while fishing out on Lanier. Nothing surprised him anymore.

Entering his lake house, Giles wondered, "What the fuck am I thinking? I'm crazy setting up a dinner with her. I could be toast – and so could she. These are scary fucks." He'd call her first thing in the morning and suggest another time and place.

He grabbed a bourbon, leaned back, and dozed off on his leather lounger. An hour later, there was a knock on the door that woke him up. Instinctively, he looked for his Glock before going to the door. It was on the table.

"Who's there?"

When he heard the familiar name, he opened the door. "Come on in, boys."

"Sheriff, you remember my cousin?"

They shook hands. "Sure do – nice to see you. What brings yawl out this way? Can I get yawl a bourbon?"

Both men nodded affirmatively. "Sorry to impinge, Sheriff. Power went out in my place. Not sure when it's coming on again. I remembered you lived not too far away."

"Always glad to have company." He handed them bourbons and sat down again in his chair while they shared the couch.

"How's the furniture business, these days?" Giles asked.

"Couldn't be better. Hard to keep up with the demand." He laughed, "If we could only get more product from our spic friends south of the border."

The three men shot the shit for a half hour while Giles refilled their glasses twice.

Then, out of the blue, the cousin asked, "You got a nice sum of money in the mail, recently, didn't you, Sheriff?"

Immediately wishing his Glock was a lot closer, Giles stammered, "Ah, yeah. How would you know that?"

The other man stood and aimed his Sig Sauer P226 at Giles' head. The cousin said, "Sheriff, why do you think you got that money?"

Giles couldn't move his lips; he knew he was in deep shit.

The furniture man smiled. "You knew what the deal was, didn't you, Louis?"

Giles gave them both a grim smile and finally said, You've been eavesdropping on me?" Giles thought about going for his gun, but it would be fruitless.

"You killed the girls down in Atlanta, didn't you?"

He stared at one and then the other. "

"Hey, you shouldn't feel bad, Sheriff. Sorta our specialty. No one's ever detected a bug of ours; it was a piece of cake bugging your office and two houses."

"You told Delacroix part of an interesting story, but of course, you won't be around to add more or to corroborate it," said the furniture guy.

There was no point fighting, trying to stave off the inevitable. Maybe what he'd told Suzanne might merit consideration for him on

Judgement Day. Maybe not.

The cousin handed Giles a bourbon, which he chugged instead of sipped. As soon as he put the glass down, the furniture man stepped directly in front of Giles and put a single shot through his forehead.

He said to his cousin, "Gotta take the ring."

Ironic that Hoover's ring he'd kept all these years as a financial insurance policy did not save his life.

The Next Morning, April 16

Midtown, Atlanta

Suzanne was getting out of the shower and toweling off when she got a call from Sheila. "Heads up, Suzy, this hasn't hit the news yet. I figured since his name was in the files I gave you yesterday you'd want to know. Sheriff Louis Giles of Woodstock was found dead in his lake house. A single shot to the forehead; not likely a suicide. The place was all busted up. Wallet, keys, and car gone. And who knows what else? Ring finger missing; probably couldn't get the ring off."

Suzanne felt like she'd been stabbed in the gut. "Who found him?"

"Anonymous call."

"Right. Thanks, Sheila. Keep me posted."

"Will do."

She slipped on a robe and walked to the kitchen to make a pot of coffee. Her doorbell rang. A voice said, "Special delivery package for Suzanne Delacroix."

At 7:15 a.m.? she thought.

"Okay, I'll buzz you up." She grabbed her "kitchen" Glock and put it in her robe pocket.

The automatic door camera showed a young blond guy who looked like he could be a poster boy for Georgia Tech sports. She opened the door before he knocked.

"I'm with Schroll Courier," he stammered. "Ma'am, all you've got to do is sign." He gave her a clipboard and pen and pointed to the top line. She signed, and he left.

She fetched scissors to cut the tape and brown paper around the slender rectangular package and then lifted the top off the lacquered black box. Inside, wrapped in tissue paper, was the huge, bejeweled ring that Louis Giles had mentioned yesterday. A bouquet of diamonds surrounded a striking blue sapphire in a platinum setting. Once J. Edgar Hoover's ring. It was still on Louis Giles' ring finger, obviously severed last evening. She'd bet her million-dollar condo that it had been sent from the same killers who'd murdered the Monroes and Sheriff Giles – and the others.

Suzanne slumped down on her couch. She was sad and mad that she'd never get to meet and eat dinner with Sheriff Louis Giles – and ask him the dozens of other questions she had about the other murders; about Orville Johnston and Derbert Hinke; and, most of all, her father. She hadn't even asked his theory of who the murderers were, and she bet he had one.

She felt ensconced in a diabolical game. Their taunts were escalating. She was going to need all the help she could get. She had plenty of guts and guns, but right now, she wouldn't mind having her badge as well.

Like Hinke before him, Louis Giles was a piece now taken off the board. He'd hung in for a long time and had helped connect the 1970s to the present. After four decades, the persons-of-light had a new

queen who could prove to be quite formidable. Miss Delacroix would likely be the first serious challenger since Hinke was anointed sixty-five years ago. It would be delicious fun! She'd known how her son still lusted for the Asian-black woman, but he would need to be patient a while longer. She would be taken off the board, too, but not yet. It was more important that the Game goes on.

Chapter 10 – The LN Group

April 17, 2015

Headquarters, Atlanta Division of the Federal Bureau of Investigation

So far, a boring morning – save Sheila calling her about Giles being murdered in his lake house and then receiving his severed finger adorned with J. Edgar Hoover's ring.

And she thought she'd retired from law enforcement.

Suzanne placed the finger, ring still attached, in a tall Starbucks coffee mug, surrounded it with ice, and screwed on the top. Beyond that, she hadn't decided yet what to do with it. She fixed a bagel with cream cheese and sipped her coffee while thumbing through the *Constitution*. The Cascade Murders were on the front page, with a byline by Bobby Price. Police spokeswoman Marjorie Shaw was quoted as saying there were no persons of interest yet, but the police were looking for a vehicle that was possibly involved. Then she could hardly hold her amusement: "Shaw confirmed that highly decorated, longtime Atlanta Homicide Detective Suzanne Delacroix, who retired in the wake of the Cascade Murders, had agreed to participate on an interagency task force, including the Atlanta PD, FBI, and other law enforcement agencies, to find the killers." No doubt there would be another call forthcoming.

She clicked on the *Constitution* website; news of the robbery-murder of Woodstock Police Chief Louis Giles in his Lake Lanier lake house was already featured. She already knew who did it; the same people involved in multiple twins murders over the years. But who were they?

She'd found out a lot from Louis Giles but had a growing number of questions. The main one: "What the hell are we dealing with here? Abominable murders of female teenagers going back to Hoover's heyday and ancillary killings as well?"

She spent an hour on her summary Board and decided to designate a board just for the Monroes and one for the other murdered twins: the Brevards, Blounts, and Haverfords. She knew the least about the Oosterhuis twins murders in 2002 and didn't include them now. At least there were more commonalities and indisputable similarities in the murders.

She was expecting her call. "Hey, Mia. Been a while. How you doing?"

"Up to my ass in alligators. Sorry to hear you left Homicide, Suzy. Dusty says you'd be willing to help us out on the Cascade Murders Task Force."

"That's what the paper says this morning, so I guess I'm already at your service."

She laughed. "Busting your chops."

"Suzy, this thing is a supreme clusterfuck so far. We got nothing, and the political shitstorm is swirling. Not nearly as bad as it could get. I'll listen to almost anything except the Aryan Brotherhood or KKK bullshit coming from your former boss, Tucker."

Suzy couldn't help laughing again. "Come on, Mia, I thought that was the party line. White supremacists strike the crème de la crème of Atlanta black neighborhoods, kill three black women, and leave their bloody rebel flags and knives?"

"Suzy, you know that's all horseshit."

"Yep. Bobby Price thinks it is, too. But I haven't shared anything with him – yet."

"Jeez, I don't need Bobby in this mess."

Suzanne decided to give it to her full bore. "Mia, I think the Monroe murders were the next in a series of killings that started as far back as

1950. At least four sets. Murders of female twins and others. Does the name Derbert Hinke ring a bell?"

She paused to let that bombshell sink in a bit, then continued. "But maybe the Bureau's not too keen on a bunch of cold cases they fucked up now being hooked to the Monroe murders. An old rogue agent with payola involved. And a couple sets of murders the FBI says are still "missing persons" cases. Parents were never even notified. Maybe other Bureau hanky-panky as well? Oh, by the way, I had an interesting chat with Sheriff Louis Giles of Woodstock, Georgia, yesterday before he got capped in his lake house last night. Giles was at the Brevard crime scene in 1974. I was supposed to have dinner with him this evening and talk more. No doubt the same perps killed him."

Mia Gonzales said tongue in cheek, "You've always been one smart, sassy bitch."

"Like you, Mia." They both laughed.

"We need to talk. And yeah, there are multiple murdered or kidnapped twins cases, possibly related, but you missed one. Believe it or not, in 1911. How 'bout you hop in your car, and we meet here for a while this afternoon? Unless you've got plans?"

"If I can come casual and you buy lunch, I'll leave right now."

"Done. God, I'd kill not to wear a suit and heels to work."

She ran Zeke down to do his business, then dressed in her favorite jeans, boots, and white blouse. She took a couple of digital pictures of her boards and brought a portfolio to jot down notes—and the coffee cup.

On the drive over, she thought about Louis Giles – likely murdered because of this thing that now involved her, too. Seemed he was desperate to finally tell his story, and she was sure he'd taken a lot of it to the grave. She thought about Orville Johnston. An innocent man was murdered in jail for a crime he had nothing to do with. Earlier, she'd pulled up the old black and white newspaper photo of him. A tall, rangy black man with a weather-beaten face, kind eyes, and a huge smile; wearing overalls, a work shirt, and work boots standing next to his tractor; perfectly content on his farm. Back then the largest black-owned farm in Cherokee County. Her dad had told her stories about infamous Forsythe County, the whitest county in all of Georgia (which borders Cherokee). She supposed Cherokee wasn't much better. Maybe not much better now. Innocent black people still dying at the hands of racist white boys. Orville Johnston deserved justice – along with all the others.

Then it hit her. Did Mia say 1911? These kidnappings and murders of twins had gone on for more than a century. How was that possible?

After ending her call with Suzanne, the second in command of the FBI's Atlanta District Office sat back in her leather chair, stunned. No question, Suzanne was the best cop she'd ever known, male or female. But how in the world had she put those pieces together in less than two weeks? More progress than the Bureau's in decades. She felt the anger spread from her rib cage up to her neck. *"How stupid could they be, for God's sake?"* Twice divorced, Mia Gonzales answered her own question: *"Fucking white men in charge, that's how. "If only one of them had an ounce more of common sense than one of his balls weighed..."* Then she thought, *"Yes, It was entirely possible the Bureau preferred to cover up these apparently linked cold cases and let them remain secrets."*

That started to make more sense.

She needed to be careful, especially after what she'd heard Tuesday during her visit to D.C. She had a daughter going to college in the fall, a mortgage, and little money in her bank account. She didn't need anything to jeopardize her job. God, she wished she'd gone to med school or taken another track to make a buck. She debated having a quick scotch. No, too much work left in the day. Tonight, she promised herself she'd go home and drink no more than two glasses of a decent Cab instead of the whole bottle she had last night.

Suzanne had never looked better. Mia hated to feel jealous of other women but couldn't help herself. How a female of her age could look like her was one of God's miracles. It wasn't fair one girl got that much.

The two hugged, and Mia said, "You keep getting more gorgeous."

"I don't know about that, but thanks, Mia. You look great yourself. Love your new digs."

Mia didn't have the typical dark, drab furniture; it was all light wood and decked out with the latest high-tech devices: two PCs and two laptops, a giant screen on one wall, and a flat-panel TV behind her desk. She also had a matching oval conference table that easily fit eight and one file on the table.

Mia Gonzales' skin tone was a shade lighter than Suzanne's; her straight dark hair was snipped at the base of the neck with short, well-coiffed bangs; she was a head shorter and two years older; she had a friendly, attractive full face, but little crow's feet kept creeping out from the edges of her brown eyes – thanks to nearly two decades at the FBI.

"Don't be too impressed. The glamour of being Number Two here wore off like maybe a month into the job."

Her admin, Wendy, came in with the salads, bread, and iced teas.

"Before we get too serious, give me the scoop about the new hot man or men in your life."

"Nada right now," Suzanne replied.

"No way!" exclaimed Mia.

"Sad but true. I got a great dog, though, that keeps me warm at night. How about you?"

"Ditto, without the dog. Well, we'll hope it turns around for both of us sooner rather than later. Never been against finding a sugar daddy or one finding me."

Mia inquired about the mug Suzanne had in front of her. "You brought your own coffee? Ours is pretty good."

Suzanne grinned like a Cheshire cat. "Nope. A present for you. Look inside."

Mia looked askance but unscrewed the top. "What the hell?"

"Go ahead, take it out. It won't bite."

Ice spilled onto the table as she pulled out the finger, blanched by cold and death, still wearing the huge ring.

"Until last night, both belonged to Louis Giles."

"You're shitting me, right?"

"Nope. A courier dropped it off at my place earlier this morning. I'm sure it couldn't be traced. A little trivia, though. The ring used to belong to Hoover himself."

"Now you're double-shitting me."

Suzanne smiled and shook her head. "Story is that Special Agent Derbert Hinke gave it to Giles as partial payment to keep his mouth shut back in 1974, which he apparently did for a long time – until he talked to me last night. FBI shenanigans from way back."

Mia pointed to the file folder on her desk. "Compliments of Special Agent Derbert Hinke, who died in 1975."

This time, Suzanne raised her eyebrows and said, "What are we dealing with here, Mia?"

"I don't know, but it's nasty. Not going to kid you, Suzy: Until a few minutes ago, I wondered what I'd show and tell. I'm all in if you are. But this is confidential; our conversation stays in this room. Right now, this isn't Task Force work."

"Sounds like a plan," Suzanne said, then dove into her Cobb salad as Mia stuffed the finger back into the mug.

The Same Day

Federal Bureau of Investigation Headquarters, Washington, D.C.

Assistant FBI Director Theodore Zirnan told his executive assistant he wasn't to be disturbed under any circumstances. He made himself a cup of espresso and sat at his semicircular, glass-topped desk on the fifth floor of the J. Edgar Hoover Building. The sound quality from the Bureau's latest and greatest surveillance bug that was hooked into the wiring in Mia Gonzales' office was perfect. Like he was sitting beside her. He'd opted not to install cameras but could access the spyware his associate had downloaded onto her phone. Excellent audio anywhere. The video worked okay if her phone was out in the open and not buried in her purse or computer bag – or if she was in front of her laptop.

Zirnan was given a summarized news account regarding the murder of Sheriff Louis Giles of Woodstock, Georgia. His time with Mia Gonzales, Tuesday, had been fascinating, and he found her quite sexy. Maybe next visit he'd delve into that. The files and evidence

Mia had dug out of an FBI storage facility in Rockville sat on a nearby table. Enlightening, but left a lot of room for cogitation. He felt sure he'd be able to decide on a direction for the case in the next few days – then let the chips fall as they may. Regardless, this one was going to be fun, like the chess matches he played long distance with a half dozen grandmasters around the globe. The difference compared to chess: He got to make up a few of his own rules on the fly – as needed. He was so looking forward to the discussion between Special Agent Gonzales and the spectacular Suzanne Delacroix.

Pushing aside her lunch, Mia said, "Got back from headquarters Tuesday evening after a strange visit that I'll tell you about."

"D.C. headquarters?"

"Yep. I met with an Assistant Director by the name of Theodore Zirnan."

Mia took a deep breath. "Except for a similar case in New Jersey in 1911, this all started in 1950 with none other than the infamous director himself."

"Hoover?"

"Yep, the guy whose ring is on ice. But let me go back to after the Monroe murders, which seems like a year ago. You saw the horrific mayhem firsthand, and I looked at the crime scene photos. I wasn't buying the white supremacy thing from the get-go, despite the bloody banners. Obviously, neither were you. This was entirely different from racial hatred. Now I'm sure about that. I ran through a couple hundred queries in the VICAP [Violent Criminal Apprehension] database. VICAP was awesome, but it wasn't too valuable before 1990. NCIC (National Crime Information Center) database goes back to the mid-'70s but has its limitations too. No doubt, you probably Googled many of the same search terms I used. Google is a much better search tool, but NCIC has the biggest library of proprietary crime content in the world. Eventually, I ran into the Brevard murders, then the Blount kidnappings – and I'd forgotten about the Oosterhuis twins' kidnapping in 2002."

"Yeah, me too. I gotta admit, Bobby Price helped shortcut my searches. He wrote a story about the Blounts back in 1973. He's on the right track and, I think, waiting for us to give him a scoop."

"A bridge to cross, perhaps, but not right now. Long story short, when I was digging into NCIC, the damnedest thing happened for the crimes in 1950, 1973, and 1974. They were each flagged."

"Flagged how?"

"Flagged 'P,' which I subsequently learned was an old designation used for Hoover's Personal files. Eyes only, executive approval required."

"Like super-duper, double-cross-my-heart, and hope-to-die secret files?"

"Yeah, Hoover, the anal fruitcake that he was, forbade the use of the word 'secret,' but that's what they were: personal, confidential, interesting cases. They were his juiciest files – and except for the CliffsNotes versions, entirely excluded from NCIC. Nothing digital. Hoover birthed the NCIC, maybe his one great accomplishment, but he also had his own, off-the-grid, manual indexing system of secret files controlled by Helen Gandy, his longtime secretary, who apparently did a masterful job of getting rid of the bulk of the most damaging files in the wake of Hoover's death. Lots of controversy about other Hoover files after he croaked. No one knows where all his 'P' files ended up. Hell, all sorts of thrillers have hypothesized about Hoover's lost files. Maybe we'll find out the real stories about JFK, and Lee Harvey Oswald, and Marilyn Monroe one day. I think that Hinke's files were a subset of or related to other Hoover 'P' files. The NCIC had bare mentions of the Haverford, Blount, and Brevard murders. How the 1973 and 1974 files got a 'P' stamp after Hoover's death, who knows?

"Anyway, when I called NCIC, the analyst I talked to had never seen a 'P' category and was interested. Said, if there was anything to be found, it would be at one of the Bureau's secure archives that warehoused the old stuff that never got digitized. I decided to get on a plane to D.C. to look for them myself. Marty Cravens, the analyst, gave me directions to an FBI storage warehouse in Rockville. Inside, it was just me surrounded by thousands of file boxes stacked two stories high on a hundred or so aisles. Took me four hours to locate the box of files and evidence I was looking for. Not all the answers, but it was well worth the trip.

"I grabbed the good stuff I found before the warehouse shut down, but as I started to pack up, I was beeped by a woman who identified herself as Executive Assistant to Assistant Director Zirnan. She asked me to return to headquarters immediately and then please attend a meeting at five o'clock with Zirnan. I told her I had a flight. She said she'd take care of that if necessary. I was already getting strange vibes and wanted to say WTF, but uncharacteristically held my tongue. Then I did a no-no. I stuffed several of the small original photos I'd found down the front of my panties and left the enlargement duplicates in the files. I also took several camera photos of the few pieces of evidence."

"You are such a bad girl," Suzanne chided. "Was the no-no stealing the photos or putting them in your panties? Jeez, I'd have had a hard time smuggling them out that way. I never wear any. Maybe I should."

They cracked up.

"There was a little leather notebook embossed with 'H,' which, no doubt, was Hinke's. It was a hodgepodge of stuff I didn't get a chance to read in full. I wish I could've stuffed the whole notebook down my panties, but I wasn't sure I could pull that off. Looked like some pages had been pulled out. The last page, though, from November 6, 1974, had a brief itinerary. He was taking a Delta flight to Atlanta and had a dinner appointment the next evening. You'll never guess who with."

Suzanne grinned. "My father, Hollis Delacroix."

"Bingo! You get to choose from any of the big stuffed animals on the top rack. I also found a small piece of torn paper tucked into the back fold of the little notebook; I put that in my bra." She placed it in front of Suzanne. It said:

Thank you for playing

Game of Twins

"What do you think it means?" Suzanne asked.

"I'd guess it was from the killers to Hinke. An invitation to play their game – or keep playing their game – or a sick thank you for having participated? Who knows."

Suzanne nodded and said the words out loud a few times: "*Game of Twins*." The note was several decades before the renowned show, *Game of Thrones*. Maybe not many similarities, but both *GOT* and *Game of Twins* she knew could be deadly.

Listening in surreptitiously from his D.C. office, Theo Zirnan clapped his hands in delight. He'd wondered where the original photos had gone. Photos and other evidence stuffed in Mia's panties. These two ladies were so fun!

Three Days Earlier, April 14

FBI Headquarters, Washington, D.C.

After locating Zirnan's office on the fifth floor, Mia Gonzales – rolling her overnight bag and carrying her computer bag and purse – was ushered to the adjoining anteroom. There, a prototypical six-foot-two, buffed, blond agent, but curiously dressed in jeans, Polo shirt, and loafers, politely said, "Special Agent Gonzales, if you'd please leave all your belongings here. After your meeting with Assistant Director Zirnan, you'll get your things back. Please leave your phone as well."

Theodore Zirnan was already standing near the doorway when she entered. He smiled and introduced himself. His impressive office looked down onto Pennsylvania Avenue. It was airy with lots of glass and white furnishings, accented by dramatic art, colorful oils and acrylics, tasteful plants, and flowers. Zirnan was a waif of a man, slender and all sharp angles. Well-dressed in linen slacks, stylish gauzy shirt, and hip gray leather shoes. Not your standard FBI attire. Quite distinctive and not unattractive. No jewelry of any type. Maybe he was gay, but he didn't seem to have the typical affect.

She took a seat on a minimalist, firm, but comfortable chair. Mia wanted to get back to Atlanta, and her patience had worn thin. After Zirnan sat across from her on a matching couch, she asked, "Why am I here? What's with the third degree taking my stuff and my phone? And who the hell are you anyway?"

He laughed and ignored her diatribe. "Special Agent Gonzales, may I get you a drink? Anything you'd like."

"No thanks. I'm good."

Zirnan moved with the grace of a ballet dancer as he walked to a tall wood cabinet. He came back with two short glasses and an ornate black bottle. "This is my favorite mezcal, Clase Azul Ultra Añejo. He poured two glasses, half full. "It's otherworldly. Try it."

Maybe it would calm her down, she figured. Why the hell not? Then, said, "Whoa, super-smooth heat. Nice," she said.

He grinned and swilled a healthy mouthful of the smoky Mexican liquor. "Agent Gonzales, may I call you Mia? First, I want to apologize for holding your things temporarily. Sorry, it's protocol. They'll be returned when you leave, I promise. Why are you here? You've been appointed to head a high-profile task force – I guess it's being called the 'Cascade Murders' by the media. It came to my attention today you've been going down a fascinating investigatory path that, should we say, is probably not politically correct in Atlanta. I want to see how I can assist."

He took a sip of his mezcal. "Now, as to who I am. Please call me Theo. I hate formalities. My group takes care of sticky wickets for the Bureau, especially relating to potential high-profile cases like the Cascade Murders. We attempt to do that proactively, not retroactively. Make sure that we protect the reputation of the Bureau and, of course, our agents. I guess you could say I'm a troubleshooter.

"I don't understand. Do you handle the media? You're part of Internal Affairs? You're Big Brother? You're a sanctioned black ops thing? What?"

Zirnan grinned. "We work behind the scenes to get optimal results for the Bureau. For all his faults, Director Hoover always made the Bureau his number one priority; he was the father of the Bureau, after all. Things happen; some are controllable, most not. Agents and others do things that could get themselves or the Bureau into trouble. We try to prevent negative things from seeing the light of day. From time to time, that means interventions."

She asked, "I've been with the Bureau fifteen years now. Why have I never heard of you or your division? Is my Cascade Murders Task Force a problem where you need to intervene?"

"We try to keep a low profile. We're not exactly on the org chart."

⧪

By the mid-'80s, most of Hoover's loyalists had exited, but there were still a few true believers dedicated to continuing his ways. It was unofficially called the "LN Group" after Lou Nichols, the longtime maestro PR assistant to the director who also headed the Bureau's Crime Records. The modern LN Group wasn't charged so much with promoting the Bureau or its director, but rather proactive damage control to protect the Bureau and its reputation from any threats. Whatever it took.

As head of the LN Group, Theodore Zirnan was the FBI's lead "fixer." He'd joined the Bureau four years before straight-arrow Robert Mueller started his ten-year stint at the helm of the FBI. Zirnan was a hand-picked legacy who had been schooled by a cadre of young Hoover loyalists who'd managed to survive the tumultuous upheavals when the director's death in 1972 left a mega power vacuum to be filled. It wasn't about the country or the American people, or politicians. It was about the Bureau: the best of all American institutions.

With his photographic memory, Zirnan had so wowed FBI Director Mueller and Deputy Attorney General Jamey Comey with his encyclopedic knowledge of global terrorism that they'd even consulted him on President Bush's sneaky, backdoor attempt to renew warrantless wiretapping under the terrorist surveillance program that the DOJ had ruled unconstitutional. Zirnan told them that Bush's ploy to railroad that through – when Attorney General John Ashcroft was hospitalized – wouldn't work and recommended that both Mueller and Comey threaten to resign. They took his advice, and the White House backed down.

After that, both men gave Zirnan an exceptionally long leash to preserve the sanctity of the Bureau. Mueller's only mandate was that he never sees nor hears about anything contrary to FBI policy. Zirnan assumed the operable words were "sees" and "hears."

At any point in time, Theo Zirnan, an MIT and Harvard Law

graduate, juggled several hundred variables on a dozen or so cases – in the chess game in his head. He used computer analytics to wade through volumes of data whenever necessary, but early on, he learned that a computer program would not spit out the optimal answer. His LN games were even more complicated than chess, especially since the rules themselves were always in flux; he loved making them up on the fly.

Mia mulled Zirnan's comment and was even more befuddled about what the heck he did but was now half-lit by the amazing mezcal.

Zirnan broke the silence. "You must be famished. I'll have hors d'oeuvres brought in. But you'll have a full meal on your flight home."

"How does that work?"

"An FBI jet will take you whenever you'd like to get back to Atlanta this evening, and I'll have a car at Hartsfield to drive you home or wherever you'd like to go."

She'd never been on an FBI jet; secretly, she'd always wanted to fly on one.

"You're kidding?"

He poured her another mezcal.

"Look, Mia. You got put in a tough spot with the Task Force in Atlanta. Your seat is likely to get a lot hotter. All I'm saying is, maybe I can be of assistance."

The hors d'oeuvres were divine. Sautéed and crusted scallops, caviar on thin crackers, crab cakes, tuna sushi, kiwi strawberries, pineapple miniature potato pancakes, and home-baked bread. All delicious and did not affect her high. She spent the next hour spilling her guts, talking about herself and the idiots in Atlanta who were convinced it was a white supremacy racial murder thing. Zirnan listened intently and then asked a question. "If not one of those types, who do you think is responsible for these bizarre murders over decades?"

She took another sip of mezcal and told him, "Don't know yet, but I'm working on it."

"Well, I'm sure you and your Task Force will solve the Cascade Murders. Maybe that will lead you to the others. Let me look at the files and evidence you found in the archives, and then I'll get them back to you in Atlanta. If anything else comes to mind that you think is relevant – or if you think I could offer a hand in any way – here's my cell." He handed her an FBI card with only the Bureau logo, his name, and his cell number.

Trying not to slur her words too much, she told him, "Probably time for me to get going, Theo."

"One of my agents will get your things for you, and a car will wait downstairs. It was a pleasure to meet you, and I know we'll talk further. Have a pleasant flight back to Atlanta, Mia."

Chapter 11 – The Game

Friday, April 17, 2015

Headquarters, Atlanta Division of the Federal Bureau of Investigation

"This Zirnan guy, is he going to help move the ball forward?" Suzanne asked.

The question troubled Mia. "Not sure. A strange bird. Can't figure him out. But I gotta keep him in the loop. If he doesn't give me back the stuff I found in Rockville by Monday, I'm thinking that's a bad sign."

After Mia filled her in on the meeting with Zirnan, she gave Suzanne the short version of the sketchy escapades of Special Agent Derbert Hinke, who worked for the Bureau from 1946 until he died in 1975. In 1950, Hinke was assigned by Hoover to devote his sole energy to investigating the murders of twin girls in Connecticut.

"You may remember that Hoover was going full throttle, believing there were Communists under every rock. At the height of his powers, he was feeding raw meat to McCarthy and the House Committee on Un-American Activities. When the Red Scare circus revved up to a fevered pitch in 1950, fourteen-year-old twins Natalie and Nellie Haverford were found brutally murdered on a pool table in the guest house of their family estate in New Canaan, Connecticut – in much the same fashion as the Monroes were found two weeks ago. The FBI got involved soon after the girls were killed, but it wasn't so much the murders that lit Hoover's fuse – it was the commie flags found on the table."

Mia opened the single file and pulled out five black and white, eight-by-ten photos. Three from before Nellie and Natalie were murdered, and the other two, after. "These are enlargements of the original Polaroids that I swiped. I made enlarged prints of these on my

PC at home. Here are the originals." She put the old black and white Polaroids on the desk.

Suzanne's eyes were glued. The "after" photographs from 1950 were nearly identical to the scene at the Monroes', except the crime scene was a pool table instead of a dining room table. The banners had the Communist hammer and sickle logo, instead of Confederate flags, on the outside of their bodies. She picked up and perused the old originals and said, "I had no idea there were Polaroid cameras back then."

"Me neither, but I checked, and they'd recently hit the market. The first Polaroid Land cameras sold like hotcakes back in 1950. I left police crime photo enlargements in the files that Zirnan now has. One sentence in one report I saw said the photos were found in the Haverfords' guesthouse."

Suzanne added, "So the killers left Polaroids like they did in 1974 in Orville Johnston's house. Classic serial murderer mentality: We are smarter, better, invincible; we're going to leave clues and still get away with it; catch us if you can, idiots. I can almost hear them laughing, but at the same time, begging us to join their *Game of Twins*. Their sick game of butchering female twins."

She placed four eight-by-ten color enlargements in front of Suzanne. "The Blount girls from Anniston, Cherry and Merry. Gruesome like the others' body positions and wounds. And the black crosses. So, as you learned from Sheriff Giles, these color photos from 1973 are proof that the Blount twins were murdered after being kidnapped. Murdered, but still officially cold case kidnappings. We may be the only ones who know that truth." Neither was sure she wanted that responsibility.

Mia lined up the set of Brevard photos. First, color photos of the identical chestnut-haired beauties, Mareissa and Mathilde. One with their arms around each other with flowing aqua gowns and tiaras, their made-up faces making them look older and exquisitely gorgeous. The other with them standing next to two beautiful palominos in their cowboy boots, jeans, and T-shirts. As pure as snow, the wind playing with their long blonde hair. Heartbreakers, they would have been.

The following four photographs were in unfathomable contrast. As Suzanne learned from Giles, the twins were found outdoors on Orville Johnston's farm on a natural sheet of black, white, and red-speckled granite that tilted several degrees—their heads toward the top of the rock. In broad daylight, gagged. Their eyes registered alarm. Their long, bare legs spread and tied down. No clothes anywhere in the picture. Then, post-mortem, covered in blood with wounds nearly identical to the other twins' murders and impaled with black crosses. Their ankles bound and arms draped out to the side, their bodies also positioned as adjoining female crosses. The speckled granite darkened with their blood flowing downhill; the human crucifixes lengthened by the blood stain that extended in a straight line below their feet. As with the Blounts, though, no banners or flags in these horrific images.

She told Mia the rest of the Giles story and added, "He called Hinke 'obsessed' by the twins' cases. He was a man on a mission to solve them. Apparently, my dad thought he was very close to a breakthrough. I wish I could have talked with Giles more."

Her office phone rang, and Mia Gonzales said, "Yes, sir. I'll be there in a minute."

"Suzanne, I gotta go next door and talk with Jeffrey. He's having a hissy fit. I'm sure you can keep yourself entertained?"

"No problem."

After Mia left, she took an iPhone shot of each enlargement and the originals without asking. That way, Mia wouldn't have to tell her no.

When Mia came back about twenty minutes later, she said, "Obviously, no coincidence that Giles got murdered last night."

"No question, but I don't think sending me Hoover's jewelry on Giles' dismembered finger was a message to leave it alone. I think it was an invitation to keep us playing their sicko *Game of Twins*."

She put three photos in front of her. The final photo from three sets of murders: Haverfords, Blounts, and Brevards. Uncannily similar. No question all the girls were murdered by the same Evil, whatever that was – even over decades. She looked at the photos of the Brevard girls and Blount girls; dead bodies splayed out on pieces of primitive stone that harkened up images of Stonehenge or another ancient place. She could only think of one word: sacrifice. They were sacrificed in a bizarre ritual. Sacrificed why?

Mia brought up the photo gallery on her phone. "There were two sets of the black wooden crosses, not identical, but pretty close. The four points are incredibly sharp. Okay, see this next picture; I was holding two from the Haverford murders. Each with a notch that fit together perfectly, like two pieces of a puzzle – forming a new cross, a black double cross with one horizontal bar. The same as the positions of their bodies, laid out as crucifixes, with their arms touching each other. And like the symbol on the hunting knives used to butcher the Monroes."

"Exactly."

Besides the two Monroe murder weapons and these photos, Suzanne had seen the unusual black double-cross symbol before. It was driving her nuts that she couldn't remember where.

"Mia, can you get an agent researching this cross design, maybe online; check out occult groups in the area? I've heard there are a bunch. Or even university experts who know symbols.

Mia said, "I already have. Nothing to report so far. Check out this photo." It showed two seemingly identical, gold necklaces. "See the KAA initials on the backs? There was a single notation in the Haverford file that mentioned that these two necklaces likely belonged to Kaitlyn Ann and Katherine Ann Abercrombie."

"Don't tell me…"

"Teenage female twins who disappeared from Port Norris, New Jersey, in 1911. Technically, it's still a cold case after a century. The necklaces were found on the pool table where the Haverford twins were murdered."

Suzanne said, "Why am I not amazed? We need to make a road trip."

In D.C., Theo Zirnan had an idea where the women's road trip was going and hoped it might help him make up his mind. He smiled as he listened to the two women talk in Mia Gonzales' office. Both were exceptionally bright and had excellent criminal investigative skills. But he was even more impressed by the people who'd orchestrated these diabolical murders over the last one hundred-plus years. He'd not run into anything like it ever. His decision would be a conundrum.

Forty Years Ago – November 7, 1975

The Colonnade, Atlanta

Special Agent Derbert Hinke, whom he called "DH," was going to meet him for dinner at the Colonnade at seven o'clock. He hadn't arrived yet, so Hollis Delacroix ordered Black Jack on the rocks. DH had called him earlier that week. He sounded excited and said he'd made progress on his three sets of murder cases and would like to get his take on what he'd found. Even better, he cryptically added before hanging up, "I might have news on your cold case, too."

The night before FBI Special Agent Derbert Hinke planned to meet Detective Hollis Delacroix in Atlanta – he wasn't exactly sure what he was going to tell him about the series of kidnappings and murders that he now believed could be traced back to 1911.

A year and a half earlier, after twenty-three years of investigating the cold cases. Hinke had traveled to Anniston, Alabama, when he heard two teenage twins, Merry and Cherry Blount, had been kidnapped. He'd wondered why he bothered – until he saw the eight-ball found in the glovebox of the drowned vehicle. Then he knew Tommy Elder's murder (which Hollis was trying to solve) was somehow linked to the Haverford twins' murders in 1950 – then to the kidnappings of the Blount twins. The unusual custom pool ball was from the Haverford guest house in 1950; it had been put in the glovebox by the murderers for Hinke to find. A breadcrumb that only Hinke would understand.

None of that information was public and would mean little or nothing to any law enforcement – and it could potentially interfere with his own investigations. A couple of weeks later, he received in the mail an Anniston area real estate brochure with one rental home circled. That led to two other breadcrumbs: another custom pool ball – the cue ball this time from the Haverfords' – and a short note in a blank envelope that read in ornate calligraphy.

Thank you for playing

Game of Twins

Hinke wasn't sure if the note signified the beginning or the end – or maybe in between – of this game the murderers were playing. All he knew was that he was on the right track. When the Brevard twins were murdered in Woodstock the following April, the game became deadly once again – and he found himself smack dab in the middle of it. Forcing him to do things that once upon a time he would have never contemplated. But over the next six months, he made more headway than he'd made in twenty-four years. He wasn't sure yet how he was going to prove any of it, but he was reasonably sure who'd been responsible for the crimes in 1911 and 1950 – as well as the latest murders in Anniston in 1973 and Woodstock in 1974 – but hadn't yet told a soul or even written it down in his journal.

Hinke had been impressed with Hollis since he first met him in Anniston and felt horribly guilty he hadn't told him about what he knew about the eight-ball – or any of the other specifics he'd learned after Anniston.

Hollis knew the lay of the land in Atlanta better than he did, and Hinke needed local help. He sipped his Old Fitzgerald and pondered what he'd say tomorrow night but realized he might be putting the young detective and his family in harm's way – if he decided to get Hollis further involved.

Derbert Hinke never made it to his plane at Washington National the following day. He died the night before and was found in his own bed. His untimely death, though, might have unintentionally saved the lives of Hollis Delacroix and his loved ones, at least for thirty-three more years.

Chapter 12 – The Other Twins

April 17, 2015

Atlanta

It was only about fifteen miles from Atlanta FBI Headquarters to Cascade Heights. But it was Friday afternoon rush hour traffic. A slog at best.

Mia's Android beeped.

"Gonzales, it's Joe Tucker. We got 'em."

"Got who, Joe?"

"The motherfuckers who killed the nig…" He caught himself. "…the black girls and their mom."

"Pray tell, Joe. Klan boys slipped on their dicks in a bar, then came in and confessed?" She winked at Suzanne and put her phone on speaker. "Joe, that's great. What's the scoop?"

"The old lady's tip came through. The techies ran through a ton of video and found a plumber's van driving about a half mile away around the time they'd have left the murders."

He waited for dramatic effect. "Van is owned by two brothers who run a mom-and-pop plumbing outfit in Covington. Two brothers, Donnie and Jeb Dixon. It gets better. We got a friendly judge to issue a search warrant. Bingo! Dixon boys had a ton of white supremacy, Klan, and Nazi bullshit literature in their garage. Under one stack of crap, we found several printed pages from the internet about the Monroe girls, including pictures that were circled. But the best is we found two pairs of panties stuffed into the back of the van seats. Running DNA now."

Suzanne and Mia both rolled their eyes. "So, Joe, did these plumber boys confess?"

"Not yet. Said they were drunk and stoned. Said they passed out and missed Easter church service. Said they weren't confessing to jack."

"Right."

"Might be your type, Gonzales. One a big ole bald boy, the other a skinny ass, neither with shit for brains."

"Fuck you, Tucker. Where are they?" Suzanne tried not to laugh.

"Already arraigned and in Atlanta Detention for now. Got a no-name lawyer I never heard of."

"Joe, if they did this, why do *you* think they killed the girls and their mom?"

"Hail, I don't know. A couple of southern white boys who hate niggers. Oops, pardon my French. Telling the world they had enough of black folks always takin' away from white folks."

"Yup, that's the story of America: black folks takin' from white folks," Mia said. She wanted to add: "You stupid racist fuck." She was pretty sure Tucker hadn't voted for Barack Obama – and that he would've loved attending get-togethers at Dixon Plumbing.

Suzanne couldn't resist saying, "Sounds like amazing detective work, Tucker."

Tucker fired back, "Is that you, Delacroix? You miss me, baby?"

"Like a swollen hemorrhoid."

Both women howled with laughter.

Mia asked, "Who all knows about this so far?"

"Well, I'm guessing a lot of folks pretty soon when CNN interviews me."

The two women couldn't help seeing the irony as they passed

CNN Headquarters.

Mia told him, "Joe, that's not a good idea until we sort this out more. You should've at least called me.'

"Cool your jets, Gonzales. Local boys caught 'em this time. No need for any task force, Feds, or females. Hail, you can go on vacation, or whatever you Fed girls do when the boys get it handled. You should be thanking me."

Steam erupted from her ears. Mia took a deep breath. "Joe, what if I told you that Suzanne and I think you got the wrong guys?"

He yelled into his phone, "I'd say you're batshit crazy and jealous-as-hell bitches. We got 'em, and that's that. Mayor and Chief are happier than pigs in shit.

"You're not going to fuck this up, are you, Gonzales? And goddammit, Delacroix, I thought I was through with you."

Mia said, "You're making a big mistake."

"Screw you, Gonzales – and Delacroix, too."

Suzanne asked, "Hey, Tucker, what about the third person? Mrs. Nethers saw three people leaving the Monroes."

"Shit, the old lady probably got that wrong."

"Hello? She got the van description right."

"I gotta go. They gotta make me look purdy before I go on camera."

Mia hung up after commenting, "I don't think anyone would have enough time and tricks to ever make you look good, fuckface."

Suzanne giggled. "That seemed to go well. I worked for that asshole my last year. Glad he's got all this figured out for you."

"Yeah, right," Mia said as Suzanne turned onto the Monroes'

pretty, peaceful street in Cascade Heights.

Mia Gonzales couldn't believe the abrupt change from the loud, crowded downtown to Cascade Heights. She felt the calm of the beautiful old neighborhood with its well-kept, mostly modest homes, lush greenery, and exquisite flowers. Like most Atlantans, she'd never been in the old neighborhood, on the footsteps of the big Atlanta skyscrapers.

After getting out of the car, the first thing she said to Suzanne as she did a slow 360 was, "Wow, I had no idea. I could live here."

Suzanne smiled. "Neighborhood's got quite a history. You got a key to the house?"

"Nope."

"Didn't think so."

Suzanne pulled a pick out of her purse and goosed the lock; they were in the foyer of the Monroes' house in less than a half minute. Suzanne glanced at the dining room she'd entered two weeks earlier but didn't dwell. She wasn't sure if she would puke again, especially if that odor of evil had hung around. She told Mia, "It's about six o'clock. Why don't you watch our Task Force buddy on the news while I check out the upstairs?"

Mia turned on the TV and sat down on the living room couch while Suzanne stood on the landing below the stairs.

It was an empty house devoid of its longtime occupants since the murders two weeks earlier; the mess in the dining room had been cleaned up – otherwise seemed normal. Until she looked up the wooden staircase.

At the top stood Lisa and Leslie Monroe, dressed in white

nightgowns, smiling and beckoning with their forefingers. Her eyes fixed on them warily as she climbed the stairs.

They weren't mere outlines like she'd imagined a ghost or apparition might be like, but they weren't exactly human either. Holographic, translucent figures with white light gently pulsing from each. When she reached the top of the stairs, each twin took one of her hands. Their hands were soft and silky smooth, almost liquid to the touch. Neither warm nor cold. Neither spoke; Suzanne was too in awe to utter a word. They turned left – Suzanne's steps creaked on the hallway floor, but not theirs. At the bedroom door, they both smiled once more and nodded their heads, telling her to go in. When she looked around, they were gone. Suzanne didn't think she was hallucinating but had no explanation for what had occurred. She also felt a peace, unlike anything she'd ever experienced.

Suzanne went directly to the small white nightstand without noticing the rest of the room. There was one drawer. She opened it and saw a gaggle of girlie teenage stuff – pens, pencils, lipsticks, nail polish, cell charger, sunglasses, coins, a devotional paperback, and a pack of gum. The cops might have briefly thumbed through the contents but had no reason to do much more. She pulled out the drawer and put it on the pink bedspread, then reached to the inner back of the nightstand. Taped to the wood was an envelope, which she peeled off. How she'd known it would be in that exact spot, she had no idea. She opened it and held her breath.

She placed each of the six color Polaroids on the bedspread and put the drawer back, then sat on the bed and looked at each in detail. The strange calm was still pervasive as she perused the horror before her. She looked toward the doorway. They smiled at her again.

"Please, please tell me who did this to you."

They turned away. Suzanne jumped up to follow, but the Monroe twins were gone.

Downstairs, she heard the voice of CNN anchor Erin Burnett. She returned to the bedroom and took close-ups of each Polaroid with her iPhone. Just in case.

The pre-death photo of the Monroe twins was almost worse than the after photo. One Polaroid screamed out in terror: the girls lay naked, tied on the dining room table; their faces etched in terror, knowing they were going to die. Then another: the girls with fresh crucifixes cut into their bodies and the horrific black crosses driven into them.

She'd seen a few pictures of the Oosterhuis twins on the volleyball courts and modeling shots. The blonde beauties exuded girl-next-door purity. The four photos of them in front of her were abominable. She shuddered because she was now positive all the dead girls were also brutally raped before they were murdered. She remembered how close she'd come to that many years ago. But she'd been lucky; unlike twelve teenagers, including the Abercrombie twins in 1911.

Thankfully, she experienced no nausea as she examined the Polaroids. She heard Mia shout from downstairs, "Tucker, you stupid redneck asshole!"

After it quieted down, Suzanne yelled back at her, "You need to come up here. Left-hand bedroom."

Mia arrived with her face flushed. "I'm gonna kill that motherfucker."

"I get that. I found these inside the nightstand taped to the back."

Mia knelt on the floor in front of the photos. "Holy shit!"

"Two of the Monroes and four of the Oosterhuis girls."

Suzanne pointed to the Oosterhuis photos. "Looks like the same place the Blounts were murdered. What do you want to bet it's in or around Atlanta?"

Solemnly, Mia nodded her head in agreement. "Well, we've got new crime scene evidence."

Suzanne corrected her. "No, Mia, the FBI has new crime scene evidence."

Mia's brain flipped into auto-FBI. "It's got to be reported to local law enforcement, and the evidence turned over to Tucker. Not doing so could be a felony rap."

Suzanne nodded. "But it's not going to make his day."

Mia hesitated. "Can you give me a minute?"

The FBI agent walked down the stairs, opened the front door, and stood on the front sidewalk of the peaceful exterior.

She dialed Theo Zirnan, who was on an FBI Gulfstream 640 in route to Grand Cayman.

"Mia, what can I do for you?"

"The shit hit the fan the past couple hours," she told him.

She filled him in on Joe Tucker appearing on national news minutes ago – telling the world he'd caught the Monroes' murderers. She and Suzanne also found new photographs at the Monroe home. Photos that pointed even more strongly to similar multiple murders over decades – the Oosterhuis photos now linking all of them.

Zirnan had listened in to their conversations in the Monroe home until Delacroix went upstairs. "Mia, thanks for the heads-up. Let's not turn that evidence over to Tucker just yet. Don't worry, got you covered. Let's see what happens over the weekend, and we'll talk Monday. You and Miss Delacroix are doing a heckuva job."

She frowned. "But this means the Dixon boys didn't kill them. No way. And all the murders are related."

"You don't need to convince me. Tell you what, for safekeeping, I'll have an FBI courier get the photos to my D.C. office. I hope that you two ladies have a nice evening." He hung up.

Now, she was conflicted, but what choice did she have? Hell, if she turned the evidence over to Tucker, which would be protocol, he would bury it. Zirnan was right.

Upstairs, Suzanne sat on the edge of Leslie Monroe's bed. She felt ensnared in this grotesque game she didn't understand. Calm a few minutes ago, she now felt rattled and knew she couldn't glance into the dining room again. She also knew she couldn't share her paranormal encounter with Mia.

On the way downstairs, the old wood creaked with each step. At the bottom, she looked back up one more time. The twins were there again smiling, then vanished. Suzanne thought, *"Maybe I've lost it and need more time at Seaside. Or maybe in the Grady psych ward.'*

Theodore Zirnan never predicted what the future would bring. He found it a fruitless exercise. But with the arrests of the white supremacists, he was getting a clearer picture of what the prudent play would be. After a couple of relaxing days on the beach at Grand Cayman, he'd make his decision.

Leaving her office, Mia told Suzanne, "You're driving, but I'm taking you to eat anywhere you want. I need to blow off a bit of steam."

"You choose," Suzanne told her.

"Can we get into the Capital Grille without a reservation on Friday night?"

Suzanne smiled. "I think I can make that happen."

"I'm sure you took photos of the Polaroids upstairs. Text them to me, will you?" Suzanne glanced over and smiled knowingly.

Silence for a couple of minutes as Suzanne wound her way through the beastly Atlanta downtown traffic, then said, "No doubt bad folks are fucking with us in their *Game of Twins*."

Mia asked, "But who? And why?"

For both women, it had sunk in that a group of people had murdered at least six sets of teen twins, as well as several other people, over more than a century. And gotten away with all their crimes.

Stuck in traffic, her cell rang. She looked down at the number but didn't answer.

Bobby Price left a message. "Suzanne, looks like the Task Force has already solved the crimes. At least according to CNN and other national news outlets. Impressive! But you and I both know this is unmitigated bullshit. No way these ninnies did this or any other murders. They got set up, and you know it. Let's talk when you can, on or off the record. Don't you think it's unusual Sheriff Louis Giles got shot in his own lake house up in Cherokee County? How convenient. You need to catch these guys, Suzanne. Tell Mia I'm going to call her too. Have a good night."

She called Dusty. "Say, partner, pretty exciting day. You think Tucker's got the killers?"

"Suzy, these guys may know how to fix toilet leaks, but they're dumber than two boxes of rocks. The arraignment happened at warp speed. They're in Atlanta Correctional for now. They better have those white boys locked up tight because I think other guests are going to be *very* interested in them."

"Dusty, on the QT, Mia and I found other photos of past murders."

"You're turning them over to Tucker?"

"No, Mia's got it covered with an Assistant Director in D.C. Tucker gets nothing for now. It was her call, not mine."

"Okay. They're running DNA tests on the underwear found in their van. The Dixons' workshop was papered with white supremacy garbage. Like a National Archives for white hate shit. You know, if the DNA comes back next week and matches to any of the Monroes, this thing is over."

She ignored the comment. "Keep me posted when you hear more about these yahoos. Remember what Yogi said. 'It ain't over 'til it's over.'"

Chapter 13 – The Wrong Guys

Thirteen Days Ago – 11:00 p.m., Holy Saturday

Cascade Heights, Atlanta

The Dixons were home passed out the last few hours. They didn't need the Dixons' van. They had one that looked identical. Her brother employed a full-time designer-painter who'd customized hundreds of vans, trucks, and other vehicles – and could create a perfect fake license plate in less than an hour. In the wholesale narco business he ran, those skills were critical.

She drove a nondescript sedan down the street to see if there was any unusual activity. All quiet. She returned to the designated parking spot at a small shopping center only a few blocks away, then got into the back seat, took off her wig, and changed her clothes.

At 11:30 p.m., they were parked in their replica of the Dixon Plumbing van across the street. She got out and walked to the right side of the house around the back, where the home phone and alarm system were wired. Within two minutes, the alarms were dead. But of course, there were the girls' cell phones.

The two men stood out of sight while she rang the doorbell. She waited as Linda Monroe arrived in her nightgown. Mrs. Monroe looked out the peephole, then cracked open the door.

She said, "Hi, I'm Tammy Keith of Dixon Plumbing. Sorry, yawl got a bad leak tonight. We'll get it fixed ASAP. I promise."

Linda Monroe opened the door further. "But we don't have a leak as far as I know. You must have the wrong house."

She started to shut the door but heard, "Ma'am, I'm sorry, they must've told me the wrong address. My cell charge went dead. Could I use your phone for one minute?"

Linda thought, *"I shouldn't do this, but it's a nice-looking white girl, not some gangbanger."* She told the stranger, "Sure, let me grab my phone and you can use it on the porch."

But before the front door was shut, the two men had entered. A lot better conditions than where they once operated in Afghanistan or Bosnia. They worked by rote. With a hand on her mouth, the woman dragged her into the living room and gagged her.

The two men had already shot up the stairs, one going left and the other right. The girls' cell phones didn't come into play – which she'd worried about. She heard the screams. Then silence. Both were injected with a dose of diazepam and gagged. They carried the twins downstairs. The twins were conscious, but the kicking and screaming had stopped. She assisted as they positioned both girls on the shiny mahogany dining room table.

"Get your fun," she said. "Then the ritual." They'd placed a small camera on the back edge of the van. She checked it on her phone; nothing unusual.

"Mrs. Monroe, would you like to watch?" one man asked demonically. He didn't wait for an answer. He sat her up on a dining room chair in the corner and zip-tied her hands and feet. Then, the woman used an old trick to tape her eyelids open. Her big brown eyes flickered with unspeakable fright.

The woman snapped photos with the old, reliable SX-70 Polaroid and a digital Nikon to commemorate the event. The men did the slicing of flesh while the twins were drugged but still fully conscious. Not deep incisions, but enough for blood to trickle out. Ten minutes later, she took the crosses from her black duffel as the men stepped out of her way.

The twins' eyes fluttered as she stood between their pair of outstretched legs, and with a black cross in each hand did her pronouncement from *The Teachings*: *"In Your name, Dark Lord, accept these beautiful twins as our offerings to You. May they be your brides forever for your eternal pleasure. May we be rewarded for these sacrifices unto You. Twins for twins. And may you bless our Tribe and your Game of Twins for all time."*

As she impaled them, the look in their eyes she thought was positively priceless. Disbelief and terror beyond all. She waited a minute and then walked around the table and cut their throats; dead, their eyes looked remarkably frozen. Her brother threw each of the beautiful knives point blank into the wooden floor, sticking below each twin. Their cousin looked at the knives, not the twins, and said, "I hate we have to leave these."

But it had been the Chief's call to leave the two custom-made knives; she said, "To spice up *Game of Twins* more."

The dining room table and floor were now bathed in blood, as were the three of them. She chose two of the new Polaroids and added them to the others she'd brought. She carefully removed her shoe covers and walked upstairs barefoot to leave the envelope of photographs. Her brother and cousin smeared the floor with a towel; then they wiped the blood off their dark uniforms and removed their shoe covers at the door. Less than a minute later, they walked down the Monroes' sidewalk with their uniforms and ball caps on. She gave no indication but noticed the old woman across the street peeking through her front window. Whether she saw the van clearly or not, she wasn't sure. It didn't matter.

Driving separately, she made a late-night trip to the Dixons' shop in Covington to plant the white supremacy shit, web printouts about the Monroe twins, and two sets of bloody panties; the panties she pushed into the back of their van seats.

ⵜ

Friday Evening, April 17

Atlanta

The two women managed to have a grand time at the Capital Grille, probably because they'd agreed not to talk shop. After all the courses, including dessert and too much fabulous Cabernet, Mia called for a car, an FBI perk that she rarely used. She'd get her own car at work tomorrow. Suzanne had eased off the vino earlier and made the short drive from Buckhead to Midtown.

Home in Marietta, Mia turned on the late news and was drunk but riveted. Ten years ago, one of the murder suspects, Jeb Dixon, had been charged with child molestation. The case was ruled a mistrial and not retried. Both Dixon brothers were members of the United Northern and Southern Knights of the Ku Klux Klan. Their photos weren't flattering. One, with a thick body and bald, blocky head, dark stubble on his fat face. The other was almost the opposite: lanky with a red beard and long hair. Poster boys for white supremacist hate groups. Mayor Cain and Police Chief John Carleton praised the effort of the APD's rapid arrests – without mentioning the FBI or other authorities. Remarkably, black activist pastor Elijah Tisdale, who had been leading protest groups in front of City Hall, also thanked the APD for quickly bringing the murderers to justice.

"You'd think these guys were already tried and awaiting execution," Mia thought as she clicked off the TV. Helped by the bottle of Turchi Cab earlier, she was sound asleep in minutes.

She and Mia were running in an empty field – scared. Then they're tied and on a big flat rock. "We can't die like this," she said to her FBI friend. Mia said, "You know, they're going to kill us." A man with a black hood stood over Mia and shoved a long black cross into her mouth. She went silent. The other man, she thinks was Tucker. A

woman came to her side and whispered something about the angels. "Maybe they can save you?" The Monroe girls were in the background, smiling. As the other man grabbed another huge black cross, she implored them to help. Then, the cross became a large knife. Tucker laughed and tried to kiss her. The other man stood between her legs. It was Thad. The knife with its gleaming blade slashed across her mid-section.

To avoid further horrors, Suzanne woke up. As she'd done so many times before, Suzanne went to the living room and spent the rest of the night wrapped up in a blanket on her sofa with Zeke asleep below her.

The Task Force was in limbo. Technically, it was the Bureau's responsibility, but APD had run with it since Friday – making it crystal clear they were in charge. It's what the local politicians wanted. Yesterday, both Donnie and Jeb Dixon were charged with multiple counts of aggravated homicide, rape, breaking and entering, and a host of other crimes. Bails set at amounts no one would ever post.

Mia Gonzales had plenty of other work to do and treated Monday as a catch-up. By one o'clock, she was making decent progress on one of the stacks in front of her when her assistant, Wendy, ran into her office and said, "Ma'am, you need to put it on CNN now."

Wendy was not one for histrionics. Mia clicked the remote on her desk, and one of her huge screens lit up. The scene was the Atlanta City Detention Center. None other than Erin Burnett herself was holding a microphone as she stood outside the center. "CNN is reporting that the prime suspects in the murders of Leslie, Lisa, and Linda Monroe two weeks ago – Donnie and Jeb Dixon – are themselves dead. Apparently killed inside the Atlanta City Detention Center. I repeat, the Cascade murder suspects are dead."

She clicked the screen blank. Wendy left without a word. Mia phoned Theo Zirnan.

"Hi, Mia. I heard the news. Puts your investigation in a different light," said the Deputy Director.

"How's that?"

He'd made his decision. "Mia, it's time to close this down. We tried. We did the best we could. But that's the way it played out."

She jumped out of her chair. "You can't be fucking serious? You know there's not one chance in a million those goobers killed the Monroes."

He ignored her outburst. "Here's the thing, Mia. Everyone else thinks they did. And got what was coming to them. The black community I'm hearing is ecstatic – along with tens of thousands of others, I'm sure."

"That everyone doesn't include me or Suzanne. How about you, Theo?"

"I'm a realist. Let me ask you this. Do you or Miss Delacroix have any better idea of who killed the Monroes?"

"No."

"Suspects?"

"Not yet."

"How about for any of the other murders you think are related?"

"Suzanne has a pretty decent profile of the killers."

"But not a single solid lead?"

"No."

"So, the FBI is supposed to ride in and piss off the Atlanta political establishment -- particularly blacks in Atlanta and nationwide, and say, 'Atlanta police got the wrong guys. But we can't tell you who committed the murders because we don't have any idea.'"

She wanted to rebut but understood.

He continued. "Look, Mia, for a long time, over the years, there were loose ends in the FBI investigations into these twins' murders. There were mistakes made and rules broken – things that should have been brought forward."

She yelled into her phone, "You mean like tampering with and withholding evidence, payola, and conspiracy? You mean stuff like that? What about the families, the Blount and the Oosterhuis families? We now know for certain their twins are dead, but they don't know that. For God's sake, Theo, they don't even know what happened to their little girls."

Calmly, he said, "It's unfortunate, but we couldn't bring them back anyway. You know that."

She shot back, "You're a cold SOB. What about justice for the girls themselves, for Orville Johnston, even for the guys who got killed in jail today?"

He let her rail.

"Mia, also, what if we were talking about several supposed serial-type murders? What if the public got wind that they might have a weird, frightening, occult bent? You know, like what happened in the '80s: a 'Satanic scare' about kids getting abducted, abused, and murdered that resulted in one of the most expensive trials in U.S. history – the McMartin Preschool Case. It would be a nightmare."

She fumed as he added, "So maybe what happened today was fortuitous." "*Occasionally, you get lucky*," he thought to himself.

"And when they murder again, Theo? What happens then? These people won't stop."

He knew there was that possibility, but the murders had been infrequent and showed no discernable pattern. If and when any similar murders happened again, he'd likely be long gone from the Bureau.

"I've already talked to your boss, Mia. I was complimentary. You're a heckuva agent, and I've got no doubt you'll head up to the Atlanta field office sooner than later."

"This is wrong."

"Not wrong for the Bureau."

Smoke billowed from her ears. "What if I refuse to let this go?"

"You need to carefully think that over. Might not be good for your career at the Bureau, Mia. And you've already broken laws. Not turning over key evidence to local authorities – the finger and ring and the Polaroids you found at the Monroes. Oh, you need to make sure Suzanne Delacroix has ended her quixotic efforts as well."

"You son-of-a bitch. I gave those to you…"

He cut her off. "This is over, Mia. I know you'll let it be." He hung up. Zirnan was pleased with the result, but he knew – despite his warnings –there was one wild card he might have to deal with down the road.

Suzanne Delacroix.

Mia sat alone in her office. Zirnan could get her demoted or fired and ruin her chances of future employment at the Bureau or anywhere else. Or maybe worse? Her imagination spun out of control. He was now her Big Brother; she had the sensation that she was being surveilled. Where, when, and how, she didn't know, but she'd try to find out.

Her solitude was broken when Suzy called. "I heard what

happened at the Detention Center. What's the word in Atlanta?"

Mia Gonzales had no idea what she could or should say.

"You and I both know the Dixons didn't commit those crimes and that they're perfect scapegoats. The wrong guys are now dead. No Task Force anymore, so your tenure didn't last too long. Don't even try to submit any expense reports."

Suzanne laughed.

"Look, Suzy, I gotta leave this alone – and you do, too. You understand what I'm saying?"

"I get it. The Dixons are an uncanny parallel to what happened to Orville Johnston in 1974 and the teacher in 1950, don't you think?"

"Yeah, listen, I gotta go. Have fun at the beach."

Suzanne sensed the pain and disappointment in her friend's voice – and something else: fear.

Later that afternoon, Suzanne sat on the screen porch of her Seaside beach home with a glass of Conundrum. Weighing her options.

On her second glass, she realized she was at a crossroads. She heard her mother's sage advice: "Be at peace – whatever the circumstances." She heard her father telling her, "Whatever it is, finish what you start."

She could call Bobby Price and blow the whole thing up in the press. It would be a circus. She'd be enveloped in media coverage and the political muck for a long time. But more importantly, Zirnan could hurt Mia and her daughter. Besides, if she tried this alone, she would be fighting public opinion, City Hall, the APD, and the FBI – with no help. Zero. Then there were the *Game of Twins* assholes, whoever they were. She had an early profile but not one suspect.

She couldn't get the visions of the Monroe twins out of her head. Weren't they expecting her help? She'd never met Orville Johnston, but how about justice for him and the others murdered? And others who'd die in the future if these monsters were still out there.

Maybe if she could remember where she'd seen the black cross emblem – the demonic union of two crosses – that was on each of the Monroe murder weapons. But she couldn't.

Then there was her father's death.

Her hope had been if she helped solve the twins' murders, her nightmares would go away. But she failed.

She sipped her wine, and Zeke jumped up next to her on the outdoor couch. He knew his owner was troubled. She would make her decision when she got back home.

Four Days Later

Atlanta

As soon as she arrived back at her Midtown condo, she plopped down her luggage and got Zeke a bowl of food. She walked into her Board Room and took a long look at each of the boards for the twins' murders and the one for her dad. The only thing she'd done in seven years was to drag his board out from her closet. She had nada; not even a hint of where to start. She wasn't even sure she was maybe being ridiculously irrational. Made a lot more sense if he'd accidentally drowned.

She prayed the Monroe twins would not reappear – and that her dad would forgive her.

Part II - The Chairwoman

Chapter 14 – The Tournament

Eleven Months Later, March 2016

Birmingham, Alabama

By mid-March, after lofty expectations, the boys' lacrosse season was in the toilet. Regardless, the Eaglewood Middle School Lacrosse Club was heading to Birmingham to play in the most prestigious middle school tournament in the Southeast, the Dan Mullins Invitational.

They drove from Atlanta to Birmingham in their 2004 Honda Pilot, still holding up after nearly two hundred thousand miles. Sarah Baldwin's eighth-grade son David, wearing his headphones, played combat video games on his tablet in the backseat – and was one hundred percent immersed. Which, that evening, was fine with her. She was also glad her husband Tim could get out of the house and play golf at Calloway Gardens with all expenses paid for the weekend thanks to a wealthy friend. But mainly, she was happy to get out of Dodge for a couple of nights. She could board her two Airedales for free at her practice's kennel for a couple of nights.

A part-time veterinarian for nearly two decades, Sarah was now employed at a twenty-four-hour emergency vet practice. Over the last many years, she worked as a part-time vet, but lately was taking more long shifts and extra calls as well. The money was now critical. Some private practice vets made a bundle; she did okay – but wasn't one of those.

Until two years ago, Tim had always been a good provider. A couple years older than her, Tim still had his handsome looks: he was about her height with a slender, well-toned body and pitch-black hair. But after getting laid off from his six-figure advertising job, he was a shell of his old self. He was different. Not a good different. Her salary alone didn't pay all the family bills in affluent Roswell, Georgia. After twenty-two years of marriage, Sarah had become the primary breadwinner. A mantle she'd not wanted to carry – and not how she'd imagined things would turn out. Especially with age fifty, only a few years down the pike. Scraping out an existence, pinching pennies, and not having nearly as much fun as her friends – or as much as she used to have. Only surviving. At least they had health insurance from her job – but they were burning through their second mortgage to make ends meet. Her son's inadequate college fund was now the family's last-ditch survival money before they were dead broke.

Sarah fantasized that Tim's decrepit parents would kick off, enabling them to inherit enough money to get David through college and dig them out of their financial hole. Stubbornly, the two old loons, who had once been loving, generous in-laws and grandparents, refused to give Tim any say in their financial matters or help in any reasonable way. They even refused to give him a copy of their will. The financial safety net they'd once taken for granted – at least for David – was now an illusion.

She knew that her situation was still among the most privileged in the whole world. So why did she feel like her life sucked? For the good of her son, a great kid, seemingly undamaged by the undercurrents of turmoil in the household, she and Tim had decided to stay together for now. They'd discussed the "D" word, but both agreed that for the foreseeable future, it made no economic sense. Worse, it would devastate David. They were stuck with each other. They were living on the edge with no margin for error—a frightening place to be.

Sarah and David arrived at the Wingate Hotel in Birmingham a bit after ten o'clock that evening. The small lobby was teeming with boisterous kids and cocktailing parents. She recognized a few of them and nodded hello. David begged, "Mom, can I stay down here for a while?"

"After you help me carry up the luggage. Lights out in one hour."

Saturday, March 19

The Dan Mullins Invitational Lacrosse Tournament, Day One, Birmingham, Alabama

On Saturday morning, after a good night's sleep, a quick shower, and a marginal self-serve breakfast in the lobby, they got directions to the tournament fields, ten minutes away. David mapped it on his iPhone to make sure. His buddy Aaron was ready to go; they gave him a lift so his parents didn't have to rush.

Sarah smiled, listening to the backseat banter of the two boys dressed in their black and gold Eaglewood Lacrosse Club uniforms. She fondly remembered the jolt she used to get putting on her high school basketball uniform and Converse shoes. Like she'd become Wonder Woman even though she was a tall twig of a girl who wasn't too coordinated.

Aaron, a solid starting defenseman, assured his teammate, "Don't worry. You'll get to play a lot. Four games today and another one tomorrow. When you do, I'll make sure nobody gets it close to the hole."

David, though, wasn't so sure and told his friend halfheartedly, "Sure hope so. Been a while."

Sarah chimed in, "Both of you play good. Let's win a few games."

"Yes, ma'am," they replied from the back seat and then were quiet. Pre-tournament jitters – she remembered those too.

If only David had started sprouting up, maybe this lacrosse thing would have been more straightforward for him. She'd been a later bloomer, too, but almost made it to six feet by the time she was a senior in high school. David got her blonde hair and bright blue eyes, his dad's athletic coordination, and, she liked to think, his smarts from both. But now, in eighth grade, he was only five-three and a little over a hundred pounds; he'd fallen behind most of his friends in size and physical maturity – and looked even more painfully skinny in his lacrosse uniform. She knew Tim wished David was bigger, too, but they'd need to have patience.

In person, Sarah loved watching most sports, except baseball and soccer, both of which she found slow and tedious. Lacrosse was twenty energetic kids with long, webbed sticks, running and passing and banging into each other on a field larger than a football field – trying to throw a small, hard ball into the opposition's net. A game she wished she'd had an opportunity to play – fast and exciting, usually with lots of scoring and often quick momentum swings. She understood enough about basketball, soccer, and hockey to see that lacrosse was a fascinating amalgam. The modern-day version still resembled the game that North American Indians played for centuries before it started catching on among Canadians and Americans in the nineteenth century. She wondered if any of her Indian ancestors played the game. If so, maybe David had that DNA.

Her work schedule typically interfered so far this season, and she'd only seen three games. David hadn't played in any of them. Tim was the optimist about David playing more this season. He kept telling his son that he'd get his chance, but it hadn't happened. This season was a far cry from last year's undefeated JV middle school season when David started as goalie in most games and improved a lot despite his size.

They arrived at 7:20 a.m. Long lines of SUVs, vans, cars, and several high-end customized buses from all over the Southeast were piling into the Birmingham park for the lacrosse tournament. She had no clue this would be such a big deal. She told the boys, "I guess this is where we unload. Get your stuff and the chairs. I'll drop the cooler and come back for it after I park."

"Bye, Mom" and "Thanks, Dr. Baldwin" were all she heard as the two boys disappeared into the multicolored throngs.

The Dan Mullins Invitational was a kids' sporting spectacle unlike anything Sarah had ever witnessed. After parking in a grass lot with a few hundred cars, she climbed back up the hill to retrieve her cooler filled with drinks and fruits (which she'd been assigned). She walked to the central snack bar and bought a cup of coffee, found a program, and headed off to Eaglewood's assigned team spot.

She'd been to only one other lacrosse tournament in Atlanta. This was a couple of levels up. A sports carnival. Hundreds of teenage boys clad in every imaginable hue of lacrosse regalia: shorts, jerseys, socks, shoes, sticks, and helmets. Plus, an untold number of parents and spectators, most bedecked in team colors, roamed the sidelines of the sixteen fields. Hearty aromas of sausages, hot dogs, brats, bacon, burgers, eggs, chicken, hash browns, and fries permeated the early morning air. Sarah couldn't help but smile. It was good to be outside in the fresh air that beautiful spring morning – and out of Atlanta. She was already enjoying this twenty-first-century medieval-like sporting extravaganza.

She located Eaglewood's spot, which had three big, rented tents and a few dozen coolers, and added hers to the collection. Not yet in full gear, the boys were doing throwing and scooping drills on the sidelines. David and his friend Aaron were joking and laughing as they practiced with their buddies in the bright sunshine.

Sarah recognized a few faces but had never been great with names – unless they were animals. She recognized Coach Frank Ezell,

Assistant Coach Tony Santucci, and Pamela Loncart, president and chairwoman of the Eaglewood Lacrosse Club. She knew who they were, but Tony, a mentor for David, was the only one familiar enough for her to talk with.

Last season Sarah had seen her a few times, but not like she was bedecked today. By any measure, Pamela was drop-dead gorgeous. Long, wavy auburn hair several inches past her shoulders, a movie star's face with a light complexion and a hint of freckles. A killer, curvy body in a pair of impossibly tight black booty shorts and a low-slung gold top. Legs with nary a blemish. She was probably a half foot shorter than Sarah but made herself look taller with four-inch wedges. A face with seemingly perfect, symmetrical features, punctuated with slight dimples à la Jennifer Garner – and if possible, an even sexier, softer version of the stunning actress. No doubt Pamela was younger than her, but how many years she couldn't guess. She had two eighth-grade boys on the team, so probably around forty, but could pass for a lot younger.

Sarah made a lightning-fast, female-to-female comparison: Pamela had her on tits, figure, and probably face because she had not one wrinkle; plus her clothes were hot. At six feet, she had Pamela on height, but unfortunately, she had long legs on which a few spider veins were sprouting. Hair, maybe a tie. Her friends (whom she believed) had rated Sarah a 9. Tim rated her a 9.5 – but wasn't sure he was objective. Pamela Loncart was at least a 10 on a 10 scale. But there was something else about Pamela. She had immediate, unmistakable sex appeal. Sarah doubted she'd ever match that.

Tim told Sarah he'd heard from another parent that Pamela was a federal agent and a widow. She certainly looked the part of a sexy agent, spy, or cop, like in the movies. Everything about her was beautiful and oozed money and unmitigated confidence. Sarah zoomed in on her interaction with the coaches and parents. No question, Pamela was the Queen Bee. Pamela smiled and chatted, not schlepping around coolers, drinks, or food. Others did that.

Inside her tony gold-with-black-trim Gucci purse, Pamela carried a few typical female necessities and other critical items: two iPhones and, tucked into an interior pocket of the bag, her Glock G26 Gen4 an extra clip. She was currently a special consultant to the Drug Enforcement Administration and formerly a special agent in the Special Operations Division. Her usual Glock 22 was locked in her Ferrari FF with an M6A2 automatic rifle and a half dozen clips. Pamela could put a strong, well-trained, unarmed two-hundred-pound man on the ground in a heartbeat but rarely went anywhere without at least a couple of firearms close by. Also in her purse was her favorite pocketknife, which had come in handy many times in Mexico.

As eight o'clock approached, the park was abuzz with excitement and electric anticipation. The first games of the round-robin tournament were imminent. Spectators from both teams sat on the far sideline, with the respective coaches and players huddling across the field about sixty yards away.

Sarah made up her mind to have a good time regardless of what happened on the lacrosse fields today. She'd enjoy the terrific weather and forget about the rest. "Try to stay in the 'now' for a change," she admonished herself. That always sounded so easy. But it never was – if you had to think about it. Her troubles would all still be at home when she returned. She put her cell on vibrate and decided not to answer unless it was an emergency.

Chapter 15 – The Games Begin

Saturday, March 19, 2016

Birmingham, Alabama

The Eagles started with a top prep school from Chattanooga. The big high school lacrosse teams used these middle school tournaments as tune-ups and to give their super-deep junior varsity high school teams extra experience, even though ninth graders were technically not eligible to play; no one ever checked. Across the board, the Rebels from Chattanooga looked older and seemed a head taller and thirty pounds heavier per boy than the Eagles. While size wasn't the prerequisite as it was in football, it didn't hurt in lacrosse either, especially if the big boys were good athletes.

The ref put the ball on the ground at midfield for the first face-off. That's as close as the Eagles got. Within the first three minutes, the Rebels were up by five goals. Like being down a couple of touchdowns with a lot of time left in the first quarter. Only groans from the Eaglewood spectators.

Early in the second half, Sarah was hopeful that David might get in since the score had quickly ballooned to 16-2 – even with the Rebels obviously saving their best players for games to come.

The final was 25-3 – with David not playing a minute. "A buttkick'n," Lana observed.

"Painful," replied Sarah. Like Tim, Sarah was no Pollyanna sports parent who believed that all kids deserved to play and deserved a meaningless, year-end, cheap trophy for showing up at a handful of practices. But come on!

By nine o'clock, it was already in the mid-seventies, the sun feeling more like mid-June than mid-March. Back at the team tents, David and his teammates tugged off their gear while Coach Frank cussed them out, not entirely out of earshot of the parent spectators.

Sarah noticed that Pamela stayed out of the fray. Her twins, Dex and Dax, were among the best players on the team, both good midfielders who always played on the same line together. Like their mother, the twin boys were model-attractive. They were similar looking, yet not identical – both big for their ages and taller than their mom. One favored his mother and had auburn, wavy hair. The other had pitch-black hair and was a bit taller and sturdier built than his twin, with a sharper-edged, slimmer face.

She put her arms around both of their shoulders, bulging with pads, and gave each a kiss. Squarely on the lips – lingering longer than a typical motherly peck.

The players were drenched with sweat as they sat, drank Gatorade and soft drinks, and munched on snacks. David walked over to his mom with his palms up and eyes wide open, silently appealing to her, God, or the lady holding the scales of justice. "Why didn't I get to play any?"

Sarah gave him a quick pep talk. "You'll play. Go get 'em next game."

During the first game Sarah had focused on goalie Randy Frederick, and she agreed, as objectively as she could, with her husband: even though David didn't have the mature male body of Randy yet, he was quicker and a better passer. More importantly, he was unafraid of balls that were rocketing in, point blank. As in hockey, no goalie stops them all, but David stood his ground. Randy, whom Tim had nicknamed "the flincher," seemed to touch nothing that came in hot with any speed. Ball after ball hit the back of the net.

Still, there were three more games today, and David was bound to play. He'd been working out and practicing – spending extra time with Coach Tony and Tim. Their dedication to the game was palpable. But without real playing time, it was hard to improve. For a thirteen-year-old kid on the edge of fourteen, David had kept a pretty good attitude so far. Sarah wondered how long that could last.

At halftime of the second game, the Flyers were up 13-0. The final score was 26-5 – against a powerhouse team also from Atlanta. David didn't play a minute at goal.

In her white capris, sleeveless blue blouse, Nikes, cowboy hat, and sunglasses, Sarah Baldwin felt like she'd been running laps with the boys on the field. It was only eleven o'clock, and she was dripping sweat. Patience was not one of her virtues; she was royally pissed off. It was ludicrous her son hadn't played in either blowout. She better understood Tim's disgust for Coach Frank Ezell.

She trekked back to the team area with the other parents and kids. Ezell, a disguised beer in hand, rounded the boys up near the green Porta Potties where Eaglewood tents were stationed. Just watching his facial expressions, she knew he was tearing them all new assholes. After he finished his diatribe, David walked over to his mom.

Checking out the big bruise on his cheek, she asked, "What in the world happened to your face?"

"That idiot Lance hit me," and then told her the rest of the story of him simply disagreeing that his friend Molly was a slut; then Lance slugged him. Sarah got a chunk of ice from a nearby cooler for David and touched it to his face. But he grabbed it from her and applied the ice himself. "Did you say anything to the coach?" Sarah asked, her emotional temperature skyrocketing.

"Yeah. He said, 'Shouda had your helmet on, and I've got better things to do than babysit little pussies on the sideline.'"

"Let me talk to the coach," she suggested.

He begged her, "Mom, please, it's no big deal. Please don't do that." She told her son she was sorry he didn't get to play but tried to remain upbeat. "This afternoon you'll play. I know it."

Eaglewood wasn't on the schedule again until two o'clock and then would play another game after that. But "Debbie Downer" was starting to overtake her thinking, and she felt like she'd lied to her son.

Sarah wandered aimlessly for a few minutes. Walking back by the tent with the boys' equipment, she noticed a few of the bags were different: each metallic gold and black with Eaglewood Lacrosse and a black emblem stamped on the gold. Kind of a strange "H" with the middle bar extending out. The same symbol was sewn into the mesh of the sticks, which were shiny gold and black like the bags. She looked more closely at one of the bags. The same symbol that hung around Pamela's neck.

It was no surprise that David wasn't at goal when the second half of the third game began. Even though the game was close, Sarah had lost all interest. With no scoreboard and paying little attention, she had to ask what the score was. She commented to Lana Cheney, "I see your son and a few other boys have cool black sticks with gold heads and matching bags. They look pricey."

Lana told her, "I don't know what they cost. We didn't buy them."

"Who did?"

"Ms. Loncart gave a bag and stick to Bryce and, I guess, to a few other boys on the team. Bryce told us it was a bonus for the odd jobs they did around her estate."

"Nice," replied Sarah, wondering how a federal agent, or whatever she was, could live on an estate.

"You've been there?" Sarah asked.

"Several times, but only once inside. It's magnificent."

The Eagles lost again without David getting into the lineup. Sarah folded up her chair. She was so enraged she wasn't sure she could stomach another minute of lacrosse today. They were spending a few hundred dollars going to this dopey tournament, and her son wasn't playing at all. "This is beyond nuts," she muttered out loud.

After returning to the Eaglewood tent area, Sarah told her son, "David, you need to go ask Coach if you are going to play in the next game. If you don't, I will."

David knew when his mom meant business and returned five minutes later. "Mom, he said I'll play the next game."

She feigned enthusiasm. "Great."

By 3:30 p.m., the mid-March sun was beating down like a sweltering day in August. Sarah's body wasn't used to the eighty-four-degree temperature this early in the year. She was beyond toasty, wet with sweat, wondering why she was wearing a padded bra in the heat and wishing she could take it off. She'd downed a half dozen bottles of water today already and hadn't even peed but was still thirsty. With another game yet to be played.

But no David in the lineup once again. And no Pamela on the sideline. Sarah was so outraged her body trembled. In the middle of a big park with hundreds of people enjoying the lacrosse games and the warm, radiant weather, Sarah couldn't remember feeling so angry and alone. The roaring sounds of the crowds were muted. The colors of the early spring day dulled. The heat was unbearable. The final score was 18-7 – with David never getting in the game.

His shoulders slumped as he walked off the field. David walked to his mom, who greeted him with an agonizing smile and a big hug.

"I'm so sorry, David. I know how badly you wanted to get out there today. It's not fair." She put her arm around his shoulders, and they walked back to the tent to get his stuff.

On the way back, he said to her in the saddest voice she'd ever heard. "Mom, Coach promised I'd play in the last game. I hate him."

She didn't say anything, but she hated Ezell, too. Maybe more than her son did. She couldn't get out of the park fast enough. She left their big cooler under the tent and walked back to the parking lot with her heartbroken son. Back in their hotel room, David took his usual twenty-minute shower while she collapsed on the bed and closed her eyes, not bothering to turn on the TV.

Out of the shower, he asked, "Mom, the team, and parents are going for barbeque at a place down the road. Can we go?" her son asked her after getting dressed.

Afraid of what might come out of her mouth if she went, Sarah had no desire to join the group. "I think I'll pass, but I can drive you, or maybe you can get a ride." Immediately, he texted Jason, who texted back to meet them in the lobby in five minutes.

She gave him a twenty-dollar bill. "Take your phone and an extra key in case I step out. Stay with the group, please."

"Okay, Mom, I will," and he was gone.

Chapter 16 – The Blood Pact

The Same Afternoon

Birmingham, Alabama

Since she could remember, Pamela Loncart loved lacrosse and, with one notable exception from her childhood, the boys who played it. Lacrosse had been in her blood since the seventeenth century when her namesake played an early version called *bedagwe* in the Mohegan (Mohawk) language. It's hardly known that female American Indians played the wild, rough and tumble, warlike game alongside their male tribesman. The legend being that because of her courage and skill at tossing the wooden ball through the bedagwe goal (demarcated back then by heaps of stones), the Mohegans came to call her ancestor *Yakonkwe Ronkwe* (the woman leader).

Today, Pamela had better things to do than watch her Eagles get drilled in Birmingham's early spring heat. She adored her twins more than anything, but there would be next year's high school team. She'd decided not to stress about her middle school lacrosse club this late in the season.

After a punishing hour session on the treadmill and elliptical in the ground-level exercise room, Pamela showered, reapplied a bit of makeup, and brushed her auburn mane. She slid on a sheer half-cup violet brassiere with matching panties, garter belt, and stockings, an *Agent Provocateur* outfit hot off the shelf for the new season. One she knew he'd adore. She laid back on the bed and warmed herself up before their video chat.

Twenty-Five Years Ago – September 3, 1991

New York City

She was an incoming freshman at CUNY John Jay College of Criminal Justice. After graduating Summa Cum Laude in Finance from the University of Miami in Coral Gables, he was starting at NYU Law School and taking a graduate course at John Jay.

The two met at a campus mixer for new students. At seventeen, she was fully developed, gorgeous, and quite persuasive. Her dark talents, though still not polished, were becoming more impressive. She had no problem getting into the graduate student mixer with the older guys, whom she knew would be a lot more entertaining than the immature college freshmen.

After only a few sips of her Bacardi and Coke, she saw him. Maybe the most striking man she'd ever laid eyes on. Ridiculously good-looking with blue-green eyes and a classic, thin aquiline nose; a strong, shaven face with chiseled cheekbones and jawbones that trumpeted confidence and strength. Maybe it was the most perfectly symmetrical male visage she'd ever seen. Six-foot-two, slicked-back raven hair, broad shoulders, slim waist, and sinewy well-muscled. And, she would discover, more brilliant and dangerous than any male she'd ever encountered.

Never shy, she walked up and introduced herself, making sure she stared straight into his eyes. "Hi, I'm Pamela Loncart. You're the most handsome man here by far."

Without hesitation, he said, "Raoul Gallardo Menendez. The pleasure is mine, Miss Loncart," and he bowed like a knight of old, took her manicured but not soft or dainty hand, and lightly kissed it.

It was lust at first sight. Theirs, a match made in Hell.

Within twenty minutes of meeting they ditched the lame mixer and were in Pamela's Upper East Side penthouse apartment. These were hardly the typical digs for a freshman, but Pamela had never lacked for money and never would. Especially after her parents' death in a helicopter crash in Switzerland the previous year, leaving their vast riches to Pamela and her brother – and to the Atlanta Tribe. Within seconds of entering her thirty-ninth-floor apartment with twelve-foot ceilings, the two were getting better acquainted as he lifted her off the floor and pinned her against the living room wall. Nothing under her skirt to impede his progress.

Minutes later, he lay naked on his back as she grazed her ruby-red fingernails over his rippling, sparsely-haired chest. "You are of the Darkness, aren't you?" he asked. Freshman to be, Pamela grinned and welcomed his lively aquamarine eyes and gave him a flavor of the depths of darkness behind her scintillating coal-black eyes.

"I'm a member of the Atlanta Tribe. Elsewhere, called a coven. I intend to be chief one day – and maybe more. Our Tribe is the most powerful in the U.S. The history of my American ancestors, originally from Hartford, Connecticut, in the 1600s, is quite a story."

He was fascinated. And he knew for a fact this amazing young woman was telling him the absolute truth in everything she'd said so far that evening. Kneeling next to him, she said, "You too are of the Darkness." That much she could divine as she probed into his eyes and soul. He smiled and told her the abbreviated version of his lineage. His father's side of the family included one of the most infamous Mexican witches from Catemaco, Esmerelda Gallardo Menendez. He grew up on stories that his *abuela* had etched in his memory – when he first learned that men could be witches, *brujas macho*, as well. She told him he had the makings to be a great one, especially after she'd realized that he possessed *Regala de Mentira*. The gift of discerning lies. He had to decide whether he'd use that power on the side of Light or Darkness.

He'd never tried to overanalyze his gift – if it was reading people's slight mannerisms, voice cadence and tone, eye movements, and other body language. He knew only that he needed to be a keen observer. His grandmother's advice was *"el reloj escucha y aprende"* (watch, listen, and learn). Given the nature of his father's business, he accepted the powerful gift from the Dark Lord and never reconsidered his decision. *Regala de Mentira* counseled him to eliminate dozens of enemies from his life – and no doubt saved his own more than once.

"I am a believer in *Principe De Las Tenielle*, The Prince of Darkness," he told his new friend. That evening she didn't mention that she, too, possessed *Regala de Mentira* – as well as other powers that he would never have.

He was enthralled by her beauty and captivated by the dozen dime-sized dark imperfections that marked her chest and back. My "Devil's kisses," she told him, following his eyes. "But enough talk."

After their next round, Raoul lay on his side, his hands massaging her exquisite flesh. "I have a confession to make. I'm not here to become a lawyer or government official or anything like that in the U.S. or back in Mexico. I'm here to soak up all I can about the American system of justice and government, understand better how Americans of power and influence think and act, and scout new opportunities for my family's business."

"Which is?"

"Drugs. Heroin, cocaine, marijuana, and even straight opium for the old-time connoisseurs. *El Sin Cuello*, my father's partner, is pondering my assertion that methamphetamine will be the next big thing. I haven't convinced him yet, but I've researched and discovered it was the drug of choice used by World War II aviators and soldiers on both sides to keep them alert and awake and even euphoric under horrific circumstances – and that it's highly addictive. So, we'll see. My family is part of a large drug operation in Northwestern Mexico. I'm being groomed to play a key role."

Pamela's brain whirred into overdrive. The opportunity of her young lifetime lay next to her. Their meeting this evening was no coincidence. Like her adversaries, the persons-of-light, she believed there was no such thing as coincidence. Why so many people dismissed the idea of the supernatural, Evil or Good, Pamela never understood. For now, she didn't tell him that her father, Nigel, and his second cousin Franklin had been the silent forces behind the drug trade in Atlanta since the 1970s. They were jointly known as "The Ghost" because they ran such a tight ship; only a handful of people ever knew of their involvement. It provided the capital for them to make tens of millions more in more conventional businesses: banking, shipping, real estate, and others that were complementary to drug trafficking. A hefty percentage of those millions were earmarked for the Atlanta Tribe.

"You look so pensive. Do I shock you?" Raoul asked.

She rose up and kissed him. After her parents had died, she'd been encouraged by her aunt and mentor, Maddie, to infiltrate and join the corrupt American "justice system" like others before her had done. "Do *His* damage from within," she advised. A criminal justice education was her jumping-off point. But she didn't have a plan. Not until that evening.

To Raoul's disappointment, she walked out of the bedroom. From the wall safe in her study, she removed the knife that had been handed down for generations. A French trade knife crafted by an unknown blacksmith, probably Canadian. It had a simple walnut handle and a razor-sharp forged, handmade blade over 350 years old. Bartered for by the Mohegan Indian who had saved her ancestor and namesake from certain death. She reentered the bedroom with the knife, which they would use to consummate a lifelong blood pact.

Saturday, March 19, 2016

El Nido de Augila Haupia in the Sierra Madre Occidental Mountains – Sinaloa, Northwestern Mexico

After rising through the ranks, Raoul Menendez became known

within the Pacific Cartel and in the international narco world as *El Oscuro,* The Dark One. Some said for his wavy jet-black hair, elegantly combed back on the sides and top; others said it was for his penchant for security and secrecy; and others said it was for reasons that shouldn't be discussed.

Long called *El Sin Cuello* (No Neck), since his blockhead sat on a pair of thick shoulders with only a hint of any connector, Raoul's uncle had a serious run going. A run even longer than the legendary Colombian Pablo Escobar – and now much longer than *El Sin Cuello's* longtime partner, Raoul's father, Armando, gunned down fifteen years ago.

But now, with *El Sin Cuello* behind bars in Mexico's most modern and purportedly inescapable prison, Altiplano, just outside Mexico City, Raoul, his longtime top lieutenant and nephew, was in the catbird seat to assume complete control of the richest, most powerful drug cartel on the planet. A cartel that Homeland Security, the Hoover Institution, and other so-called experts estimated grossed about $5 billion the previous year. A number that wasn't even close. He chuckled at their assumptions and attempts to gauge the ever-escalating wealth of the Pacific Cartel, whose finances, he thought by 2020, would break into the top few dozen countries' GDP in the world.

Raoul eschewed the popular narco wardrobe of leather slacks, open silky shirts unbuttoned with gaudy gold chains, huge rings, Rolex watches, and tattoos. He sat with his brown caiman alligator boots propped on the edge of his huge Kingwood desk. He wore blue jeans, a belt studded with turquoise and opals, and a white linen shirt, looking like he just walked out of a Calvin Klein ad.

Known as the man with ice water in his veins, but now feeling like a foolish schoolboy, he was nervous with anticipation of seeing her again, if only online. The love of his life and blood partner for more than two decades. Five more minutes until their scheduled call at one o'clock, *El Oscuro* knew Pamela would be punctual. She also liked to tease him.

Wearing the little diaphanous outfit she knew he'd like, she sat cross-legged, Native American Indian style, with her laptop in front of her on the bed. She logged into one of her many Darknet accounts and launched an untraceable video chat app.

She sank her flawless, ivory teeth into a succulent apple, her favorite fruit that she truly believed was essential to health – and always had been since that ancestor of hers, Eve, had taken her first bite. She hit a ten-character authentication sequence, and within a minute, Raoul Menendez appeared on screen.

When his Mac Pro beeped three times, he hit his own sequence of keys. Pamela appeared on each of his three huge monitors. She was ravishing. Even more desirable as she bit into the fruit again, allowing the sweet juices to drip down her chin and between her spectacular, natural breasts.

"Ojos Bonitos (he called her "Pretty Eyes"), *Eres encantadora!"*

"My *Valiente Matador*, you don't look so bad yourself," she giggled playfully. "It's good to see you and hear your voice, even if from so far away."

He only got better looking with age. Her pet name for him was Valiente Matador, Brave Matador, which she gave him after hearing stories of his youth. As a teenager, he'd trained to become the next Carolos Aruzza, *El Ciclón* ("The Cyclone"), from decades ago. He showed great promise, but his father decided that bullfighting was too dangerous for his only son. Still, his skills with banderillos and swords came in handy – not on 1,500-pound bulls but rather on enemies when his business was threatened or he was disrespected. His signature kill he saved for the most egregious offenders.

"I'm not sure I can wait six weeks before we meet again in person, *Valiente Matador*," she purred.

"I think of you all the time and when we are together once more," he told her, soaking in her face, her auburn hair, and her thinly veiled breasts on screen.

Four years ago she had her husband Darrell killed while he thought he was making a big drug bust in Guadalajara. She and Raoul rendezvoused more often than in the past: on his private island off the coast of Baja or in Rio or Milan or Granada or Paris or Zanzibar. But even with Raoul's skill for disguise, her own wealth, and carte blanche to set her own schedule as one of the DEA's top, semi-retired operatives, there were limits on how much time they could spend together – surreptitiously mixing business and pleasure – under the radar scopes of their respective organizations. Regardless, their collaboration continued to pour hundreds of millions of dollars into the coffers of the Atlanta Tribe just as Pamela envisioned it that evening back in 1991 when they first met.

In front of her laptop, in her skimpy lingerie, she asked, "How do you think *El Sin Quello* will enjoy his vacation in the United States?"

They both chuckled before discussing the scenarios it would take to have him removed from his top spot once and for all, including extradition to the U.S. Pamela, told him that it might take more of Mary Jo's help but that wouldn't be a problem. Mary Joanne "Mary Jo" Cogburn was in her fifth term representing Pamela's congressional district, one of Atlanta's most affluent and the most conservative in the North Atlanta burbs. She was a member of the House Armed Services and House Budget Committees and ranking member on the House Permanent Select Committee on Intelligence. More importantly, she was also a member of the Atlanta Tribe.

Chapter 17 – The Close Encounters

The Same Day, 6:00 p.m.

The Wingate Hotel – Birmingham,

After a day that began with much hope and levity, Sarah Baldwin was hot, beat, and annoyed. She peeled off the perspiration-soaked clothes and let the warm shower dissolve away the dirt and tension. The tall blonde toweled off and stood in front of the vanity mirror.

Forty-seven-year-old Sarah was no hourglass, hard body like Pamela, but she kept herself in decent shape walking or doing yoga most days of the week. She had long, slender legs, a beautiful broad face with high cheekbones, crystal blue eyes, and a generous forehead, no doubt an inheritance from her great-grandmother, a full-blooded Seneca. Thick, ash blonde hair cascaded over her shoulders – hair that females and males had told her for years was to die for. She'd always wanted bigger tits. Even more, she wanted to erase the bags under her eyes and a few unwieldy spider veins on her legs. With no discretionary money, though, not likely soon – if ever.

While lotioning her bare skin from toes to neck, front and back, she took a long look up, down, and around in the side mirror as well. She was proud of how she wore the 147 pounds on her nearly six-foot frame, especially at her age. She wished Tim would notice her like he used to. For more than twenty years, he'd rarely been able to keep his hands off her for more than a day or two, and she loved his physical attention. Could those days be gone forever?

She stuffed her purse and valuables in the small hotel closet safe and took only her room card, car keys, and wallet. She texted David and said she'd be back in an hour or so. At a nearby fern bar, she ordered a lemon drop Grey Goose martini and an entrée she rarely ate: a half rack of pork ribs and greasy skillet fries. With a cocktail and comfort food in her tummy, she calmed down. It was just nice to sit peacefully and alone in the air conditioning after the long, hot, miserable day at the tournament.

Upon her arrival back at the hotel, David was coming in, too. She pulled him aside and asked her son point blank, "David, do you want to go home? It's up to you, and I completely understand if you say 'yes.' I can't tell you how disappointed and upset I am you didn't get to play today. I know you've heard it before, but life sucks sometimes." A lot of the time lately, she thought.

"Mom, you already paid for the room, and it's too late to drive home. I just wanna have fun tonight and hang with my friends."

She examined the big black and blue half-circle under his right eye. "Please let me put ice on that eye."

"Later, Mom."

She smiled. "Go have fun but stay on the premises and be back in the room by 10:30 p.m." Surprisingly, he reached up and kissed her on the cheek and told her, "Thanks, Mom. I love you. It'll be okay."

She was unable to avoid smiling. The wondrous resilience of youth. She couldn't remember hers.

In the hotel lobby where they only served soft drinks, cheap wine, and beer, Sarah ordered a glass of Chardonnay she'd never heard of. A few moms smiled, and she politely nodded, but she had no interest in conversation. Being back in the lobby of the hotel reignited her earlier anger. Why not keep drinking?

The small lobby bustled with activity. Boisterous boys had already forgotten their defeats of earlier and were running around, cutting up, and having a big time. She saw David off and on; he seemed to be enjoying himself with a few of his teammates. She asked Lana Cheney and the Swensons if they'd seen Pamela Loncart tonight, but no one had.

Okay, if no Pamela, then I'll at least have a little chat with Coach Frank Ezell, Sarah told herself. On the verge of ordering another glass of wine, she saw the coach stroll in, beaming like he'd won all four games earlier – instead of losing them all. He sat down with his entourage of players, including the Loncart twins and four others. Sarah thought, ah, the boys with the special sticks: Dex and Dax Loncart, Randy Frederick, Lance Earl, Bryce Cheney, and Kevin Westerman.

Hoping for an opportunity to corner the coach, Sarah ordered a water instead. Twenty minutes later, he got up. As nonchalantly as she could, Sarah walked over and asked him if they could talk outside for a minute. Ezell checked her out from top to bottom. "Sure, Mrs. Baldwin."

He followed her out, his eyes glued to the tall blonde from behind. She stopped at the hotel's small, illuminated fountain out front. Face to face, Frank Ezell thought to himself, *"Man, I'd like to tie up this hot mommy and fuck her all night long."*

"By the way, Coach, since I used your appropriate title, it's not Mrs. Baldwin; it's *Doctor* Baldwin. Just to make that crystal clear." Her bright blue eyes bore into his brown slits, glazed with booze.

She hadn't planned this out and just started talking. "Coach, I'm just wondering what the deal was today with Lance slugging David on the sideline for no reason and you doing nothing? Did you see his eye? Then telling him he'd play in the last game today. He didn't get one goddamn minute of playing time in *any* of the four games. David was the only player on the freak'n team who didn't get to play today, Coach. Oh, maybe you noticed that we got toasted in all of them. Lemme see. I think you've lost seven of eight games in the last three weeks. How's that goalie working out for you, Coach?" Sarah was spitting nails but stopped.

The decent-looking but full-faced, beefy coach, an inch taller and outweighing her by at least eighty pounds, took a threatening step forward. "First, *Doctor* Baldwin, that was just little boys' bullshit on the sidelines. Lance told me your pissant son was in his face, and so he gave him a little kiss. No big deal. Second, I play who I want to play. Your son wouldn't have helped us at all in any of the games today. End of story."

Sarah hadn't belted a male in a long time, but she came within an eyelash from cussing him out, then swinging at the buffoon standing in front of her. Instead, she took a deep breath and asked one more question. "So, Coach, did you tell my *pissant* son why you decided not to play him the last game?"

Ezell sneered, his squinty eyes crinkling. "Look, lady, you're fucking kidding, right? I don't baby these boys. That's for their mommies, like you, to do. I'm the goddamn coach. I work for Miss Pamela. Randy is the number one goalie this season. Live with it, bitch. Oh, sorry, *Doctor* Bitch." He walked away just as a group of people exited the hotel and a few others entered.

Taken aback by his language, tone, and insolence, Sarah knew if he hadn't walked away, it would've gotten ugly. She wished she'd been carrying her pepper spray, which she'd left in her hotel room safe upstairs. She would have loved to see him writhing on the pavement for all to see.

She stood alone and forlorn by the fountain. There was no one to corroborate either of their stories as to what had just transpired. Her immediate thought, other than wanting to kill the SOB, was to scream to the heavens. To anyone who would listen. Sarah was so upset her body shook with rage. Her teeth clenched. She felt completely helpless and immobile.

Then came the thought: *Now my son won't play another minute the rest of the season. What have I done?"*

Back inside, sipping another glass of acidic wine, ignoring the other parents and wondering what the heck to do, Sarah got a tap on the shoulder from none other than the Eaglewood Lacrosse Club President and Chairwoman.

Sarah swiveled on her bar stool, faced her, and realized it was the first time she'd seen Pamela indoors – and without her expensive sunglasses. She'd changed outfits since the morning and was now in a figure-hugging, short, button-up dress with a high collar and cutout, accentuating her cleavage; a sort of Asian look, her dress shiny golden and charcoal, black stiletto heels, and black jewelry. Perfectly coordinated, she was tastefully adorned with the Eagles' colors. Accented by faint freckles, her fair skin glowed.

Sarah's deep blue eyes stared directly into Pamela's, which were unlike any she'd seen in her life. Often, beautiful auburn-redheads like her have those enchanting, sparkling, emerald green eyes. Pamela's weren't like that at all. Hers even more unique; her irises, flecked with a myriad of dark, liquid crystals; coal black, barely differentiated from her pupils. Sarah was mesmerized.

Looking into her clear blue eyes, Pamela sensed the near-blinding pulse of a person-of-light. An adversary not to be taken lightly.

"Dr. Baldwin, why don't we step outside? I heard you've been asking about me."

Pamela's request seemed genuine, which surprised Sarah as much as her uncanny eyes. The two comely lacrosse moms stopped near the small hotel fountain, only steps from where Sarah had her unpleasant chat with Frank Ezell twenty minutes earlier. They stood a pace apart; Sarah got a closer look at the unusual black pendant on Pamela's necklace. The same symbol she saw on the boys' bags and lacrosse sticks. She wished she'd been wearing her beautiful gold cross necklace studded with diamonds and emeralds – an heirloom from her grandmother – as a tit-for-tat, but she'd left it at home.

Pamela said, "Dr. Baldwin, I apologize that I couldn't make the games this afternoon. You may have heard I work for the government in law enforcement. I must answer the call even if my twins are playing in a big lacrosse tournament. I'm sure you understand."

Sarah nodded but said nothing.

The chairwoman continued. "Lacrosse is a passion of mine. It's been a family tradition for a long, long time – going back a few centuries. My twins are still a little raw, but they're going to be great players, maybe All-Americans one day."

Sarah thought about telling her that lacrosse was likely an ancient tradition of her family as well, but strangely, Pamela beat her to it. "Maybe the game was part of your heritage as well, Dr. Baldwin?"

"Possibly. My great-grandmother was a full-blooded Seneca."

Ah, I am right about her, she congratulated herself. "You have the beautiful high cheekbones of our Native Americans. A tribe of the Six Nations known for lacrosse."

Before Sarah could thank her, Pamela's eyes latched onto hers. She listened and watched Pamela's remarkable black eyes transmute into something different altogether. Now seething, pulsing with unfathomable malevolence; even darker, yet incandescent, flickering with red flame. Like she'd flipped a switch.

"Dr. Baldwin, I want to ask about your altercation with Coach Frank. But you need to understand something. When it comes to my lacrosse club, you have no say in who plays or doesn't play or how much they play or anything else for that matter. No parent does. Frank Ezell is the coach, but this is my club. He does what I tell him. He said you cursed at him and were disrespectful and demanded that your son play more. I won't tolerate that kind of behavior from my club's parents. I'll grant you this one reprieve. But if you or your husband or your son ever complain again about how I conduct the Eaglewood Lacrosse Club, that would be a mistake. Is that clear?"

Never one to tuck her tail and run, Sarah fired back, "I haven't a clue what Coach told you or not, but he was the one who cussed me. I never demanded that David play today. I wanted to know *why* he didn't play him in even one of the four games. Especially when we've been losing virtually every game lately, even after he promised he would. David works hard, and he's a good goalie, a better goalie than Randy. Your club is a train wreck right now, Mrs. Loncart. But, of course, you were busy and missed most of the action today."

Pamela smiled disdainfully, her ebony eyes pulsing sinister darkness, "Yes or no, Dr. Baldwin? I'm not sure you're getting my drift on this. Would you like your son to remain on my lacrosse club or not?"

"Pardon me?" Sarah asked incredulously, "I'm not going repeat myself."

Silent for several seconds, she bit her tongue but managed to stammer back, "Yes, of course, Tim and I want David playing on the team, but more importantly, David wants to play."

Pamela's strange, frightening eyes retreated to their more approachable, even friendly, state. "Excellent! I know that you'll be able to follow my simple rules. I'm sure David is having a terrific time with his lacrosse pals tonight, regardless of what happened on the fields earlier. You never know what might happen tomorrow, Dr. Baldwin. I have other important business in Atlanta. Regrettably, I'll miss the final game, but please enjoy rooting my club on."

The chairwoman turned and walked back into the hotel, oscillating her perfect, round butt, and joined the crowd inside.

Chapter 18 – The Witch

March 19, 2016

Birmingham

A piece of jewelry with a cross would have protected her, though Dr. Baldwin didn't know that, thus paving the way for Pamela's witchcraft. She detected a forbidden hunger veiled deep within Sarah; a small, soldering slit Pamela would titillate into a full-blown, dangerous crevice that would suck Sarah in and consume her. Pamela chuckled at the fun it would be toying with Sarah Baldwin's clandestine craving, one she was familiar with; one of the reasons she kept her dark-skinned servant, Tariq.

In her encounter, Pamela also experienced a first in her forty-two years: one of the more arcane decrees from The Teachings that her ancestor Pamela added three centuries ago; her namesake ordered that Indians were forever exempt from the wrath of the Tribe. She was forbidden to spill her blood or blood of her blood. However, even witchcraft was subject to interpretation over time. Dr. Sarah Baldwin and her son had Native American lineage, but she could live within the rules and still make Sarah's life, and the lives of hers, living nightmares – without bloodletting – if she chose to do so.

Her mother Phoebe and her father Nigel had taught her to savor the destruction of persons-of-light, their arch-enemies and true believers in good and the God who, by definition, opposed their Dark Lord. Only a minute percentage of self-proclaimed worshippers of the God-of-Light weren't preposterous hypocrites, raving lunatics, or closet heathens – or all the above; false believers, sheep easily led and dominated. Even better, the herd could be quickly mobilized to help trample the true believers.

Pamela had always found her battles with persons-of-light more arousing than sex, her favorite daily activity. The clashes aroused every fiber of her soul – and honored the Dark Lord she worshipped. But she was also taught their God-of-Light was formidable; never to be underestimated. If she could help tip the balance, her Dark Lord would move closer to his endgame.

Pamela's ability to divine the darkness of others' souls and was what her Tribe called *Tenebris Clairvoyance*, or Dark Telepathy. Hers was a strange, powerful type of telepathy enabling her to delve into the human soul and discern hidden hungers, temptations, addictions, and fears that racked them. Eye-to-eye, one-on-one, at her whim, she had the power to turn those cracks, often hidden from others, into cataclysmic chasms. Fault lines that became so wide and deep they could swallow their victims' souls. If she was able to keep repeating her maul splitting, the damage could be irreparable.

Many who truly believed in witchcraft and the Dark Lord thought there were six well-defined primary powers, six spell powers, and six potion powers. Not so. Instead, there were unlimited permutations of those with boundless ranges of strength, depending on the witch's innate skills, her practice and honing of those skills, the victims themselves, and the environment.

Pamela spent endless hours lassoing her own Dark Telepathy and her brand of sexual mind control, *Sexus Imperium*. By age fifteen, Pamela had impressive abilities to control the actions of others, male or female, telepathically, after she'd lain with them – but the effect and longevity varied substantially from person to person. Years ago, her first "laboratory" had been an Atlanta high school lacrosse team; an experiment that got a bit out of control when she was sure a lacrosse boy was going to kill her; she discovered she had another rare power, called Black Widow (aka *Coitus Mortem*) – the ability to telepathically kill while in a sexual act.

Pamela was the progeny of an original Tribe family, and no one was close to her powers except Mary Jo (not a Tribe family descendant). They both could discern lies and do some basic telekinesis (moving small objects, shutting a door and the like). Still, Mary Jo had the unique telepathic ability to read minds of any person in her presence – without physical contact. And yes, "talk" with them if they had any telekinetic ability. That power helped make her political career.

Both witches knew that only one would eventually be tapped as chief, their powers being an important criterion, but not the only one. Eventually, Maddie would decide. Pamela was sure she would be chosen.

Chapter 19 – The Spoils

The Same Evening

The Wingate Hotel—Birmingham

It was her reward, sanctioned by the Tribe after the birth of her twins and her success kidnapping the Oosterhuis girls in Birmingham. But it was a dozen years until she had her own game; her own lacrosse club; her lab to practice and expand her powers – and to enjoy every second of it. This season had been a bust in terms of wins and losses, but she had come so far. Now, it was all about preparing for high school and the Pecan Valley Lacrosse Club, which she planned to head. She wanted more wins, more titles, and more trophies, but that would happen next year. She had her core boys and would recruit many others. And pay whatever it took to be a great team. And mold the club she'd always wanted. And continue to expand her powers.

After her set-to with Dr. Baldwin, Pamela texted Coach Ezell and gave him five minutes to arrive in Room 506, the extra suite that she'd paid for in cash. Frank had put on thirty pounds or so after his lacrosse college days, but he was still a cute young guy with a classic lacrosse "I'm fucking hot shit" attitude. He was well-paid and would do anything she said.

Upon his arrival, Pamela told him, "I had a little chat downstairs with Dr. Baldwin. I took care of it for tonight. You know I won't be there tomorrow. Unless he doesn't show up or isn't able to play, Baldwin plays goalie tomorrow. We're going to get murdered anyway. That will put an end to all the nonsense with his mother when he plays and gives up a couple dozen goals. I'll chat with Randy. After that, Randy plays out the season at goal. Understood? And if you want to skip the game tomorrow, I'll leave that up to you – Tony can coach, but let Baldwin play goalie."

Frank nodded to his boss. "Yes, ma'am." Pamela poured him a

half glass of Macallan and a few fingers for herself and clinked his glass.

"Not a good day. Sorry, Miss Pamela."

"No worries," she lied. The verdict was already in on Frank Ezell. But for all his faults, he was splendidly endowed. The auburn beauty stood up. She unzipped the back of her short skirt and stepped out of it. As she removed her yellow thong, his eyes zoomed in on her inviting, new trim: fiery red pubes, perfectly trimmed in the shape of the Loncart emblem.

She grinned and tossed him a black Lifestyle Tuxedo from her bag. She sat down on the big chair facing him, draping her bare legs over the chair's arms. The coach was mesmerized. With enthusiasm, Frank did exactly as she commanded. Any spell on him would be overkill.

The six boys in (what she called) "The Club" were under strict instructions to communicate with her only using their retina-secured iPhones. With extra apps, Pamela could GPS track each of them even when their phones were off and conduct periodic audio and video surveillance. She could immediately erase all texts and emails sent and received to and from her—as well as disable any photography (forbidden within her premises).

To each, she made it clear what it meant to belong to The Club. There were many benefits but also consequences if anyone broke her rules. Off and on, she gently interrogated each of them alone about their pledge to her – not to discuss the club or its games with anyone outside the club. She also quizzed them about their other sexual activities, not precluding them from other pleasures but rather impressing the importance of "playing a clean game." Like any good interrogator, she knew their answers before the questions.

Dex and Dax were under her total mind control. Over time, she learned how to focus her powers to manage her other four club members, too. She knew, though, there could always be gaps. But she'd thrived living on the edge for many years. And this was such a fun game she'd chosen. This varsity middle school season was her preparation for next year at Pecan Valley. She would add bigger, stronger, faster – and even better-looking – boys to her high school club. Nothing would get in her way. Not Ezell – and certainly not the annoying Dr. Sarah Baldwin.

A few weeks earlier, as a reward for his progress, she promised Randy Frederick he'd play the whole Birmingham tournament, but she'd easily convince him that missing the last game tomorrow would be worth his while. Randy's parents weren't at the tournament. A piece of cake. Other than her twins, Pamela thought Randy was the best-looking boy in her club: nearly as tall as Dex and Dax, with a hard body, sandy hair, and a handsome face with amazing cheek and chin dimples. When she heard him knock on the door, she pulled him inside and placed his hands on her breasts, then between her legs. He was hard before he got to the sofa. Randy would forever remember this evening and forget about needing to play lacrosse the next day.

After her recent sessions with Coach and Randy, the hot shower felt incredibly refreshing. Since she'd first watched the film with her father as a young teen, she'd often thought of Marilyn Chambers' iconic, breathy, wanton lust in the classic *Insatiable*. *"Please, more. More. More. I want more!"* she demanded from John T. Holmes' monstrosity. She missed her father calling her "My Adorable Dark Princess." Since her teen years, no one else, except Raoul, came close to exciting her the way her daddy did, but her sons were closing in.

More pretty much summed up her view of life on earth: more power, more money, more pleasure. Sex central to her club games.

More a literal command from her Dark Lord.

She would always hunger for *more*, and her darling twins were more than happy to oblige that night. They made her the Oreo center of their cookie. Her husband, Darrell, had provided the right genes and had been fun while he was around, but after he balked at her sexual activities with their sons, he became expendable. Raoul was happy to do it himself in a phony narco bust. Now she had two men of her blood in her life – all for herself. And she had her other club boys. And Raoul. And Tariq. And she wanted others.

Two floors below, Sarah Baldwin, was inexplicably, insanely horny. She couldn't remember the last time she'd even wanted to touch herself. She hurried to the door, checked the lock, and hooked the chain – in case her son arrived back early. Alone, with no one to answer to in a strange hotel room, she sensed an overwhelming, uncontrollable carnal urge bubbling up from primal parts.

She wanted to be wanted again. Needed. Taken. Held. Kissed. Touched. Caressed. Licked. Fucked. Fucked more. She craved wild, passionate sex. Even snuggling in bed at night with Tim was a thing of the past. Barely a peck on the cheek from him, but she wasn't exactly doing her part either. They'd been drifting apart for a long time. Neither seemed to give a damn or knew what to do about it. Sarah had never broken her vows or seriously contemplated the possibility but more often had fantasized about having sex with other men. One was her coworker, Dr. Bill Allison.

A chiseled, coal-dark black man. Six-foot-six and a former second-team All-Big East small forward at Villanova, he played ball three years in Europe but returned to the U.S. and went to vet school. Bill had a shiny, shaved head, a confident, angular face with no facial hair, and perfect, large white teeth. She found him intelligent, pleasant, funny, and impossibly gorgeous. She'd always been attracted to athletic black guys, which she'd joked about with a few girlfriends for years. She knew very few who didn't want what she did.

She'd never personally worked with or known a guy like Bill, who'd joined the clinic six months ago. She got subtle vibes that he found her attractive, even though he was fifteen years her junior. Despite the drab, shapeless pink or blue scrubs she usually wore with her beat-up Nikes, Bill – unlike her husband – complimented her daily about something: her hair, her jewelry, her eyes, her clothes, her smile, her laugh. The last few weeks, she'd upped her game. She'd taken to wearing skirts or slacks and plunging blouses with a white lab coat instead of her scrubs. Bill's compliments increased.

A couple of months ago, Sarah had friended him on Facebook, and he immediately accepted. She was floored by one of his photo albums, "At the Beach." Not a big fan of Speedo-type suits, which less than one percent of the male population on the planet should, or could, ever wear, she'd made an exception. In several posed stills and short video clips, he looked like a Greek god. Positively Herculean. Popping biceps, muscular legs, ripped abs, trim waist, especially for a man of his height. His itty-bitty sunburst yellow suit left little to the imagination. Hung like a horse, stretching the thin fabric to its maximum. "Oh my, how big is that at full mast?" she wondered.

Showtime.

The delicate lacy cups of her demi bra now scooched down, exposing the entirety of her small breasts and erect nipples; Sarah stood panty-less in the hotel mirror. She widened her stance and with her right hand she switched from his Facebook page to video on her iPhone. She took a step back and pointed her iPhone at her reflection in the mirror until the camera focused. Then hit video and let her fingers do their thing.

Still breathing hard after she finished, she'd lost count of the orgasms she had standing in front of the mirror. Oh my, she told herself, I am still hot. But hot enough for a stud a half-generation younger?

Did she have his cell number? Scrolling down her contact list, yes, he was there. She typed a text to her colleague: "For your eyes only, please. Enjoy, Sarah." and attached the steamy video.

It was wrong. It was dangerous. It was wicked. It was nutzo. It was counter to all she'd ever believed. Yet sinfully exhilarating. Overtly seducing another man this way. On the verge of hitting "Send," she heard a cacophony of old and new voices raging inside her. At the last instant, she deleted the sexy text and collapsed naked on the bed, still clutching her phone. She slipped on her PJs, took the chain off the door lock, and climbed into bed to watch TV and wait for David.

David returned to their hotel room, his bruise worsening. Sarah grabbed ice from down the hall and let him press it to his cheek. They giggled together while watching a rerun of *Modern Family*. After the show, Sarah asked her son if she could say a prayer.

"Sure, Mom."

"Lord, thank you for this day and the beautiful spring weather. Jesus, we know that you can make good from all things as bad as they can seem. We pray for your protection of Tim tonight, and we pray that David will play tomorrow like your warrior of old, his namesake David."

They both said, "Amen." Seconds after his head hit the pillow, David was out like a light.

But not Sarah. Staring at the dark ceiling with slivers of light creeping around the edges of the cheap hotel curtains, Coach and Pamela were stuck in the forefront of her brain. She kept replaying excerpts of her disturbing confrontations outside the hotel. Why did she get in the asinine coach's face like that? But it was too late now.

Pamela's dark, intrusive eyes gave Sarah the sense that something didn't bode well for her son – and maybe not for her either. But thank God she hadn't sent that video.

Two floors above, still savoring the fruits of having been the center of her twins' "cookie," Pamela also prayed before falling asleep. But to a thing with many names: Satan, or Lucifer, or Beelzebub, or Ruler of Demons; God of this World; or Diablo – her Dark Lord. *"Give me the strength to destroy this person-of-light you have put in my path – without touching a hair on her head. Already, she had crossed the line in defying my authority and interfering with my club, my own game, the spoils that you granted me. Amen, my Dark Lord."*

Chapter 20 – The Goalie

Sunday, March 20

The Dan Mullins Classic Lacrosse Tournament, Day Two – Birmingham

Sarah awoke to a rare Nor'easter bearing down on Birmingham. It was windy and already thirty-five degrees colder than yesterday. Mountains of steel-gray clouds marched toward the city like they were Sherman's army. Without thunder or lightning in the area, they'd probably still play, but Sarah hoped the game would be canceled and that she and David could jump in the car and drive back home to Atlanta – and forget about lacrosse.

She hadn't told her son anything about her disturbing conversations the previous night. Some things were better left unsaid, but she still hated fibbing by omission. She had no idea what would happen that cold, blustery Sunday morning. She tried to leave that outcome in God's hands, which she had a harder time doing lately.

They arrived at 7:30 a.m. for the final day of the Dan Mullins Classic Lacrosse Tournament. In the parking lot, Sarah hugged her son and told him that she and his dad couldn't be prouder of him. Trying to be positive, she said to him, "Play well today, son. Remember your namesake."

"Yeah right, Mom," he told her with a wry smile, doubting that he'd ever get to set foot on the battlefield.

Walking in the cold, damp chill, Sarah played back her conversations of the previous night with the coach and Pamela. The stark reality slapped her harder than the wind whipped the trees as she realized what those words would likely mean for her son today and the remainder of the season – and beyond. Flooded with rage and guilt – and certain she'd screwed it all up for him – Sarah dreaded the game this morning. But at least they'd soon be home.

A few minutes before the start of the game, Coach Frank Ezell told Randy, "No sense wasting our number one goalie. You're taking a break today, Frederick." Per his private session with Miss Pamela the night before, Randy wasn't surprised and said nothing. Besides, his right shoulder ached from the punishment he'd taken in yesterday's games. Watching from the sideline today, bundled up in his coat, was okay with him. Ezell, his head still throbbing from last night's alcohol binge, looked around and fingered David to come over. "Okay, Baldwin, you wanna play today? Stop a few of these. They'll be coming a lot harder in a few minutes."

David double-checked his mouth guard, chin strap, and cup and stepped to the front of the goal, outside the crease, to warm up. The coach threw a few eggs, slow ones, at him that he caught easily. But then, from only about eight yards out, he rifled three in a throw, each alternately right past David's ears at hyper speed. Ezell scoffed at his second-string goalie. "Come on, pussy, gotta stop those if you wanna play against Mountview."

Stepping up to only five paces outside the box, Ezell cocked his stick and took dead aim at David. As in other sports, the most difficult shot to block or defend was the one that came in at top speed, dead at you. Like a line drive straight back up the box at a baseball pitcher. With no more than a couple hundredths of a second to react, the missile grazed the edge of David's stick's head but then ricocheted and hit him squarely in the nuts. Sizzling pain shot through his groin. Even wearing a cup, the pain pulsed through his whole body, and he fell to the wet ground.

On the far sideline, Sarah couldn't hear what had transpired but was relieved to see her son get vertical. Then, she thought, oh my Lord, he's going to start. Yes, this morning, she and David were getting what they wanted. David was going to be in front of the Eaglewood goal, playing the formidable Mountview Mustangs.

Ezell decided to take Pamela up on her veiled "get out of jail free" card to bail on this game and go nurse his hangover. His team was going to get killed anyway. The tournament had been a debacle so far and could only get worse today. On the sideline, the wind and rain gusting harder, he told Tony, "It's all yours today, hot shot. I'm feeling sick as hell and need to go lie down."

"You're leaving?" Tony asked incredulously.

"Yep, you're the coach today. Make sure you play that little shit Baldwin at goalie. Miss Pamela wants him there. I don't know why." Frank Ezell stumbled down the far sideline without saying anything to his team and didn't look back.

In his two decades of playing and coaching lacrosse, Tony had never seen a coach bail like that. Fuck Ezell. He'd taught virtually all the Eaglewood players. He knew their talents and weaknesses – a lot better than Ezell. Sure, they'd lost key players this year, but he still had guys who could play.

Chapter 21 – The Battle Royale

Sunday, March 20

The Dan Mullins Classic Lacrosse Tournament

As the horn blared for the game to begin, Tony yelled, "Let's go win this game." Many looked around for Coach Frank. He wasn't on the sideline. Most thought that was awesome.

At midfield, the first face-off went to Mountview. A crisp pass to a slanting midfielder, and then another to a cutting attacker. A couple of confused Eaglewood defenders weren't even near the goal before the ball sizzled past David's right shoulder and into the top of the net. Across the field, Sarah thought: this could be ugly, real ugly. Please let it start thundering and lightning, she prayed.

After a beautiful wrap-around goal, Mountview was up two-zip after less than a minute into the game. Sarah did the math in her head. The Eagles could lose by eighty.

David stood up before the horn started the game, but Ezell's literal ball-busting was only now wearing off. So far, no chance to stop any of the blistering shots, unhindered by his outmatched defensive teammates. Nobody, but especially D-pole player and team bully Lance Earl, seemed to be helping.

After Mountview's big star, No. 45 Dalton Rice, blasted little Nick Hamilton and scored a goal, he picked Nick up by the shoulder pads, patted him on top of his helmet, and told him, "The peewee tournament was last week."

Tony called a timeout. A few minutes into the game, his boys already looked crushed. The rain and wind added insult to injury. Tony gathered his already drenched and bedraggled troops around him and yelled, "Listen up! No motherfucking, piece-of-shit, dirt-bag, asshole prick ever disrespects any member of our team. Ever! You all got that!" Their eyes widened – they'd heard Coach Frank cuss that way daily, but never Coach Tony.

He assigned his best athlete, Garrett Lumley, to make sure No. 45 saw the error of his ways. At six feet and about 150 pounds, Garrett was the only player he had who was close to 45's size and athleticism. He reassigned little red-headed spitfire Jay Mason to the front line and told him to run the "Cross" offense and told the defense to play a box with Garrett shadowing 45. He said to his Eaglewood players, "I want you guys to go play your butts off as a team. Lance, by the way, you're out." Lance took his helmet off and threw it down the sideline.

The next face-off went to Rice, the fifteen-year-old ninth-grader, who at six-two and 180 pounds, looked more like a senior in high school; he was (illegally) playing in this tournament for additional practice. He took a pass in full stride and came in from the right, heading straight at David. It was too late when he realized his folly. He'd locked in on the goal and momentarily lost sight of the guy coming at him from the left side.

Garrett walloped Rice so hard with his body and stick that Rice's helmet popped off, and his mouth guard disengaged from his helmet. Even with the rain beating down, Sarah heard the collision from fifty yards away, a legal but teeth-rattling hit. The big kid from Mountview tumbled to the sloppy turf. The Mustangs' superstar midfielder hadn't been belted like that one time in the entire season. Rice lay motionless in the mud until he was helped up by two teammates. As he walked away from the collision, Garrett followed and grinned at him." By the way, that was for my 'peewee' teammate, fuckwad."

Over the next ten minutes of the first half, the Eagles fought like Sarah and others had never seen nor imagined. They scored five goals and held Mountview to none. Lance Earl was gone from the park with his father, and the defense was jelling and getting a little rest with the improved offense. David made a half dozen great stops of Mountview fireballs.

To the amazement of all spectators, it was a ballgame. The score at halftime, Mountview seven and Eaglewood five. On that wild, rainy Sunday morning in Birmingham, the Eagles, who'd gotten pounded in four games the day before, had come alive. So had their fans. "Go, Eagles!" their continuous, growing war chant. Several dads went out of their way to fist-bump Sarah, one saying, "That goalie son of yours is playing a whale of a game. Don't understand why he hasn't been playing more this year."

She nodded and wondered the same thing. Now soaked to the bone, Sarah couldn't be more thrilled to be at this game. "Go figure," she smiled to herself. Then thanked God, regardless of what might happen in the second half.

With his team still leading by two goals at halftime, Mountview Coach John Sandoval strode to the far end of the players' side of the field. The huge check on his star player woke him up, too. They were in a dogfight for the first time this year. Out of the Bobby Knight school of coaching, Sandoval went ballistic on his nationally ranked lacrosse team. He picked up two nearby lacrosse sticks and threw them over his team's heads and then hollered, "We're up a couple of goals, but you goddamn pussy assholes are getting the shit beat out of you by a pitiful, no-name public school. They're kicking your tails. You pricks won't win this tournament, and we won't keep any kind of national ranking unless we kill them this half. I mean, murder them."

Tony was almost as astonished at the score as Sandoval – but didn't let on. He huddled his team on the other end of the far sideline. Each player was drenched to his jock, uniform soaked and smeared with mud and globs of turf. But he saw intense excitement in their eyes.

"You all having a good time in the crappy weather?" They all shouted, "Yes, Coach!"

Tony always carried his ancient midfielder stick with him. He pointed it at David. "This guy will make the stops if we play good defense. You all got that?"

"Got it, Coach!" they shouted back with enthusiasm.

Then he pointed his stick at Jay MacDonald. "Jay is our quarterback and will play multiple lines. Stay alert, and he'll get the ball to you middies and attackers to stick it in the goal. Got it?"

"Got it, Coach!" even louder.

Next, he pointed his stick at Garrett. "He is going to hound No. 45 hard wherever he goes. He can't do it by himself. We can beat these guys if we all play together." Then, he broke into a gigantic smile. "First and foremost, have a blast. This will be a lacrosse game you'll tell your grandkids about. That I promise you."

Their sticks pointing into the dark skies, the Eagles roared.

Before the horn went off, Sarah watched her son standing alone in front of the goal he'd defend the rest of the game. With the winds howling and the rains still beating down, out of nowhere, a man walked toward David. He was dressed like a Native American Indian. He wore a headband with feathers and loincloth, no shirt, and long black hair. He stood in front of her son and put his hands on David's shoulders. After a few seconds, her son pointed his lacrosse stick to the heavens and yelled, "We are Eagles!" The Eaglewood players turned toward her son. Their sticks rose to the sky. The Indian was gone.

"What in the world did I just see?" Sarah wondered.

The horn boomed to start the second half. When Eaglewood broke their huddle, cheers from the crowd were deafening. The overwhelming number of spectators weren't rooting for the hometown favorite. They were cheering for the unlikely underdogs from Roswell, Georgia.

Mountview scrambled for the first face-off of the second half, and it went to their most dangerous player. Rice raced downhill, sprinting dead at Eaglewood's goal and David Baldwin. Coach Sandoval watched and licked his chops.

Garrett and the other Eagles defenders tried their best to stop Rice, but after making extraordinary spins and dodges, he kept going, cutting and juking while skillfully cradling the ball with his stick. He was not going to pass it; he was hellbent on the goal in front of him. Five paces from the goal, with clear daylight in front, he rifled a laser at David.

He had to guess, but somehow David knew where the shot was going. Rice would try for the knockout punch. Right at him and low. The ball screamed at his feet at ninety miles per hour. He didn't flinch. He'd flipped the head of his stick down as Rice let it loose.

For a few seconds, everyone assumed the ball was in the back of the net.

But walking back into the crease in front of the goal, David held his stick high; the ball captured in the mesh. The crowd went wild. The seldom used, second-string goalie had stopped a point-blank breakaway heater from Mountview's best player to start the second half. Rice shook his head and headed back down the field as David cleared the ball to his defender and best friend, Aaron, who gave him a thumbs-up with his free hand. Eaglewood marched back down the field to their offensive end, soaked and muddied but looking like a revitalized team.

With only three minutes left in the game, the Eagles knotted it on a goal by Dex Loncart. Thirteen all, the clock running.

Mountview's coach screamed, "Timeout!" A risk because the time clock ran during his called timeout. For Mountview, a tie would be as bad as a loss, likely knocking them out of first place in the tournament and any top national ranking. He told his assistant to rev them up. Then, instead of addressing his players himself, he ran to the head referee. Not in his wildest imagination had Sandoval thought he'd have to play the card he was going to play, especially this morning against an unknown team. But there was too much at stake.

Tony tried to stay calm. When Sandoval called timeout, he huddled up his team and told them, "One more goal. That's all we need. One. Help your teammates out. You got this."

Out of the corner of his eye during the short timeout, Tony spied Sandoval talking to the lead ref and not his team and wondered what was up with that. He told his Eagles, "After Garrett wins the faceoff, run the offense. Don't rush. Plenty of time to score. I'll yell out the time left in case you can't hear the ref. There won't be a tie in this game. We're going to win it."

On the face-off, Garrett scraped it back to Jay. With an almost imperceptible nod, he indicated he wanted to start the Eagles' best play, The Cross ("La Crosse"). After getting his screen, Jay threaded a pass to Dex. Nick circled the goal to give him a target. Dex found him as he rounded the right side. A defender contested but was a step late. Nick cocked his stick to take it point-blank into the goal. A step outside the crease, though, he got planted, hit in the back by a Mountview D-pole player with his stick and driven into the sloppy turf. An obvious penalty.

The ref blew his whistle.

Tony was ecstatic. It would be a sixty-second penalty on

Mountview for hitting Nick. The Mustangs would go a man down. The Eagles on the power play with the ball, now less than two minutes in the game.

Inexplicably, the ref called a slashing penalty on John Harold, an Eagle attacker, who hadn't touched any Mustang player. Mountview got the ball out of bounds and, instead, Eaglewood got a full-minute penalty and went one man down. Boos rained in from the spectator sidelines. Sarah screamed with the others, "No way! Terrible call!"

Even the usually calm Coach Tony was incredulous. Instead of cursing the refs, he simply put both of his palms up in the air, silently indicating, "You can't be serious?" The lead ref blew his whistle again. He came over to the sideline and called Tony for unsportsmanlike conduct. Unheard of, without a warning first.

Eaglewood went two men down in the penalty box for the duration of the game with little time left. Mountview had the ball. The sideline boos, now deafening, when spectators realized Eaglewood had been penalized again.

Tony told his remaining three defenders to pack it in tight around the box and help David protect the goal. Playing only four against Mountview's six on that side of the field. The ref yelled there were thirty seconds left. A Mountview midfielder sent the ball to Dalton Rice, who went one-on-one toward the goal. Rice faked left, spun right, and headed full tilt at the net. Garrett jarred him enough on the way to force him to pass to a teammate, who immediately got the ball to Rice on a give-and-go. Rice zeroed in and nuked another missile at David's feet. David guessed right again and blocked it with his stick, but not cleanly. The ball popped into the crease in front of the goal. In a wild scramble with several players from both teams colliding, jolting, and hacking with their sticks, a Mountview attacker – clearly inside the crease and pushing David, and in blatant violation – got the rebound. In the traffic, he shoveled it low into the right side of the goal. The horn went off.

Final score: Mountview 14, Eaglewood 13.

It was like all the air got sucked out of a gigantic balloon. Hundreds of spectators groaned—pleading with open hands or offering prominent middle fingers.

Traditionally, after a win, a lacrosse team raced to their winning goalie, mobbed him, and buried him with their bodies, or put him on their shoulders – or all the above. Sarah watched and wept as David's teammates rushed in mass to elevate her son on their shoulders and yelled, "Eaglewood, Eaglewood, Eaglewood!" She'd never seen anything like it after a loss. Tears flowed as the crowd chanted, "Eaglewood!"

Also, per tradition, after the applause, the players on both teams walked single-file past each other, shaking hands. In a genuine gesture of good sportsmanship, Dalton Rice stopped the line and shook Garrett Lumley's hand. "You all played awesome. We were lucky to win."

Garrett smiled. "Helluva a game. You're a great player."

"You're not too bad yourself. I hope we play again one day."

The two stars bumped gloves and rejoined their respective teams.

Near the sideline, Tony gathered his guys, each one of them caked with wet mud and grass. "I've been playing and coaching lacrosse now for two decades, since I was younger than you guys. I've never seen a team play with the heart you all did today. You played like men. I can't tell you how proud I am of you." He pointed his lacrosse stick to the heavens again, and his team did the same. "Go, Eagles!" they chanted over and over.

Tony knew that Sandoval had given instructions to the ref, but there was no sense in complaining; the game was over. Despite the disappointing loss, Tony felt like a switch had been flipped. He knew that he could coach at any level and would never doubt that again.

For the sake of the team, Tony would finish out this season, but he was done with Frank and Pamela after it ended. A couple of months ago, he'd overheard a handful of players talking in the locker room – saying things that had made him more than a little queasy. He wanted to get as far away from the chairwoman as possible.

Sarah hugged her son who, especially without his equipment on now, looked like an underfed, filthy drowned rat. She tried to be upbeat, telling him, "You and your team played great today, David. You should've won. You deserved to win. You'll get more playing time now."

But she wasn't so sure about her last statement, and neither was her son. Neither Ezell nor Pamela had attended the game. So, no one who mattered saw the best lacrosse game of the year. What version of this morning's epic battle would they hear from others?

The Baldwins wanted to get back home to Atlanta; the sooner the better. They said a few goodbyes, got their cooler and headed to the parking lot. She couldn't resist asking her son, "David, you're going to think your mom's crazy, but as the second half was going to start, I think I saw a man, a Native American Indian, come up to you and put his hands on your shoulders, then vanish. Pretty nuts, huh?"

Her son smiled in the back seat. "Yeah," he said. "Hosgeegehdoh."

"Say what?"

"In Seneca, it means, 'I am a warrior.' That's what he told me."

Sarah was too dumbfounded to say more. Indeed, David had battled like a true warrior – like his biblical namesake.

As Pamela Loncart stood naked in the bathroom mirror of the ornate, black quartz bathroom accented with whites and dabs of red, she received a text from her sons. "Driving out of B-ham. Tony coached. Lost 14-13 in last few seconds. D&D."

The score was astonishing. Putting Baldwin in the ball game she knew could backfire. She couldn't have a defiant lacrosse mom like Sarah on her hands – a mom who could influence others. Not when she was already planning what she wanted to do at Pecan Valley High. She needed another plan. Sarah and her son were interlopers in her club. Her game. But she chuckled to herself and wondered how far the crack she'd divined in Dr. Baldwin had already widened. Tomorrow the real fun would begin.

A tall, rangy, good-looking man walked in naked from the bedroom. He picked her up as if she was a mere child and sat her on the vanity. He eased her legs apart and stood between them. She needed to keep the Pacific Cartel's sixth biggest distributor, and a fellow member of the Atlanta Tribe, a happy boy – as she'd done for so many years. She aroused him with her hands and fitted his erection with a black condom.

He stared into her dangerous, dark eyes as he slid in and out of her. "You know, Sis, this has always been my favorite position with you." She knew that and much more about her twin brother.

Part III - The Dismissal

Chapter 22 – The Hero

Monday, March 21, 2016

Roswell

Tim Baldwin woke up more chipper than he'd felt in months. Nothing like getting laid after a long hiatus to put a guy in a better frame of mind. He rolled over and watched his beautiful wife, still asleep. He carefully lifted the sheet to gaze at her bare breasts, slowly rising and falling. Last night seemed like a dream. He had no idea what had gotten into Sarah but wished he could bottle it. Standing naked in the bathroom mirror, he checked himself out. His five-eleven body wasn't what it was twenty years ago, but he was still well-toned for his age (and better than any of his friends); he had a few age lines that Sarah said made him look distinguished, and amazingly, a full head of black hair with only hints of gray. Maybe he still had it after all.

Still half asleep, she smiled at him. Her fifty-two-year-old husband, who looked forty-two was still the guy she'd fallen for twenty-four years ago. But last night, she'd fantasized about Bill while making love to Tim and wasn't sure how many times she came. That made her even hornier. She would have liked Tim to fuck her brains out again, but he was taking David to school this morning, meeting a friend for breakfast, and said he was running a few errands and would be back home late morning. Her twelve-hour vet shift didn't start until ten o'clock.

She got up at 7:30 after the boys were gone and was alone in her own home for a change. She sat at the kitchen table reading the morning paper, sipping coffee, and noshing a toasted bagel with butter. After her peaceful breakfast, she hung her silky robe on the hook near her vanity and scrutinized herself naked in the mirror. Last night's sex with Tim was nice, but she yearned for more. Since the weekend, even with all the lacrosse nonsense, she'd felt insatiably hyper-erotic without pretense of sexual inhibition. Bill kept bubbling to the forefront.

She felt manic. She rushed to her closet and threw stuff out of her secret drawer until she dug out a big dildo she hadn't used in ages. It was flesh-colored – not black flesh, but it would do. She roughly touched her tits and nipples and got herself wet with her fingers. With her foot braced on the vanity, she slammed the toy in and out until she moaned, "I'm cumming. I'm cumming *big*."

She stared at her iPhone on the vanity and then typed the text, "Hey, good morning. Thought u might enjoy the vid. Loved making it! Wondering what the real thing is like? CU at work." With three naughty smiley faces and "PS for ur eyes only." It was Sarah unfiltered. The video from Saturday night. This time she hit "Send."

Usually a quick dresser, she took an extra half hour to primp. No scrubs today. Instead, she picked a sleek, fashionable, above-the-knee blue skirt and flesh stockings with a black garter belt. No panties. A half-cup black bra and silky light gray blouse with the top buttons undone. And black heels, even though she knew she'd pay for that extravagance by the end of the workday. All perfectly professional but as sexy as she could get with her lab coat. "That's as good as it gets," she told herself.

When she turned on the car ignition, a text warbled in, and she grabbed her iPhone before zooming off.

"U are hot & beautiful. Been on my mind 2. CU soon." Then, a dozen emojis of brown thumbs-ups. Sarah felt her cheeks warm. Now, what was she going to do? His short response, an invitation? "Sometimes you get what you ask for," an inner voice told her. But did she want this? Before pressing the accelerator, she felt compelled to text back several emojis with smiley faces and hanging tongues. Who was she kidding? She wanted it bad.

At 9:55, Sarah pulled into the parking lot of the Roswell Emergency Animal Clinic and regretted the high heels. Worse, she was petrified of seeing him in the flesh after sending her X-rated selfie video.

She greeted the clerks up front and walked swiftly down the hall to her small office to stash her purse. But then, they were face-to-face in the hallway. She stopped in her tracks and stared. He grinned. "Hi, Beautiful. I hope I catch you later." As he passed her, he glanced back, and seeing no one, gently grabbed her backside with his massive hand. Then he was gone.

The brief ass grab sent shock waves of excitement through Sarah's body. She realized she hadn't said one word to him but figured the video had said plenty. How she'd keep her mind on her work the rest of the day, she had no clue.

David had never felt like a hero – until that Monday. After his dad dropped him off, he walked into Eaglewood Middle with his shiny black and blue eye and his head held high. Before reaching his locker, it seemed like he'd turned into a rock star. News had spread that Eaglewood, led by David, Jay, and Garrett, had nearly knocked off one of the top lacrosse teams in the country. Only to be cheated at the end by an illegal goal. That news went viral, at least in his school. Coach Tony had written an online blurb about the game that was posted on the school's website, and he posted several photos on social media as well. The best one was of David, after the game, holding his stick high, with his helmet off, looking up into the sky.

His eye didn't hurt much, but it sure looked nasty. A badge of honor he wore proudly. Even super-hot Caroline Connolly stopped to say, "I heard you were amazing yesterday. Cool."

Her smile nearly melted him. Humbly, David managed, "We played a good game but didn't quite get it done. A lot of guys played good."

She smiled. "Is your eye okay, David? Does it hurt?"

David told the petite brunette cutie, "Naw, it's fine."

Without asking, she lightly touched his cheek under his eye with her fingertips. He'd felt nothing like that in his whole life. His entire body tingled.

"I'm coming to your next game," she winked and walked down the long hallway. Transfixed, he watched her perfect little butt swish rhythmically down the hallway to algebra class. She stopped for a second, looked back, and blew him a kiss. David stood in the middle of the hallway, staring at one of the hottest girls in the school. She'd never said a word to him until this morning. He could care less that he'd miss the bell for his first class.

As Pamela walked back to her Escalade, she looked at her watch; she needed to hustle to the Eaglewood practice. She was pleased that her first-ever meeting with the principal of Pecan Valley High School went so well. After promising a substantial donation to their SportsPlex Building fund, she was the new chairwoman of the Pecan Valley Lacrosse Clubs – boys and girls. The Pecan Valley *Predators*, she laughed to herself. How apropos.

Chapter 23 – The Temptations

Monday, March 21, 2016

Roswell

At practice, Coach Frank Ezell went after David as soon as he saw him. "Hey, Baldwin, I heard you fucked up and let in the winning goal yesterday. That's why you're not starting goalie, you little cunt."

David knew better than to mouth back to Coach. He said nothing. Nearby, though, Tony overheard the exchange. He walked up six inches in front of Ezell's face. "Baldwin played awesome, as did the other kids – even though you were a fucking drunk no-show." Never once had David heard Coach Tony get into Coach Frank's grill like that. Frank himself was taken aback and ordered Tony, "Get the damn drills going, you skinny cretin. Now."

David noticed that Mrs. Loncart was at practice. He'd only ever seen her at games, and she didn't attend all of those. Even though his mother had told him nothing about their conversation on Saturday evening, he'd gotten the vibe that his mom wasn't a fan. Ten yards back from the sideline, she talked with her twins and then a couple of her other favorite players, Lance and Randy. Neither he nor his other teammates were oblivious to the fact that there was a "Loncart" clique within their lacrosse team. When Randy, the latest to join the clique, got his gold stick and fancy bag a couple of months ago, David knew playing time was going to be even tougher to come by – though he hadn't mentioned that to his dad.

That her team had almost pulled off the middle school lacrosse upset of all time – with Baldwin playing well at goalie – was still hard for Pamela to believe. Water over the dam. After hearing more about the surprising Mountview tournament game from her twins, she'd hatched a backup plan. She didn't care about wins and losses the rest of this season. Job One, she needed to underline to all involved – kids, parents, and coaches – exactly who directed Eaglewood's lacrosse club and who would be in charge at Pecan Valley next season.

Dr. Sarah Baldwin had pissed her off. She didn't want to hear about her son starting as goalie for her club from her or anyone else. That had to be nipped in the bud. No mutiny in her ranks. She'd already promised Randy he'd be at goal the rest of the year, and she kept her promises to her *Lacrosse Club* boys.

She asked Dax to tap Coach on the shoulder. With a slight turn of her neck, Pamela indicated for Coach to follow. He jogged over. Facing away from the western sun, she slid off her sunglasses. "Frank, here's what's going to happen." She took two minutes to tell him as she munched her honey crisp apple. He nodded several times and said nothing. She took a few more bites of the sweet fruit, tossed the core into the woods, put her Pradas back on, and started walking to the far edge of the field.

Toward the end of practice, with the sun slipping fast and the lights now on, Ezell whistled, "Baldwin, Lance, Randy." They hustled over, and he told them, "Do a half lap. You guys get out of running suicides. Take the equipment back up to the locker room." David had a good practice alternating with Randy. Maybe Coach would cut him slack after all. He was fine not running the punishing sprints.

Inside the locker room, the three boys began pulling off their practice jerseys and pads before the others arrived. After pulling off his shoulder pads in the cramped, gamy room, Lance, who was several inches taller and forty pounds heavier than David, jawed, " Baldwin, I hear it was you who complained about my defense to Santucci. Got me kicked out of the game Sunday, and my dad kicked out of the park. You fucking little prick. You'd have never gotten in the game if Coach and Miss Pamela had been there." He purposely forearmed David in the back while he reached to stuff his gear in the locker. David turned, accidentally bumping Lance's arm. "Get off me, you little pussy," he shouted, and slammed David up against the lockers. Hard enough to make them rattle.

As Lance combed his long black hair out of his eyes, David yelled, "That's all bullshit. I never said anything to anyone about you or Randy." Lance pushed him again, his shoulders with no pads clanging against the lockers. He was ready to defend himself against the much bigger guy when his goalie rival, Randy, surprisingly slugged Lance in the mouth, drawing blood, halfway spinning him around.

More strangely, Randy moved aside while Lance went after David again – not Randy, who had hit him. Lance punched David twice in the face and planted the much smaller boy on the cement floor; sitting on David's midsection, prone, Lance was poised to pummel him further. While Randy stood by watching, David heard him say, "Easy. Remember what she said."

"Get off me, douchebag!" David yelled as Lance grabbed him by his practice jersey and bounced the back of his head on the cement floor. At that point, all three heard the raucous voices of other lacrosse teammates entering the dingy, claustrophobic locker room.

Laying on the floor, David couldn't see what was happening but realized that a couple of guys were prying Lance off him as he lay on the hard floor. Aaron banged Lance up against the metal lockers and yelled, "What the fuck are you doing, asshole?"

Lance spit back, "The little prick cold-cocked me for no reason. Maybe he's still sore at me for cussing his girlfriend at the game on Saturday. Who the fuck knows or cares? He's fucking crazy."

"Yeah, right, dickhead." Turning to Randy, Aaron asked, "What happened?"

"Not sure. Baldwin bumped him or whatever, then cussed him. Then he wailed at Lance and hit him in the mouth. Lance popped him and got on top of him on the floor. I was trying to break things up, but

Lance was pissed," the starting goalie lied.

Aaron looked at him with more than a bit of disbelief. The little locker room was now jammed with two dozen players. Noisier than usual, the boys jostled to find out what was going on.

"You okay, David?" Aaron asked, helping his friend to his feet.

"Yeah, thanks. They both lied. Randy hit Lance then did nothing while Lance slugged me and pinned me down. I didn't do crap other than get hit."

The bruises from Lance's blows were darkening on David's face and blood dripped from his lips. Lance had the beginnings of a shiner – from Randy's punch.

Aaron, who wasn't as tall as Lance but had more heft, got two inches from Lance's face. "Lemme get this straight: David sucker-punched you?"

Lance spit back, "Out of nowhere. Little punk should know better than to fuck with me. "

Aaron stared at Lance, "You haven't heard the last from me, dickhead."

Randy and Lance pushed their way out of the crowded locker room into the cool, early evening air. They'd played their parts well, and outside the locker room Randy gave Pamela a subtle, from the waist, thumbs-up. The two sauntered over to talk with her and Coach Frank.

Last evening Sarah and David had given him a blow-by-blow report on the Eagles' lacrosse game. He'd have given anything to have been there but was glad Sarah got to see it. Maybe David's lacrosse, even in defeat, would help bring the family close again. And he was keeping his fingers crossed for more hot sex that night.

Tim arrived at the back of Eaglewood Middle School near the small locker room to pick up his son, Aaron, and Bryce. Usually, it was a bunch of boys piling into SUVs and exiting quickly, but tonight, several adults and kids were milling about the small, crowded lot. Hard to tell what was up. He stepped out of his old Honda Pilot and saw the boys – Aaron carrying David's stick and holding him up by the elbow. His son approached with fresh bruises on both sides of his face and a big cut lip.

Tim asked him, "What in the world happened?"

"Lance beat the crap out of me for no reason at all," he told his dad.

His son had never been a troublemaker.

"I believe you," he told his son.

He told David and the two other boys to get in the car and stay there. He marched up to Ezell, glaring. "You need to get control of him," he said, pointing to Lance, who was standing over near Pamela's Escalade. "Everyone knows he's the team bully. And he just beat up my son again like he did at the tournament."

As he'd done with Sarah two nights before, Ezell took a step forward. "Get out of my face, Baldwin. The way I heard it your son started it in the locker room. Your bitch wife was warned in Birmingham. It's handled."

Tim shot back, "Right. Like you did in Birmingham. If you call my wife a bitch again, I'll..." But his voice trailed off before he finished the sentence as Pamela appeared next to Ezell. Tim redirected his anger at her. "*You* need to get that kid under control." He pointed at Lance.

Her black eyes attacked his and ferreted out plenty. Immediately, she knew which crack would destroy him – one that killed thousands of people a year without her help. She glared back at Tim with her glittering, pitch-black eyes pulsing. "Mr. Baldwin, you need to calm down, go home, and have a couple drinks. I'll sort it out." With that, she turned around and went back to chat with several other parents, whom he knew were on the Eaglewood Lacrosse Club board.

His heart galloped, and he sweated like a pig in the suddenly chilly evening air. "You do that. I'll be back in touch," Tim yelled back at her, but he decided to leave ASAP to avoid further escalation. He turned his back on Pamela and other staring onlookers and got back in his car.

Tim thought about calling his wife, who was still at work, but she'd texted she was busy and probably wouldn't be home until late. What could she do at this point anyway? David's wounds were superficial, and being a former Army medic himself, he saw no signs of serious injury.

What he did see was that he'd probably made things worse for his son. Like his wife, he too had seen inexplicable, captivating darkness in Pamela's eyes. He understood why his wife had been frightened. What was it about her? He tried to think of the right word – but could only come up with *evil*.

As Tim drove away, Pamela beamed and without a word winked at Frank, "Good job." He hoped maybe he could get off her shit list – and even get to fuck her again. Hope sprung eternal. With the slightest motion of her forefinger, she ordered Lance and Randy to follow her around the other side of her car. She asked for a quick debrief, then put her arms around both teens and told them, "Thanks, guys. I mean it. Sorry, Lance, you had to take the punch, but it was necessary."

"No problem, Miss Pamela," he replied in a rare polite tone. She knew she'd probably made a mistake with Lance, but with his dashing, chiseled face, long black hair that he could never quite keep out of his eyes, and broad shoulders and small waist, he was the hottest of her club. He was her problem child, but she'd seen him as a challenger who needed even more attention, which was more than okay.

"Guys, why don't you both tell your parents you're coming over for dinner tonight and I'll have you home by 9:30 p.m. sharp. There might be a special treat for each of you." With no hesitation, Lance and Randy told her, "We're coming for dinner." They grabbed their iPhones to call home while Pamela walked toward the three board members.

After overhearing the parking lot rumblings, Tony walked up to Frank Ezell and said, "This thing with Baldwin and Lance is complete bullshit, and you know it."

Ezell barked back, "Shut the fuck up, Tony. Remember who butters your bread. You want your stipend to vanish tonight? You've got no say in this. Got it, dickhead?"

Tony took a deep breath and didn't respond. Instead, he walked away from his asshole boss, wedged his gangly frame into his bright orange 1992 280Z, and drove away. Pissed off, but not knowing what to do, he would try to finish out the season. But he was no longer sure he could keep quiet about conversations he'd overheard one evening a few months ago in the same locker room. He hated Ezell; he hated Pamela more.

Chapter 24 – The Email

Tuesday, March 22, 2016

Roswell

After kissing her boys goodbye, Sarah was out the door for her early shift. As she drove to work, her mind was a mishmash of thoughts and feelings. She hoped Lance, the bully, would get what was coming to him after hitting David again – but doubted that witch Pamela would do anything. Maybe the school would.

After tending to David last night, she'd been insanely horny once more; after priming him with her mouth, she rode her hubby like a wild filly.

Earlier, she'd had wanton sex with Bill in the storage room at work – in a position she'd not thought possible: he stood holding her under her buns with his blacksmith-like arms, her feet off the ground while he pogoed her up and down on his huge cock.

She thought, "*I just got banged by two different guys within a few hours.*" She was incredulous. She didn't understand what was happening and felt powerless to fight off her illicit desires. She knew right from wrong but wanted what was taboo; inexorably and inescapably, she was caving into an unfamiliar, overpowering lust. She was anxious and excited about seeing him again. And didn't feel the least bit guilty; what was up with that?

Tim woke David and made a cup of coffee. He decided to take the dogs on an early walk before schlepping his son to Eaglewood Middle School. He fetched the newspaper and sipped his coffee – knowing it would take at least one more attempt to roust his son. Now sporting two black eyes and a nasty purple bruise on his cheek from his latest beating at the hands of Lance, David looked like hell. On the short drive to Eaglewood Middle, Tim told his son to stay cool about all the lacrosse stuff, even if provoked. As David grabbed his frayed backpack and disembarked, his dad said, "I'm proud of you. What happened to you last night won't happen again, that I promise." David nodded, then was lost in the crowd of kids entering the school. As he left the drop-off lane, Tim saw Ezell talking with Pamela as they walked toward the teachers' parking lot. What was up with that? The sight of them darkened his mood.

Back home, Tim felt better once he opened the blinds, letting the sunshine stream into his spacious, cluttered office. As they often did, Grant and Zeke, his Airedales, encircled his chair. He pet both of their wiry-haired bodies. His laptop was alive; he scanned his Outlook Inbox and saw a new email pop up. Sent from Pamela Loncart and cc'd to each of the Eaglewood lacrosse board members and Coach Frank Ezell. The subject: "Lacrosse Club Dismissal." Fantastic, he thought; Lance was finally getting kicked off the team. He wished he could slap a few high-fives.

But Tim read the lengthy email in mounting horror and disbelief; Pamela Loncart ticked off an array of team rules that David had supposedly broken and accused Tim and Sarah of threatening the coach and incessant complaining. But it was the last line of the lengthy email that made Tim jump to his feet: "Last night, the Board voted unanimously to dismiss David Baldwin from the Eaglewood Lacrosse Club. He needs to turn his uniform into the school by this Thursday."

"No fucking way!" Tim yelled. His dogs exited his office in search of safe haven downstairs.

Stupefied, Tim sat back down and blinked to clear his contacts and reread the email. Then he read it a third time. Surely, this couldn't be happening. They never even talked to David or him or Sarah about last night or anything after the lacrosse tournament. His mind reeled as he tried to figure out what to do next. His overriding thought: It's my fault. If only I hadn't been there after practice last night, this would've never happened.

Last night he'd been pissed off at Coach Frank, but did he threaten him? He told Ezell not to call Sarah a bitch again – and maybe was on the verge. That was athreat? There were a few parents around, but who could or would corroborate a "threat?" Sarah had complained about David getting no playing time the first day in Birmingham but said she made no demands. And he knew the other stuff in the email was pure bunk. A unanimous vote? There had to be a way to fix this injustice.

Tim's all-too-familiar anxiety erupted and superseded the other processes of his body and mind. He paced through his office and upstairs hallway. His brain couldn't focus. His chest tightened. His feet felt numb. He knew his own signs. He'd been doing better but needed to self-medicate. He yanked open the bottom drawer of the large red metal file cabinet in the corner of his office and shoehorned out a bottle of Patron that lay buried under old files. He poured out the remnants of his coffee into the toilet in the guest room. Then returned and filled the mug half full of tequila.

He tried to call Sarah on her cell, but she didn't pick up. Regardless of the puzzling, sizzling sex the last two nights, his wife hadn't been happy with him for a long time. The email wasn't going to help their flimsy marriage.

He calmed down and let the tequila do its magic. He started a new document, naming it "David Baldwin – Lacrosse Club Reinstatement." He listed the names of a few people he should try to contact ASAP. Then, he broke his own cardinal rule: when angry, wait at least twenty-four hours before responding in writing to anyone online. His short email response intended for Pamela, board members, and the coach read: "There is obviously a misunderstanding as to the events of last evening and at the tournament in Birmingham. Sarah and I would like to meet in person at your earliest convenience so this can be cleared up and David can remain on the lacrosse team." He decided he better change the email's subject from "Dear Queen Bitch and Asshole Board Members," but otherwise thought it was fine. He spellchecked the short email and read it a few more times. He was proud of his restraint and hit "Send."

Tim phoned the main office at the middle school and asked for an appointment with Principal Mulhaven. After a couple of minutes on hold, her assistant, Cheryl, told him, "Mr. Baldwin, Principal Mulhaven would be glad to meet with you. How about eleven o'clock?"

Tim replied, "Thank you. I'll be there, hopefully with my wife, if she can get off work."

His other attempts to reach the lacrosse club board members went to voicemail. Tim was simply asking each if they might have a couple of minutes to talk. Then the obvious struck him: David might not even know about his dismissal from the lacrosse team. The email he'd received went out to only a handful of adults. He wasn't sure he'd get to talk to him before meeting with Principal Mulhaven. What a fucking nightmare.

Chapter 25 – The Middle School Principal

Tuesday, March 22, 2016

Roswell

David walked swiftly down the hall to the principal's office after first period. Lance Earl passed him in the crowded hallway and smirked, "Hey Baldwin, been nice having you on the team, pipsqueak. Maybe you can be a cheerleader, pussywad. I'll get you pink pompoms and tampons."

What the hell did that mean? David wondered.

Earlier that morning, Pamela and Frank Ezell had paid a visit to Edith Mulhaven. With Pamela's generous donations to the school's music program (besides the lacrosse team), Edith had little choice but to meet. She'd not yet heard what had transpired in the boys' locker room the previous evening. Pamela gave her version, apologized for the boys, and assured her she would handle it. After meeting with Loncart and Ezell, Edith met with Randy and Lance individually. The three stories were remarkably identical. There was something fishy, but she couldn't put her finger on it.

She cringed when she saw David with his two black eyes and bruised face; his story didn't come close to matching the others'. She did not think he was lying – which meant the others were. It pained her to tell him, "David, I'm sorry about your face – but I think we're going to put this whole thing to bed. If anyone had gotten seriously injured, that might be different."

He stared at the principal in disbelief. "You mean *nothing* is going to happen to them?"

She told him, "Whether I like it or not, it's a lacrosse club matter, not the school's. I'm not going to take any actions against you, Lance, or Randy. That's the best I can do." She felt nauseous after she said it.

David started to walk out her door but then turned and said, "Mrs. Mulhaven, I mean no disrespect, but if you don't do anything, that says that you don't believe me."

"Back to class, young man," she told him.

She was even more sure David was the only one telling the truth, but she didn't know what else to tell him. After David marched away, Cheryl informed her that Mr. Baldwin and maybe Dr. Baldwin would be there at eleven o'clock.

Edith sighed. "Might as well get this crap over with." She sat back down in her office chair, her right hand involuntarily groped into her purse to locate her pack of Camels and lighter. God, she needed a cigarette and longed for the days she could smoke on the premises.

Sixty-year-old Edith Mulhaven didn't used to smoke so much when her husband was alive, but he died twenty years ago in a car accident. Back in the day some folks even considered her "cute." Not these days. At five-foot-four and now thirty (maybe more, she never used a scale) pounds overweight, she bought clothes at Target and occasionally got her short brown hair cut at a cheap salon. She'd been principal at Eaglewood since it opened twenty years ago. She didn't have any kids herself but knew that she'd had an impact on hundreds over the years and would never do anything else.

Still, there were some days when she felt she wasn't getting paid enough to do this job.

Tim arrived at Eaglewood Middle School about ten minutes

before his appointment. He got Sarah's text saying she was too busy at work, and that he should talk to her by himself. After two cups of coffee, water, and Advil, Tim was sober after his early morning binge.

The principal met him in Cheryl's office. "Coffee, Mr. Baldwin?"

"No thanks, I've had my quota for today."

He sat down in the old black chair in front of her desk. He smelled the unmistakable odor of tobacco, which he despised, and realized it must be the principal. To each his own vices, he thought.

"How is your lovely wife, Sarah?"

He tried to have patience chatting for a couple of minutes and explained that Sarah was stuck at her vet clinic.

She broke the ice. "I know that you're here about David. I'm glad he's okay. Let me put your mind at ease. I've already decided not to take disciplinary action against any of the boys. Just something we don't want to repeat."

A good poker player, but not when pissed, Tim scrunched up his face and eyes and looked at the principal like she was dogshit he'd scraped off his shoe. He was at a total loss for words. Edith continued, "This morning I talked to each of the boys, separately, as well as Pamela and Coach Ezell. Mrs. Loncart assured me that there was no need for the school to discipline the boys, and after talking with all parties, I agree – and have told David and the others. She said that it was a lacrosse club matter and that she'd handle it with Coach Ezell. Frankly, it is a club thing; not one for the school to get involved in."

Tim, whose blood had been simmering went to boiling. He tried to stay calm and yearned for a drink, but said, "Mrs. Mulhaven, you do know what Pamela already decided in the way of punishment for the boys?"

She could tell from his tone he wasn't a happy camper. "No, sir, I don't." He believed her.

"She already made that decision, either late last night or early this morning, before she even talked to David, me, my wife, or you."

"What?"

He pulled out a copy of the email he'd received earlier and told the principal, "This, by the way, is unmitigated – excuse my French – horseshit," as he got up and laid it in front of her.

After reading a few sentences, Edith knew she'd gotten played by Pamela Loncart, but unless she wanted to start World War III with her, she had to play nice. She pretended to read the remainder of the email but could smell a pile of crap, especially if it was right in front of her. She didn't have jurisdiction to get involved in club matters unless she wanted to go draconian like suspending or dissolving the club. That could be a real shitstorm. And, likely, the money spigot for the music program would dry up. David was going to be the sacrificial lamb in this thing, whatever was going on. He was royally fucked, and she hadn't a clue how to help.

Finally, she looked up and handed back the email. "Mr. Baldwin, I honestly don't know what happened other than a couple of kids have black eyes, and no one got seriously hurt. I already decided not to discipline any of them, but I don't control the lacrosse club. I'm sorry your son had to be part of it." It was all she could muster at this point. His jaw muscles were tight as a drum. She could tell he was seething, and she could hardly blame him.

He glared at her. "Mrs. Mulhaven, that sucks, and I think you know it. Maybe not a broken arm or leg or concussion, or whatever, but my son got hurt, and I'm not sure how that hurt will heal. He got kicked off the team for no reason at all. And nothing is going to happen to Lance or Randy." He took a deep breath. "Will you at least call Mrs. Loncart?"

"Mr. Baldwin, if I could make all this disappear, I would. I like David. I like you and your wife. Between me and you and the fencepost, I'm no fan of Lance Earl, trust me. Yes, I will call her, but I don't expect she'll change her mind."

And, of course, she was right about that. Pamela had made up her mind. Tim felt like he'd had the air knocked out of him. The principal was a dead end. He managed to say, "Thank you. Mind if I have a few minutes with my son?"

"Certainly, and if you'd like to take him home with you, the absence is excused...by me. I'll have Cheryl locate him for you. Again, I'm sorry about all this. If I hear anything from her, I'll call you."

She watched the distraught father shuffle out in defeat. She called Pamela and briefly told her of the meeting and that she wouldn't discipline the boys. She came within an eyelash of asking her, "Why? Why only David? And jeez, kicking him off the team versus having him run extra laps or whatever?" But decided that would be a bad idea. Preemptively, Pamela told her, "Dismissing David was for the good of the lacrosse club. Thank you, Mrs. Mulhaven, for letting me handle it." And she hung up. "For the fucking good of the fucking lacrosse club," the Principal repeated out loud to herself. Right.

Events of the morning didn't add up. What the hell was going on? Edith sat twirling her pencil but then grabbed her purse, told Cheryl she was going out, and lit up as soon as she was out of the parking lot. The Camel was delicious. Now, maybe she could figure this thing out.

David saw it in his dad's eyes. It was true. He was off the team. Tim put his hand on his son's shoulder. "Let's go walk outside."

Still fuming from the injustice, Tim told his son, "The lacrosse club board voted to dismiss you from the team. Here, you read it," which his son did – then balled it up and slammed it into the green can nearby.

"It's what I heard early this morning from that asshole Lance but didn't believe it. Dad, this can't be happening. That whole email is a lie." Tim gave his son a recap of his discussion with the principal. "David, your mom and I are going to do all we can to get this fixed ASAP."

David felt numb, like he was stuck in the middle of a bad dream. Through the fog that was enveloping him, he heard his dad say that he could go home for the rest of the day if he wanted. "Mrs. Mulhaven said it would be okay."

He told him, "No, but I guess another parent will have to drive my friends to practice today." Tim hadn't thought about that, but no, he wouldn't be driving.

"Pick you up, usual time then," Tim said to his son, who'd never had such a forlorn look in his eyes. David turned and trudged back into Eaglewood Middle School. All of it was starting to sink in. No practice today. No putting on his gear, which always made him feel great. No game on Thursday. No Caroline Connolly watching him play Thursday, or ever. Why was this happening to him? It wasn't fair. They'd all lied. And his parents, they'd probably made it worse.

After the short drive home, Tim called Sarah to give her the scoop. Simultaneously, the two heads of the Baldwin clan had parallel thoughts: *I had a hand in this, but my spouse is the one to blame. Otherwise, David would at least still be on the team. This all sucks and David's the one paying. We're both shitty parents, but my spouse is shittier.* But neither said what they were thinking.

"If I saw that flaming bitch right now, I'd strangle her," Sarah shouted into her iPhone.

"I've got an idea. But I'm still swamped here and may be late again tonight. Keep me posted by text. I'm going to get this fixed," she said and hung up. Not "we," but rather, "I am going to get this fixed." That's what Tim heard his wife say and felt about an inch tall. Maybe alcohol would help.

Chapter 26 – The Bad News

Tuesday, March 22, 2016

Roswell

Sarah wasn't even sure she had his cell. They hadn't talked in the last couple of years. The two cousins were best buddies growing up together in Atlanta. Over time they'd seen less and less of each other, especially as he climbed the Atlanta pecking order and became a senior partner at one of the city's most prestigious firms. Not surprising since his father had once been a partner. Cousins and confidants growing up, they'd drifted apart – even living in the same city. They weren't exactly estranged, but after he'd canceled her attempts at lunch three times in one month, she gave up. She'd never liked his Barbie doll, gold-digger, super-southern belle of a wife, and she knew his wife didn't like her either. They exchanged Christmas cards but might as well have been living on separate planets. She missed seeing his two beautiful twin daughters, Saville and Sarah (her namesake). Did he miss seeing his nephew?

She dialed, but it went to voicemail. "Hey, it's Sarah. Been a long time. Hope you're doing well. I need your legal advice – sort of a family emergency. Please call me. Thanks." She had no idea if or when she'd hear back from her cousin.

She went back to work on the scheduled skin mass surgeries, tooth extractions, and whatever else was on the docket while Bill worked with Charlie to care for the walk-ins that seemed to be endless today. They exchanged a few surreptitious knowing winks, but in the bustle of the day, that was about it. Even with all the crap going on with David, God she had a constant craving.

This lacrosse thing was tipping him over the edge again. Today,

Tim felt the need for alcohol like never had before. Sarah had texted that she'd likely be late again, probably at least nine o'clock or so. More free time for cocktailing.

He opened Outlook and brought up the email he'd sent earlier. After a few more sips, he decided to send another follow-up, trying to bend over backwards to be reasonable. Once more, he asked as politely as he knew how: Could the lacrosse club board please hear David's side of the story so that the misunderstanding could be cleared up and put to rest? Then he tacked on, "We plan to take whatever steps are necessary to get a quick resolution to this situation to have David reinstated on the team ASAP." He had no idea what steps those might be. He hit "Send" to the same group as earlier: Pamela, the other board members, and the coach. He opened his office windows for a breeze of fresh air, then sat back and listened to the kids playing outside. He thought back to happier days when David was romping on that playground – and dozed off at his desk.

Tim woke up to a text from his wife. "Still crazy here. Hope 2 be home by 9 or so."

He fed his Airedales and let them out the porch door to run around in the backyard within the invisible fence. My most loyal friends. No, my only loyal friends, he thought. During his waking hours, day in and day out, Tim spent a lot more time with his big dogs than any other creatures. They were good-natured and loved to hang out and get a few pets and treats. They walked with him for miles. Lately, they'd been the only things that made his lonely days bearable.

Sarah walked in at 9:30 p.m. wearing tight jeans and a sleeveless T-shirt with no bra, her long blonde hair now wet and pulled back in a ponytail. Looking more desirable than ever, not dressed in the clothes she'd worn in the morning. She kissed him gently on the cheek and said, "I'm famished. Never got a bite. I was a walking disaster, so I took a quick shower at work."

Well, she thought, only a small fib. The shower with Bill hadn't been quick at all.

Sarah wolfed down leftover pizza and gulped a glass of wine while Tim gave her the scoop. He refilled her glass and got one for himself. She listened to his whole story without interruption, which was also unusual. With grit and hatred in her voice, she said to him, "No one does this to my son, no one. I'm going up to talk with David."

Returning twenty minutes later, she said, "David says he's okay, but he's not. I know it. I assured him I'd get this all straightened out, but he's a big enough kid now, Tim. He knows this won't go away by magic." She hesitated. "I called Kip."

Tim had always liked her cousin but knew that he and Sarah were no longer close, and he avoided, like the plague, getting into her family business. "What did he say?"

"Only got his voicemail."

"Try him again. It's not that late." Hell, he hadn't thought of Kip. He wasn't sure what a high-powered criminal attorney could do for them, but it was worth a phone call.

Sitting cross-legged on the bed, she punched his number on her iPhone "You want me to leave?" Tim asked.

"No, it's okay. I'll put him on speaker."

He answered, "Blondie, how are you? Sorry I couldn't get back to you earlier." Sarah was shocked he'd picked up.

"We're good but have a problem. I've got Tim here too, on speaker."

"Hey, Tim. So, what's going on?"

She tried to summarize in about fifteen minutes.

Silence.

Kip listened but then said, "Let's cut to the chase here, Blondie. You all are upset. I can tell. I get that. Hell, last year at one of the girls' soccer games an idiot father punched out a ref and put him in the hospital with a broken jaw. That probably became a lawsuit settlement. But this sounds more like a few boys fighting where nobody got injured; David probably got screwed, getting booted from the team. The way I understand it, it's a private club sponsored by the school but not a school sport, per se. Sure, you could sue the lacrosse club or the Loncart lady who runs it – probably a bad idea, especially if she's a Fed. Or sue the school or the school board, or the kid who beat up David. I don't think that's going to get him back on his team any time soon. Legal stuff would be a waste of a ton of time, money, and energy – and maybe end up a lot more negative than positive. Sorry, Sarah. I'm not sure there's much to do if they won't even talk to you."

"But there's gotta be something?" she pleaded.

He recommended trying to talk to the Loncart lady again, then started prattling on about his twin daughters who'd recently started eighth grade. Straight-A students, cheerleaders, soccer stars, prettier than their mom, won this and that...yak, yak, yak for another ten minutes while Sarah and Tim sat on the bed, patiently, and listened. Tim, with his palms up, saying silently, "This is a waste of time."

Sarah butted in. "Hey, Kip, I need to get my beauty sleep. Thanks for your advice.

"Oh, right. Well, yeah, we need to get together soon. I'll call you."

Sure, she thought.

"Bye. Thanks again," and hung up. "Well, that was a big fucking help. I should have known better."

"At least you tried."

Her pathetic cousin offered no hope at all. She got into her PJs and hopped in bed; she was in no mood for sex with Tim tonight. Her mind raced for an hour until she got up and took one of his Clonazepams to let her sleep. She finally drifted off and had a spectacular dream, starring Bill.

At her estate, Pamela reread Tim's latest email, which enraged her more. How dare he threaten her? She didn't care how late it was. She hit the number. After four rings the Sheriff of Fulton County picked up.

"Lonnie, it's Pamela. I've got a thing I need you to do tomorrow."

Chapter 27 – The Cops

Wednesday, March 23, 2016

Roswell

After taking David to school, Tim arrived home and plopped down in his cozy front sitting room with a cup of coffee. Sarah was still in bed, and it was peacefully quiet. Peace being what Tim craved more than anything that morning. After twenty minutes of solitude, listening to the birds chirping outside the front window, he felt relaxed and ready for the new day. He'd wait for Sarah to get up to think about the lacrosse abomination.

The silence ended when the doorbell rang. His Airedales stormed to the front door and barked to high heavens like they did when a UPS or FedEx guy arrived in uniform to invade their property. They could each get a bird's-eye view of a potential intruder from the set of slender windows bordering the door. Then, they'd calm down once a package was dropped off. But the doorbell rang again, and they got louder. Grabbing his big dogs by their collars, Tim opened the door. There stood the two largest policemen he'd ever seen up close and personal; both well over six feet with serious heft; wearing all blue and jangling with handcuffs, nightsticks, flashlights, mace canisters, tasers; and big handguns on their belts.

"Mr. Tim Baldwin?" one asked.

"How can I help you, officers?" As the dogs barked even louder, he said, "Excuse me, let me put my dogs in the bedroom and I'll be right back."

He dragged them down the hallway to the bedroom and shut the door.

"Tim, who in the world is at the door?" Sarah asked.

"Two cops. Two big Fulton County cops," and before she could ask why, he shut the door, leaving Grant and Sam barricaded.

Tim rushed back to the door, almost out of breath. "Sorry about that."

"May we come in, sir?" the big blond one asked politely but already had a foot on the threshold. Tim had no experience dealing with police and was flummoxed. He ushered the two giants into the front sitting room.

"I'm Officer Zilensky. This is Officer Harmon," said the beefy, round-faced blond cop.

"Please have a seat, officers," but they stood while Tim sat. Both now looking even more imposing in the little room.

"And you're here why?" asked Tim, who was getting less thrilled by the second about cops being in his home.

Sarah hustled in as the officers were about to answer Tim's questions.

"Mr. Baldwin, we've gotten a complaint that you've been sending threatening emails," said the block-faced, paunchy, dark-haired cop. He handed Tim a folded copy of a single piece of paper.

Tim read it, rolled his eyes, and handed his wife the email he'd sent last evening to Pamela and the lacrosse club board members. She read it. "How in the world could this possibly be threatening?" she asked – not knowing Tim had sent any emails until that moment.

"Your husband wrote that he 'would take whatever steps are needed…' Those words were interpreted as quite threatening."

"You can't be serious," said Tim, failing to take a cue from his wife to shut up. "We may or may not decide to take legal action or go to the press or post information online about the injustice done to our son. We have the right to take any of those steps."

"Well, here's the thing, Mr. Baldwin," said Harmon. "There's a formal complaint filed against you, and I'd advise that you cease and desist from writing any more inflammatory emails. You don't want this to become a bigger problem. The next step could be quite unpleasant. Threatening digital correspondence, by the way, can get you a visit from Homeland Security. Then it can get worse."

"Who filed the complaint to send you officers out here?" Tim demanded. "We aren't required to tell you that sir," said Zilensky.

Tim asked, "Pamela Loncart sent you, didn't she?"

Chad Zilensky could hear the fear in his voice and see it etched in his face. "Don't know a Pamela Loncart. Our Sheriff sent us. Just following orders."

More than a bit peeved at all three of the men in her sitting room, Sarah asked, "Officers, is that it?" She got up and went to the front door and opened it, inviting them as nicely as she possibly could to vamoose.

"Yes, ma'am. You all have a good rest of the day."

As they got back into their squad car parked in front of the Baldwins', Walt Harmon told his partner, "That was completely bogus, but I think we made our point."

Chad Zilensky replied, "Yeah, I know. I wonder what the hell Loncart has on Lonnie to call in that marker. What a bunch of horseshit."

As they drove off to Dunkin' Donuts before continuing the rest of their typically boring shift in the North Atlanta burbs, Chad noted, "I'd love to frisk Mrs. Baldwin and put her in handcuffs. For warm-ups. That's one hot-look'n mamma."

His partner agreed. "I'd nail her in a heartbeat. I'll call Lonnie and tell him what they said. Maybe he can figure out how we could put her under arrest for a couple of hours." The two big cops heehawed while driving to their favorite stop of the day, where they'd never paid for a single donut or cup of coffee in their lives.

Pamela smiled when she got the report. She wondered how the Baldwins were handling their own personal addictions that she'd thrown gasoline on – especially after a little wake-up call from the police. Never one to be in a hurry, Pamela would find out in due time. She loved being the big cat playing with little critters, especially persons-of-light. Chasing them, batting them around; terrorizing them; even more fun than devouring them.

"Tim, my God, she sent cops into our house. Our fucking house!" Sarah yelled, still standing, her voice trembling with anger. "The lady is evil!" Then an accusatory, "Why didn't you tell me about the email? No more emails to these assholes – got that, Tim?"

"Got it." He knew that making any comment about the email would simply make things worse.

Chapter 28 – The Lawyer

The next day, Wednesday, March 23, 2016

Law Offices of Stuyvesant, Knight, Fitzpatrick & Burns – Midtown, Atlanta

At 8:00 a.m. criminal defense attorney Kip Davies walked into her office and shut the door. Not wanting to ask what he was about to ask. He and Suzanne had happily coexisted as boss and employee for about a year, working together on dozens of cases. Weather permitting, they played golf together every couple of weeks and ate lunch together at least once a week. They both wanted the same thing. This wasn't going to help either get there.

Suzanne Delacroix was the most exquisite woman he'd ever known. Over a dozen years he'd never so much as kissed her though he thought about that and much more, many times. He plopped down in the chair, facing her desk. "Suzanne, I have a favor to ask."

She stared into his deep blue eyes. "What kind of favor, Kip? I'm not going to surveil your wife again. I shouldn't have done it the first time."

"No, no. Nothing like that, I promise." He hesitated. "But it is a family matter."

She rolled her eyes as he explained what he knew and what he needed. She took a few notes as her mind wandered back two decades to the sport of lacrosse. She liked most sports except a few like car racing, bowling, and curling. Lacrosse, she despised for a different reason. Kip had no idea of that history and how it still haunted her dreams. No one did.

She sat and tried to pay attention to the story of an upper-middle-class kid, Kip's cousin's son, getting axed from his middle school lacrosse team, supposedly for fighting. Most of her legal investigations were tame compared to the homicides she'd dealt with at Atlanta PD. But this one took the cake. Part of her employment deal was that she had a choice of which cases she took. Regardless of her distaste, she knew she'd have to swallow this one. Before Kip finished, she shut her portfolio, which he'd never seen her do before the end of a meeting.

She'd kept her yap shut for the past twenty minutes. He could see she wasn't thrilled. Before she could say anything, he tried to placate her. "Listen, Suzy, I know there's virtually no chance of getting what they want. I'm not asking for a miracle. Don't spend a lot of time, but I need you to go talk to David, Sarah, and Tim tomorrow. Frankly, I've been a dick to my cousin for a long time, and I want to get back in her good graces."

"Trying to get her son back on the team is going to do the trick?"

"I don't know. Maybe you can give them a ray of hope."

Suzanne fidgeted and chewed her lip. She was annoyed. "Okay, Kip, I'll talk with your relatives. I'm assuming you don't want me to use the firm's name and go nuclear on this Loncart lady or the school?"

"No, no, we're not going to do that."

"You're the boss," she said with sarcasm, which was unusual for her. "Send me their contact information, and I'll go out and meet with them tomorrow."

"You're a sweetheart. I told the Baldwins you'd call them this evening and set up a time to meet."

She frowned. "What if I'd have said 'no,' Kip?"

"I know you better than you think, Suzanne."

She gave Kip a wry smile. He winked back. She had a new client whether she liked it or not.

But Jeez, a suburban lacrosse kid who allegedly got unjustly kicked off a middle school sports team? She was supposed to investigate *that*?

After stewing a few minutes, though, the new case had already wormed its way into her brain. She was curious about the lacrosse lady DEA agent whom Kip mentioned. She picked up her iPhone and called her best DEA buddy, Rondo Blackman.

Rondo was a diminutive black guy and strictly a by-the-book agent. She knew he wasn't into excessive DEA pilfering, and she'd liked working with him. Plus, she knew he'd always had the hots for her. Maybe not as bad as Kip Davies did, but still bad. If he was undercover, she'd be out of luck, but he answered.

"Tigress! My most beautiful blast from the past. How is the world's loveliest ass, baby girl?"

"Rondo, with my cushy gig now, I get to work out more than ever. It's even rounder and firmer than it used to be," she teased. But it was true. In her early 40's, he'd never been in better shape and probably never looked better.

"No way! Not possible! You're giving me a hard-on thinking about it."

Like most straight male law enforcement types, Rondo was incorrigible – rarely politically correct – and always hunting pussy. He was cute enough, but unfortunately, Rondo was about the same height as her old partner Dusty – the top of his head maybe reaching the top of her boobs when she wore heels. At five-foot-six, it wasn't happening.

They caught up for a few minutes. Then she popped the question. "Pamela Loncart, you know her?"

The hesitation spoke volumes. "Rondo, you there?"

"Ah, yeah, Suzy. Let's catch up in person. How 'bout tomorrow at five? The Sound Table downtown. Wear your hottest outfit."

In her most sensual voice, she told him, "Baby, you better wear your steel jock, so you won't embarrass yourself in public. I'm going to rock your world." She clicked off.

Rondo answered part of her question. He knew the name Pamela Loncart. And she was thinking it wasn't good. Now she had to know more. It was like her brain began clicking back into gear after being in hibernation.

For kicks, she Googled a couple dozen iterations of "Pamela Loncart" with and without "DEA." She came up a few times in context of her role as chairwoman of the Eaglewood Lacrosse Club, which she'd assumed three years earlier, but not much else. Not one picture. Suzanne grinned. Touché. Her own persona as chief investigator for Stuyvesant, Knight, Fitzpatrick & Burns Stuyvesant was a mere whisper in cyberspace. She'd gotten Dusty's tech friend, Arnie, a hacker extraordinaire, to erase her own digital footprint. She didn't even appear on the firm's website. Instead, she used multiple online aliases depending on the case she was working – all thanks to Arnie.

Game on, Pamela Loncart, she grinned. Then admitted to herself, Kip Davies, *"You do know me too well."*

On her way out of the office, she caught a quick glance of a tall dark guy in a beautiful gray suit who was opening Walter O'Malley's office door, then shut it. She didn't know all the lawyers but knew he wasn't one. She saw only part of his face. She couldn't place him, but he looked familiar. She'd find out from Walter's admin who he was.

In her relaxing hot shower, Sarah heard her cell ring twice. She let the calls go to voicemail. The first was from her cousin Kip who told her she should expect a call later from his top investigator, Suzanne Delacroix, who was going to see how she could help. Suzanne, he said, was a longtime friend and used to be the top Homicide cop for the Atlanta Police Department.

"Interesting," thought Sarah.

The second message was from Edith Mulhaven, principal of Eaglewood Middle School, who wondered if she could meet this morning around ten o'clock tomorrow. Sarah texted back, "Certainly, see u then."

Earlier that morning, David arrived at Eaglewood Middle School still wearing his black eyes badges of honor, but the adulation had dried up. Aaron and a couple of guys on the team acknowledged him and said it was bull crap he'd been booted off the team. Caroline Connolly stopped and said she was sorry to hear the news but was quickly gone without a smile or wave. Last night, David didn't even tell his parents about Tony. Aaron had called and told him that Tony had punched out Coach at practice, and it was positively epic. Then Coach screamed and fired him. After leveling him, Tony gave Ezell the finger, pointed his old lacrosse stick to the sky, and left without any goodbyes. David admitted to himself that it might have been fun to see but wasn't sure how Tony's exit could be a help. Might even make it all worse.

But then, how much worse could it get?

When Sarah arrived at Principal Mulhaven's office, Edith sat in her chair and took a deep breath, like she'd sat down in a Catholic confessional, and said, "Look, I know David's a good kid and he's got good parents. I'm one hundred percent sure that David got screwed in this lacrosse club thing. But why?"

Sarah shook her head. She wondered what the principal would think if she knew David's dad was careening toward alcoholism and that she was having a torrid affair with a coworker – and her family was teetering on the edge of financial ruin.

Edith asked, "Did you know Pamela Loncart has already been named Chairwoman of Pecan Valley's lacrosse clubs for next year? And she also donated a huge sum of money to the proposed Pecan Valley SportsPlex. I'm not going to kid you, she's a big contributor to Eaglewood too – but I decided last night, screw her if she thinks I'm on her goddamn leash."

"Like to say I'm surprised, but I'm not," Sarah said glumly. "That's the end of David's lacrosse career. What kind of contributions are we talking about?"

"To Eaglewood, including the lacrosse club monies which I don't see, probably around $40,000 a year. She pledged $5 million to the Pecan Valley Sportsplex."

Sarah's eyes widened in disbelief. "You're kidding."

Edith shook her head and asked, "Is there anything you could tell me about the lacrosse club that I might be missing?"

Sarah considered. "There's a group of boys on the team who – I've heard from one mom and David – are Pamela's pets. Six of them. Her twins, plus Lance, Randy, Bryce, and Kevin. They get super-expensive lacrosse equipment, other goodies, and hang out at the Loncart place a lot. Here's the thing that struck me again. Their gold-handled lacrosse sticks have pockets with black patterns sewn into the mesh. I picked one up in Birmingham. Like a weird-looking 'H.' It's on their lacrosse bags, too. Or two black crosses vertically pressed together."

Edith raised her eyebrows, which said, *So?*

"The pattern is exactly like the black jeweled necklace she wears. Unusual. Pricey, I'm sure. Strange, huh?"

Edith tried to digest and in her mind's eye she saw the black necklace Loncart had been wearing. "Well, what do we make of that?"

After they both gazed off, Sarah said, "Whatever it is, this thing is all about Pamela Loncart."

On the short drive home from Eaglewood, Tim asked his son how the day went. "Okay," David lied. It had been miserable. Like no one knew what to say to him or if they should talk to him at all. He felt alone and isolated and angry with his coach, Lance, Randy, Mrs. Loncart, and his parents, too. He just wanted to play lacrosse. They'd ruined it for him. All of them.

"You didn't tell me what happened to Coach Tony last night."

"What difference does that make?" his son shot back. "They can get rid of whomever they want. Screw'm all."

Tim was pretty sure he and Sarah were included in "all." He tried to turn it around. "Hey, guess what. Uncle Kip's chief investigator is going to come over tomorrow and see what can be done. We're not giving up on this, son."

David said nothing. He thought, *"Jeez, like how is a stranger going to magically fix this, especially by the next game tomorrow?*

"How about a burger at Sonic?" Tim asked

David never turned down Sonic, but this time he did.

Arriving home, David went directly to his room and locked his door.

He escaped into his world of *Call of Duty*, where he had a big gun, buddies, and control over what happened to him, good or bad.

After getting off from work early, then three hours of ecstasy that included the best full body massage in the history of womankind, Sarah showered with Bill, who made sure all nooks and crannies were well attended and spic and span. In Bill's bathroom mirror, once dressed, she looked like the perfect prim and proper suburban lacrosse mom again. Then shook her head and looked at herself. *"Is that you, Sarah Baldwin?"*

On her way from Bill's condo to pick up Dreamland Bar-B-Que, she texted Tim that she'd be back with food in an hour. She splurged on a few racks of ribs instead of pulled pork. David's favorite food of all time, especially from Dreamland.

Tim wasn't sure how his words were going to come out, so he let her do the talking at dinner. She reiterated the positive to David. Suzanne Delacroix, who works for Kip, used to head the Homicide Division at the Atlanta PD. Pretty cool, huh?"

"Pretty cool, except nobody got murdered and I won't get to play in tomorrow's game. Or probably ever again," David fired back at his mom.

He gnawed through a few of the wet spareribs like he hadn't eaten in weeks and then grabbed a few slices of white bread and a Coke and left without excusing himself. Tim and Sarah sat silently eating their ribs, neither knowing how to comfort their son and wondering if anyone could undo what they were blaming each other for that had been perpetrated on their son.

"I'm going to take a shower," Sarah told her husband. Her body didn't need another cleansing. Bill had done a fine job of that and then took her another time under the hot spray. In her own shower now, she was trying to digest what was in front of her. She could tell Tim had been drinking again today. But talk about the pot calling the kettle black – for the third straight day, she'd fucked another man. She was now a serial adulteress. But it was all so primal; so sensual; so naughty; so forbidden. Indeed, she'd tasted the apple and liked it. She didn't care. She wanted more. That was what started to bother her – that it didn't bother her at all.

Part IV - The Crosshairs

Chapter 29 – The Pocketknife

Thursday 8:30 a.m.

Eaglewood Middle School – Roswell

As soon as Cheryl arrived, Edith asked her for the locker numbers and combinations for six students. It was five minutes after the first-period bell. The halls were empty, and Edith was on a fishing expedition.

She started with her least favorite, Lance Earl. His locker was a pit. Oh, surprise. Inside, a few of his brand-new, unstudied books, a couple of pens, unsharpened pencils, candy wrappers, a phone charger, a grungy Braves baseball cap, and a 3-pack of rubbers. Oh, surprise.

Randy Frederick's nearby locker was tidier, but nothing out of the ordinary. *"This is a waste of time,"* she told herself, but dragged herself to the other side of Eaglewood Middle and located Bryce Cheney's locker.

Bryce, also one of Pamela's pets, was a mediocre student and had only visited her hot seat a couple of times over his three years. There were books and stuff at the bottom of the locker and a light black jacket. "Shit," she said out loud. But before shutting the locker door, she grabbed the jacket and checked the pockets. "Voila." She pulled out a big pocketknife, the mere presence of which could get Bryce suspended for the rest of the year.

She'd inspect it more closely in her office, but there was no question the unusual symbol on the white handle was the same shape as the one on Pamela's necklace – and the same as what Sarah had told her was on six kids' lacrosse gear. She thought: *"This is getting fucking weird."*

╫

That morning, Suzanne dressed a tad more conservatively than usual for her visit to the Baldwins. Designer jeans, scoop neck top with a gray silk jacket, and flats instead of heels. After walking Zeke, she followed her GPS and drove up I-400 into the Roswell burbs. Without much traffic, she was there in thirty minutes.

Sarah met her at the door, and they introduced themselves, both checking each other out from head to toe. After the auto-assessments, Sarah said, "I love your necklace."

"Thank you. It was a gift from my father to my mother years ago. They've both passed away."

She gave a knowing "I'm sorry" look. "Platinum and diamonds?"

"It is."

Sarah realized she hadn't been wearing her gold cross necklace that week and made a mental note to put it back on. Hers, a twenty-four-karat minimalist gold cross with small diamonds and emeralds, was nice but couldn't hold a candle to Suzanne's.

"So, you're like Kalinda was on *The Good Wife*?" Sarah asked.

A question she'd gotten more than once. "Sort of, but a lot less colorful, and I'm taller and not nearly so devious," she chuckled. But she knew that Kalinda was minor league compared to her.

The two women took a seat in the front sitting room and made small talk for a few minutes. Sarah couldn't resist. "You've known my cousin awhile?" However, what she really wanted to know was if she was sleeping with Kip. She wouldn't blame her or him, knowing what a bitch Kip's wife was.

"We met several years ago and play golf together off and on. When I left Atlanta PD, Kip hired me. I'm a contractor, not an employee, and I work on a retainer basis. Kip is golfing buddy and a good guy, a little full of himself off and on, but he knows I was a cop and could kick his sorry ass anytime."

Sarah laughed. "Yes, he is that. We were best friends for a lot of years growing up. But we haven't run in the same social circles. I called him on a whim to see if he thought we could do anything about this lacrosse thing. Look, I know it's a longshot, but if you think there's any way we could get David back on the team…" Her voice trailed off.

"We'll see," Suzanne said evenly, not meaning to sound either optimistic or pessimistic. "Sarah, do you mind if I drop by the school and talk to David first about the lacrosse stuff – and talk to the principal? Then, I'll circle back and chat with you and your husband. I want to hear a few things from him firsthand. I've read the emails, and Kip gave me a little background. Then I want your perspectives."

"Fine with us. I already okayed it with Principal Mulhaven. I'll call her and confirm. It's a short drive to Eaglewood. Tim's up in his office, but he'll be ready to talk whenever you're back."

"Edith," Sarah said, "there's a woman by the name of Suzanne Delacroix who's on her way over to Eaglewood to talk with David for a bit if that's okay. She's an investigator for my cousin's law firm. Used to be an Atlanta Homicide cop. She knows the situation and is going to see if she can help. Just met her, but she's sharp."

"Sure, I'll have Cheryl get him out of class."

"She'd like to talk to you, too, after that."

"Perfect. I'll show her what I found in Bryce Cheney's locker."

"Which is?"

"A pocketknife with the same design as on Loncart's necklace and what you also described on the lacrosse equipment."

"Really?"

To Sarah's surprise, the principal responded, "Yep, no shit."

When Cheryl told her that Bryce was on his way, Edith tried—with mixed results—to figure out how to spin the pocketknife between her middle fingers like she could effortlessly do with a #2 pencil. She put it in front of her on the desk as Bryce walked in and sat on the hot seat.

She went for shock and awe right off the bat. "Bryce, you know why you're here?"

"No, ma'am," the lanky, blond kid said politely.

She picked up the knife, rotated it vertically, and watched his eyes expand.

"Bullshit. I found this in your locker. Know what that means? Automatic suspension and probable loss of your whole school year."

He stammered, "Ma'am, I can explain."

"Go for it."

"Please, Mrs. Mulhaven, I must have forgotten to take it out of my coat pocket at home. I didn't mean to bring it to school. I didn't. I swear. I'm not a terrorist or anything like that."

She considered the knife for about a minute and said zilch while Bryce fidgeted on her hot seat.

"Nice knife, Bryce. You buy it, or it was a gift?"

Without thinking, the boy said, "Miss Pamela gave one to me and the others."

"That would be Mrs. Loncart who gave it to you?"

Too late. He couldn't backtrack. "Yes, ma'am."

"Special occasion?"

He repeated the party line. "No, ma'am, we hang out there and do chores, and she gives us stuff sometimes."

"You and Lance and Randy and Kevin all got pocketknives like this one?"

"Yes, ma'am. And I guess Dex and Dax, too."

"Of course, I forgot her twins. So, the six of you?"

"Yes, ma'am. Tariq, her servant, taught us how to play mumblety-peg."

"Interesting." Edith pulled the knife open, examined its entire length in detail, and closed it again. "You all play the version where you try to stick the knife as close to your foot as possible?"

"Yeah."

She held it up to him. "You know what the black symbol on the handle means, Bryce?"

"Ah, no, ma'am. It's on our lacrosse stick webs and our bags, too."

"Like a team insignia?"

"Well, not the whole team…" Again, he knew he'd fucked up.

Edith pursed her lips and tried not to smile. She may have found a bit of leverage. She dismissed the boy and told him she'd think about his punishment – then picked up the pocketknife and tried twirling it again.

After getting directions to the nearby middle school, Suzanne found the principal's office. Cheryl ushered her into a little conference room in the back of the administrative area. There were no one-way windows, but it did vaguely remind her of the cramped, sparse interrogation room downtown where she'd spent way too much time for way too many years.

David was already there. He stood up and politely shook her hand, then shyly said, "Nice to meet you, Miss Delacroix."

"Call me Suzanne, okay? Nice to meet you, David."

It was hard for her to tell, with his two shiners, but he seemed to be a handsome boy – maybe looked like his mom, but she hadn't met his dad yet. A little guy with a mop of his mom's thick blonde hair. A kid she'd bet would sprout any day but didn't have much meat on his bones yet.

"Looks like you've been in a prizefight, young man."

"Yeah, but I didn't do much of the fight'n. Am I being interrogated?" he blurted out.

She smiled and tried to loosen him up. "Yep. Maybe you've heard that I used to be a Homicide cop and now work with your Uncle Kip. I'm going to sweat you out in here till I get exactly what I want to know."

David's eyebrows jumped, but then he grinned and cracked up. "Yeah, right."

She laughed with him. "You know I'm kidding." She already knew this was a sharp kid.

"I'm trying to figure out how we can maybe set this lacrosse thing straight. You game?"

"Okay. You don't look like a homicide cop." Another line she'd heard a time or two.

"What do I look like?"

"I don't know, maybe a movie star or a singer or a model," the young teen blushed.

She shot him a good-natured, ear-to-ear smile. "I'll take that as a compliment and maybe give you an autograph before I leave." For now, she gave him a friendly smile.

"Tell me about Monday in the locker room." He gave the same version he'd told to his parents and then to Mrs. Mulhaven.

"Sounds like you got set up. You know why?"

"I told Dad that night it was real bizarre. It's like Randy has the sole right to play goalie. He lied about me, not him, hitting Lance, which got me in trouble and not him. I forgot to tell Mom and Dad, but when I was on the floor getting popped by Lance, Randy told him something like, 'Remember she said – take it easy,' and Lance told him to fuck off, and he hit me again before the other guys walked in and broke it up."

Suzanne had little doubt who "she" was, but that was enough for now. She could see he was a good kid who was having fun, starting to live his dream of finding a sport he could enjoy, and the adults were fucking it up royally.

"One more thing, David. Tony, your assistant coach who got fired, you have his phone number?"

"Yeah, on my phone in my locker."

"Do me a favor and text me his number. Okay?" She wrote down hers and gave it to him.

"Yes, ma'am."

Suzanne stuck her hand out, and he shook it. "Hang in there, David. I'm going to talk to Mrs. Mulhaven, then your parents and a few other folks." She had no intention of going out on this limb but told him, "David, I'm going to do whatever I can to get you playing again. Soon, okay?"

He beamed. "Thanks, Suzanne." He used to think that Mrs. Loncart was the prettiest lady he'd ever known other than his mom.

He changed his mind. Suzanne was off the hot scale, and he even had her phone number!

She asked Cheryl, "Do you think Mrs. Mulhaven might have a few minutes?"

"Yes, she said she'd make time."

Even without her heels, Suzanne towered over Edith when she met her at the door.

Holy shit, Edith said to herself. *"It was like Charlie's fucking Angels this week with Pamela, Sarah, and now this woman.*

They stepped into her office. "Sorry about the accommodations, Miss Delacroix. Been meaning to get new furniture for this hole."

"Suzanne, please. Hey, this is the Ritz compared to places I used to hang out when I was a cop."

Edith grinned and caught a good vibe.

"Kip Davies, my boss, is Sarah's cousin, and he asked me to see what, if anything, could be done about David's dismissal from the lacrosse team."

Edith considered the stunning woman. "I'm thinking you didn't pick this gig, did you, Suzanne?"

Sharp lady, Suzanne thought. And said, "I'm doing a favor. What can you tell me about Pamela Loncart?"

Edith told Suzanne about her brief history with Pamela, the donor, and talked a bit about David and his family. Then she pulled the pocketknife out of her top desk drawer and handed it to Suzanne. "I found it this morning in Bryce Cheney's locker."

Suzanne turned the pocketknife in her hand. She was transfixed.

The same type of handle; the same cross symbol, and the tiny writing was there on the base of the shaft.

Edith said, "You look like you saw a ghost."

Suzanne tried to regain her composure. It was a different style of knife, but the rest of it was all too familiar. "Let's say I've seen knives like this before. She didn't add that the other knives of the identical design were used to carve up twin girls and their mom last year in Cascade Heights.

Suzanne sat twisting the pocketknife in her fingers, then asked, "Edith, can I borrow this?"

"It's all yours. Loncart, she contributes money to the school, but she's a witch."

Suzanne grinned. "Trust me, we're going to fry her sorry ass and some other sons of bitches too – and figure out how you won't lose contributions."

For Edith, it was almost surreal as Suzanne rose from her chair. Like this beautiful woman had put on a cape and turned into Superwoman. She smiled. "I don't doubt that for one minute."

Suzanne winked at her and headed out the door.

She sat in her Honda in the Eaglewood Middle School parking lot, adding up what she knew at this point. Too many coincidences with the black double cross symbol. For the past year, she'd been sleepwalking – handling investigations any competent investigator could do. That's not what her dad or mom would want right now. That's not what she wanted. She knew one thing: Pamela was now in her crosshairs. She made up her mind, then and there, in the school parking lot. The Tigress had been in hibernation, but no longer.

Later that morning, Suzanne listened to Tim and Sarah's stories, jotted down notes, and asked a few questions. She learned a lot more. The love they had for their son and the guilt they felt was palpable.

She also knew neither would ever blame or manipulate a coach so that their son could play. They were convinced this predicament was about Pamela Loncart. She already had little doubt about that but didn't let on. She told the Baldwins she'd be back in touch tomorrow.

Leaning against her car, she texted Kip a cryptic message. "Love your relatives. Thx for connecting me. Small world. Tigress on the job."

Driving back down I-400 toward the city and East Lake Golf Club to get in nine holes, she pondered the Baldwins' life and living in the burbs – something she'd never wanted. But she felt jealous. They had a nice family, and their neighborhood was beautiful. Her clock was ticking. She had more money than she could ever spend. She anonymously gave considerable sums to hunger and relief organizations that her mom had championed. She volunteered at Ebenezer Baptist. But she was thinking she would trade it all for a loving husband and family. The Baldwins, she knew, would get over this hurdle.

What Suzanne didn't realize was that the Baldwin family was unraveling before her eyes.

Chapter 30 – The Curs

The Following Day: Thursday, March 24

Roswell

When Sarah got back from treating herself to a late lunch and a little shopping at Perimeter Mall, her son was sitting on the floor in front of the big screen with his Xbox controller in hand, deep into a video war game. Sarah had never tried a video game in her life and didn't get the attraction, which made her feel old. She looked at her son, still sporting two black eyes – the blacks and purples starting to fade. It was a longshot, but she asked, "David, how about you and I take a walk today with the dogs – and go see your lacrosse team play? You've got lots of friends who know you were treated unfairly. Let's show we won't back down. What do you say? Besides, the dogs need exercise."

He started playing his video game again, but then the automatic gunfire ceased. "Okay, Mom. Let's go."

She beamed, "Great. We'll leave in a few minutes. That should get us there right about face-off time. Why don't you get the dogs' leashes, and I'll get a backpack for waters and snacks."

David wasn't sure he wanted to do this, but he too wanted to show he was no coward. Sam and Grant rushed to David when they heard the collars and leashes jangle and whined with anticipation, both wanting to escape the house and walk in the worst way.

The warm, breezy spring air felt wonderful on her face and bare arms. Vegetation was on the verge of turning green again, finally. Winter hadn't been bad, but she missed the longer, warmer, sunnier days. The Eaglewood lacrosse game started as they walked up to the aluminum grandstands near midfield. Sarah, David, and the dogs walked up behind the Eaglewood sideline to the edge of the bleachers as the game started. Sarah scanned the area but didn't see Pamela

Loncart anywhere.

She decided the dogs, who loved humans big or small, would be fine tied to the back of the grandstand in the shade. It wasn't crowded; she and David took a seat. She saw Bryce Cheney's mom, Lana, on an upper right-hand row. She waved to her, but no response. Others brought their folding chairs or were standing about twenty yards down the sideline from the Eaglewood team. She watched the black and gold and the blue and white clad boys run back and forth and wondered why the hell she'd dragged David with her to this stupid game.

David sat with his mom and watched in silence. There's no denying he missed it. He missed wearing his gold and black jersey and shorts and feeling his spiked shoes gripping the turf; his caged helmet protecting his head and face; his lacrosse stick always in his hands, like a soldier with his gun; going through the pre-game drills; standing on the sidelines with his teammates and coaches; yelling encouragement; hearing the guys chattering to each other out on the field; the shoulder pads, helmets, and sticks cracking together; the rush of being in action on the field in a real game guarding his goal like it was Fort Knox – and like his team depended on him as if all their lives were at stake. He missed all of it. Terribly.

The Eagles played decently the first two quarters, coming back from a five-point deficit to trail only by two goals, but were losing to an inferior team from a nearby public school in Alpharetta. Watching Lance Earl play made Sarah sick to her stomach; he should be off the team along with Randy Frederick, not David.

Toward the end of the second quarter, Frank Ezell, phone in hand, turned around and looked back toward the grandstand. He was a good forty yards away, but their eyes met.

"The tall blonde bitch came to the game." He hit speed dial.

During the short halftime break, Sarah walked up a few rows and over an aisle to say hi to Lana, who took a quick look at her and then started yapping with the other moms. She wasn't being ignored; she was being shunned. Climbing back down, she saw Darlene Mason and said, "Hey Darlene, good to see you." Darlene nodded without response and walked off.

Fucking bitches. Sarah wasn't returning to the bleachers.

Others she noticed not only didn't speak but also avoided eye contact. She and David were full-fledged pariahs. She went behind the grandstand to check on Sam and Grant, where she also found David. She suggested they walk to the other side of the field and watch. No one was dthere. On the way, several of his teammates waved and stuck their sticks in the air. David grinned and shot his fist into the air, too. He hitched the dogs to a grandstand facing the adjacent field. The big Airedales flopped down to lay in the cool green grass. Sarah and David stood almost a football field apart from the Eaglewood crowd. She felt like a mangy leper. She despised every parent of every kid playing.

She appeared as the third quarter began. Wearing shimmering gold metallic jeans, a skimpy black tank top, black wedges, and a gold cap with her auburn hair pulled back in a ponytail. Pamela walked up the sideline to chat with Ezell, Drake Lynch, who Sarah knew was on the board, and another guy she didn't know.

Sarah's reaction was visceral. As the second half of the game went on, she fantasized about watching Pamela being trampled mercilessly by a mob, shot in the forehead, and knifed in the gut.

As the sun slid down the orange-painted sky, Pamela talked with Drake near the main grandstand. After giving him a couple of directives, she removed her Prada sunglasses. *"How dare Baldwin come to the game with her pitiful son?"* Pamela was galled, but her Dark Lord never promised "easy." Sarah was proving to have more backbone than many of the Mexican narcos she'd corralled, intimidated, and killed over the years. Indeed, a person-of-light to engage in further battle. It might take longer, but then again, it would be so much more painful for Sarah Baldwin and her family – and so much more fun for her. She had the Baldwins in her crosshairs.

After the game, with most spectators gone, Pamela sensed it from behind. Dog. No, dogs. She was terrified of only one thing on this earth. Like her female ancestor namesake, she was terrified of dogs – and tried to stay away from them whenever she could. Over the years, she'd learned firsthand what her mother had told her. Wisdom handed down through the ages. "The smarter the canines, the better their sense about our kind." She knew they could divine her fear and her Dark nature. She could still feel the bite of the German shepherd on her leg from years ago. Then the deafening blast from her father's shotgun in front of their home. Her father had taught her many things. One was to beware of dogs. The other: terminate when necessary.

Pamela whirled around to see Sarah and David, each holding a dog. "Wretched curs!" she yelled with loathing. Sarah saw genuine fear in her dark eyes. Her normally docile dogs went rabid: growling, snarling, and baring their immense incisors, wanting a piece of Pamela; rearing up and pulling hard on their leashes. Airedales are great companions and love people. They also have the largest teeth of any canine breed on the planet. Sarah's "down" and "stop" commands, which always worked, failed. It took every ounce of her and David's strength to rein them in. They continued to growl and flash their huge teeth, their eyes fixed on Pamela as she reached into her purse and pulled out her Glock. She alternated pointing at one dog and then the other; and in so doing the gun also waved at Sarah and David. Pamela screamed, "Get your damn cur mongrels away from me!"

Shocked at having a gun pointed at them, Sarah and David managed to pull the dogs to the grandstand and securely tie them. Sarah told David to stay with the dogs. By the time Sarah returned to the field, Pamela had stuck her gun back in her purse. The two women went toe-to-toe on the lacrosse field sideline. A few other bystanders looked on but couldn't hear the conversation. "I have no idea what got into my pups. They like all *people*."

Pamela's black eyes spewed evil, and she replied, "Curs are typical of your whole clan, Dr. Baldwin. None of you, including your mangy beasts, act civilly." From behind the grandstand, the dogs' barking grew louder.

The pleasant vision of her dogs tearing Pamela limb from limb danced across Sarah's mind. Once more, their eyes locked for several moments. Sarah asked, "Why?"

"Why what?" Pamela looked up at the tall blonde who towered over her. In this statuesque woman, she saw an antagonist who needed to be dealt with brutally. Unfortunately, *The Teachings*, the ancient book that guided her satanic Tribe, told her she couldn't physically harm Sarah or her children. No, she would take down Baldwin and her family by other means.

Sarah's blue eyes peered into Pamela's pitch-black kaleidoscopes. "I want to know *why* my son got kicked off his team and why you sent police to my home."

Tonight, the gold-jeweled cross around Sarah's neck blocked Pamela from further exacerbating the crack she'd laid open the night at the tournament. Still, Pamela believed that her initial foray into the darkness of Sarah's heart would be plenty for the fissure to initiate a cataclysmic collapse. Only a matter of time. Sarah couldn't resist.

Pamela decided to fly it up the flagpole: "Dr. Baldwin, they say once you go black, it's hard to go back. No wonder your pitiful husband drinks – with a slut like you for a wife." Even with her powers nullified, Pamela could tell she'd already hit the right nerve.

In the tree line of the upper fields, Tony Santucci had been watching the game on and off with his binoculars. He saw but couldn't hear the discussion between Pamela and Sarah – and Loncart pointing a gun at them. He made up his mind.

Tony sent a text to Sarah. "News about P u need to hear. Tomorrow eve 7 at Bernie's. Thx Tony S."

Sarah didn't know what to make of it.

Unfortunately, she wasn't the only one to read his text. Pamela's brother intercepted it and then forwarded it to his sister. He smiled, hoping that their Sunday afternoon get-together would be much longer than usual.

Chapter 31 – The Dancers

The Same Day

The Sound Table, Edgewood, Old Fourth Ward – Atlanta

It was less than three miles away from her condo but far enough to be a hassle with Atlanta's traffic and parking at rush hour. Suzanne cabbed it down from Midtown to the Sound Table. She'd heard of it but never been there. Supposedly a high-class pickup joint, which wasn't her thing. Jeez, how old was she acting? Guys had been on the back burner for way too long, but sifting through the letches, morons, and hotshots hadn't been appealing. Regardless, she decided to have fun with her date, Rondo Blackman.

She wore a short, skin-tight dress, plunging to the bottom of her D-cup breasts with classic white heels. Nothing else besides her minimal makeup and necklace.

She arrived at the Sound Table about fifteen minutes early, sat down at the bar, and ordered a Kettle One vodka up with a twist. She'd put her little purse on the adjacent stool, but that didn't deter a half dozen guys from giving it their best.

At 5:05 p.m. Rondo called. "You're going to kill me."

"That's possible. You forgot the time, or are you standing me up?"

"All-hands-on-deck thing. Sorry, I couldn't even call till now. I owe you big-time."

"You do, but first, you owe me information about Pamela Loncart.

"I gotta get back in a few five minutes."

"CliffsNotes version."

"Okay, okay. Why do you want to know, by the way?"

"We'll get to that. Hold on, lemme walk outside." She asked the good-looking millennial guy next to her if he'd save her seat for a few minutes. He was more than happy to oblige.

Rondo began. "I haven't seen her for a while. We worked a few cases together. She was a rocket at the DEA until her husband, also an agent, got killed in Mexico a couple of years ago. A setup outside of Durango. She went semi-retirement. I hear she now picks her own gigs on a part-time basis. Still sits on the Organized Crime Drug Enforcement Task Force (OCDETF), the interagency thing masterminding our unwinnable war on drugs. She's *the* go-to gal for wetback cartels. Supposedly knows the major players down there as well as anyone. Pretty much a legend at the Fed level. Dangerous, and not to be fucked with. Off-the-charts, stone-cold scary. I heard she's offed more than her fair share of narcos. Nobody knows how many. Doesn't look the part – but mean as shit and fearless. So, sort of like you. Sorry, forget the "mean" part. Has a ton of money, I've heard – they say family bucks. Got a mega crib with a couple of kids up in the north burbs. Heard she has a twin brother who was a special ops guy. No clue why she hangs around the DEA if she has that kind of bread."

He stopped.

"What else?"

"Checked in with a couple buddies I trust to see if they'd run into her lately. No luck. Bad idea to do any government database search on her. Shit, if she knew I was checking her out for any reason, I could end up minus my tongue or my dick. They say she likes knives better than guns but uses both quite well."

"For you, not sure which would be worse," she jibed.

"Why are you interested?"

"Short story, she's also a lacrosse mom – think soccer mom on steroids. Runs a middle school lacrosse club and kicked a friend's nephew off the team she controls. For no reason. Doing a favor for my boss. You remember the twin girls and their mom who got murdered in Cascade Heights last year?"

"Sure. Done by a couple of Klan types who got popped by brothers in jail."

"Nope, but you didn't hear the rest of this."

"Okay."

"That was complete and utter horseshit. Those crackers could no more have murdered the Monroes than get into Harvard. FBI and APD wanted the murders off their plates, and they were convenient. I'm pretty sure a set-up by the actual murderers, but who knows? A case no one is interested in anymore except for me and a couple of others. I was there at the crime scene. Worst I've ever seen. This morning, I was given a pocketknife taken from a lacrosse kid's middle school locker. Serious custom piece. The handle and the symbol on it were *exactly* like the knives I saw impaled into the floor below the two girls who were found desecrated on their own dining room table. The initials on the blades are identical. Made by a guy who lived in Santa Fe years ago. The kid got his pocketknife from Loncart. This bitch has not only fucked with my friend's nephew; she's involved in the twins' murders. I know it."

She paused, then, "I don't know why anyone would murder those girls and their mom, but *could* she have done it?"

Without hesitation, he said, "Absolutely."

"Thanks. You're off the hook for now, Rondo."

"Suzy, please don't go after her. She is big-time bad news."

"Oh, I'm not going after her tonight. But I am going after her."

She returned to her bar stool, thanked the guy who saved her seat, and ordered a fresh martini. She liked the funky vibe of the Sound Table. It was nice being out. Hotlanta had always been a cool city. Her view of it, though, was darkly colored by her occupations as a cop and now an investigator.

A cute couple had taken over the little dance floor at the Sound Shop. She wasn't sure if she'd ever seen dancing like that in person – the couple wearing tap shoes and clicking up a storm to a Flamenco-style song she'd never heard. She clapped with the rest of the bar.

Listening to the dancers tap, an idea germinated. On the way home, it grew.

Chapter 32 – The Boot

The Same Day

Midtown, Atlanta

On her way back to Midtown, Suzanne's brain was racing so fast that the cab driver had to remind her to pay. She pulled out a fifty and slapped it in his hand. She ran upstairs, ripped off her little dress, and put on a sweatshirt and jeans to take Zeke out. Back upstairs, she calmed down after she opened a bottle of Conundrum, poured herself a glass, and entered her Board Room. For the first time in a year, she opened the big closet that housed her evidence boards.

Eight years ago, after her father died, there was no Hollis Delacroix cold case. It was written off as a sad drowning. Suzanne had asked the ME to box up his personal effects. His gun, shield, cuffs, clothes, etc. Suzanne gave her mom his wedding band, watch, and car keys. When the Monroes were murdered last year, and she tried to help Mia Gonzales solve those cases, she'd intended to take another look at her dad's death. She never even tried. Maybe couldn't handle another failure? She wasn't sure.

There were three boxes on the top shelf inside her closet. One labeled "Dad" she'd never opened. It had been taped shut since November of 2008. She hauled it down and ripped off the tape. Inside, on top, was a large manila envelope. She could guess what was inside but wasn't ready to open it yet.

Polishing agates, which he found around Summerville, was his cold-weather hobby when he wasn't watching football. He always wore a black and red checkered wool shirt, jeans, safety glasses, and work boots. They were heavy, low-cut boots that she was surprised to learn he'd also worn while fishing. But why not, since he wasn't one to wade around in the water and fly fish. Boots. It never hit until an hour earlier at the bar. Boots – not with taps on the bottoms like the dancers' shoes, but with metal parts.

She rummaged to the bottom of the cardboard box and dug out the lone boot. Georgia Boot brand, low to medium height with six sets of metal eyelets, brown leather with a thick hard rubber, and a waffled bottom. Heavy and firm and still in good shape. The laces were obviously undone when the ME or an assistant pulled it off his foot. She Googled "*Georgia Boot*" – the online version, maybe a little updated. Indeed, it had a steel shank and toe beside the islets. A sturdy boot made with a lot of metal. The exterior of the short boot was heat, water, oil, and chemical resistant. The laces on the boot weren't rawhide but rather had a plastic exterior. Maybe even more interesting, his white sock was stuffed into the boot; it was thick and long enough to go halfway up his calf.

She sighed and took a deep breath before opening the envelope. Thank goodness the ME hadn't included autopsy photos, but there were four from different angles of his lifeless body on the rickety, weather-beaten dock. And a copy of the short APD file about his death. She flipped through photos of her dad lying lifeless, wearing a waterproof Bass rain jacket and pants, and one boot with a white sock. His other foot bare. The digital versions might be in police archives, but a magnifying glass would do. The one boot looked to be tied firmly and double-knotted at the top. She knew her dad did that with all his shoes. He was good with knots and fastidious about his own possessions, whether it was his dress police uniform, his golf shoes and clubs, or his fishing or rock equipment.

Where was the other boot?

There were reasonable explanations for why her was wearing only one boot as he lay dead on the dock. The laces were loose, and one slipped off in the water. Or the divers pulled one off while dragging his body out of the water.

Or his assailant pulled the boot and sock off while drowning him.

She pondered as she touched his checkered shirt and Braves cap. The theory she wanted to test might be the biggest stretch of her investigative life. The odds of success were probably worse than winning the Georgia lottery. She didn't give a rip.

Suzanne picked up his heavy brown boot and talked to it like it was her father. *"Daddy, I gotta know if you were murdered. I will find out."*

First thing tomorrow morning she would make a phone call. She found his number on one of the police notes. She didn't care if it was the mother of all longshots.

A year ago, she'd given up on the Monroe case – and the other related cases. She didn't want to, but she couldn't risk getting Mia in trouble, and regardless, she had no idea who the murderers were. She'd failed to revisit her dad's death; she told herself she had no angle. Instead, she escaped to Kip's firm, where investigative work was easy. she played golf at least twice a week. She volunteered a lot, and she contributed a bunch of money to local charities. There was no man in her life. Her nightmares had continued unabated. She wasn't happy or unhappy – but she was without peace or real purpose. She'd tried to tell herself she didn't care, but she did. She was done playing it safe.

A year ago, she felt she'd been inserted into their bizarre *Game of Twins*; then she bowed out. Back then, she'd started to erase the information on her boards but stopped. Now, the Tigress was ready to play.

She pulled out the three big boards and flipped one around so she could write on the back.

Tomorrow, she'd start reorganizing and cleaning up the board, including her father's. She looked at the images of the six sets of twins and touched their faces: Abercrombies (1911), Haverfords (1950),

253

Blounts (1973), Brevards (1974), Oosterhuises (2002), and Monroes (2015). She promised them, *"I'm going to find your murderers."*

But she swung one of the boards around and, in a stream of consciousness, wrote, underneath PAMELA LONCART: Serial Murderer?

Super rich – huge estate Roswell

Beautiful – 40ish

Unusual dark eyes – usually wears dark glasses

Twin teen boys

Lacrosse mom on steroids; domineering head of club

Twin brother – Special Forces…violence not foreign to the family

DEA heavy hitter – Mexican narcos expert, speaks Spanish

Widow, husband was DEA too

Vindictive; nonempathetic

Ruthless, Dangerous – likes knives & guns and knows how to use them

Could she kill? Rondo said yes (she killed many in Mexico)

Then on another side, she couldn't stop and scribbled more notes:

Could have killed Oosterhuises & Monroes, but what about the earlier murders?

Could have been the 3rd (shorter) person Mrs. Nethers saw?

Signature/MO similarities – similar murder method, knife(s) murder weapon, body mutilation, sexual control/domination; torture; body positions posed as horizontal crosses; black crosses impaled inside victims

Black double crosses…an occult thing?

Sick game – murderers leave clues: knives, photos, etc.

Significant planning; multiple murderers

Bodies (sometimes) left at murder scene (unlike many serial murders)

Differences: Inside and outside, flags, leaving murder weapons

Victims – all teenage, female, attractive, visible, chosen randomly? "Virginal"?

She stopped for now. Loncart had the means, the smarts, the arrogance/ego to murder the girls – but why? What would drive her and others to slaughter twins who were probably strangers?

Black double cross symbol appears on: PL necklace, PL lacrosse gear; PL pocketknife – same as two custom long knife murder weapons made by the same guy in NM.

Maybe set up the Dixons in prison…like Orville Johnson was set up 40 years ago? And the teacher in the 1950 murders?

Pamela couldn't have done the old murders, so who did?

On the way out, she hit the light switch, but turned around. She saw several lilting apparitions in the dark. Pairs of girls holding hands walked slowly around her boardroom, then stopped in front of her. Each pair clasped their hands in front of them like they were praying. In the blink of an eye, they were gone—the second paranormal experience in her life: *the ghosts of all the murdered twins.*

Zeke sat on the floor next to her. When she looked down at him, it was like, "What's the big deal? Oh, and I need to go out and pee…"

It had been a couple of weeks since she had one of her nightmares. Until that night.

Women she didn't know walked around brandishing all sorts of knives in a medieval setting with lots of crosses and candles. She plays mumblety-peg with a huge knife that sticks into her own foot. It doesn't hurt, but she can't pull it out of her foot. The crowd roars, then becomes quiet when a tall man dressed in black appears with a bigger blade and strolls toward her.

Suzanne screamed and woke up sweating and shaking.

Chapter 33 – The Pie Maker

The Same Night

Roswell

Pamela called her brother to make sure he'd do the task that night. "Incommunicado, a long way away?" he asked. "Okay, but wouldn't it be better to just make him disappear for good?"

She cut him off and said, "Let's have fun and give him a head start. Make him sweat more. You'll track him; his time will come sooner than later. Here's what you should tell him…"

Her second request struck him as even more unusual. He wondered what had gotten into her but knew better than to protest.

Pamela realized she was asking a lot and reassured him. "You'll be even more happy on Sunday, my darling. Maybe even a holiday soon. Just the two us. Keep me posted."

She hung up before he could say goodbye. But Philip Hawthorne was already getting excited thinking about having his sister to himself on holiday. He always did whatever she wanted. She knew he would. He had no choice.

Tony Santucci couldn't dispute that he'd lived a charmed life since moving to Atlanta. A couple days after arriving from Towson – while staying at his buddy's, a guy he'd known from college – he was exploring his new environs after rush hour. He saw a hole-in-the-wall pizza joint named Bernie's in a strip mall off I-140. Lots of cars, though – usually a good sign – so he walked in. Bigger and nicer than he'd ever thought from the outside. Waiting for a table, he spied a small sign tacked on the wall. "Need Experienced Pie Maker. Talk to Bernie."

He liked the thick, old-fashioned, Sicilian-style pizza that was cut into squares. He added anchovies, Portobello mushrooms, and onions to the tomato and potent caciocavallo cheese to his order. He was pleasantly surprised and had no idea anyone could make that kind of pizza in the South. A thick, husky man with snow-white hair, dark complexion, big ears, and a black eyepatch greeted customers at several tables and eventually got around to Tony. In a muted but distinct Italian accent, he asked, "How's the pie?"

"Great. I need a job. I can make pies," Tony answered back, maybe a bit too directly. The old Sicilian sized him up, grinned, and walked away. Then turned and said, "Hang around 'til ten."

An hour later, the place had thinned down to a few tables, and the man with the eyepatch returned. "Okay, Mr. Pie Guy, make me one. Oven's all yours." Tony followed him to the kitchen. It had been a while since he'd been in front of a giant pizza oven, but it was like being at home again. His mom had taught him to make pies; then he worked in high school and college at a local neighborhood pizzeria in Salisbury, Maryland.

He made a pizza and brought it to the table, where the man sat drinking red wine. After a bite, he said, "Not too bad." In his distinctive Italian accent, he asked the tall young man only one question: "You do drugs?"

"No, sir. I smoked a little weed in college, but no more. No other drugs."

"Good. Any drugs and you're fired, capiche?"

He told Tony, "Joey, my main pie maker, he gotta have surgery next week. See you Monday at 10:00 a.m." The proprietor, Bernie Scally, hadn't even introduced himself.

The rest was history. Making pies at Bernie's was a steady job that offered him the flexibility to do his coaching. The base pay was good, but even better were the bonuses. On the first Tuesday of each month,

Bernie held a little get-together in the small banquet room. Tony made the pies, served them, and poured expensive Chianti Classico. Coming in and out of that room over three years, he heard bits and pieces of colorful stories about old Sicilians who'd been through mob wars – back in the day. One had immigrated to New Jersey from Sicily and lost his eye in a knife fight in an alley in the Bronx. Tony had little doubt who that was.

The tips he made those Tuesday evenings doubled his typical earnings for a week and went directly into the bank. As Tony closed on Tuesdays, Bernie would always ask him what he got in tips. Then, he'd open his wallet, always flush with cash, and double it. "Don't spend it all in one place, kid," he told him.

By pure luck, he ended up at Eaglewood as the JV coach and assistant varsity coach via a Craigslist ad. The interview with Frank Ezell consisted of a few basic lacrosse questions and pitching the rock around the field at Eaglewood – then a few beers. From the get-go, Tony didn't like Ezell, but he got over it because he enjoyed coaching the JV kids and was left to handle that by himself. Then there was the pay, which he thought was terrific for an assistant middle school lacrosse coach: $500 per month (all months) the first year, which became $600 the next year and culminated to $750 per month this year – every penny of which he saved, as he lived solely on his pizza job wages. He had no illusions about where it was coming from.

Tony had never spoken more than a few sentences at a time to Pamela Loncart in three years. Since the incident a couple of months ago, he had tried to avoid her as much as possible. He replayed it in his head over and over. But after the Birmingham tournament—then David getting booted off the team based on phony accusations—it was haunting him more. No, it was eating him alive. There was something rotten about the Eaglewood Lacrosse Club, and the rot started with its chairwoman.

Eight Weeks Earlier – January 28

Eaglewood Middle School, Roswell

It was a bone-chilling evening, the second week of lacrosse practice. Most kids who hadn't played in an indoor winter league were still rusty and out of shape. So far, it had been mostly conditioning and simple drills. No plays or scrimmaging yet. It bored Coach Frank Ezell, who spent a lot of time huddled in his parka and talking on his cell phone while Tony ran drills. Tony paced the field with a trusty fifteen-year-old, beaten-up middie stick during practice, where it almost never left his hands.

That frigid day in January was pitch black at 5:30 p.m. when Tony left. Driving home, he was only a couple miles from Eaglewood when he panicked. He looked in the front seat, twisted his head to the back, and didn't see it. He took an immediate right and popped his front trunk at a Shell station. It wasn't there. Where was his lacrosse stick? His most prized possession. He needed to get to work, too, and it was rush hour traffic. He hustled back to Eaglewood as fast as the traffic and his 280Z would let him. After practice, he'd gone into the locker room to see if there were more lacrosse balls in the equipment locker – for practice tomorrow – otherwise, he'd need to pick up a bag because Frank wouldn't think of it. His stick must be in there.

He was back in less than ten minutes. No cars in the lot, but the door was still open, lights on. Typical that Frank had forgotten to lock up again. What a moron. Good thing he came back to do that, too. He parked in front of the back door. Walking up, he heard a few voices in the locker room, but before turning the corner and entering, he stopped for a second to listen. Bags, sticks, shoulder pads, and shoes banged around; then he heard the familiar voice of Lance Earl.

"Hey, Dax or Dex, isn't it weird, you know, doing your mom? But she is so hot! What tits and pussy she's got. Never thought any female liked cum that much. I always save mine for her instead of jacking off."

Dax glared, and his twin brother slammed his lacrosse stick into Lance's locker, "Shut the fuck up. You know the rules!" Dax pushed his lacrosse stick into Lance's neck.

"Easy, buddy, okay. I got it. It's just the six of us."

But Lance continued until Dex told him, "If you don't shut up, I'll make sure you're left out tonight and maybe for a long time."

Remaining quiet as a mouse, Tony had listened for another minute – not believing his ears. He quietly stepped back outside to check out the parking lot; no one. He took a deep breath and before re-entering and yelled, "Anybody still here?"

"Coach?" asked another voice. Tony walked in to see Lance, Bryce, Kevin, Randy, and the Loncart twins. Pamela's own secret lacrosse club, the boys with the golden sticks. Before they said anything, he told them, "Guys, I think I left my stick in here. You see it?"

In less than a minute, Bryce found it. "Musta slipped between the lockers. Hey, Coach, your stick is such a piece of crap. It's older than my dad. You ever going to get a new one? You oughta get one like ours."

"Thanks – this one's always worked fine. You guys get out of here so I can lock up. How come you're all here anyway?"

Lance piped in, "We're waiting for Miss Pamela to pick us up. I call shotgun!" He shooed them out and locked the door. Sure enough, Pamela's black Escalade was now parked next to his Z. All six boys piled in, with Lance dashing to the front passenger seat. Often, other parents drove Dex and Dax, but it was her turn that night. She lowered her tinted black window and said, "Thanks for locking up tonight, Coach."

"Yes, ma'am," he managed. "Have a good night." Tony stood in the empty parking lot. He was sure he'd heard what he heard, but he had no idea what to do about it.

Driving home, Pamela asked them, "I was a little late. Coach Santucci was waiting with you?"

"He came back. Forgot his stick and said he'd lock up since we were there late," Dax told his mom.

She promised, "I've got a surprise for you guys tonight."

Later, after tending to her lacrosse flock individually, she freshened up and drove each of the boys home, her twins accompanying her. With automatic audio access on their phones, she knew the gist of the conversation in the locker room. On the way back, she asked her twins, "So, my Dark Princes, did Coach Santucci hear any of Lance's nonsense?"

Both twins told her they didn't think Coach Tony had heard anything. She nodded okay but wondered about that possibility. Trying to control Tony sexually and read his mind might take a lot of time and effort – and might not even work. And then there was the small gold cross he always wore. No, her powers weren't the answer with Tony. She'd keep on him in case.

Thursday, March 24

Alpharetta

Since that night in January, Tony had become more observant of the six boys on the team with the fantastic lacrosse equipment perks, a small fortune per boy. He first thought the black symbols woven into their nets and imprinted on their bags were a strange version of the letter "H." Maybe, but they also looked like two overlapping black crosses. Brought up a staunch Catholic, Tony try to attend Mass once a week. He was no choir boy but considered himself a person of faith. He always wore a necklace with a small gold cross, which his uncle had given him when his dad died. Guys on his college team used to kid him about it in the shower, but he ignored the abuse; it was in memory of his dad. He wondered about the unusual black crosses.

Tony didn't regret laying out Frank Ezell with one punch and quitting on Tuesday, but tonight, it felt strange and lonely watching the Eaglewood game with his binoculars. When he saw an apparent confrontation between Pamela and the Baldwins and their dogs, he sent the text. By the time he'd gotten home, David's mom answered and said she'd meet him after work the following evening. He breathed a sigh of relief. He had to get this burden off his chest.

Before going home, he stopped by work to see if they needed any extra help. They were swamped, so he helped with making pizzas, waited on tables, and cleaned up until 10:45 p.m.

Back in his modest apartment at 11:15, he turned on Alison Krause and got a Dos Equis with a submerged lime. He flopped down on his old Barcalounger and pondered. If he said nothing, he would be like Joe Paterno and the cowardly administrators at Penn State who ignored and swept Jerry Sandusky's horrific deeds under the rug. But Tony was no idiot. He knew he'd heard way more than he should have. The truth could be dangerous. Pamela might be a sexual predator, but she was also rich and powerful and a federal agent to boot.

Sitting amid thought, Tony felt cold metal against the back of his head. As he lurched, a man with the muzzle of his gun silencer pressed into the back of his head said calmly, "Don't turn around, don't move, and listen up, or I'll blow your head off. If you'd like to remain among the living, you're going to do exactly as I say. Got it?"

Tony held off the urges to both piss and shit in his pants. His throat suddenly parched, and he choked out a "yes."

Chapter 34 – The Kiss

Friday, March 25

Atlanta

At 9:00 a.m., Suzanne called the number she'd found in her dad's postmortem file. A man answered, "Dive Shop, Rick speaking."

"Rick Waller?"

"Yes, ma'am."

She was in luck. "Rick, you may not remember me, Suzanne Delacroix. I used to be an APD Homicide Detective."

"Yes, ma'am, sure do. It was your father who drowned in the lake fishing. I think it was November 2008."

"You've got an excellent memory. Do you recall where in the lake he was found?"

"I think so. Good fishing area, that inlet off the northwest side."

"If you have a few minutes, I have a few questions." "No problem."

"You were the one who found my father, right?"

"Yes, ma'am. There were three of us who dove; a couple others in the boat. God, I remember the weather was horrible that day."

"Yes, it was. How exactly did you all bring him up?"

"Well, apparently, not much time from when he drowned, so his body hadn't hit the bottom yet. We looped a rope underneath his arms, then we guided him up, and he was pulled up by two other guys on our boat."

"Do you recall that one foot was bare, without sock and boot?"

After hesitating, he said, "Yeah, I think I do."

"Think you or another diver pulled it off?"

"I don't know, but I doubt it. That's not how we'd grab anyone."

Suzanne tried breathing more slowly. So far, so good.

"Rick, I've been looking at the photographs of him after you pulled him out. How do you explain him not having a boot and sock on one foot?"

"Well, I suppose that boot wasn't tied well, and it slipped off in the water."

"With his sock, too? It was a sock that went halfway up his leg."

"Hard to say, ma'am."

"You may or may not have known, my dad couldn't swim. He would fish but was scared to death of being in water. What if a guy pulled his sock and boot off while drowning him – and the laces were still tied?"

She let that sink in a moment. He said, "I suppose that's possible."

"The boot is made from tough synthetic and has steel plates as support and on the bottom."

"Okay."

"Diving to the bottom of Lanier wouldn't be a stretch for an experienced diver?"

"No, ma'am. Only about sixty or seventy feet deep in that section. Parts of the lake are three times that deep."

"I'm assuming you could use a metal detector to find things at that depth?"

"Yeah, there are guys who dive to see what's on the bottom, mostly for kicks. Off and on they'll find a few pieces of jewelry and watches; all sorts of fishing gear; bullets, guns, and other Civil War artifacts. I heard once, even a prosthetic leg. Who knows what else? I've done it a few times but didn't find any pirate's treasure."

Bingo. "Rick, here's what I'd like you to do, if you're interested. Understand this is not a police matter, per se. I'm an interested civilian."

They talked for another ten minutes about her request. Rick reiterated, "Even with three more divers, it would be like finding a needle in a haystack."

"Rick, I get that. Give it your best shot for a couple of days with a few of your best diver buddies. If you don't find it at least, I'll know we tried. Tell you what, sleep on it and let me know. Money isn't an issue; whatever you think is fair. If you're game, I'll get a check to you this weekend. Thanks."

Suzanne was starting to wonder if she'd lost her mind. Even if they found the boot, it might have its laces undone, or maybe they were simply gone. And if they found the boot, it might only tell her whether he *was* murdered. Not who did it.

Or maybe it would.

She didn't get a chance yesterday, but on her way to grab a cup of coffee, Suzanne stopped by Walter O'Malley's office to speak to his assistant, Gloria. "There was a tall, dark-haired, well-dressed guy who walked into Walter's office a couple of days ago, but I only saw him for a second. Thought I recognized him. Would you remember who it was?"

Gloria told her matter-of-factly, "Brand new client. Thad Sutterland. You know, son of Franklin. Billionaire family. Walter thinks Hawthorne Industries can be the firm's biggest client within a year. Thad, like his dad, is easy on the eyes," she winked.

Suzanne felt like she was going to retch but tried not to let on.

"You know him?"

She had no idea what her face looked like but managed to say, "No, I thought it was someone else. Thanks, Gloria."

She left quickly to avoid any further conversation and calm her stomach. Hotlanta, with its five million-plus people, could be such a small town. She returned to her office and did something she rarely did at work. She sat at her desk, brought out the bottle and a glass, and poured herself three fingers of Noah's Mill, her favorite bourbon.

Thad Sutterland. Unfuckingbelievable! Since she worked under aliases as an investigator, she wondered if the bastard knew she worked there, but if so, she wondered why he hadn't stopped by. She called Kip on his cell and asked him if he could drop by her office for a few minutes. When he arrived, she already had a glass waiting for him when he sat down on her small couch. She sat next to him and clinked glasses.

"What's the occasion, Suzy?" he smiled.

"I hear the firm has a new, big corporate client."

"Yeah, it's a major deal. A good reason to celebrate. Walter just hooked Hawthorne Industries whose CEO is Thad Sutterland. Similar to Trump, except Thad and his family have *a lot* more money. He'll be a pain in the ass but could easily make our year and maybe our next few years."

She turned her head to him. "I know Thad. Let's say we are past acquaintances." She took another big sip.

"How so? You go out with him once upon a time?"

"Not exactly. In college, he assaulted and tried to rape me at a Tech frat party. Got off scot-free."

"Holy shit. I'm so sorry." He realized this was not good.

"Kip, maybe one day I'll tell you that whole story."

He nodded his head almost imperceptibly, not knowing what to say.

She gulped the bourbon, then said, "Kip, I'm quitting as of today."

He was stunned. Coddling his drink, he finally managed to say, "Please don't leave, Suzy. I can keep you insulated from Sutterland, and you'll never have to work on a case for him, I promise. At least sleep on it, please."

She shook her head. "No. I gotta leave. Time for me to move on, but I'll continue to help the Baldwins. There's nasty stuff going on that I'm trying to get a bead on. The lacrosse thing may be entangled with the murders of the Monroes."

"You can't be serious."

But he knew she was. "Are they in any danger?"

"I don't think so, but I'm going to meet Sarah for dinner this evening and make sure she'll be extra careful not to piss off the head of the lacrosse club, Pamela Loncart. Hopefully, we can learn more from the assistant coach who asked to meet with Sarah; he got fired a couple of days ago."

"Can you go to the police?"

"No, I don't have nearly enough, and I could be wrong. Besides, except for a couple of people cops, the boys downtown believe the Monroes' murderers were the guys who got offed in jail before they stood trial. And they aren't going to care about any lacrosse stuff. Don't worry; I won't let anything happen to the Baldwins, I promise. Hey, you still have your cottage up at Lanier, don't you?"

"I do," he said with anticipation. He'd take her there in a heartbeat.

"Might be a nice gesture to offer it to your cousin for the weekend, even if they can't go. I think they need to get away for a bit. Your idea. Boy, that's a nice family. I wish…" She stopped her thought.

Deflated, he said, "Great suggestion." He fumbled for the key on his chain and pressed it into her hand. "Tell Sarah I said 'hi,' and I'll text her directions."

He stood up and asked her, "Will you give me a hug on your way out?"

She got up close enough so that her breasts were mashing into his chest. She loved the smell of him and the bare hint of musky cologne. Before releasing the hug, she took his head in her hands. Then her lips were on his and her tongue was in his mouth that tasted better than any man she'd ever kissed.

She broke off the passionate kiss. "I've wanted to do that for a long, long time."

He smiled sheepishly, "You and me both."

"Please box up any personal stuff for me if you would. I don't have much."

"Sure, will do. You be careful out there, young lady, and keep me posted."

"Yes, sir." She smiled and left.

Kip Davies walked back to his office and went to his small fridge where he had a couple bottles of Stoli in the freezer. He poured a healthy tumbler, slumped down on the big chair in his office, and sipped the silky Russian lightning. His thoughts ping-ponged. God, he'd miss seeing her around the office. Was that mind-boggling kiss a one-time thing? If so, would she drift away? If not, how could he get divorced from his bitch wife without losing a ton of money and his precious daughters? He couldn't answer any of those questions. Had she loved him for as long as he loved her? One day, he intended to find out.

Thad Sutterland. He'd talked with Thad only a couple of times. He wasn't surprised at what Suzanne had told him. If Sutterland were here right now, he'd love to punch his lights out, regardless of the consequences.

He took another gulp of his vodka. One way or another, Sutterland was going to pay for what he did to the love of his life. It was bittersweet about her quitting, yet the mind-blowing kiss gave him a little hope.

Chapter 35 – The Proprietor

Friday, March 25, 2016

Alpharetta

Sarah was glad to work a reasonable shift at the vet clinic. She needed to keep her mind off David's situation, off Pamela's seeming knowledge of her affair with Bill, who, thank God, was on vacation for a few days – and off her husband Tim, who was drinking way more than he should.

She zipped home so she could preen for her rendezvous with Suzanne and Tony at Bernie's. She Googled the address of Bernie's and arrived before seven o'clock. Located in a nondescript strip mall, it was cozy and comfortable inside. There was even a violin player near the long, old-fashioned bar, and seats filled with an eclectic group of patrons.

Suzanne arrived a few minutes later. Sarah watched many heads turn like they were checking out a celebrity. She wore skin-tight brown leather pants, a white chemise with a black bra, and heels. Her long, raven-black hair bounced as she walked. Sarah thought, *Oh Jeez, I'm not in the same universe.* She stood and politely held out her hand but instead got a pleasant hug.

"I've lived in Atlanta my whole life. Never been here. Nice," said Suzanne.

"Me neither. David and Tim say the pizza is awesome."

They both ordered a glass of wine, red for Suzanne and white for Sarah. Within minutes, they were gabbing like fast friends, avoiding the purpose of the meeting until Suzanne asked Sarah what she knew about Tony.

Sarah replied, "Not a lot. Nice guy. Single. Polite. David and Tim think he's a great coach. He's helped David a lot one-on-one. He works here making pizzas. Moved from up north a couple of years ago. Apparently was a big lacrosse player in college, but doesn't give off the same vibe as Frank Ezell, the asshole head coach at my son's school."

"I completely get that," Suzanne told her without elaborating.

At 7:30 p.m., as they ordered their second glasses of wine, Sarah asked the waiter, "Have you seen Tony? We were supposed to meet him here at seven o'clock."

The middle-aged, bald waiter, dressed in black trousers, a bright white shirt, and a black bowtie, politely said in his Italian accent, "He was supposed to work today but didn't show up." Then, he was gone in a flash.

Sarah looked perplexed. She tried texting him and told Suzanne, "Sorry. Hopefully, he'll respond back."

Not a minute later, a barrel-chested, older man with a wrinkled, swarthy complexion, prominent nose, white hair combed back, and black eyepatch approached their table. He announced with an Italian accent, "Ladies, let me introduce myself. I'm Bernie Scally, the proprietor. I hear you've been looking for Tony. May I sit down?"

Both women nodded.

He looked at one and then the other. "I haven't heard from him. He's never missed a shift in almost three years. His phone doesn't ring. I've texted him. I sent a guy over to check his apartment. No sign other than it looks like he packed and left. Something is wrong. Would you ladies like to enlighten me?"

More wine and a pizza magically appeared at their table. Both women were starving, and the Sicilian-style pizza was delicious. Sarah told him her abbreviated story, and Suzanne told him she did contract investigative work for a big law firm. One of the senior partners asked her to help Sarah, his cousin, and the Baldwin family.

She avoided the fact that she became a free agent as of today.

He looked directly at her. "Miss Delacroix, I'm guessing you were a cop before becoming an investigator?"

"Homicide detective, APD, for seventeen years."

Oh my, she was an exquisite beauty, thought Bernie, maybe one of the most gorgeous women he'd ever laid eyes on. But cops were cops. He hated most of them and distrusted the rest. While telling her part of the story, she chose her words carefully. She was a pro, he could tell. She clearly knew more than she was telling him. Tony hadn't told Bernie he was no longer the assistant coach of the kids' lacrosse team Tuesday – and didn't seem to be himself. As he'd just learned from the two women, Tony could be in trouble with a Fed named Pamela Loncart, who directed his lacrosse club. Still, he was hoping Tony had left Atlanta to maybe sort things out and would call him later. He wasn't only his best pizza maker; Tony had become his surrogate son – all these years after his boy and wife were gunned down. Today, Bernie Scally was a pizza shop proprietor. But four decades ago, he'd been one of the New York mob's most feared hitmen. He'd retired, yes, but was not without contacts. He would find Tony Santucci if it was the last thing he did on this earth.

Suzanne looked at Bernard Scally and knew they were thinking the same thing: he'd been taken and could be dead or alive. Bernie leaned back a bit in his chair and pondered. Sarah was a professional mom who hurt for her child. He got that. Suzanne was doing a favor for a colleague, but there was more to it.

On the way out, Sarah went to the ladies' room. Now, standing facing each other outside, the ex-mobster said to Suzanne, "You and I need to talk alone. I need to know whatever else you know."

She smiled. "Okay, if you tell me your real name."

He smiled back. "Scalise. Bernardo Conti Scalise."

"Bernardo, I'll see you at Bones in Buckhead at 7:30 p.m. tomorrow evening."

He took her hand and kissed it. "I look forward to it, Miss Delacroix."

On the way out, Suzanne said to Sarah, "Kip asked me to give this to you. A key to his place up on Lake Lanier if you would like to get away for the weekend. Or another time that works." She handed her the key. "He'll text directions."

"Wow, thanks. Yeah, I'm off this weekend. I'll see what Tim wants to do. David's staying at a buddy's."

Suzanne smiled. "We'll get this figured, okay?" Sarah nodded but wasn't optimistic.

Bernardo Scalise had a boatload of chits he could call in from across the country. First, he called his best-connected Atlanta compadre and then another who was still wired into federal law enforcement. Each was eager to help him find Tony. The first was assigned to check out Delacroix and report back before midnight. Indeed, he learned she had followed in her father's footsteps and had the highest homicide close rate in the city's history. She was also rich from her inheritance.

He smiled. Maybe she was the exception to his rule. An ex-cop whom he could trust? Wealthy and not influenced by others' money? He fully intended to find out why she really quit APD. And figure out how they could work together to find Tony.

The second call was to find out more about Loncart. His friend told him it might take a couple of days. Bernie impressed on him the need for speed.

His friend said, "Okay, maybe tomorrow."

From the safe in his office, he brought out two items. One, a handgun he hadn't fired in over two decades. He spent an hour cleaning his .357 Magnum revolver, like the one Eastwood used in *Dirty Harry*. Indeed, with the right rounds, it could blow a man's head to smithereens. He could vouch for that firsthand. The second item was his go-to killing weapon of choice, a black Italian stiletto, eleven and a quarter inches when open. He hadn't oiled it in years, but it slung open on the first try when he pressed the button. He used oil on the knife, too.

He was glad he'd met the two women but felt helpless. He had no clue where Tony was. He knew Tony would never leave without at least saying goodbye. He could be dead. His gut didn't feel good about any of this, but he'd try to be patient at least until his dinner with Suzanne. If he wasn't already dead, she might be his only hope to find him.

After his wife and son were taken from him, he swore that he'd never do this again – but also knew how foolish it was to ever say "never." He sat in his little office in the back of the restaurant, his head in his hands, and cried. He got down on his knees and prayed, fully understanding God didn't have a single good reason to listen.

At home, Suzanne Googled Bernardo Conti Scalise. Wikipedia indicated he had been a hitman extraordinaire for Carmine "Lilo" Galante of the Bonanno crime family. When the Five Families Commission put a hit on Galante, they put one on Scalise as well. He survived the hail of bullets that hit his Cadillac, but his wife and young son did not. He had killed an estimated thirty men by a variety of methods. A photo from 1974 showed him with thick, dark hair and no eyepatch. He was quite good-looking. This evening, she wouldn't have guessed he was a stone-cold killer.

She smiled. *"Okay, so he's no Boy Scout. I'll take him any day over the cops and FBI."*

The Same Evening

Driving West from Atlanta

At ten o'clock, as the two ladies were leaving Bernie's Pizzeria in Alpharetta, Tony Santucci was driving on Highway 29 north of Omaha, Nebraska.

The man who'd stuck a gun in the back of his head the previous evening had been weirdly friendly – after he'd scared the crap out of him and told him it would be a good idea not to turn around. "You think you overheard a few boys giving each other grief in a locker room, but you know how horny teenage boys are. You've already quit as coach and should stay out of lacrosse around Atlanta. Take a long road trip. Drive somewhere you want to go. You have the iPhone I gave you. Keep it but use it carefully. Amazing what can be learned from people's smartphones these days, only knowing their cell number. Don't communicate with *anyone* in Atlanta other than checking in daily with me, by text. I'll get you the number." Then he tacked on, "It would be a shame if anything happened..." He paused, then continued. "David is such a nice kid. By the way, do you like your pizzeria boss...?" Then he dropped five thousand dollars in his lap. "Traveling money. Everything you do is cash, and keep in touch, like I told you."

Tony took off. He'd gotten a few speeding tickets over the years, but he'd never been in any kind of trouble with the law or anyone else. He had no idea what to do but decided he'd head west. His first stop was Murfreesboro on the outskirts of Nashville, where he crashed at a Motel 6 for a few hours, ate breakfast, and was off again.

His destination was Yellowstone National Park, which he had always wanted to visit. A friend told him a great place to stay was in Chico, Montana, north of the park. Chico Hot Springs Resort & Spa had a huge outdoor pool fed by the hot springs, but even the thought of it couldn't calm his racing mind. He headed toward Kansas City. He loved driving his Z but couldn't relax with the music on or off.

Tony knew he could be monitored with the iPhone GPS, plus the new phone could probably be used as either an audio or video device as well, but he couldn't get rid of it. He could get a burner phone, but he couldn't safely call the Baldwins or anyone else in Atlanta, including Bernie. The guy with the gun was not dicking around. He couldn't go to the police or the press. Even if they believed him, he might put David, Bernie, himself, and others in jeopardy. He could try to get on a computer somewhere and email or Skype, but he didn't have contact information and was scared if he did *anything* digitally, he might compromise others.

Then he got an idea. It was already rush-hour in Kansas City. Off I-170, he spied a big strip mall and took the exit. He left the iPhone in his Z. In CVS he bought a cheap burner cell phone with cash. In Kroger, he got a cooler, a six-pack of Becks, Cokes, ice, and snacks, along with a pack of envelopes, a pad of paper, and stamps. He put the food and drinks in his Datsun and walked over to Starbucks with the rest.

He ordered a cup of Verona and sat down in the corner where, for the next hour, he wrote, in as much detail as possible, what happened starting that night in January – and what could happen; plus his new burner phone number, cautionary instructions, and where he was heading. He didn't see a postage store and figured it wouldn't be open at this hour anyway. He decided to drop the letter he addressed to Bernie Scally at his pizzeria's address into a mailbox outside the grocery. He hoped it would arrive by Tuesday or Wednesday. Worst case, they would know what happened to him – and the truth about Pamela. Best case, Bernie would call him on his burner phone once he received the letter and rescue his ass. He might be overly paranoid, but he couldn't take any chances.

Per instructions, he texted the unknown number on his iPhone and received a smiley face back, immediately, from the bad guy in Atlanta. It erased the smile from his own face. After mailing the letter he grabbed a Whopper with cheese and fries at Burger King and was off. It took another twelve or thirteen hours until he reached Chico, Montana.

Chapter 36 – The Calm Before the Storm

Friday, March 25

Buckhead, Atlanta

Bones was hopping on Friday night when Suzanne walked in a few minutes after 7:30 p.m. Bernie Scally, who'd already been seated, stood and tenderly kissed her hand. "Suzanne, you look *fantastico*!" Politely, he pulled out her chair at the cozy, two-person table and scooted her in.

"Bernardo, you look great yourself." His white hair looked freshly trimmed and complemented his silky gray sport coat, open-collar white shirt, and, of course, Italian loafers. And his black eyepatch.

"No doubt the patrons think I'm your father or grandfather."

She winked. "I don't know about that. Or my date. Maybe the 'most interesting man,' like in the Dos Equis commercial."

Bernie Scally laughed. He'd already ordered a bottle of Ruffino Reserva Ducale. "I hope you like red."

"I do." She tasted it and pronounced it "wonderful."

Along with the rest of her, he noticed her platinum, diamond, and emerald cross necklace. "That's a beautiful necklace, Suzanne."

"Thank you. A gift from my dad to my mom. They're both gone now."

He bowed his head knowingly. "Tell me about your policeman father."

She relayed information about her dad and his death, ending with, "I think he was murdered; I've always assumed it was a bad guy who wanted revenge."

Without missing a beat, he asked, "Who benefited the most?"

She hadn't looked at it from that angle. "His longtime fishing buddy, the guy who got the job he was supposed to get – who is now chief of APD." It was so obvious, but she'd never even considered the possibility. He hadn't been out on the water with her father. But still. Then it hit her like a ton of bricks. Two different stories from two fishing buddies about her dad's vest.

She added, "My father was by himself and couldn't swim, so the assumption was he fell off the boat and drowned." She told him about her probably being crazy hunting for the missing boot.

His only comment: "I hope you find it, but even if you don't, go with your gut."

She nodded, "Do you like red meat, Bernardo?"

"Of course."

She suggested the filet mignons medium rare, crabmeat cocktail, and Bones salad.

He said, *"Perfezionare."*

Waiting for their meal and drinking the Italian red, Bernardo asked, "Suzanne, what made you quit being a cop?"

She looked down at her plate and then started slowly. "My partner and I were briefly in charge of the Monroe murder cases. I'm sure you remember from last year. Atrocities unlike anything I'd seen or could ever imagine. They were butchered with two knives that the killers left." Her voice tapered off. "I snapped – I don't know. She continued, "Back in college, I was assaulted and almost raped at knifepoint. The guy who tried to rape me belongs to a wealthy, powerful family in town. He got off scot-free. And as of this week, his firm is a big new client of Stuyvesant, Knight, Fitzpatrick & Burns, where I've been working. I can't condone that, so I quit yesterday."

"May I ask his name?" Bernardo asked.

She hesitated. "Thad Sutterland, of Hawthorne Industries." Why would she tell a virtual stranger about being assaulted and almost raped? She hadn't talked about it with anyone in over two decades until Kip yesterday and now Bernardo. It felt liberating.

He nodded. He was sure Suzanne could be trusted. He had a half dozen people digging into all they could about Pamela, now a DEA consultant who sat on Homeland Security's OCDETF. The Task Force was currently working to extradite the Pacific Cartel's Joaquin Romero Menendez, *El Sin Quello, the* most powerful narco on the planet.

He asked, "Did you know Pamela has a brother named Philip Hawthorne? Ex-Marine RECON who runs a big furniture import-export business and trucking operation based out of Woodstock – with a dozen Southeast locations. An unsubstantiated rumor is that he's one of the largest drug distributors and money launderers on the Eastern Seaboard, second only to Miami. He's also rumored to have a lot of Atlanta metro area cops – and beyond – in his hip pocket." He smiled. "It never changes with underpaid cops."

"I never took a dime, nor did my father," she shot back.

"Sorry, I didn't mean to accuse you. There are exceptions to the rule. You and your family are one of them. Of that, I have no doubt."

She tried to digest that along with her delicious filet mignon. *A DEA agent whose brother could be a huge drug player – and have protection from the cops and maybe even Homeland?*

"That's not all." He took a big sip of wine and then grinned. "Twins Pamela Loncart and Philip Hawthorne are cousins of your assailant, Thad Sutterland, whose father and mother control Hawthorne Industries. Thad has a twin, too. Appears he changed his name years ago. Didn't find anything on him."

Suzanne fumbled her glass of red wine and nearly spilled it. All she could do was bat her big, amber eyes like she was trying to clear her head. The implications, she couldn't immediately fathom.

"And you know this *how*?"

"I know people who know people."

"Thad Sutterland, she almost had to laugh – what a surprise."

While waiting for dessert, she pulled the custom pocketknife out of her purse and handed it to him.

"Nice knife." He opened the blade. "Should I divide our dessert with it?" he kidded.

She smiled. "Check out the symbol on it. The two black crosses jammed together. Ever see anything like that?"

He shook his head. "I don't think so."

"I saw the symbol on the two long knives that were stuck in the floor at the Monroes' murder scene, custom-made by a guy in Santa Fe more than thirty years ago. Do you have a pen?" He handed her one from his inside coat pocket.

On the white napkin, she drew the stick outlines of two bodies. "That's how the girls were found on their dining room table. Same shape as the knife crosses. This pocketknife was found a couple of days ago in the middle school locker of one of Pamela's lacrosse pets, one of the boys who helped screw over David, Sarah's boy. The exact same handle, emblem, and engraved signature. The same black double cross symbol is also on the boys' lacrosse gear – and the shape of the pendant on Pamela's black necklace."

Deep in thought, each took a forkful of their nearly foot-tall frozen pie. *"Delizioso,"* he said.

"I read online that you know knives."

The corners of Bernardo Scalise's small mouth turned up a bit but not voluntarily. "You can't believe everything you read, Suzanne."

"Your wife and son were killed?"

His dark brow dropped, and he said softly, "Yes, many years ago. It was my fault and always will be. I shouldn't be alive. I mourn them daily."

Clearly, a subject he didn't want to talk about. Bones was thinning out at ten o'clock. They sipped coffee. He demanded to pay the bill, so she let him.

"That brings us back to Tony. This is about Pamela Loncart, don't you think, Suzanne?"

"Yes. I haven't met her in person, but I plan to do that Tuesday afternoon at the Eaglewood Middle School lacrosse game. I'll be using one of my aliases."

"Suzanne, I'm not trying to make a boy's lacrosse thing right or solve a series of murders. I'm trying to find Tony. I cannot lose him, too."

"I know. I'm thinking Tony knows or saw something he shouldn't have."

He nodded. She said to him, "Bernie, do you believe that all things are interconnected?"

"Yes, in one way or another, I know they are..."

She could see the tears well up in the ex-hitman's warm, brown eyes. He couldn't help wiping them with his napkin. Getting up from the table, she put a hand on his shoulder. "We'll find him. We'll find Tony."

But neither were sure about that.

After she got home and took Zeke out, Suzanne was bushed. She had dozens of thoughts she needed to get on her boards tomorrow, but they'd have to wait. She was asleep in five minutes. But then it happened again.

She's on a stretcher in a medical room surrounded by all sorts of equipment. Her long legs are up in the stirrups, not even a sheet covering her. She's in a truck or van, parked on a golf course. The windows are open; she's freezing. She glances over and sees several sizes of knives handles laid out on a surgeon's tray; others hang on the wall. A man in scrubs wearing a surgical mask and a golf visor says, "Hello. It's nice to see you again, Miss Delacroix. You'll be back to playing golf in no time." He picks up one knife and the blade flicks open. It's huge. "Don't worry, this won't hurt a bit." She begs, "No, you forgot to give me anesthesia, and I'm going to miss my tee time." Thad takes off his mask and picks up the knife again. "Suzanne, you've been such a naughty girl," he grins.

She bolted upright, waking Zeke. He got up and licked her face. He handled her dreams of terror a lot better than she did.

Saturday Morning, March 26

Alpharetta

Bernie Scally didn't sleep well last night either. At 5:00 a.m., he drove to his restaurant. He fired up the cappuccino machine and made himself an Italian omelet with sausage, prosciutto, four cheeses, onions, peppers, and mushrooms. He walked down the street to get a *Constitution* and had another cappuccino. He decided to give his pie maker the weekend off, hoping that doing the work himself would help take his mind off Tony. He was torn. He hoped Tony simply left town by himself and was safe – but couldn't believe he left without saying goodbye. He made a few more calls, redirecting friends to find out quietly whatever else they could about Pamela, Philip, the Sutterland family, and Hawthorne Industries. They had all the leverage now, and he knew it. He had nothing, yet, to bend the will of Loncart. Unless maybe he had her point-blank with his .357 pressed to her forehead, or his switchblade pressed against her cheek below an eyeball.

After going for a run with Zeke in Piedmont Park, Suzanne got a text from Rick Waller. "Dive Mon-Tues. Cost $3000/man and $3000 more expenses. $15k. Will that work?" Waller still rated the chances as infinitesimal, but it was hard to turn down that kind of money for a few days of diving.

He was surprised she didn't have sticker shock, but she texted back, "Yes. Will get a check to u tomorrow. Thx. S."

Unemployed and free as a bird again, she escaped to East Lake, where she played a good round of golf in the pleasant, cool spring air.

The Same Day

Chico & Gardiner, Montana

When he left Atlanta, Tony hadn't thought about snow; he had other things on his mind. It was only the first week of spring but still cold and snowy in southwestern Montana. Twenty-five degrees and about a foot of snow covering the ground. At least the main drag, Interstate 89, was clear from Gardiner to Chico. His 280Z wasn't great in the elements but did okay. In Gardiner, he bought a couple pairs of jeans, boots, heavy socks, a decent winter coat, gloves, and a hat. He signed up for a snowmobile tour on Sunday and spent the rest of the day hanging out at Chico's famous outdoor hot springs pool. After a couple of beers at the pool, he'd almost forgotten about his plight but knew he better text. This time he got a response. "How's the weather in Montana? DB is fine BTW." Not surprising they knew exactly where he was. His iPhone tracked him – they listened and watched – and he was sure his Z was bugged, too. He prayed nobody was physically following him but kept his head on a swivel, like he was taught playing lacrosse.

Tony woke up on Saturday night sweating, in a total panic. Pamela and her crew had let him leave Atlanta, but he was still on a tight leash. If only he'd sent his letter FedEx. His paranoia spiked. God, he hoped the mail was fast. Eventually, he fell asleep trying to envision the bison, elk, wolves, and other animals he'd seen on his snow coach tour tomorrow in the snow-covered beauty of Northern Yellowstone.

He slept for a few hours and then awoke. He was sure they'd get rid of him sooner than later. There was no more sleep that night.

Sunday Afternoon, March 27

Roswell

On most Sunday afternoons "Uncle Philip" made the twenty-five-minute drive from Woodstock to Pamela's estate in Roswell. Dex and Dax were expected to make themselves scarce while he was there. They'd have their alone time with Mom later. Pamela and her twin brother usually spent it indoors in her huge, private playroom on the lower level. In his whole life, Philip had ongoing sexual relationships with only two women: his sister and his dear mother, who'd been gone many years. Those started when he was twelve. He'd never seen or met any woman who was as desirable as either. Not even close. He was taught all the nuances – but used them sparingly over the years with females – and only when absolutely needed. The rugged, lanky ex-Marine RECON looked forward to Sundays with Pamela even more than killing people who dared step in his way.

Then there was Thad, whom he'd also lusted for since the two grew up together in the West Paces area of Atlanta. He wasn't sure why, but Thad floated his boat almost as much as his sister. Jeremy, Thad's twin, was not into boys, but Philip always dreamed about taking the two Sutterlands at the same time. Maybe a threesome with Pamela and Mary Jo, his "stepsister" (now U.S. congresswoman), might be fun, too.

Sunday, after their two-hour sex session, there was more official business than usual. He assured her it was all set for tomorrow morning, and there were a couple of backup plans. Sitting naked on the bed, Pamela cooed, "Philip, darling, I know you will make my request happen tomorrow. And Santucci, he's been a good boy so far?"

"Yes, he's in Montana."

"I wanted to make it sporting and thought it would be nice to let him dangle longer in my game, but perhaps he could disappear this week?"

"I'll get our guy from Denver."

"Splendid, and before you leave, maybe more of your potion, my dear?"

The Same Afternoon

Atlanta

After golf, Suzanne took Zeke out and then drew a long bath. She ordered Chinese takeout and pulled the cork on a bottle of Zin. At

10:00 p.m., with a black marker in hand, she perused her boards. Before writing, she thought: It's like *they want* to connect the murders over time for us. They've left more than a few breadcrumbs for law enforcement – and are especially enamored with pornographic, Polaroid snuff photos.

She could hear them: "Even though we've gotten more outrageous, no one has caught us in over a hundred years." The narcissism and psychoses was palpable. They even liked to implicate others for murders – not necessarily to ensure their tracks were better covered, but rather to torment investigators. Sounded like they drove an FBI Special Agent nuts, then maybe put Derbert Hinke out of his misery when he got too close. They weren't going to do that to her.

But what was "it" – this game of killing twins – all about? Not money, that's for sure. Revenge? For what? The victims had no apparent connection. For grins? Maybe. Weird occult sacrifices. Could be, though last year Mia's person had found no local connections to known occult groups in the area.

She spent an hour weaving in and out of her boards, adding and deleting and re-organizing items. Then on a spare side she hadn't used she wrote underneath *Game of Twins*:

TWINS

BLACK DOUBLE CROSSES

PAMELA LONCART

It was all about those three things.

Part V - The Storm

Chapter 37 – The Airedales

Monday, March 28, 2016

Roswell

The always well-organized Loretta Moriarity screwed up and knew she was in a world of shit. Despite having the patience of Job – learned over the years bringing up her autistic son Carter – she was in a complete panic. On her synched digital schedule, she forgot to update Cumberland Academy's teacher in-service days. Atlanta's preeminent school for kids who have autism, Asperger's, ADD, and other special needs was out today, and she had to be at work.

As vice president of Human Resources for a local software company, Loretta had slaved all weekend on a huge presentation. Not going to work today wasn't an option unless she wanted to get fired. There was no way she could take Carter; she'd tried that before and was told not to do it again. Her high-tech company wasn't exactly family-friendly, which was going to be part of her HR pitch.

She called her best sitter, who got along well with her twelve-year-old but only got voicemail; then tried a couple of acquaintances from the neighborhood. Again, no answers. She said to herself, "*Goddammit, Drew*, and was immediately aghast that she could get pissed off at a man who had died five years ago of brain cancer, for leaving her in such a lurch.

Carter Moriarity was already dressed as usual in baggy jeans and a Falcons T-shirt. His Nike high-top shoes were on the wrong feet. He ate three strawberry Pop-Tarts, gulped down a quart of chocolate milk, and was ready to hop on the small bus that picked him up each weekday morning before Loretta drove to work. She sat her son down and slowly explained there was no school today, and she had to go to work.

"Where did the school go?" he asked.

She re-explained, "No, Carter, it's like a Saturday or Sunday today. No school for you today. I have to go to work."

"Monday. He wants to go to school."

"I know you do, but not today. I'm going to leave you alone, but I need you to stay in the house and keep the doors locked. Okay, Carter? I'll bring you a surprise later."

"He likes Ashley," Carter told his mom, who hoped she would be back home by noon or so.

"Carter, listen to me; Miss Ashley can't come over this morning. You need to stay by yourself inside for a few hours while I'm at work."

Carter nodded but started to rock a tad, which was never good. Over the last couple of years, she started leaving Carter alone, off and on, to run to the grocery store or do a few quick errands, and he seemed to do fine. But she'd never left him home alone for a half day.

"I'll call you from work this morning, so please keep your cell phone close." Carter Moriarity stared at the ceiling and told his mom, "He likes Sonic."

"Yes, Carter, I will bring you onion rings, a double cheeseburger with extra pickles on bread, not a bun, and a large Kiwi Coke slush. Carter, do you remember when we visited Yellowstone Park last summer? Show me when I get back." He grinned.

Loretta Moriarity felt guilty as hell, but she grabbed her purse and computer bag and ran back to kiss her chubby, bespectacled son on his forehead. No rocking and he was at his desk as she hoped — oblivious to all else now, including her. She locked the front door from the outside and took off to work, praying that her son would be okay for a few hours. But she knew Carter wasn't exactly the ideal latchkey kid.

Philip Hawthorne had done his reconnaissance on Friday morning by checking out the inhabitants of the three families through a variety of sources not readily available to the average Joe. He was thankful he could get this nuisance out of the way and get back to real business: trafficking drugs, laundering money, and making millions. That was the game he'd been granted.

Even a good plan could go wrong, and that morning it did – right off the bat. Roadwork on I-140 delayed him by fifteen minutes. Still, he saw what he needed. He already knew that the Baldwins' neighbors on the left were on vacation; Dr. Baldwin had the early 7:00 a.m. shift at the vet clinic; and her son was at school. He watched Loretta Moriarity walk out of the house on the right and zoom down the street like she was in a hurry. Her kid would already be off to Cumberland Academy. About fifteen minutes later, Tim Baldwin backed out of his driveway and headed to his volunteer job at HungerWorks.

Showtime.

Philip drove his nondescript, white Fred's Heat & Air van up the Baldwins' driveway to the back of their two-story home. He parked it with the backend angled to block any line of sight from the street between the Baldwins and the Moriaritys next door. Depending on a couple of factors, he figured he could be in and out in five minutes. He decided not to wear a uniform but instead jeans, boots, and a blue denim work shirt with a Braves ball cap – but added a mustache and glasses just to be careful. He opened the back of the van and pulled out the ramp.

The dogs could be in three spots: inside the house (the least preferable), on the back screened-in porch, or in the backyard, which he knew had an invisible fence because of the sign. He heard them both bark. Perfect—they were on the porch. With a simple pick, he quickly pushed up the inside hook on the screen door and dropped a couple of small pieces of meat on the landing. He lured them down the stairs, and their barking ceased as they devoured the pieces of sirloin cutlets. Unlike his sister, he got along with virtually all dogs and kidded her about her fear of canines, which she called "curs." He chided her, "It's witch pussy they hate."

The two Airedales were maybe sixty to seventy pounds, but he could tell they were house dogs, not hunters. Once they were on the driveway, he lured them with more meat onto the grass. While they ate, he went to the back of his van to get his Sig Sauer P226 with a suppressor.

It took ten seconds. *Thwack. Thwack.* One headshot per dog. No way to even hear the sounds across the street. With a small towel, he mopped up the little blood that spilled on the grass. He grabbed their front paws and backwards, dragged each of the limp bodies up the ramp, and then shut the back of the van. On his way down the driveway, he jumped out and picked the side door lock. Within twenty seconds he found the invisible fence control and loosened two wires – hoping to exacerbate the upcoming confusion.

He hopped back in the van and glanced at his watch. Five minutes on the dot. Even he was impressed. After the initial delay, the little op went well. Child's play compared to the stuff he used to pull off in Bosnia and Afghanistan. As he drove down the Baldwins' street, he called his sister. "It's done."

Pamela told him, "Excellent." She fantasized about the end game. For kicks, maybe she'd help *her Dark Lord* rid the planet of all cur breeds. Or better, make their owners do it before they were brought to slaughter. In the meantime, she was merely warming up for the Baldwins. None of her Tribe relished destroying persons-of-light more than she did. They represented the only real threats on this earth to her Dark Lord – *and* she would make *Him* proud.

Carter Moriarity loved Sam and Grant, the Baldwins' Airedales. For seven years now, the Baldwins often found him in their backyard, sitting on the ground petting the two regal dogs that were seemingly mesmerized by whatever he told them. Loretta thought about getting Carter his own dog but realized he already had two wonderful pets next door, and she didn't need the hassle of caring for another creature. Besides, the Baldwins told her many times that Carter was welcome to come over and spend time with the dogs anytime he wanted.

When the dogs started barking, Carter gave a half-twist to the closed blinds in one set of the windows in his second-story bedroom that looked out on the Baldwins' driveway and backyard.

He saw it all.

When the man left, he did exactly what his mother had told him not to do. He unlocked the front door and went outside. For the next two and a half hours, he sat alone on the grass on the spot where he usually petted his two furry friends. His body rocked back and forth like a maniacal bobblehead.

Tim found him at 11:40 a.m. He parked in his driveway and saw Carter sitting in the backyard rocking back and forth with his hands over his eyes. It wasn't unusual to see Carter in the backyard petting both Sam and Grant, but it was a school day. Why was Carter alone in his backyard? Tim raced up the porch stairs where he had left Sam and Grant nearly four hours ago. No dogs on the porch or in the yard. Maybe he forgot and left them inside. He yelled their names. They weren't inside either.

Panic gripped him as he ran back downstairs. Carter was still sitting, legs crossed, rocking, as the cool breeze freshened, and the clouds grew more ominous. "Carter, are you okay? Is your mom home?"

He said nothing and kept rocking. Tim yelled for his dogs. "Carter, did you see Sam and Grant this morning?"

Tim noticed the bite marks on his forearms. "Oh shit." He asked the boy, "Carter, did the dogs hurt you? Carter, please!"

He sprinted to the Moriarity front door; no one answered the doorbell. He tried the knob, which was unlocked, and cracked the door open. "Loretta, Loretta, are you there?" Nothing.

Tim hustled back. "Carter, where's your mom?" But the boy had escaped deeper into his own world. He might as well have been on Mars.

Tim hit his wife's number on speed dial. For a change, she picked up at work.

"Hi, babe, what's up?"

"Sam and Grant are gone," he told her.

"What do you mean, gone?" she asked with alarm in her voice.

"I mean, not here. Gone. I had them locked on the screen porch. They're nowhere I can see."

Her first inclination was to blame her husband, but she bit her tongue. As Tim stood in the driveway talking on his cell, Loretta Moriarity drove into hers. He told Sarah he'd call her back.

During a break in the presentations an hour and a half ago, Loretta had tried to call him. No answer. She didn't like it but knew Carter wasn't crazy about phones. Her presentation went well; then she tried her son on his cell immediately after it was over. No answer again, and she was worried. She made her excuses to get out of lunch and knew she was lucky not to get a speeding ticket flying back home. When she saw her neighbor waving her over, she knew there was trouble.

Tim told her he had found Carter like that a few minutes before he came home and that his dogs were gone. He had no idea where they were. Not once in the seven years they lived in their house had Sam or Grant ever run off – or certainly ever hurt anyone. Both dogs knew the precise boundaries of the electric fence. He couldn't believe they bit Carter.

Loretta knelt in front of her son on the grass. "Carter, what's the matter? Where did the dogs go, Carter?" She hadn't seen him act like that in many years. He rocked like a metronome set at high speed. His hands still covered his eyes. "Carter, let's go back to the house," but he didn't respond. Loretta told Tim, "I'll stay with him out here until he calms down. You go look for your dogs. And don't worry, your dogs didn't bite him. He bit his arms himself."

A tad relieved that his dogs hadn't hurt Carter, Tim called Sarah back and told her the situation. Again, she came within an eyelash of chastising her husband but held up. She said she'd have the gal up front call the area shelters.

"I'll post a missing dogs blurb on the Nextdoor website, then start riding around. We'll find 'em," he said. Tim walked up to his office and made another phone call. This one to Suzanne. He got her voicemail and told her that it might be nothing, but their dogs were missing. It had never happened before. He remembered she was a dog person, so he thought she might want to know.

Tim felt edgy. He heard that soft, seductive, comforting voice creep back into his head telling him, "It's okay. You'll feel so much better." He followed directions, then posted online and printed off a couple dozen simple signs with his dogs' photos. "Sam & Grant Missing, Please Call…" The first glass of vodka was gone in less than two minutes.

Sarah got off early and when she arrived home an hour later, a chill ran down her spine. She stared at Carter Moriarity, who was sitting with his mom – exactly where he always sat with Sam and Grant.

She feared this was all about Pamela Loncart.

Sarah and Tim spent the rest of the day driving and walking their Roswell neighborhood, talking to anyone who was outside. Unfortunately, it started to drizzle shortly after David arrived home from school. They went out with coats and umbrellas and rotated, with one of the three staying home in case the Airedales or someone showed up. At seven o'clock they were all hungry, wet, exhausted, and needed a break. Tim made them breakfast for dinner.

At the dinner table, David was the first to voice the unthinkable. "Do you think she took our dogs?"

Tim didn't know what to say and glanced at his wife. "It's possible."

He discovered the electric fence wasn't operating correctly, but he also knew his dogs hadn't simply wandered off.

David abruptly excused himself and left the table – with a piece of cinnamon toast, which he loved, still on his plate. Sarah started to get up and follow, but Tim gently shook his head, and she took his hint.

The front doorbell rang. The last time he heard his doorbell, it had been the Fulton County cops. They could come again if that would bring back his Airedales. His heart pounded. Please, God, let it be someone who's found them, he prayed.

It was Loretta. She stood holding a thin folder. Tears streamed down her face. "I am so, so sorry about your dogs. Carter has been in his room since we left your yard. He wouldn't even come out for dinner. He hasn't said a word about what happened."

She handed him the folder. "I found these on the floor outside his room. I gotta get back."

Tim pulled out the content and looked at the top piece of paper, which was detailed and realistic enough to be a photograph of a van parked in their driveway. A full-color drawing rendition of what Carter saw that morning from his bedroom window. Tim knew that a small percentage of autistic people were idiot savants – able to do complex math calculations in their heads or recite complete chapters of books – but he had no idea that Carter had this extraordinary artistic skill.

Indeed, Carter Moriarity could draw anything he chose to remember.

The eight intricate ink drawings showed a white van parked in the driveway in the back of their house; a man with a dark mustache and ballcap getting out of the van; the man at the top of the landing with the dogs coming out; the man throwing pieces of food to the bottom of the stairs and the dogs running down the stairs; the dogs on the grass with the man pointing a gun; the dogs laying on the grass; the man dragging their bodies up a ramp into his van; and the man stopping at the garage side door. The back of the van with the sky blue, peach, and white Georgia license plate with the black letters EYX8603 and Cobb, as in the county. Then the final ethereal drawing: the bodies of his beloved dogs floating skyward from the place they'd lain on the grass.

Sarah walked down the hallway as Tim sat on the stairs with the pictures in hand. Tears poured down his face as he told her, "They're gone. She had them killed."

Sarah looked through the drawings and didn't shed one tear. Instead, she went numb. She managed to say, "Tim, I want her to pay for what she's done to David and to our dogs."

"I know," he sobbed. Then managed, "I'm glad David didn't come down. Let's not advertise this right now."

Sarah agreed.

Wiping his face with his shirt sleeve, he said, "I'm going upstairs to make a call."

Through his tears and glazed alcohol haze, the prayer formed: *Please send an angel to help us.*

Earlier the same day

Atlanta

Suzanne listened to Tim's voicemail that the Baldwins' dogs were missing but wasn't quite sure what to make of it. She itched to play a round of golf, but the weather wasn't great, and East Lake was closed for play on Mondays. She was on pins and needles waiting to hear from Rick Waller but resisted the temptation to call him. She worked on her boards more and then called Dusty Rayfield, whom she hadn't talked to in the past couple of weeks.

"Dusty, I need you to pull the two knives used in the Monroe murders out of evidence. Nobody should care. The case is closed. Right?"

"Suzy, nice to hear your voice too."

She asked if she could take him to lunch and suggested the Atlanta Breakfast Club at 11:45 a.m.

Dusty didn't fall off the turnip truck yesterday and asked, "You're not going to try and solve the Monroe murders again, are you? Please tell me no."

"Not only that. Solve a bunch of other twins' murders as well and figure out why the hell a good kid got kicked off his lacrosse team for no reason." She did not add that she also intended to solve the mystery of her father's death.

He didn't understand all that she was talking about but smiled. He heard a voice he hadn't heard for a while. He heard the Tigress. "That's it?" he laughed. "I'll be there with bells on."

"With the knives, Deadeye."

She hung up.

At the Atlanta Breakfast Club, they enjoyed a tasty lunch. Sipping his sweet tea, Dusty listened and was intrigued by what she told him. After lunch, in the parking lot, Dusty gave her the two long hunting knives wrapped in a white cloth. She thanked him and pulled the matching pocketknife from her purse.

"See what I mean?"

He nodded. "Watch your back, Suzy. I might not be there to save your spectacular ass. But remember what's around your neck."

After returning to her condo and a long walk with Zeke, the temptation was too great. She texted Rick Waller. An hour later, he texted back. "Sorry, Suzanne, we made about sixteen dives among the four of us today. No boot, but we'll be back at it in the AM."

She shook her head. She was fucking nuts authorizing those dives to find a boot that had been underwater for eight years.

At 9:30 p.m., Tim called and said, "Suzanne, she had them killed."

She could tell he was distraught and maybe over-cocktailed. Though, she couldn't blame him. He told her about the drawings that only he, Sarah, and Loretta had seen so far.

"Take photos of each and text or email them to me. Yeah, let's keep quiet about the drawings. I wouldn't tell David right now. I'm sorry, Tim. We'll get to the bottom of all of this. I'll be back in touch tomorrow."

After the photos came through on her phone, she enlarged them on her laptop and was amazed by what the boy had drawn. She scrolled through each of the drawings several times. She enlarged one and shook her head – incredulous that the boy could draw such detail: as the man with the Braves cap and mustache pulled one of the Airedales up the ramp and into the van, the back of his wrist was exposed; on it was a black double cross.

"Fuck this bitch," Suzanne said to herself."

She sat down on her sofa with Zeke at her side. Sipping a glass of Ridge Zin, she assessed the day. She felt horrible for the Baldwins. She couldn't imagine how she'd feel if anyone took or killed Zeke. She checked in with Bernie. He told her that he hadn't found much except that the Hawthorne Industries empire was a maze of hundreds of corporations across the globe. More than he could check out. Otherwise, he found nothing new on Pamela or her twin brother Philip—or their cousin Thad. She had nothing new, either.

She put the three custom knives on her dining room table – and circled several times. What was it about the knives she couldn't put her finger on?

It was late, but she called Dusty and was glad he was still awake. She filled him in on the latest. He asked, "So, this Loncart lady. You think she would go to the trouble of having a couple of dogs killed?"

"No question."

"That's pretty sick."

"Like all else in all this sick *Game*. Hey, I'm not expecting much, but will you run a plate for me? Georgia EYX8603. I'm betting it's expired or fake but let me know."

"Will do."

Tomorrow, she planned to jump headfirst into this *Game of Twins* that Pamela Loncart and her people were playing.

Chapter 38 – The Fun

Tuesday, March 29, 2016

Roswell

Sarah had an early shift and got up a few minutes after Tim. She walked into the kitchen to warm up a cup of tea; she brought her phone and looked through her text and email messages before she went back into the master bath and started the shower. Tim reappeared from his office upstairs. Her phone was on the counter. He was loath to ever spy on anyone else's phone, even David's, but was curious if she took any good photos at Lake Lanier over the weekend. He flipped through a few of the lake in the morning from Kip's dock, including a selfie she took of them both. Inadvertently, he scrolled back further.

It was evident Dr. Bill was more than just her vet colleague.

He turned her phone off and left it exactly where he found it, back on the counter. He got it. He'd been kidding himself. The great sex the past week wasn't about him at all. It was about Doctor Bill. He grabbed a fresh glass and several cubes of ice, then returned to his office to find his hidden booze.

Their marriage was deeper in the toilet than he'd thought.

The Same Day

Alpharetta

The mail was delivered to Bernie's Pizzeria at 1:10 p.m. After the lunch rush, Bernie sat down at his desk and thumbed through a few bills, bank statements, and vendor ads. There was also a handwritten letter postmarked Kansas City, Missouri. No return address. As he sliced the envelope with his stiletto, he tried to think of who he might know there. His eyes widened, and he grinned. It was from Tony. He was alive – or at least he was on Saturday when he mailed it. He read the two pages twice. Then, combing his fingers through his thick white hair, he decided what he needed to do.

12:00 p.m. MST

Chico, Montana

It was twenty-five degrees in Chico. But the hot springs water was at eighty-seven degrees. After getting out of the big outdoor pool, Tony sat at the inside pool bar sipping a beer when the call came into his burner phone. He slid the iPhone under his towel and shoes, two empty stools down – in case the bad guys were monitoring audio or video. Only one person had his new number. He stood when he heard Bernie's voice and walked outside into the cold.

"So, I guess this means you're going to miss your shift again tonight?" Bernie asked. They both managed a laugh.

Tony reiterated what he wrote in the letter with the ominous comment, "I'm scared. They know exactly where I am. They could get rid of me anytime they want."

Bernie had to hold back his emotions. "Don't worry, I'm coming to get you, my son."

Tony smiled at the figurative nomenclature, but Bernie did not mean it figuratively at all. He'd go through hell and high water to find him and punish whoever did this.

"Be safe. I'll call you again later this evening. Stay in your hotel with other people around if you're not in your room."

"Will do. Thanks, Bernie." Tony almost said he loved him but stopped short of that declaration.

Bernie Scally needed to get to Montana ASAP. He made a phone call to a friend in town who called another friend. Then he called Suzanne and told her about Tony's letter and their call. She didn't say it, but thought, *I'm shocked he's still alive. Umm, Pamela likes teenage boys, maybe among other things?* In a strange way, that seemed to fit the bizarre puzzle perfectly. Would any of the boys be willing to come clean, she wondered? Hell, she probably had them scared shitless about ever saying anything. Or had them under a spell?

Bernie volunteered to put a 24/7 watch on David. "I've got it handled" is all that he said, and she had no reason to doubt it.

"She's a piece of work, isn't she?"

"No shit. I'm guessing her brother Philip is the one who ushered Tony out of town."

"I'm flying to Montana, leaving about six o'clock."

"Good luck. Stay in touch. Say 'hi' to Tony for me when you see him."

Suzanne called Sarah and told her, "Please don't contact Pamela or show up at the game this afternoon. I'm going to be there. Trust me on this, please."

Much remained unsaid between the two who'd recently met but already liked one another. Suzanne couldn't tell her about her plan to find out more about Pamela and crew, and she decided to let the surveillance go unmentioned – at least until Tony was okay. Sarah couldn't tell her about what was going on between her, Tim, and Bill and their family issues.

"Sarah, I'm going to sort it out. I'm going to get David back on the team. Bernie is going to get Tony back. Pamela is going down. Okay, Sarah?"

"With no hesitation, she said, "Okay. Tim said you were our angel. I trust you. We trust you."

Suzanne clicked off. The steely determination to always finish the job, which she had learned from her dad, kicked in: *They're not getting away with any of this. None of it. I promise, Daddy.*

Chapter 39 – The Photojournalist

The Same Day, 4:00 p.m. – Game Time

Roswell

Suzanne arrived twenty minutes before face-off with her Nikon and telephoto lens. She scanned the lacrosse field and small crowd and was relieved not to see any of the Baldwins. But no Pamela.

The fifty or so boys ran their pregame drills – the Eagles in their gold and black and the Knights in their blue and white. She was able to snatch a one-page program that featured the player names and numbers. She was only interested in Dex, Dax, Lance, Randy, Bryce, and Kevin. She roamed the far sideline, getting the lay of the land and taking dozens of shots of the field, crowd, and players.

Just before the face-off, Pamela arrived and stood on the sideline with the coach. Suzanne took a couple dozen photos of her: the DEA agent; chairwoman of the current Eaglewood Lacrosse Club; future queen of the Pecan Valley Lacrosse Clubs; mistress of her own teenage sex club that included her own twins; and Suzanne believed, stone-cold murderer of the Monroes and others.

Looking through her telephoto lens, she had to admit that the woman was beautiful. Flowing auburn hair, great figure, perfect face, partially hidden by sunglasses, and the black cross necklace. She walked to the far side, taking more photos of the game, then back around the Eaglewood goal.

Pamela Loncart was taught how and what to observe. She noticed the tall woman across the field taking pictures. No lacrosse mom she'd ever seen. After the game, the woman walked toward her and introduced herself. Pamela couldn't remember seeing such a gorgeous creature. Her ethnicity, she wasn't sure. Asian with a darker complexion. Pamela also noticed, not that it made a difference, no wedding ring. Instead, a beautiful diamond and emerald ring complemented by a matching jeweled cross necklace, which unfortunately would block any of her powers. Before she could open her mouth, Pamela was smitten.

She stuck out her hand. "Mrs. Loncart, my name is Natalie Myers. I wonder if I could have a couple minutes of your time?"

"What can I do for you, Miss Myers?"

"Please call me Natalie. I'm a photojournalist and do freelance writing about the Atlanta sports scene. I'm doing a piece about the growth and popularity of lacrosse in Atlanta. As the newly appointed head of the boys' and girls' lacrosse clubs at Pecan Valley, I'm sure you would have an interesting perspective."

Pamela slowly took off her ubiquitous sunglasses and smiled. "Word gets around fast about my involvement at Pecan Valley High, which I'm looking forward to. Natalie, are you a fan of lacrosse?"

She smiled, "There was this boy I knew a long time ago who played. It's a great game. I like most sports, and lacrosse seems to be the up-and-comer."

Pamela asked, "How about dinner tomorrow evening at my place, and we can talk more. Under two conditions."

Suzanne waited to hear what was coming next.

"Your article can include as many photographs of this lacrosse game as you want, but none of me. And two, I can approve your article before it's published."

"Ah, but you are such a beautiful woman," Suzanne said as seductively as she could. "Okay, no pictures of you in the article, I promise. For sure, I'll let you read my piece first."

"Splendid. Give me your card, and I'll text you about tomorrow.

I'm Pamela, by the way." She extended her perfectly manicured hand with alternating black and gold nails.

"Thank you, Pamela. See you tomorrow." As she released her handshake, she made a point of lightly grazing her hand with her fingertips. Then gave her "Natalie's" business card.

Suzanne grinned as she walked away. It had been a while since a woman flirted with her, but there was no question she'd piqued Pamela's interest. Now, she had to figure out how to catch Pamela at her own game.

In the parking lot before climbing into her car, Suzanne let temptation win out. No news was probably bad news since she hadn't heard from him yet, but Suzanne called Rick Waller – instead of texting.

"Suzanne, sorry, I was about to call you. We got in a little late after our last dives today."

"You didn't find the boot, did you?"

"No, ma'am. I'm sorry, we didn't. If you want your money back, we all agreed to oblige."

Bummed, shaking her head at herself for trying to win the lottery, she paused, then said, "No, you guys did what I asked. You find any pirates' treasure?"

"We found a couple of pretty good watches, a bracelet, and what I think's a real diamond and ruby ring. You paid for 'em. They're yours if you want 'em."

"No, Rick. They're yours."

"We also found a bunch of Civil War artifacts. Maybe the coolest thing we found was a knife."

"An old knife?"

"Well, no, I don't think so. It's a stone-handled knife with a serrated edge, maybe used as a diver's knife."

Suzanne gasped and tried not to get too excited. "Could you text me a couple photos of it?"

"Sure."

"Thanks again, Rick."

She was about to try the Baldwins again before leaving the park when the text came through. She enlarged one of the photos.

Its steel needed shining, but it was a straight knife with the same type of handle and the black double cross – like the Monroe killers' knives and the pocketknife Edith had given her.

She called him back. "Hey, Rick, the small initials at the bottom of the blade; JRH. It was made in Santa Fe, New Mexico, years ago. Do you see it?"

"Yep. It's there."

He didn't have a chance to ask how she knew that before she chimed in, "Rick, all I want is the knife. And I'll pay you another grand. Deal?"

"Yes, ma'am. Sounds good."

"Rick, one more question. My father's blue life vest, I forgot to ask you. It was on his little fishing boat, right, when you got there, and not in the water?"

"Yep, it was on the deck with his personal stuff. Unsnapped like maybe he never put it on."

She smiled. "Thanks, Rick."

Even though it was lost forever at the bottom of Lake Lanier, her dad's boot would never be found. Suzanne knew that. She looked up to the heavens: I'm going after him now, Daddy. I know who got you killed. I knew you never went near any water without your vest on. Sheriff Giles knew that, too. Another friend lied about it.

In the struggle to drown him, her father likely tried to grab the knife. It dropped to the bottom, where it had sat for eight years. No coincidence. He wasn't stabbed, but he was murdered. Then, the murderer left the vest on the boat. Very smart.

She was convinced her father's murder was related to the other murder cases – and what had happened to David and Tony. The only problem was she couldn't prove anything about any of these crimes. What she did know was that the gloves were coming off. She was sure that her dad would approve.

It was time to take things into her own hands.

It was time to go Old Testament.

On her way back to town, she called Dusty and said, "Where are you?"

"Drink'n a beer at the Buckhead Saloon. You find the boot?"

"Nope, even better. A matching knife. The exact same handle design as the Monroe knives and the one the principal gave me. I know my dad was murdered, and I know who was involved. His murder, all the twins' murders, and this lacrosse mess in Roswell – they're all related. I'm one hundred percent sure of that, but proving it is another matter. But I need another favor, Deadeye. A cell number and any other cell numbers and addresses attached to it."

When she told him the name, he spit beer from his mouth. "You're kidd'n me, right Suzy?"

"No. He and I need to have a chat. Get whatever current contact info you can."

She hung up before he could invite her for a drink. On his barstool, Dusty took big swig of Bud, then said out loud, "Holy fucking shit!"

Chapter 40 – The Hitmen

Wednesday, 12:30 a.m., March 30, 2016

Bozeman-Yellowstone International Airport – Bozeman, Montana

After talking to Tony six hours earlier, Bernie Scally boarded a Bombardier Challenger 350 at DeKalb-Peachtree. He was the only passenger. Two thousand miles later, he arrived at the sleepy Bozeman airport, where it was fifty-five degrees colder than when he left Atlanta. He wore a thick wool sweater, black leather jacket, black cap, black gloves, and black boots – and, of course, his black eyepatch. All rental car agencies were closed, but outside the terminal, a black Mercedes was waiting for him. He put his small bag and flat, long, rigid case in the back seat. An unknown man in dark clothes handed him the keys, then jumped in an identical car and was gone.

Bernie had caught a little shuteye on the flight but was dog-tired. It seemed colder than he was used to in New York and New Jersey back in the day – or maybe he'd turned into a spoiled pussy living in Atlanta for so long. Thankfully, he was mentally keyed up enough to drive east on Interstate 90 and then turn onto Highway 89 South toward the resort in Pray, Montana.

It was like he was traversing another planet. For a half hour, he saw dozens more elk than he saw cars. He almost ran over a family of raccoons scurrying across the highway. He was sure the snowy landscape was beautiful in the daylight, but at nighttime, it was starkly and primordially grand.

After getting onto Highway 540, he almost missed the turn onto Chico Road. It was utterly dark, but the moonlight glare off the snow made headlights nearly unnecessary. Only a few more minutes on the two-lane road until he'd reach the Chico Hot Springs Resort & Spa.

The resort was a laid-back getaway in Old Chico (population 15), adjacent to Pray, Montana, population, 681 – yet not far off the beaten path between Bozeman and Gardiner, the north entrance to Yellowstone National Park. It included a sprawling two-story, white-with-green-trim, green tin-roofed main building, plus a newer rustic lodge, separate cabins, chalets, and cottages, all with their hip, western ambiance. Wildly popular during the summer and early fall, the resort was also a hidden gem in the winter where you could ride horses, cross-country ski, snowshoe, and even dogsled – if you weren't touring Yellowstone, forty-five minutes away. Many simply chose to indulge in the large indoor and outdoor natural hot springs pools, blanketed by steam in the cold weather. The adjacent, informal saloon provided plenty of entertainment for guests and others who visited for the day. The resort wasn't fancy, but it was priced to keep out the riffraff.

1:30 a.m., Wednesday, March 30

Chico Hot Springs Resort & Spa – Old Chico, Montana

No sign of anyone or anything outdoors when Bernie Scally arrived at the resort. There were several snow-covered spots available in the lot about fifty yards from the main lodge. He looked at the Chico website and knew Tony was staying on the second floor of Warren's Wing, attached to the main lodge. As he cut across the grounds to the alternate entry at the far end of the wing, the only sounds he heard were coyotes in the distance and his boots crunching the top crust of half a foot of snow. Using the burner phone, he called Tony. He could tell he'd woken him up.

"Down in a minute."

When Tony opened the exterior door dressed only in jeans, Bernie couldn't help himself. He hugged the young man hard and said, "Thank God."

Bernie needed a few hours of sleep but wanted to be out of the hotel before daybreak. He insisted that he sleep in the chair and that Tony get back in the bed. Years ago, he learned to nap almost anywhere, in any position for any period. Always with a gun and a knife in his lap, he would listen for the unexpected. But he didn't want to further alarm Tony, so he kept the bag by his side. It carried his fully loaded .357, switchblade, and dopp kit. Within two minutes, both men were asleep.

Two Days Earlier

Denver, Colorado

When Philip Hawthorne called on Monday afternoon, Orrin Dean was dropping off his oldest daughter, Michelle, at Cherry Creek High School in Denver. After letting her out, he listened to Philip's request. It wasn't typical, but then, nothing was typical in his line of work. His first inclination was to turn it down, but he'd been a little stir-crazy cooped up in his six thousand-square-foot home, and he'd always wanted to see Yellowstone with snow. The job wouldn't be dangerous, but it could prove challenging given the parameters Philip laid out. He agreed to the standard, no-frills rate of $300,000 plus expenses – the same rate he'd received for the judge in Atlanta last year who failed to play ball and was found floating in his swimming pool and ruled an accidental drowning. Philip told him the money would be in his Grand Cayman account within the next five minutes. And it was.

5:00 a.m., Wednesday, March 30

Chico Hot Springs Resort & Spa

Bernie stirred at 5:00 a.m., got up, and hit the john. He felt a lot better; his body fueled by adrenaline; it was like old times. Tony was still zonked, so he gave him a few more minutes. An old instinct told Bernie to get moving. He woke Tony up and waited until he was vertical. "Take a quick shower if you want. But let's get moving in ten minutes."

Bernie's tone told him not to dally. After a one-minute shower, Tony felt better. He got his bag and began stuffing his clothes in it but forgot the iPhone was wrapped inside a shirt in the drawer. It tumbled to the floor.

"Jeez, I'm sorry."

Bernie put a finger to his lips and took the iPhone from his hands. He stuffed it in one of Tony's gloves on the bed and put the bag on top. "No big deal." But he knew that a doctored smartphone could be a big deal.

Orrin Dean jumped out of his bed when he heard a bang and Santucci's voice. *Sorry for what? Was he talking to someone?* Orrin wondered. He was staying in the one-story Fisherman's Lodge, perched on the hill overlooking the other Chico Resort buildings. He chose it mainly because it was separate, and he could keep an eye out without Santucci ever noticing him.

He walked outside in the dark in his long johns, shirt, and boots – and heard nothing – but didn't like it. Didn't pass his smell test. In two minutes, he was packed, out the door, and into his Lexus parked ten paces away. He rechecked his iPhone GPS. All copasetic. He took the winding drive down around the horse stable and headed down the gravel drive past the front entrance. He had toured the whole place on foot yesterday and knew he could park back behind the saloon. If nothing happened in the next twenty minutes, he would drive back up the hill and climb back into his warm bed. He rechecked the GPS app. Santucci's car hadn't moved, and the second tracker showed him still in his room. He got out of his Lexus, quietly shut the door, and positioned himself for a decent angle to see the main lot and the lobby entrance.

But then the GPS app lit up, indicating that Tony was on the move. At the same time, a man dressed in black appeared from the wooden walkway bordering the small lobby. With purpose, the husky man wearing an eyepatch and carrying a small bag walked toward the main lot. He used his automatic key to open the door of a Mercedes sedan. Before getting in, Eyepatch turned and did a slow three-sixty scan of his sight line. Orrin ducked behind the edge of the saloon. Eyepatch sat in the car for a couple of minutes and then drove to the front of the small lobby, which was now blocking most of Orrin's view, and got out of the Mercedes. Tony came out the door and Orrin could see him hand Eyepatch something. Eyepatch dropped it on the gravel and smashed it with his boot. The iPhone went dead. He walked back toward the main lot and threw the remnants into the snowy brush.

Orrin didn't wait to see more. He eased back behind the saloon toward his car and made an executive decision.

Chico Road went through a valley, relatively straight, but with shallow ups and downs. The moonlight reflected off the covered hills on the left and pastureland on the right. Bernie told Tony to accelerate until he got to sixty.

"Okay, what's going on, Bernie?"

Bernie didn't answer the question. He asked, "Is the car behind gaining?" Tony checked his rearview mirror.

"Yes. Shouldn't you be driving?"

"Drive."

Bernie knew this was a dangerous game, and they were quickly running out of runway – but figured it was his best play. He popped his head up enough to look out the back window. Less than a hundred yards separated them from the rapidly approaching vehicle.

He told Tony, "I'm going to open the back window on your side. No matter what happens, keep driving." He hit the automatic button, and it was like they both walked into windy Antarctica.

Then came the shots from Orrin Dean's Glock 18, fully automatic pistol, which he angled out of his Lexus driver's window, peppering the Mercedes' backlights and panel. He aimed for the tires first and missed, then moved closer. The next burst came from forty yards away and shattered the top of the back windshield, most bullets grazing over the hood. Bernie yelled, "Faster! Go!"

"Fuck," Dean grunted after his second volley missed its driver's side target. He considered accelerating alongside and firing horizontally through his passenger side window but stayed behind. He grabbed the other fully loaded Glock 18 from his passenger seat and, with his left hand, edged it out into the bone-chilling cold. Dean hit the gas harder and figured, worst case, the Mercedes would careen off the road, about a fifteen-foot drop. If that didn't kill them, he'd need to clean up any mess to make sure they were both dead. But better here than the upcoming Highway 540 or I-90. Not his precise plan, but that's the way it worked out sometimes. The guy who paid him, Philip Hawthorne, only cared about results. Eyepatch couldn't drive and shoot backward with any accuracy. Santucci would be worthless in a firefight like this.

But then, what he hadn't foreseen.

A long gun jutted out from the driver's side back window of the Mercedes and pointed directly at him. Eyepatch wasn't driving. There was no time to react. The M16 volley shattered the front windshield of the Lexus and hit Orrin Dean in the face. His foot suddenly off the gas, the Lexus spun like a helicopter firecracker and went airborne; it flipped when it hit the snow-covered ground and then erupted into a fireball.

"Go, go!" he yelled at Tony.

"Holy shit, Bernie!"

As he turned onto Highway 540, Tony held the steering wheel with a death grip so that his hands would not shake.

Wednesday, March 30, 2016

Roswell

Sarah wasn't looking forward to going to work even if it would keep her mind off David and Tim. Bill was back on the schedule, and she had no idea what to do when she saw him. She put her stuff in her locker and then went to the break room. As she put her lunch bag in the fridge, there was a hand on her ass. She almost jumped out of her shoes and spun around.

"Hey, baby, I missed you. I missed you a whole lot." His hand went between her legs. She shoved it away.

"What's the matter, Beautiful?"

In no mood, she lost it. "I'll tell you what the fucking matter is. My son is still crushed by the lacrosse fiasco getting kicked off his team. My dogs were shot and killed in my backyard. My husband's a nice guy, but he's a drunk who isn't making any money. And me? I'm fucking a guy I shouldn't be fucking. What could be the matter?"

Bill backed off two steps with his palms up. "Hey, sorry. Thought you'd be happy to see me again." He left without another word.

Sarah seethed with anger. He had no idea.

Bernie Scally made only one phone call before taking off from Bozeman on the same private jet that brought him – the return trip, this time with him and one other passenger. He filled her in on the events in Montana. After listening, her thought was: this thing is escalating, but we're getting closer.

Bernie told her, "Suzanne, I never got a good look at the guy, but no doubt he was a pro. It was kill or be killed. Maybe it was the guy who sent Tony out of town? He was dead before his car blew up. Probably a crispy critter – hard to identify, at least for a while. You might want to check your sources to see if there was anything reported out of that part of Montana."

Suzanne thought to herself: *"Wow, that would be awesome if Bernie had taken out Philip Hawthorne"*.

"I could have stashed Tony out of town, but maybe he can be of help," Bernie said. "Got a friend who has a nice condo in a Buckhead-high rise. He'll make sure nothing happens to Tony, who will be on friendly house arrest with no phone allowed."

"Sounds good. And we both know the Baldwins don't need to know about this now. The best way for us to figure this out is to work together, right?"

He liked her style. "Yes, ma'am."

"I got invited to the Loncart estate this evening. Using my alias. I'll see what I can learn."

Bernie's tone changed. "Suzanne, these people are as cold-blooded as the ones I used to run with. Or worse. You gotta be careful. Call me later, okay?"

"Will do."

"If you don't, I'll have a small army sent to her place."

"Thanks, Bernie. I can handle it. I'll call you later."

Part VI - The Battle

Chapter 41 – The Hunger

7:30 p.m., Wednesday, March 30, 2016

The Loncart Estate – Roswell

Suzanne used Google Satellite to get a lay of the land in and around the Loncart Estate. On a bluff above the Chattahoochee, it was mega compared to other properties nearby: the large house with a clay tile roof; a rectangular, manicured sports field on one side and what looked like a large indoor and outdoor pool; and a long tree-lined drive entrance. The Google Street View showed little.

Suzanne was acutely aware of the peril she was courting with her fabricated identity, complete with a counterfeit Georgia driver's license ID, false plates on her Honda, bogus business cards, and even a sham website. This elaborate ruse had always served her well in past investigations, fooling the unsuspecting with ease. But Pamela was a different breed.

It was another warm March day, so Suzanne wore as little as possible. A short taupe skirt with a tight, white spaghetti strap top. No lingerie. A taupe linen jacket tossed over her arm. That was it, except for her favorite cross necklace. Her long black hair was blown out two hours before. She was ready. The evening would require channeling her best Marilyn Monroe, whom she'd always admired. She had no grand plan in mind, at least yet. Suzanne needed to learn anything that could help take Pamela down. Whatever it took.

The tall rod iron gate – with the Loncart emblem on one side – opened automatically. She parked her car to the right of the front entrance. A tall, slender black man dressed in brilliant white greeted her with a friendly but formal tone. "Good evening, Miss Myers. I'm Tariq. Please follow me. Mrs. Loncart is waiting for you."

♰♰

The indoor-outdoor pool was unlike anything she'd ever seen. Huge glass doors opened to the main twenty-five-meter pool and an open retractable roof. The queen of the estate stood and smiled. "Ah, Natalie, how good of you to come." She took Suzanne's hands with both of hers and said, "Please, sit."

Pamela had a hard time not staring. This exotic woman was no doubt a gift from her Dark Lord. She'd never seen or touched a more sensual female. Her sexy attire and eyes indicated mutual interest. With her cross necklace on, though, it was a pity she wouldn't be able to divine more. But tonight, that mattered little.

"Here, let me pour you my specialty cocktail. Belvedere vodka and Plantation rum, with a touch of nutmeg and a twist of lime. An old family recipe." She smiled as she handed Suzanne the drink. "Tell me about yourself."

Instead of a complete fabrication, Suzanne decided to tell parts of it straight and see if she'd get any reaction: "I grew up in Buckhead when it wasn't so outrageously expensive and went to public schools in the city and college at Spelman. Dad was a cop. Mom was a teacher. I once thought that I wanted to follow in my father's footsteps, but well, things happen. Both of my parents died much too young. I was married once but have no children. I'm not a person of your means. I barely scrape by with my photography and writing but enjoy both."

Pamela asked, "You are such a beautiful woman. I'm curious. What is your lineage?"

"My father was black. His great-grandfather and two generations before him were slaves on a plantation outside of Roanoke, Virginia. My mother was second-generation Chinese. My grandparents emigrated from the province of Jiangsu when she was three years old."

"Such a stunning combination."

She asked, "Pamela, what about you and your family?"

"My princes, my twins, Dex and Dax, you saw playing on the Eaglewood lacrosse team. I expect them to blossom next year at Pecan Valley High with a new coach and better resources. With injuries and other unfortunate events, it's been a tough lacrosse season that will be forgotten."

She debated saying more but added, "I was in law enforcement for many years and now do some consulting. My husband was killed in the line of duty. My twin brother is a successful businessman in Woodstock. My aunt is in Atlanta – we are quite close-knit – and my uncle lives in the city. Their sons, my cousins, were accomplished lacrosse players in their day. I lost my parents in a plane crash when I was a teenager. I'd appreciate it, though, if you could keep my personal details out of your article.

"Absolutely. Strictly lacrosse – and you get to review and approve it before it's published."

Pamela smiled and suggested, "How about a swim before dinner, Natalie? I'll go check on Tariq about dinner."

"Sounds wonderful," Suzanne fibbed but would go along; she was starting to get a vibe on Pamela.

"There are suits in the bathhouse. Take your pick. *If* you need one. Totally optional on the premises."

There were plenty of sexy suits to choose from, but she decided to push the envelope.

On a remote video feed into her downstairs office, Pamela watched her exquisite guest remove her heels, skirt, and top as she walked back out to the pool, put a toe in the water, and then walked in from the shallow end. Naked, she was even more spectacular.

The saltwater was comfortably warm, and stars filled the skies.

Under different circumstances, it would have been a perfect romantic evening, but not this one.

Also nude, except for her black necklace, Pamela walked toward the pool. She strode in and inched toward Suzanne until her breasts were close enough to nudge the bottom of Suzanne's. She mashed her boobs into her guest's as her hands gripped her ass. Their tongues danced as Pamela's hands reached between her legs underwater. Suzanne let herself be fondled but then gently broke their embrace and said, "Pamela, you are more beautiful than any woman I've ever seen or known in my life, but can we take this a little more slowly? I've always wanted to, but I've never been with another woman." Then kissed her tenderly on the lips.

Pamela wished she knew more about what was going on in Natalie's pretty head but smiled back, "I apologize for being so forward. Why don't you get dried off and back into your clothes. We'll talk more at dinner so that you can prepare your article."

Suzanne didn't bother with a shower and was dressed in two minutes. Tariq appeared and told her, "Mrs. Loncart will be back downstairs in about fifteen minutes. May I get you anything, Miss Myers?"

"No, thank you. Would it be okay if I wandered around a bit to see this beautiful home?"

"That would be fine, Miss Myers. Go anywhere you'd like."

Back in the kitchen, he rang Pamela to let her know.

The stone-tile hallway branched two ways. She took the right fork. Stark but stunning, the interior was in black and white with streaks of red. Twenty feet down the hallway was a big-screen digital mural framed in red, with slowly changing black and white images. Two boys, her twins, in their lacrosse gear. Another of them, each kissing her cheek. A teen beauty flanked by a handsome boy. It had to be a young Pamela. With her brother Philip? A man and a woman, maybe forties, both gorgeous. Her parents? The teen girl with the older man; yes, her father. Then, one with her mother. A photo of Pamela more recently with her arm around a tall man about her age. Philip again? Then same tall man with his arm around another dark, good-looking man. She gasped. One was clearly an older Thad Sutterland.

She was in the belly of the beast.

More images kept sliding by as she heard Pamela's voice. Pamela found her. "Ah, there you are, admiring my family." She was now wearing skin-tight black pants, a gold top that accentuated her cleavage, and stiletto gold heels.

"Are you hungry, Natalie?"

"I'm starving!"

Pamela took her by the hand as they walked into the dining room.

The dining room was small but perfectly decorated like the rest of her home. A Southwestern red woven rug covered much of the black stone floor. The oval table, itself a two-inch slab of shiny rock, was adorned with red roses and set for two. But what caught her eye were the place settings. Brilliant white cloth napkins and shiny black wooden utensils paired with gleaming steak knives; knives with white handles adorned with the black double cross – as on the other knives – she was all too familiar with.

Tariq seated her across from Pamela. Hers were the most striking eyes she'd ever seen—pitch black with irises scintillating swirls of black crystals. Behind them, Suzanne knew there was Evil like none other.

The dinner was to die for. Marinated, thinly sliced bison cooked rare with a piece of grilled pompano in lime and olive oil, a Caesar salad with heavenly anchovies, mushroom buttons, and home-baked bread. Suzanne asked a few general lacrosse questions about Pamela's Eaglewood team and her plans for lacrosse at Pecan Valley. Pamela okayed her mentioning a large (non-specific amount) contribution to the Pecan Valley SportsPlex that would be built and should be open by the end of next year.

Suzanne debated asking – then went ahead. "Pamela, your beautiful black cross necklace is quite extraordinary. I also see the cross on the steak knives – and your front gate. Is there a story behind it?"

Pamela wished she could listen in on Suzanne's thoughts – but her brilliant cross necklace precluded that. She didn't see the harm: "Yes, it's a kind of emblem that has been in the family since the 1600s. A colorful old wives' tale about an ancestor accused of witchcraft – and that the unique cross was hers."

"Fascinating," replied Suzanne. She decided not to press for more – but she didn't think it was a wives' tale.

The dessert was a key lime pie with raspberries, dabs of chocolate, and thick whipped cream. Then Tariq brought demitasses of espresso and Fonseca port. They chatted more about lacrosse in Atlanta, other sports, clothes, fashion, and even current events.

Pamela couldn't keep her eyes off her; her hunger for Natalie Myers was growing, but she realized she'd have to complete her conquest another evening. At 10:30 p.m., Pamela walked her guest to the front door. Suzanne figured a peck on the cheek wasn't going to cut it. She leaned down slightly and planted her lips on Pamela's, then her hands were on Pamela's derrière, her breasts, and between her legs. They groped like two unbridled teenagers. Suzanne moaned, "I can't wait to see you again."

6

Inside her car, Suzanne wiped her mouth with a Kleenex and couldn't wait to get home to gargle several times and take a shower to clean off the stench of Pamela Loncart. She then fantasized about plunging each of the custom steak knives through her black eyes.

Pamela, by contrast, went to her bedroom and flicked on a full-color video of their escapades in the pool and Natalie in the dressing room. She was glued to the big screen that showed the spectacular woman. Her Dark Lord knew of her hunger.

Philip texted her again, so she called him. "Yes, my dear, what's up? Tony thing done?"

"It appears he's gone. Vanished."

"How's that possible?" she said with both surprise and alarm.

"His two GPS signals went off the grid, and so did Orrin's. I found out this evening that there was an accident not far from the Montana resort where he was staying. One man was dead in a burned-up Lexus. Not sure yet, but Orrin would have contacted me. I told Tony in no uncertain terms that his failure to play ball might be detrimental to David, his boss, and anyone else he knew, but apparently, those warnings weren't good enough. I'm thinking the dead man is Orrin. I'll get a guy to Montana tomorrow morning to see what is known."

"Come on, Philip, you're telling me Tony, who makes pizzas and coaches kids lacrosse, got the drop on one of the top assassins on the planet?"

He hated to admit it, but he had no other explanation. "Maybe. With help. It was no accident."

"That's troubling, my dear." She paused. "But hardly cataclysmic.

Tony's story is hearsay anyway." She did not add but thought, *"Unless one of my lacrosse club boys corroborates it.* That would be another possibility she'd try to head off.

"Please find him soon and get rid of him once and for all."

"Okay, sis."

Math was not her strong suit, but driving back to Midtown from Roswell, Suzanne tried to do the simple addition and subtraction in her head – and almost wrecked her car driving down Peachtree. She couldn't wait until she got home. She pulled into a Shell station and used her phone to do a few simple calculations. The digital photographs at Pamela's had pointed her in an interesting direction. Pamela could pass for thirty-two, but Suzanne supposed she could be ten years older. Pamela and her twin brother Philip, and Thad and his twin brother, her cousins, were all about her same age. The two sets of twins could have been born in 1973 or 1974, the years that the Blount and Haverford twins were murdered. Pamela's twins, Dex and Dax, were maybe fourteen, so they were born about 2002. The year the Oosterhuis twins were murdered.

She did a few quick Google searches and, within five minutes, had the answer to her central question: yes, Thad had twin girls, Martha and Marla, by his third marriage. They were one year old. The Monroe twins were murdered after the births of Thad's twins. In this *Game of Twins*, with the birth of twins, beautiful teen twins were sacrificed. That would explain the time gaps.

Sitting in her car, she shook her head. No one would believe her. Well, maybe one person, but she couldn't tell him yet. She checked in with Bernie to let him know she was okay but reiterated that he needed to keep a close eye on Tony and David. She was gaining ground on Pamela and her band of murderers but couldn't prove any of it.

On the way to her bedroom, she first stopped at her Boardroom and meandered in and out of the large, rolling bulletin boards, pausing periodically to read a bit or stare at the photographs. What was she missing?

She stood in front of the horrible Monroe crime scene photos, trying not to grimace but instead sensing a peaceful presence. Lilting apparitions of the two beautiful twins approached her from the doorway.

It was the third time she'd seen apparitions within the last year. This time, they seemed even more extraordinary, more luminous. Maybe more hopeful? Each took a hand as they guided her to the closet, then opened their free hands, seemingly indicating she should look inside. They both smiled and then they were gone.

She wasn't sure how long she stood in front of her closet door before she slid it completely open. Nothing inside got her attention. It was emptier because the boards were set up in the room. Her winter clothes, seldom worn dresses and gowns, and other clothes hung on the back and two sides. A large rack of shoes and several boxes of miscellaneous stuff on the shelf above them. She had to get on the top step of her ladder to check out the top shelf. There was another box that had been pushed toward the back. She could barely reach it but finally inched it forward and managed to walk it down.

She used a box cutter from her desk to slice the tape. The heavy box contained several of her dad's beautiful agates, a few raw stones, and others cut, wrapped in old newspaper, like Christmas ornaments. At the bottom were four of the old wooden boxes her dad had collected. She put three boxes on the desk, then pulled out a fourth. It was slender and maybe a foot long – and made of sleek, black ebony. She slid the top off and opened it. There was nothing inside, but the box seemed too heavy not to contain something. She examined it more carefully. There was a faint line across the exterior of the short side. She tried sliding the panel sideways. Didn't work. Then, after fumbling around with it more, she applied pressure and slid the panel down and the top off. The box had a false bottom. The contents were coiled in a soft white cloth.

When she removed the cloth, her blood ran cold.

Confirmation linking all the mysteries in her Board Room: Thad's switchblade with the same onyx white handle and the Loncart cross. The handle that she'd never been able to see in her nightmares was in her hands. She pressed the release button, flinging open the sharp, shiny steel that had tormented her dreams for twenty years. She'd only ever seen shiny steel blades.

She scrambled to find a recorder and then listened to the microcassette that was also in the black box. She had to smile while her dad's old buddies beat the shit out of Thad and made him whimper like a baby. Then, Thad's reluctant apology. She knew it was no coincidence. She was in the vortex of past and present, life and death, good and evil.

An evil that led straight to Pamela Loncart.

Chapter 42 – The Gossip

Thursday, March 31, 2016

Atlanta

Suzanne arose early and well-rested and took Zeke for a three-mile run before the sun was completely up. With the five knives lying on her dining room table, she ate a breakfast of oatmeal, blueberries, and coffee – then attacked her Board Room, trying to make more sense of what was before her.

She looked at her timeline again and was even more sure of the connection between the twins' murders and the births of twins in the Loncart-Hawthorne-Sutterland clan. But while walking around her boards, she became increasingly frustrated. She had five knives made by the same guy in Santa Fe. Two were used in the Monroe murders, which were linked to five other sets of twins' murders. The switchblade was used in her attempted rape. The diving knife was owned by her father's murderer. The pocketknife was given by Pamela to a lacrosse kid she was molesting. Plus, she saw two other knives last night while dining with Pamela. All still circumstantial. No hard evidence. Nothing. Tony's hearsay would help, but she needed a lot more. She didn't care how she got it.

She got an idea and called Sarah. It went to voicemail. She called her husband Tim and asked, "What if we play a game with Pamela—and rock her world?"

"How?"

He listened and smiled broadly. "Absolutely. How can I help?"

"Which lacrosse mom would be most willing to talk with Tony in person; and then most apt to gossip; and most likely to warn Pamela about Tony?"

"Lana Cheney. So, Tony's okay?" Tim asked.

"He's fine, but neither of you can mention that, especially to David. Not right now."

"Got it."

Suzanne called Tony's bodyguard, Gus. "Lemme talk to him a minute." He came on the phone. "Tony, how would you like to get a bit of fresh air?"

Tony had been cooped up in the Buckhead condo for the past twenty-four hours and was glad to get out. Bernie's guy, Gus DiSalvo, parked a block and a half away, and Tony walked up to the two-story brick Colonial in the heart of Roswell suburbia, only a few blocks from the Baldwins. If Lana wasn't home, they'd go to Plan B.

He rang the doorbell and immediately heard a dog barking. She grabbed her inbred golden retriever by the collar and opened the door.

"Hi, Mrs. Cheney. Could I have a few minutes of your time?"

The pixyish, plump mom peeked her head out. The dog barked louder and bared his teeth. "Hold on, let me stash him in the bedroom."

He remained standing outside on the top step until she returned.

"Sorry about Freddie. He's not real crazy about strange men. Coach Tony, what would you like to talk about?"

"Bryce," he said flatly.

With a little frown furrowing her forehead, she opened the door for him and led him into the dining room.

"Can I get you anything?" She invited him to take a seat.

"No, thanks. I'm good."

"What about Bryce?"

"Mrs. Cheney, I think your son and other boys on the Eaglewood lacrosse team are being sexually abused."

She shook her head in disbelief. "What? Good Lord, by whom?" He heard the alarm in her voice and saw her eyes widen.

"Pamela Loncart."

He let that sink and then told her, "I overheard her sons along with Lance, Randy, Kevin, and Bryce, talking about having sex with her. You know they go over there a lot, and you've seen the extra stuff she gives them. Like they're her pets."

"Well, she's apparently quite wealthy and generous. I've picked up Bryce and others from her place a few times. She calls it her estate. It's immense. I hardly know her, but I can't imagine she'd ever do anything like that."

"Mrs. Cheney, I'm telling you what I heard. If you could maybe keep him away from her house, that's what I'd recommend. Ask him about what goes on there. Bryce or one of the others needs to come forward."

She pondered but had no reply.

"I'll show myself out. Thanks, Mrs. Cheney."

Lana sat in her kitchen. Pamela was a super-sexy, gorgeous woman. She wasn't that naïve; she could understand why Pamela would be attractive to males of any age. She knew that Bryce was on porn sites too often; he did go over there a lot and kept coming home with new things. Like it was Christmas every month, he never talked about Mrs. Loncart. Could what Coach Tony said be true? She had a hard time believing it. She wondered if he had spoken to any of the other parents. She forgot to ask.

In her last email to parents, Mrs. Loncart said she was going to head up the high school lacrosse teams next year and pay all expenses, including extra coaching and camps. Lana didn't want to interfere with Bryce's lacrosse. She hemmed and hawed for a few minutes, then sent a short email since she didn't have her cell number. She wrote to Pamela that Tony had stopped by her house unannounced and told her disturbing things that sounded farfetched – but she wanted her to at least know.

She picked up her cell to call Eileen Westerman about the news, but she didn't want to piss off Mrs. Loncart by spreading a story that probably wasn't true. Lana put her phone back on the dining room table – despite yearning to use it in the worst way.

Back in the Mercedes, Tony sat in the back seat with Suzanne. She'd heard their conversation on the wire he was wearing. "Sorry, Miss Delacroix, not sure I convinced her."

She knew better. "Tony, you did awesome."

Her other iPhone rang. "Natalie, I'd love to see you again tomorrow?"

Suzanne put a finger to her mouth and had to hold back a chuckle. Playing hard-to-get, she asked, "Pamela, how about Saturday?"

"Five o'clock? I'll make sure my boys are at their uncle's."

"Umm," Suzanne cooed. "Shall I bring my own suit this time?"

Pamela giggled. "No need." She hung up and immediately clicked on the big screen, which displayed the video of them in the pool. Then, she began touching herself.

Suzanne knew Tony was curious about the call. She smiled. "I've got a second date with Pamela at her place."

It was almost three o'clock before Pamela checked the latest emails on her phone.

She called Lana Cheney, who then spilled all the beans about her earlier conversation with Tony. Pamela thought: Well, at least he's in Atlanta.

"Lana, I'm so glad you contacted me. I'm sure you know Tony lost his coaching job after assaulting Frank Ezell; no doubt he wants to get back at me. He demanded I appoint him head coach next year. He's been leaving me threatening phone and text messages. So far, I haven't called the police. But now I may have to. He's trying to smear my name. I can assure you that there's nothing inappropriate going on at my residence."

"I'm so, so sorry," Lana stammered. "Thought I'd let you know."

"Thank you, Lana, you did the right thing. For now, can we keep this between you and me?"

"Yes, ma'am."

"Thanks again, Lana. Oh, Bryce and a few others are going to come over after practice tonight to have dinner. I hope that's all right. I'll get him back by 9:30 p.m. or so."

"That's nice of you," she said without thinking.

After hanging up, Lana put her phone down on the table again, conflicted about what she could or should say to whom. It would be hard to resist, but she would try to wait until she could talk to Bryce later.

Pamela called her twin brother. "Santucci is in town. Did you even know that?"

He admitted he didn't.

"Find him and take care of him yourself this time. Regardless, let's powwow tomorrow and see what the others think. I know you can sweet-talk Thad to come; I'll check with Mary Jo. Maddie and Franklin are on their Pacific island; maybe I'll conference in Raoul if he's available. My place at 7:00 p.m. Keep me posted on Santucci."

Philip Hawthorne again teetered on the edge of telling his sister to handle her own mess for a change, but he didn't. Once again, as always, he would do her bidding. But to find Tony, he needed a lead. Maybe start with the obvious?

Pamela had other duties to make this all go away. There would be extra treats, gifts, and private sessions with her club members. She'd check if they were lying about seeing or talking with Tony. Her phone monitoring of each hadn't indicated so. She'd again ask the most critical question: "Have you ever told anyone about our games here at the estate?" There was only one correct answer.

That evening, she'd double down her sexual control of one boy in particular, Bryce Cheney.

Chapter 43 – The Scales

Thursday, March 31, 2016

Atlanta

Over her year as an investigator at Stuyvesant, Knight, Fitzpatrick & Burns, Suzanne found Arnie Friedlander so valuable that she paid him a quarterly cash retainer from her own money. Arnie worked out of a nondescript storefront in a Sandy Springs strip mall. From the outside, it looked very mom-and-pop. Inside, however, was a cornucopia of computer equipment with a bank of large flat-screens; it was where Arnie developed high-security software and monitored security projects for organizations worldwide. And he mined Bitcoin, which she understood nothing about.

Last year, Dusty Rayfield, who played pool and drank beer with Arnie, asked him if he could turn Suzanne's expensive necklace into a remote GPS transmitter without wrecking it. A week later, Arnie told him it was ready. After work Dusty drove to Sandy Springs to pick it up. Arnie placed It on a polishing cloth. "I had the jeweler next door do his best cleaning and polishing." The platinum and diamond necklace was dazzling.

When Arnie picked it up, his iPhone beeped and brought up a map of their location.

"So, what did you do?" Dusty asked.

Arnie showed him the tiny, almost imperceptible, bump on the back middle of the cross. "If, and only if, she firmly presses the middle of the back of the cross, GPS coordinates are sent to your phone, which in turn will continuously tell you where she is, assuming she's wearing it." He wasn't positive but figured it would work twenty miles away or so.

"Cool. Thanks, Arnie."

A few weeks later, after chastising Dusty for getting her necklace altered without her permission, Suzanne asked him for Arnie's number. They lunched at a Thai place near his office and hit it off immediately. He'd told her, "Any tech stuff. Lemme know what you need, Suzy, and I'll get it done." And that was the beginning of their yearlong friendship and partnership. His first task was to totally wipe out her online footprint and create two alternate identities, one of them for the reporter/photographer, Natalie Myers.

But the best thing Arnie did for her wasn't in the realm of being legal. She could never use it in court, and it could get her in a world of hurt if exposed. But it helped solve cases and cut immense time and effort from her investigative work. She could track a cell phone's GPS and remotely access any information on that phone – by only knowing the cell number. Suzanne tried to understand when Arnie explained how that worked for iPhones and Androids. What she could decipher was that it was an ongoing cat-and-mouse game played by world-class hackers and developers, on par with those at Apple and Google. Hackers took advantage of the continual series of minute security flaws in the big operating systems. Arnie knew the right hackers on the Dark Web who were always a step ahead. This took periodic updates of apps that Arnie downloaded onto Suzanne's iPhones. The app he named "Suzy" could serve up any digital data, including phone calls, texts, logs, emails, photos, etc. – of any person she needed. All it took was the cell number.

Today, that came in handy after Dusty had gotten her the number.

First, Suzanne dug through his old texts. Right off the bat, she found one from today: "Bitch wife gone for weekend. Lake Fri eve. May fish Sat Sun." Five minutes later she found what else she needed. A few weeks back he texted a friend the lock code to get into his house and the alarm code. She needed to do a little reconnaissance, then she'd be ready.

The Same Afternoon

Roswell

Six months ago, Special Agent Mia Gonzales ascended to head the Atlanta field office and hadn't had a drink since. Her daughter was thriving as a sophomore in Athens. In addition to booze, she gave up men and realized she didn't need them as much as she thought. With zest, she'd already turned in three special agents for sexual harassment. She was happy for the first time in a long time.

She looked at the number on her cell – one she hadn't seen for a long time – and picked up.

"Suzy, how in the world are you?"

After they exchanged pleasantries for several minutes, then Suzanne dropped her bombshell. "Mia, I know who killed the Monroe girls – and, I think, all the others too."

Silence.

"Mia?"

"So, who?"

"Promise me you'll have court orders ready to drop for these people and addresses." She gave her the four addresses and names in Atlanta, Woodstock, and Roswell.

"When?"

"I don't know. Soon. Promise you'll be ready."

"Okay, but you're not getting yourself into a situation you shouldn't, are you? I'm the cop; you're not."

Suzanne dodged the question. "Look, I don't want to tease, but I'd rather do this in person. I've got a story to tell on the evidence boards in my home office. What I know, you'll know tomorrow, I promise."

If it had been any other person on the planet, Mia wouldn't have said what she did. "I gotta make a day trip to Savannah tomorrow and won't be back until late. How about Saturday?"

Suzanne said, "I'll order good Chinese. My place around five o'clock? Red Zin good for you?"

"Not doing much drinking anymore, but I'll be there," Mia told her.

"I'm sending you a few texts. See you Saturday."

Mia hung up and looked at the texts. Photos of four different knives with the same handle and design. The two Monroe murder weapons, and three others – all with the same black double cross design. And the text notes with them:

2 from the Monroe murders

1 from a boy on a lacrosse team in Roswell via Pamela Loncart

1 from the bottom of Lake Lanier owned by my father's murderer

1 that was used 20 years ago, in a sexual assault…of me

Excludes 2 others I saw last night.

"Holy shit!" Mia said out loud. Suddenly feeling uncomfortable, like her professional life could tip one way or the other. But she asked Wendy to get warrants ready for signing and tell no one else. When she asked for what crimes, Mia told her, "For now, put 'Murder' and 'Conspiracy to Murder' on each and leave the dates blank."

Since last year she was tempted to turn in Zirnan but didn't want to get cut off at the knees. More than once, Mia thought about the whitewashing of the Monroe murders – and the others – and it turned her stomach. It was time to rebalance the Scales of Justice.

The Same Evening

Alpharetta

He walked in at eight o'clock. He was surprised he hadn't been there before – only about twenty minutes from his ranch and business. The place was hopping, but there was one table for two. He decided to relax and ordered a half-carafe of good Chianti.

Philip asked his middle-aged waiter for a pizza recommendation. "You like meat?" Nunzio asked. His customer gave a thumbs-up. Twenty minutes later it arrived. He preferred thin-style, but this thick-crust pizza was stellar. At least a half dozen meats: sausage, Italian sausage, bacon, salami, ham, and of course pepperoni with interesting cheeses, mushrooms, and onions. Bernie's pizza was delicious.

After eating half of the pizza, he rested. When Nunzio asked if he wanted anything else, he said, "Box the other half. I'm still thinking about a cannoli and coffee, black. I wonder if the owner is in? I'd like to have a word. Nothing about service, and the food is great."

Five minutes later, Bernie Scally appeared and walked to his table.

"You're Bernie?"

"That's me."

"I'm Duncan Mittendorf. Your pizza is excellent."

"Thank you."

"My younger brother played lacrosse up north with Tony Santucci."

Philip Hawthorne noticed the name brought recognition to Bernie's one eye.

He continued, "I've got business in town, and my brother told me to look him up. His phone number, though, doesn't seem to work. He remembered he worked at a pizza place called Bernie's."

"Tony's off. On vacation." Bernie was going to stop there but added that Tony told him he was going to Montana to see Yellowstone, a place he always wanted to visit. "Staying at a place called the Chico Resort. You could maybe try him there."

Bernie saw the man's dark eyes go steely, and he detected a slight smirk.

"I need to get back, Mr. Mittendorf."

"Nice to meet you. Thanks again."

Bernie told him, "Dinner's on me. Let me show you to the door."

Outside, he faced the tall man, standing toe-to-toe only a few inches away from Hawthorne's face, and told him, "You fool with Tony Santucci again, I'll kill you, and it will be slow. And there will be no guns involved. Capiche?"

Before getting an answer, Bernie turned away and went back inside – though he'd wanted to grab Hawthorne and bounce his head off the pavement. The former RECON was a little shell-shocked; a feeling he wasn't accustomed to. He smiled as he walked away. Little doubt Bernie was the guy who punched Orrin's ticket. Go figure. He would know where Santucci was, no question. But not a man to be trifled with.

She made one more call that evening.

He saw the ID. "Suzanne Delacroix. Been quite a while…"

Instead of chitchatting, she asked, "How would you like to win your Pulitzer Prize?"

Bobby Price knew the ex-APD Homicide detective was not one for hyperbole.

"I'm listening…"

"Bobby, my father didn't drown accidentally. He was murdered. By the same people who murdered the Monroes and the twins in Woodstock, Anniston, and elsewhere – going back who knows how long. Same people got an innocent kid kicked off his lacrosse team up in Roswell."

"What?"

"Believe it or not, that's how I got involved again. A boys' lacrosse thing in Roswell. There are a boatload of moving parts, Bobby, and I'm going to need your help if you're game. Exclusive, I promise. But I'm a source, and this is off the record for now."

He didn't have to think about it. "I'm in. Lemme ask one question."

She waited.

"I'm thinking this is about a family."

"Even better. A family of witches."

"You're kidding?" But he knew she wasn't.

"I'll be back in touch. Dust off your old notes about all of the twins' murders. Hold off going public for now."

"I'm on it."

If she was unable to root out the killers herself, she would no longer have any compunction about telling her the story to the *Atlanta Constitution*.

The Same Evening

Roswell

Lana Cheney heard her son in the shower. After it stopped, she went upstairs and knocked on Bryce's bedroom door.

He was sitting in front of his laptop which is where he always seemed to be. "What's up, Mom?"

"You boys have fun at the Loncarts?"

"It was great. Steaks, lobsters, fries, an this amazing chocolate dessert."

"Bryce, can I ask you a personal question you might find strange?"

"Sure, Mom."

"Do you think Mrs. Loncart is hot, or I guess, what I've heard called a MILF?"

"Miss…." He almost said Pamela. "She's good-looking. Hard to argue with that."

"Bryce, do you have sex with Mrs. Loncart?"

He turned back from his screen. "Mom, you're kidding me, right? That's so weird. No way. Where would you get that idea?"

"Tony Santucci."

"Coach Tony? Mom, he's old news. Probably sore about the season and getting fired."

Lana Cheney always had a keen sense whether her only son was fibbing or not. She kissed him on the forehead and headed for her own bed. With her husband Fred out of town, she lay alone on her back under the covers. She wasn't sure if she believed him. Then had her own bizarre thought. "Are there any boys who see me as a MILF?" She doubted it.

In bed, Bryce Cheney looked up at the ceiling and relived his private session with Miss Pamela earlier that evening. He had lied to his mother and did exactly what Miss Pamela had told him to do; he had no choice. He couldn't wait for next time with her.

He chuckled to himself about what he'd tell his mother in the morning.

Chapter 44 – The Alias

Friday Morning, April 1

Atlanta

That morning Bryce Cheney told his mom what Pamela Loncart had directed him to say. He'd heard rumors that Tony molested a teammate and maybe other boys. That's probably why Tony made up the story about Mrs. Loncart. He was vague about the specifics. When pressed, he told his mom he couldn't say more. He didn't admit to being molested himself. He said that nobody he knew had seen or talked to Tony since he left the team after punching Coach Frank and insulting Mrs. Loncart.

Lana Cheney kept trying to pry as much as she could from her son until he said, "Mom, I gotta catch my ride to school."

For fifteen minutes, she sat at the dining room table worrying and wondering what she should do. She couldn't believe she'd let a pedophile into her home yesterday. Her Galaxy was begging her. She couldn't resist.

She made her first call to Eileen Westerman, Kevin's mom. She led with, "Eileen, have you heard the news about Tony Santucci?"

It went viral, first among lacrosse parents, then the Eaglewood Middle School parents, then across the school district – then to hundreds or maybe thousands tuned in on Facebook, Snapchat, and Instagram. As if by magic, the bogus story exploded into many versions. The online and telephone grapevines promulgated a host of them: The former assistant lacrosse coach at Eaglewood Middle was fired for having molested: a) one boy on the lacrosse team; or b) several boys on the team; or c) an undetermined number of other boys in Roswell.

Other stories purported that he was hiding out in Atlanta hoping to get revenge for losing his coaching job; he was a serial sex offender up north and was now using a false identity; he kidnapped a boy in Roswell who disappeared last week; he escaped Atlanta and was being hunted across the country; he may have already left the country as a fugitive; he was armed and dangerous.

Such was the juicy, suburban scuttlebutt wicked up by gossiper-in-chief Lana Cheney. Despite no boy coming forward and no one except Lana having talked to Tony. No one had breathed one negative word about Pamela. In fact, she was a sympathetic character in several versions.

David first heard the rumors about Tony when Toby Condurelis, an obnoxious kid in his American History class, asked if Santucci had butt-fucked him. David wanted to take a swing at the twerp, but he knew it wouldn't help. He texted his father a few of the things he'd heard at school and wondered if he'd heard any news about Tony.

His dad had to keep it under his hat but texted, "Total BS. I'm sure Tony is okay."

David replied, "Okay," but the rumor mill ripped at unhealed wounds. He hated whoever shot his dogs; he hated Coach Frank and Mrs. Loncart; he hated the lacrosse club; he hated lacrosse; He just wanted to disappear.

All Tim could do was shake his head and say to himself: Tony, David, their dogs, their marriage... He'd gone a couple days without a drink, but that was about to end.

Sarah got home at 6:00 p.m. As she walked down the front hallway Tim said, "You can't believe what shitty rumors that got started about Tony."

She kept walking and without turning her head yelled back, "I'm taking a bath. I don't want to hear about it."

"Nice," he said not nicely under his breath.

The Same Day – 7:45 p.m

Lake Lanier

After pouring himself a healthy Eagle Rare bourbon on the rocks from his well-stocked office bar, he plopped down behind his desk, put his feet up, and pressed the remote to turn on Fox News. He loosened his collar, yanked off his tie, and took a big sip.

She came from the adjacent alcove used as a small coat room. A movement caught the edge of his eye, and he immediately pulled open his right-hand drawer. Dressed in black, head-to-toe, she stood in front of his desk and said, "John, it's been too long."

Startled, the Atlanta Chief of Police reached inside the drawer. "Suzanne?"

Then, from the back of her waist, she pulled out a Sig Sauer. His handgun.

"Looking for this?"

He tried a jovial pivot. "Hey, Suzanne, lemme get you a drink. We'll catch up. What would you like?"

He started to stand up, but she said firmly, "Sit the fuck down, John!" He dropped his fat ass back in his desk chair.

Thirty seconds passed with neither saying a word nor making a move.

"Whaddya you want, Suzanne? You're already in a heap of shit breaking into my house."

She smiled. "Let's talk."

She put his Sig back in her belt and meandered about his big office that even had a skylight opening for a telescope.

"Lemme ask you, John. How is it that a cop, even a top cop like you, could afford a couple million-dollar lake house with its own observatory?"

"Got lucky on a few good investments. What's wrong with that?"

She walked behind him, and he started to get up again.

"John, if you get out of your chair, I'm going to make sure you never see another planet or star from your telescope."

"Is that a threat?"

Her right elbow slammed into his left jaw, knocking him sideways.

"Fuck!" he screamed. "You fucking bitch!"

"Put your palms down on your desk, or I'm going to put a bullet through your head and make it look like a suicide. Piece of cake for an old Homicide cop like me."

He froze.

"Do it!" she screamed.

He slid his hands onto his desk.

"John, I need you to answer a few questions. If you tell the truth, I'm going to leave you in peace to drink your bourbon."

"The fuck you say. Your pretty ass will be in jail tomorrow morning – and then for a long time."

She slipped the Sig out of her waist again and banged the barrel against his head, not too hard but more than a love tap.

"Goddamn cunt!" he shouted.

"You wanna play it this way, John, fine. Here's the first question: Who did you work with to murder my father?" She knew the answer but wanted to hear it from him.

"What the fuck are you talking about?" he snarled. "He fell in the lake when he was fishing. He couldn't swim a lick for God's sake. He fucking drowned."

Suzanne pondered giving him another love tap with his own Sig but deferred.

"John, I'm going to admit, I messed up on this one. It was right in front of me, but I finally got it. Without my dad around, you'd be chief. And hell, you were the only one who knew he'd be up at your lake house alone and exactly what he'd be doing when and where. You knew he never had his blue vest off when he was on the boat. *Never*. But lied to others that he sometimes didn't wear it. Then he supposedly drowns without wearing it. Really? You didn't need to be there in person. I didn't see that years ago. What else is going on here, John?"

Carleton said nothing.

From her small black bag, she pulled out the knife that Rick had found at the bottom of Lanier and one from the Monroe murders and held them up for Carleton to see.

"John, you ever see these knives before?"

"No, you fucking cunt."

"Ya know, John, I might actually believe that."

She put down the big one and held the smaller knife. You know whose knife this is, don't you? Found it at the bottom of the lake a couple days ago – almost exactly below where my father was fishing that day he supposedly drowned. Who drowned him, John?"

"Suzanne, I'm gonna try to forget all of this and give you a break."

"And I'm going to ask you one more time, who murdered my father?"

"He wasn't fucking murdered. He drowned."

"Wrong answer."

She slammed the tip of the smaller knife into the middle of the back of his right hand, impaling it on the desk. Tendons, bones, and tissue crunched like she'd squashed a bag of chips. Blood sprayed and ruined his custom dress shirt.

Staring at the knife stuck in his hand, Atlanta Chief of Police John Carleton was in such shock he was unable to talk. Then bellowed, "Goddamn you! Goddamn you!"

He tried to stand. She shoved him back down in his chair and held him by the neck with her other hand.

"I didn't hear you, John. Gimme a name, or you'll be singing soprano after I use the big knife. I'm guessing the same guy owned it. It was found at the Monroe murder scene. John, I know you had a hand in getting your friend killed. You're working with nasty folks."

"I didn't. I swear," he moaned.

When she rotated the handle a bit, she made sure the knife was solidly stuck in the back of his hand.

Carleton wailed.

"Who did it, John?"

Sitting at his desk, his head slumped in defeat, he blurted out, "Hawthorne, Philip Hawthorne."

"You told Hawthorne where and when your friend, Hollis Delacroix, would be fishing on Lake Lanier, didn't you?"

He nodded.

"I didn't hear you."

"Yes."

"So, you helped get my father murdered, didn't you?"

"Yes."

"You're on Hawthorne's drug payroll, too. Aren't you, John?"

Moaning louder, he nodded.

"Fucking say it!" She wanted to pull out the knife and stick it in his heart but refrained.

"I want you to say out loud that you conspired with Philip Hawthorne to drown Hollis Delacroix and you bought this house with drug money you got from Hawthorne."

He hesitated and tried to slide his left hand off the desk; the pain horrible.

"Move it again and I'll put the big knife through your other hand, then I'll cut your balls off. *SAY IT, MOTHERFUCKER!*"

He obeyed and then whined, "Please get it out of my hand."

She looked down at him and shook her head. "How can you live with yourself, you sorry sack of shit?" Out of her black bag, she got a pair of zip ties. After extracting the knife, she put a towel around his right hand and then tied his hands and feet. Carleton groaned like he was going through childbirth.

"Now, we're going to have an interactive phone chat with your buddies. Whaddya say, John? That should be fun, don't you think?"

The Same Evening

The Loncart Estate—Roswell

The meeting at the Loncart estate started promptly at 7:00 p.m. Mary Jo Cogburn had to attend a big political fundraiser downtown; it was Pamela, Philip, and Thad. Raoul had other business, too. They sat in the interior portion of her pool complex while Pamela got both up to speed on her lacrosse game. Never apologizing, only reporting the news and asking where Philip was on finding Tony Santucci.

Philip told them that he was positive Bernie Scally, Santucci's boss, killed their assassin in Montana, then got Santucci back to Atlanta. Regardless, Santucci showed up at the home of one of the lacrosse kids, so yes, he is around. After the Scally guy threatened him last night on the steps of his restaurant, Philip took photos of the plates on the four cars furthest from the restaurant and put GPS bugs on two. This morning he had one of his cops, Mack Hines, run the plates for him. It turned out that the well-kept '67 Caddy was Scally's. Scally drove from his place in Virginia Highlands to Buckhead, where he stopped for a half hour before heading to his restaurant in Alpharetta. He added, "Santucci is being guarded by pros. So, taking him out won't be easy."

Thad said, "He needs to go, and we'll need a good plan."

Philip added, "We've got plenty of manpower; I'll figure it out."

Pamela chimed in, "Santucci's face has already hit social media and gone viral. I've turned him into a child molester extraordinaire. Wherever he is, I'm doubting he'll wander far from his current location."

Before excusing herself to check on the dinner Tariq was preparing, Pamela said, "If you boys are bored, you might want to hit 'Play.'"

Thad grabbed the remote and pressed the button. The huge screen on the opposite wall came to life with Pamela frolicking in the pool with a tall, lovely, dark-haired woman. As the woman stood naked facing the camera, he hit "Stop."

Initially mesmerized, Thad lurched to his feet and yelled, "It can't be."

"What can't be?" asked his cousin.

Thad got up and walked toward the big screen. "Philip, do you know who that is?"

"A friend of Pamela's, I guess. Quite beautiful. You know her?"

"Yes, but let's wait for your sister."

Pamela returned and saw the two looking at the huge nude image. "Isn't she spectacular? My new friend, Natalie."

Thad gave both his cousins a sly smile, then the bad news. "I'm not sure who you think she is, but her name isn't Natalie."

Pamela looked at him quizzically.

Pointing at the screen, Thad said, "This beauty is none other than Suzanne Delacroix. Formerly APD Homicide detective who was initially in charge of the Monroe investigation. Most recently, investigator for the law firm that now represents Hawthorne Industries. I had an encounter with her two decades ago. Her deputy chief father had me severely beaten for my liaison with his daughter in college. A few years later, Philip drowned her father in Lanier as approved by Dad. The drowning was a late payback – but more importantly, put our boy, Carleton, in the top spot."

Looking at the screen, Pamela stood dumbfounded. She'd heard the Delacroix name. She couldn't believe how badly she'd been played.

Thad said with sarcasm, "It appears, Pamela, that you and I lust after the same woman."

"I wonder what she knows?" asked Philip.

Pamela admitted, "A lot. She even asked me about our Loncart emblem around my neck, on the gate, and on the steak knives."

But she recovered quickly. "Another vagary of the *Game* is all. Let's sit down and eat – take a break from business until after dinner."

As the three pondered and Tariq cleared the table, Pamela received a call. She knew the number but hadn't yet assigned it a name.

The Same Evening, 8:30 p.m.

Lake Lanier

Using her "Natalie Myers" iPhone she hit Pamela's cell number. Carleton's eyes filled with terror. His damaged hand shook uncontrollably.

"Pamela."

Her voice cold as ice, she replied, "Suzanne Delacroix, what can I do for you?"

"Pam, you must have finally caught on to my alias. Maybe Thad filled you in? I'm here with Atlanta Police Chief John Carleton, who I think you, your brother, and cousin know. I apologize, he's not too talkative right now. I slammed one of your custom knives through the back of his hand when he wasn't being a good boy. Here, let me play back a little of our conversation."

"She made me say it!" he screamed like a banshee.

With her phone on speaker, they listened while Carleton ratted out Philip which in turn, ratted out all of them.

"Let's see, I now have five of your custom knives all with your black double cross symbol and all with the same initials as the custom designer. I'll text you a picture of them and one of John, in case you think I'm bullshitting you. I thought about stealing a steak knife at dinner Wednesday but figured I had plenty. How many knives did the guy in Santa Fe make for your pathetic family anyway?"

Silence on the other end.

"Well, after I text you the images, I'm taking off. I'll leave the front door open in case you wanna talk to Carleton. I guess this means our date for Saturday is off. Huh?"

"You have nothing on me," Pamela spat back.

"Au contraire, Pam. Tony is alive and well, and one of your boys spilled the beans about you playing naughty games at your place. I think the jig is pretty much up, Pam."

"You're bluffing. Or a cop would've knocked on my door."

"Ya think? You and your brother and whoever else, I'm thinking, own cops all over Atlanta. Right now, there's only one cop in town I trust."

"Thanks for the heads-up, Suzanne. Good luck keeping yours."

Suzanne clicked off – hoping her bluff would rattle their cages even more.

Pamela told them, "She could ruin my lacrosse game – and our *Game of Twins*. She's the only one who matters. We must get rid of her ASAP."

Thad and Philip looked nervous as cats, but then Thad stood and said confidently, "Philip and I will handle Suzanne Delacroix. Then we'll get back to Santucci."

She smiled. "Chill, you guys got this."

With his hand bandaged, Suzanne popped Carleton in the shoulder with a syringe of methaqualone and then taped his two palms together so that none of the knuckles or fingers could move. Carleton moaned pitifully, "God, my hand's killing me. Don't leave me like this, please! You've no idea what these people will do."

"Oh, I think I do. But if they don't bother to pick you up, you might want to consider getting out of Dodge. Probably ought to get a doctor to check out that hand first, though. I'm leaving your phone for you over at the bar if you wanna give it a shot after you wake up. Too-da-loo, John."

On her way back down I-85 from Carleton's lake house, she tossed her "Natalie" phone out the window. Now, no question she had a target on her forehead, but she wasn't going to endanger anyone else – not the Baldwins or Tony or Bernie – or go to the cops, whom she didn't trust. Depending on how things went with Mia tomorrow afternoon, she might need FBI protection. She still needed the Loncart bunch to make another big mistake; she was confident they would.

Until then, she was on her own. She was accustomed to that but slept with Zeke and two loaded Glocks on the front sofa – just in case.

The *Game* had been the brainchild of Pamela's great-grandmother after she gave birth to her twins in 1911. Penelope Loncart was a woman of great beauty and wealth, but her occult powers, she felt, were going to waste. Penelope wanted more of everything: pleasure, money, and power. She sought a Renaissance based on the ancient *Teachings* – but modernized for the young century. She preached *more*, but also more discipline. She looked around at the gaudy robber barons, like the Rockefellers, Carnegies, Dukes, Astors, Morgans,

Mellons, and the rest whom she saw as inferior humans. She wanted even *more* than them. Much *more*. She loved the old Indian stories about her ancestor, Pamela Loncart, in the late 1600s – and named her revitalized occult group *The Tribe*. If the Tribe followed *His* ways, *He* would give them *more* than they could ever imagine.

When she bore twin girls at the ripe old age of thirty-four, Penelope saw the twins as a sign: the ultimate gifts from her Dark Lord. In *His* name, they kidnapped the Abercrombie twins from Port Norris, New Jersey, and brought them back home to New Haven. She and her husband Phineas enjoyed the Abercrombie girls so much, she decided on a dramatic kick-off for her Tribe. She'd read the old tale about her witch ancestor being impaled with a black cross. She had Phineas make two black crosses out of wood; they sacrificed the pretty twins on the deck of their yacht and threw their bodies overboard after extracting the crosses. After, she got the idea of fitting the black crosses together – and it became their emblem.

Her Tribe would trumpet sex and revere incest with their own twins. Once Priscilla and Patricia bled, she and Phineas enjoyed teaching their twins the joyous vagaries of familial sex. But it was about more than sex.

Penelope recruited women and men, primarily part of the family lineage, but also others whom she identified had occult gifts that could become satanic dark gifts – particularly any version of telepathy, the ability to read thoughts and "talk" to others with the gift. In her recruits, she looked for intelligence, good looks, and the genetic propensity for twins (she'd read enough about the new science of genetics to know that fraternal twins were much more genetically common than identical twins; likely fraternal twin genes handed down over generations). She encouraged her witches, male and female, to train in weapons, warfare, and clandestine operations; and choose among business, law, government, and law enforcement – where they could do the most damage from the *inside*.

Her efforts started bearing fruit within the next few years. One of her recruits became a close confidante of J. Edgar Hoover. Hoover had no clue. But she had to wait thirty-nine years to see another set of family twins – until Priscilla bore Maddie and Phoebe -- right under the nose of the director of the FBI.

Pamela had no doubt *Game of Twins* had already exceeded Penelope Loncart's wildest dreams – and that she would be thrilled to know the *Game* had been inculcated into her Tribe's DNA. Though the births of twins could be unpredictable, the *Game* made the Tribe tick. Pamela knew the Tribe hadn't even scratched the surface of its potential yet.

Sitting alone poolside, she had to smile that – until that evening – Pamela Loncart hadn't known how integral Suzanne had been to the *Game of Twins*. She was glad that she finally met this person-of-light in the flesh, and yummy flesh it was.

But now it was time to take her off the board. There was so much more to be done to pave the way for her Dark Lord in the twenty-first century. And sooner than later, she would lead the Atlanta Tribe to its inevitable dark greatness.

Chapter 45 – The Showdown

Saturday, April 2, 2016

Atlanta

On Saturday morning Suzanne woke up alert and refreshed – and full of hope. Instead of a run with Zeke, she took him on a short walk, ate breakfast, and decided to play golf. She didn't have a tee time, but she never had trouble joining a group that needed a single. It was a glorious, sunny spring morning, and there was almost nothing else she'd rather do. And it would keep her mind off Pamela Loncart and crew. She thought Zeke would have fun outdoors, too, and so she dropped him at a nice doggy daycare – something she did off and on when she was playing golf. Besides, she didn't want him alone in her condo – not today.

She hadn't noticed the man in the black Honda SUV who'd been parked on Piedmont and then jumped into traffic several cars behind her. He'd already put a tracker on her car and gave her plenty of leeway in front. After she dropped off her dog, he followed her to East Lake. Then made the call.

At his home on West Paces, Thad smiled – wondering if she'd play nine or eighteen. Regardless, Philip's man would follow her until she left the course and keep him posted.

Four hours later, after playing eighteen holes and enjoying a vodka and tonic and a burger with her golf foursome in the East Lake Grille, she took a shower at the club, then picked up Zeke. Driving back west on I-20, reality hit her between the eyes. NPR was reporting that Atlanta Police Chief John Carleton had been found dead in his Lake Lanier home that morning. The only word so far was that he had died of a gunshot wound that did not appear to be self-inflicted.

She'd like to say she was surprised, but she wasn't. She'd like to say she felt guilty, but she wasn't. She had Carleton's confession recorded on her iPhone, but knew, out of context, that could make her out to be his killer. She needed even more evidence to catch Pamela, Philip, Thad, and the rest. She could hardly wait to talk with Mia in a couple of hours.

Seeing her on Pamela's big screen last night was exhilarating. Thad often fantasized about meeting in her Midtown condo. Just the two of them. Her condo complex was four stories with only twenty-four units. Posh, but too small to have a person in the lobby. A keycard was needed to get into the building, then the elevator, and then each unit. There were cameras outside, in the lobby, and in the hallways. He and Philip would wear disguises today; they both loved to dress up.

A year ago, after chatting about locks with a security professional who was fortifying his mansion, Philip was thrilled to learn that he could use a small gadget to plug into the bottom of the lock on any keycard-type door and, within seconds, click the lock open. He was more than happy to pay ten grand for the keycard gizmo. Once, he'd gotten as far as her fourth-floor door and opened it. But he resisted the temptation to enter. He'd heard her dog bark when he shut the door again.

Philip Hawthorne was impressed that his cousin had a plan. They needed to be waiting inside her condo. Philip assured him the dog wouldn't be a problem. And from the phone call, it sounded like the dog was gone, anyway. Two hours later they had no problems getting into her building and condo. Philip took off his ballcap and fake mustache; Thad took off his glasses and long-haired wig. They could put their disguises back on later.

Both men were fascinated by her room filled with rolling boards that documented parts of their family story they didn't know or remember. Thad photographed each board with his iPhone and then erased the boards. They stacked the photographs (that had been pinned or taped) into a pile and put them on a dining room chair. Thad observed, "Mom is going to love these for the Museum!"

Forty-two Years Ago, October 31, 1974

Atlanta

Halloween. As she waited in the immense subterranean room, the young woman examined the Haverfords' shrine – one she'd looked at many times as a child. At first, it bothered her, but she gained appreciation as she learned more. The tall, circular glass case contained a few dozen photographs of Nellie and Natalie, their nightclothes and other garments, their jewelry, one of the pool balls, and several photos of their parents rollicking in Havana. The Blounts showcase was more colorful. Merry and Cherry with their red and white cheerleading uniforms, saddle shoes, pompoms, undies, and photos. The Brevards showcase for Matilde and Mariessa Brevard was a pile of clothes, boots, jewelry, dozens of photos, and a unique dog tag and collar – not yet organized. She thought they were the most beautiful of all the twins, and she'd been honored to participate in their sacrifice – as well as the Blounts.

Maddie Sutterland walked across the huge stone-floored room they called the Museum. On the wall hung a large plaque. She knew them by heart but read them out loud. The words burned into a simple square of lacquered pine wood, accented with overlapping silhouettes of two identical girls:

Game of Twins – The Teachings, April 1911

In remembrance of Molly, Abigail & Pamela –

Find, enjoy & sacrifice

The loveliest two

Draw the enemy close

Spread breadcrumbs

They can't follow too

Be disciplined

Wreak havoc, have fun

'Til the next twins come

She loved the verse and repeated it as her husband, Franklin, and brother-in-law, Nigel, walked into the cavernous underground room with Priscilla. Her mother kissed each of them on the lips and told the three, "You played with aplomb—two times in two years! Your names will be remembered for all time. Your rewards will be great!"

She faced her daughter, Maddie, and told her, "You will take my place one day."

Saturday, April 2

Suzanne's Condo – Midtown, Atlanta

On the dining room table were the five knives that Suzanne Delacroix had collected -- with their double-black-cross symbol, the ultimate sign from their Dark Lord. He was showing favor by returning their precious knives to them. Anticipating his long-awaited, unfinished business with her, Thad picked up and caressed his long-lost stiletto, the switchblade that had been taken from him years ago. He clicked it open, and from a dozen paces, he flung the knife at a kitchen cupboard and stuck it dead center. He grinned. He hadn't lost his touch.

Philip checked out her mini wine cellar and pulled out a bottle of Turley. He poured Thad and himself healthy glasses. Thad toasted,

"To a fun afternoon with Suzanne Delacroix," and they clinked glasses.

It would be another couple of hours until they got the warning call they'd been waiting for. Thad stayed in the kitchen to the right of the entrance, and Philip stood in the hall that led to the bedrooms and study hall foyer.

Zeke followed her down the hallway to her door. Nothing seemed amiss, but she had a Glock 17 in the back of her jeans just in case. Zeke ran through the doorway and immediately started barking. She pulled the Glock from her jeans, but it was already too late.

Barking louder, Zeke ran toward the left hallway. She heard two suppressed shots. Her dog wailed. She turned toward the hallway but heard from behind her a voice from the past. "Drop it before you turn around, Suzanne." She was outflanked. She placed her Glock on the floor.

From her bedroom, ahead of her in the hallway, came another tall, dark-haired man who also pointed his Sig at her.

She managed to say, "Philip Hawthorne, I saw your photo at the Loncart place. A neighbor boy watched what you did to the Baldwins' dogs and drew you perfectly, by the way. Takes a real man to shoot a dog. Seems to be your specialty. She could see her Aussie down the hall, not moving, and covered with blood.

"Suzanne, it's so nice to meet you, and good heavens, you've got your clothes on."

Thad chimed in, "Not for long."

Philip told her wickedly, "My sister is pissed at you, by the way, and she wanted to make sure I popped your dog."

She lunged at him but stopped and spat back, "Fuck you, asshole!"

Gun in hand, Thad grabbed the iPhone stuck in her back pocket. He smashed it on the floor and ground it with his heel. He told her to walk slowly with her hands in the air – into the living room.

On the way, she asked, "Wondering who fucks who in the ass the best – between you two?"

Philip stepped up and slapped her across the face. "Keep your fucking hands in the air, bitch!" he yelled.

Thad told him, "Chill. Don't damage the goods yet."

Thad perused the table and again picked up the switchblade he'd once brandished in his Georgia Tech frat house years ago. "Your father probably wishes he hadn't kept this one – it was my favorite – because I'm going to put it to much better use this time."

Thad told Philip, "Keep a gun on her but take it easy. I've got this. Oh, Suzanne, the Sig Sauer on the table, that's Carleton's gun. You know, the one you used to shoot him." He laughed, devouring her with his eyes, and said, "I can shoot you now, or we can have some fun."

She hesitated, looking eye-to-eye with this monster who'd returned from her past.

"What will it be, Suzanne?"

"Sure, Thad, I love games. Whatever you want to play."

"That's the spirit! Here's one for you: Suzanne Striptease."

Suzanne rolled her eyes but knew what she had to do. She conjured up her sexiest version of Marilyn Monroe. What would she do in a spot like this? Distract, delay, seduce, hope? She knew one thing she'd never do. She'd never give up. Marilyn Monroe was drugged to death; she didn't commit suicide. She didn't give up. Of that, Suzanne was sure. She hoped Mia would arrive early but likely wouldn't get there two hours early.

After showering at the club, Suzanne wasn't wearing many pieces of clothing but said in her most sultry voice, "Anything for you, Thad. Can I bring my hands down now?"

"By all means."

She had one, and only one, shot. She slowly fondled her own breasts through her sheer blouse and unbuttoned the top button.

"This is going to be fucking awesome," he told Philip. "Hell, you might even want a turn. Oh wait, we gotta get Pamela on video for this."

She stalled as long as she could while Thad turned on the laptop and launched the Dark Net video app. "Thought we'd tune you into the festivities, Pamela."

From her estate in Roswell, she smiled. "Now, who's playing with whom, Suzanne?"

Suzanne couldn't help herself. "Pam, curious who has the smallest dick of these two pathetic boys, I'm sure you know?"

She ignored the question.

"Take it off," her cousin Thad commanded.

Suzanne extended her long arms above her head, slowly lowered them, and eased them behind her neck.

If there was any hope, it was her cross necklace. She unclasped it in the back, grabbed it with her right hand, hid it in her palm, and pressed the back before she let it drop to the floor. She repeated a short prayer to herself, "Please, Lord Jesus, I ask for your peace and protection."

Pamela announced via her web video feed, "It was so nice of you to remove your necklace. You realize it prevented me from getting to know you much better. But that's moot now."

Dusty Rayfield was sitting in his Vinings condo watching a March Madness basketball game when he heard two distinct beeps. The custom GPS app automatically popped up on his phone, which he'd never seen it do. A Google map appeared and then disappeared; the screen went gray. No app. "Fuck!" he yelled. He called her phone, but it went straight to voicemail without a ring. Like it was dead. The only thing he could think to do was call Arnie.

"Dusty, how's it hang'n, bro?"

"Arnie, your app beeped twice. I saw a map, then it went blank. She could be in deep shit. I think her iPhone is dead."

"Give me five minutes. Lemme see what I can do."

"I'll give you two." Dusty grabbed his two Colt 1911s and his phone and bolted to his Mustang.

As his phone rang, he slapped an extra emergency blue light bar on his hood. "Where the fuck am I going, Arnie?"

"More!" Thad demanded like he was in a raucous Atlanta titty bar. "Come on, take it off, Suzanne."

She saw a black wooden cross on the table with the knives and pondered taking a bullet. But instead, she decided to pull off her skin-tight jeans. Even in normal circumstances, this was a challenge. It was all about the tease.

Arnie told him the app couldn't be fixed quickly, but he had the last location of her iPhone when it went dead: "It's her condo building in Midtown."

"Lord Jesus," Dusty said out loud. "Please let her be alive." By the time he reached Paces Mill Road, he'd run two lights and passed four cars by driving over the double line. So far, he'd managed not to kill himself or anyone else.

Stalling for more time, Suzanne said, "Philip, Carleton told me you drowned my father in Lanier with his help."

"I wondered if anyone would ever find my diving knife. Thanks for returning it. Maybe if your dad knew how to swim, it wouldn't have been so easy," he laughed.

She wanted to kill the motherfucker, but first, she needed to stay alive.

Thad added, "Carleton got what we both wanted. He became the head boy at APD. He was well compensated for overlooking, aiding, and abetting Philip's drug operations. The revenge was sweet – getting your pop killed."

She struggled to maintain her composure but asked, "And the twins' murders over the years? That was all revenge, too? Sacrifices after two of your ancestors were murdered a long time ago – like in the wives' tale you told me Wednesday. So, a group of witches?"

Pamela said over video chat, "We're called the *Atlanta Tribe*. For revenge, yes, but there's so much more to our *Game of Twins*."

She looked at the men and then Pamela's laptop screen. "You two and Pam murdered the Oosterhuis and Monroe twins after Dex and Dax were born fourteen years ago and after your twins were born last year. Right, Thad."

"You're so smart, Suzanne. We even fooled the FBI. They've been fooled since 1911. Now let's get those pants off."

Dusty couldn't remember how fast he'd ever driven on Interstate 75, but he was weaving in and out of cars across four lanes of traffic over 100 mph. He realized he was going too fast for many drivers to react to the pulsing blue lights. He might be too late already, but he couldn't waste a second.

Slowly, she unzipped her jeans. The men were mesmerized. Thad stood about fifteen feet away, leaning on the table with Philip off to his left. After putting both hands under her jeans, she rubbed her crotch over and over. Unfortunately, she had no panties on a day she wished she'd worn more clothes. She inched her Gucci jeans down to above her knees.

Thad said salaciously, "Nice kitty!"

"Mind if I sit down?" she purred. She procrastinated as she methodically tugged off her Saint Laurent jeans. "Who murdered the Brevard and Blount twins? Lemme guess, Thad, your folks, and who else?"

Pamela said, "Maddie and Franklin Sutterland and my father, Nigel."

She tried to keep them talking. "How about the Haverford twins back in 1950?"

Philip liked to brag. "That was Grandmother Priscilla and her husband Reggie. And Raymond Sutterland, Thad's grandfather, my great-uncle."

"The Abercrombie twins in 1911?"

"Penelope Loncart, Phineas Hawthorne, and Alfred Sutterland. Great-grandparents and great-uncle."

"I guess with you monsters, incest is best," Suzanne laughed.

From her Roswell estate, Pamela snapped at them, "Enough history. Let's get on with this."

After blowing down I-75, weaving in and out of cars like he was in a high-speed movie chase, he exited onto I-85, where traffic was at a complete stop. Why was he not surprised? He was in Atlanta.

After she removed her jeans, Thad told her to stand up and do a three-sixty. Bottomless, she spun slowly, and he said, "The greatest legs on earth. No question. Let's see the rest."

She bought more time by turning away from Thad, grabbing her ankles, and looking back through her long legs.

"Fantastic!" he exclaimed.

Then she turned back and slowly stroked the length of her slit as she licked her lips.

"You are getting me hard," Thad told her. "But I'll be a good boy and wait until I touch it."

Button by button of her blouse, as slowly as possible, she undid each while she looked at the laptop screen. "Pam, you pretty much destroyed the Baldwin family. Why?"

"The lacrosse club means more to me than you could imagine or understand. They meddled in my *Game*, not once but several times. And I love taking down persons-of-light, you included."

Suzanne forced a smile after having distracted them, but then Thad ordered her, "Take the shirt off."

Dusty tore down the shoulder lane and finally exited the freeway. He parked for ten seconds and yanked the blue light off his Mustang. He had no idea what he'd run into but didn't think he should go into her condo hot. He debated calling it in, but there was no time to explain, and he had no idea who they'd send. And frankly, he didn't have a lot of confidence that they'd do what he told them anyway. He had to go in alone.

"Twirl around again," Thad directed.

After undoing all her buttons as slowly as she could and dropping her white blouse on the floor, Suzanne had one more piece of clothing: her demi bra. That was it. Dramatically, she eased the straps off each shoulder and then deliberately unhooked the flimsy black bra in the back. She began fondling her D-cup breasts, still covered by the sheer fabric. She had their attention.

"That's what I'm talking about, Suzanne. You are unbelievable, my dear; even sexier than when we first met."

She let her brassiere drop to the floor. She had no more cards to play. Where the hell was Dusty? He was her last ray of hope; she was out of clothes and out of time.

He drove by Suzanne's four-story condo building adjacent to Piedmont Park and then circled the block again. Parked on Piedmont was the same black Honda SUV with the same guy; the driver, he had no doubt was a watcher. Time was critical, but he took it as a good sign. Maybe she was still alive. He could neutralize him but didn't want to make a scene or waste time. Wearing his beat-up gray sweatpants, Nikes, and a red Georgia hoody with a front pocket where he had the guns, he jogged up to the entrance like he was a tenant who'd been out for a run. Thank God he still had the keycard copy she'd given him last year; there was no time to figure out locks.

Over the video app, Pamela told Suzanne, now completely nude, "You've been granted a great honor as the best player in our *Game of Twins* – at least so far this century. Derbert Hinke won that award last century. You also win a death we usually accord only to twins we sacrifice."

"Tie her hands," Thad told Philip. "Be careful – she's not going to play nice anymore."

God, where was Dusty? Maybe the GPS tracker didn't work. She looked down on the floor at the platinum and diamond necklace that was once her mom's. She thought, *"It couldn't end like this; being raped and murdered by Thad and his cousin."*

She was strong and skilled, but so were both men. With her wrists tied, Philip bent her right elbow inward, almost to the breaking point, as they laid her down on her dining room table; her legs dangling and facing out toward the windows looking down on Piedmont.

Thad grabbed one of her thighs and Philip the other as Thad stood between her legs, prying them apart. He freed his erection from his pants. "You remember this schlong, Suzanne? Maybe if you'd have let me fuck you that night at the frat party instead of puking on it, none of this would be happening today."

Dusty Rayfield took the elevator up and ran as quietly as he could to her unit. He put his ear to her door and thought he heard a voice. He stuck one Colt 1911 in the back of his sweatpants. With his right hand, he slid in the keycard while holding the other Colt in his left hand.

He took a deep breath and went in kamikaze.

From twenty paces, the first bullet hit Philip Hawthorne at the bridge of his nose. His head snapped backward. He was dead before he hit the floor. Thad was already ducking and grabbing her tied arms. He yanked Suzanne off the dining room table, her legs flailing, causing two of the knives and the Sig Sauger to slide off the table. He stood up while using her as a shield, his Glock pressed against her temple.

"Drop it!" he yelled. "Or she's dead!"

Dusty followed directions. Sort of.

Instead of bending down, he dropped it and let it bounce on the wooden floor. Suzanne scissored her legs enough to distract Thad. In the same instant, Dusty pulled the other Colt from behind his back. With only a couple inches of Thad's head showing behind hers, Dusty didn't hesitate. He fired, hitting him at the edge of his right eye orbit. Thad spun and lost his grasp of Suzanne as she, too, tumbled to the dining room floor.

Dusty rushed toward them from across the room. Laying on the floor, dazed and gushing from his head wound, Thad groaned and fumbled to find one of the weapons. His fingers located the Sig. On his back, he sprayed bullets blindly. One hit Dusty in the shin. He went down hard. Suzanne kicked the gun from Thad's hand, then twisted her body on the floor to reach the knife that he'd dropped. On his back, he attempted to sit up. But it was too late. Suzanne was on her knees, holding the knife with her tied hands. With every ounce of strength she had, she buried it into his chest.

Her naked body was splattered with blood; Suzanne was the only one in the room not dead or shot or even injured. She stood and asked, "Deadeye, you okay?"

"Yeah, but you probably ought to get some clothes on before the cavalry arrives, Tigress."

Suzanne liked hearing her old nickname.

"By the way, she told him, "You sure took your time getting here."

They both managed to laugh. After Dusty called it in on his phone, she told him, "I need to borrow your phone. Mine's not working."

He said, "That's how I found you."

"What?"

"Tell you later."

Still naked, covered with Thad's blood – and even though it was a crime scene – she stopped and picked up her cross necklace, which was on her living room floor and untouched by any of the blood or the bodies. She pressed it to her lips. She ran down the hallway to see her pup. She sat down and petted his head and said, "I'm so sorry, Zekey," and began to cry. She knew how the Baldwins must feel. Then she made some calls.

The first went to Mia Gonzales. Within twenty-five minutes of her talking to Mia on Dusty's phone, FBI agents were cordoning off the two Sutterland homes on West Paces. In another fifteen minutes, FBI and DEA agents had reached Philip Hawthorne's ranch, formerly owned by Baron Brevard in Woodstock. But when FBI agents and

Atlanta SWAT reached the Loncart estate in Roswell, it was already a five-alarm fire with a dozen fire trucks from Roswell, Alpharetta, and Marietta trying to put out the blaze.

Next, she called Bobby Price and gave him the go-ahead to use any information she'd already given him. She suggested he go to the Sutterland homes, where he'd be given access per the FBI. Suzanne agreed to grant him as many exclusive interviews as he needed.

She called Bernie Scally and told him it was all clear for Tony. Tony needed to show up at the next lacrosse practice so that David and his buddies would have a good coach this season. The former Mafia hitman cried.

She called Sarah Baldwin and told her that her own dog, Zeke, was dead, but their nightmare was over. David could play in Eaglewood's next lacrosse game, and Tony would be coaching. She'd be there to root him on. Sarah sobbed.

Her next call went to Kip Davies. She told him she'd stuck a knife in the heart of his firm's big new client. Literally. But maybe they could grab a bite to eat later, and she could tell him what else happened that day. Of course, the whole story might take a few more dinners and rounds of golf together.

A Note From The Author

This book is a work of fiction. Names, characters, businesses, locales, events, and incidents are either the products of the author's imagination or used in a fictitious manner. Any resemblance to actual persons, living or dead, or actual events or locales is entirely coincidental.

Version 2- July 2024; the original version was published in January 2020.

Game of Twins © Copyright by Tom Ranseen

This is the first novel in my thriller series, *Game of Twins*. The other three books in the series are two sequels, *Game of Twins – Kidnapped* and *Golden Frog Poison- Game of Twins –* in addition to the prequel, *Game of Twins – The Special Agent*. *Game of Twins* is also available in audiobook format

Thank you for reading (or listening to) *Game of Twins*, and I hope you enjoy more books in this series. - For more information, please go www.gameoftwins.com

Epilogue

Two Years Later – April 6, 2018

Roswell, Georgia

It was a cool, breezy spring day in Roswell. A perfect afternoon for lacrosse. On their home field, the Pecan Valley Predators were playing the West Forsyth Flyers. The two teams were not only ranked one and two in Metro Atlanta and in the South – but were also ranked among the top five high school lacrosse teams in the country. Pecan Valley's stock rose further after winning the prestigious Dan Mullins Classic Tournament in Birmingham, Alabama, two weeks prior.

Now a high school sophomore, David Baldwin was eight inches taller, thirty-five pounds heavier, and skilled beyond his years. He'd already been contacted by several top Division I lacrosse programs – and was entertaining full-ride scholarship offers. That fine spring day, the team that beat them by twenty points in Birmingham two years ago got demolished. David gave up only four goals, and the Predators won handily, 13-4.

Besides a dozen Division I coaches, several other people attended the game to watch David play. Sarah and Tim, who was now the Chairman of the boys Lacrosse Club at Pecan Valley, couldn't be prouder of their son. Their marriage, once on the verge of collapsing, wasn't perfect, but on solid ground. Tim was working on his drinking and Bill was long gone – now a vet in Miami Beach. Kip had helped Tim get a good-paying job, and Sarah was able to ease off her vet hours. The Baldwins' Airedale puppies, Kyrie and Irving, were tied to the back of the grandstand and entertaining several little kids.

There were others in the stands that day. Edith Mulhaven, who was shocked when the school district asked her to take the helm at Pecan Valley High School; Bernie Scally had become a fixture at games – and was particularly proud of Tony, who was named Georgia

High School Lacrosse Coach of the Year; Bobby Price, who won the Pulitzer Prize in Journalism for Investigative Reporting for his series about the twins murders going back over a century and had become a lacrosse fan. And, of course, Suzanne Delacroix and Kip Davies attended -- now as a married couple. She had no idea she could be that happy. And she hadn't had a nightmare in nearly two years.

After the convincing lacrosse victory, Tim Baldwin and Suzanne Delacroix had the same idea. A coincidence? Probably not.

Both ended up parking in front of the brand-spanking new Delacroix-Johnston SportsPlex on the other side of the high school. Tim, who led the fundraising, saw it as the accomplishment of his lifetime. But it took a lot of people to make it happen. The original funds contributed by Pamela Loncart got buried in "General County Funds," and so he had to start from scratch. The breakthrough was a nonprofit foundation that Kip Davies helped establish. He sued on behalf of the estate of Orville Johnston, whose incredibly valuable land in Woodstock, Georgia had been illegally obtained by the Sutterland family after his death. One stipulation of the funds was that all athletes at Pecan Valley were expected to contribute time to educational or athletic programs for underprivileged students in the Atlanta area.

Suzanne personally funded the two life-size statues in front of the SportsPlex: one of Orville Johnston (1909-1974) and one of her father, Hollis Delacroix (1946-2008). Orville Johnston's epitaph read: "Father, Husband, Farmer, Soldier, Neighbor, Friend, American Hero." Hollis Delacroix's read similarly: "Father, Husband, Policeman, Neighbor, Friend, American Hero." Coretta Scott King and other luminaries spoke at the dedication. Former President Barack Obama sent a plaque, now displayed inside the school, to honor both men. Another honored attendee was Flora Nethers, who was still going strong at ninety-three.

That day in March, Suzanne Delacroix and Tim Baldwin stood in front of the two statues holding hands and together cried tears of sorrow and joy.

That same April day two teenage boys were playing in another high school lacrosse game in another city. Fraternal twins who had assumed different names and played for different high schools. An overweight blonde woman in a bulky white coat wearing huge sunglasses watched alone on the sideline and answered a phone call.

The call came from his retreat in the mountains of Sinaloa, Mexico. "*Ojos Bonitos.*"

"*Valiente Matador!*"

"*Cómo están mis gemelos?*"

Pamela Loncart patted her belly and told him, "*Valiente Matador, your twins are fine.*"

THE END

Author bio

Tom Ranseen is a longtime Nashville, TN business guy who now writes crime thrillers. His *Game of Twins* series includes *Game of Twins*, *Game of Twins – Kidnapped*, *Golden Frog Poison – Game of Twins*, and *Game of Twins – The Secret Agent* – and he's working on the 5th in his series. He loves that his two grown kids live in the Nashville area, and he spends a lot of time with his Airedale Terrier, Keri. As a Duke graduate, he's a fanatic college basketball fan.

The books are all available online at your favorite online bookseller as eBooks and paperbacks. The "anchor" book, Game of Twins is also available as an audiobook. Go to www.gameoftwins.com for more information.